W9-CDI-498

Also by Shayla Black

TEMPT ME WITH DARKNESS

Look for
POSSESS ME AT MIDNIGHT
the next book in the Doomsday Brethren series

Coming November 2009 from Pocket Books

SEDUCE ME
IN
Shadow

SHAYLA BLACK

POCKET BOOKS
New York   London   Toronto   Sydney

Pocket Books
A Division of Simon & Schuster, Inc.
1230 Avenue of the Americas
New York, NY 10020

This book is a work of fiction. Names, characters, places, and incidents either are products of the author's imagination or are used fictitiously. Any resemblance to actual events or locales or persons, living or dead, is entirely coincidental.

First Pocket Books paperback edition October 2009

POCKET and colophon are registered trademarks of Simon & Schuster, Inc.

For information about special discounts for bulk purchases, please contact Simon & Schuster Special Sales at 1-866-506-1949 or business@simonandschuster.com

The Simon & Schuster Speakers Bureau can bring authors to your live event. For more information or to book an event contact the Simon & Schuster Speakers Bureau at 1-866-248-3049 or visit our website at www.simonspeakers.com.

Illustration by Chris Cocozza.

Manufactured in the United States of America

10 9 8 7 6 5 4 3 2 1

ISBN 978-1-4165-7844-4
ISBN 978-1-4165-7862-8 (ebook)

To my Nana. Because you believed I could.
I would never have started this series without your encouragement.

Acknowledgments

To some of the most supportive beta readers and fans out there: Susan, Natalie, Denise, and Alice. You all have dropped your lives more than once to read for me, make sure I'm coherent, point out typos and inconsistencies, things that could be stronger or taken out altogether. You give me reactions and tons of friendship. Can't thank you enough.

Again, to my standing lunch date Lee Swift, you're the best. Though schedules have become tighter and lunches less frequent, I'm so grateful for your willingness to listen to me when I ramble, give me the guy's point of view, offer suggestions, agree (or not) with what I'm thinking, then make me laugh.

To Melissa Schroeder, thanks for your enthusiasm, your feedback, and all the snarky fun. Days just aren't the same without our IM chats.

A special hug for all the wonderful people on the Wicked Writers loop. I marvel at how funny, diverse, interesting, and chatty you are. I'm thrilled that such special readers have joined this online community with me. You're the best!

As always, to my family. This book, like all books, isn't without some sacrifice. I'd apologize for the fact that we're perpetually out of groceries and that birthday gifts are often late . . . but I'd just be repeating myself. The *Twilight* watching and Guitar Hero playing help me keep my sanity—and you're always so wonderful to play along. You know that I love you bunches and could not live without you!

SEDUCE ME
IN
Shadow

CHAPTER ONE

"WE HAVE PROBLEMS."

Caden MacTavish rolled his eyes. If Bram Rion thought that was news, it came two weeks too late.

Hovering on the edge of a bottle green armchair, Caden watched Merlin's grandson slam the door to his palatial home office, locking the Doomsday Brethren into the edgy silence with him. Each were warriors in their own way, most magical. All had the kind of mettle that would have been welcome in the Marine platoon in which Caden had served.

Without Bram's Hollywood smile, magickind's Brad Pitt looked both jumpy and grave. In fact, all the wizards, and Marrok, the former immortal and King Arthur's champion, looked grim. The tension ratcheted up, and Caden's thoughts drifted to his absent brother Lucan, a Doomsday Brethren warrior.

Please God, let this end soon.

A loud crash upstairs thumped the ceiling, shook the walls. A woman screamed, terror bleeding from her voice. On the upper floor, a door crashed open, the shrieking grew louder, and footsteps pounded above him. She was running down the stairs. Heading out the door.

Tearing out of the library, Caden raced to the shrieking blond woman, ignoring Bram's shout calling him back. He grabbed the frantic witch by her shoulders. Though likely over two hundred, she looked deceptively young. Her wide green eyes were glazed with fear.

"Wait. Please." He caught her anxious gaze. "My brother—"

"I can't." Her voice quivered. "He's big and feral and—snarled that I smell of another man. He ripped his ch-chains." Her words broke with new tears. "And lunged for my throat."

Caden closed his eyes and held in a curse. The fifth energy surrogate Lucan had frightened away in two weeks. Now what?

At the top of the stairs, Bram's sister Sabelle appeared. Her lace shirt and golden hair were askew, but her demeanor was calm. "I have Lucan under control. Let her go."

Instead, Caden clasped the witch tighter. If he released her, what would become of his brother? "He needs her. Without the energy she generates . . ."

Caden couldn't finish the sentence. The thought.

"He'll die." Sabelle sighed. "He misses Anka so deeply that it's unhinged him mentally. My Aunt Millie says she's never seen a case of mate mourning this severe."

More dreadful news. Where was the freaking light at the end of the tunnel? Bram and Sabelle had dragged him away from his peaceful life in Dallas two weeks ago; the hell hadn't let up since. Frustration ate his gut like acid. He didn't want to fail Lucan. Years ago, he'd been unable to save his younger brother. Damned if he'd let his older one die, too.

"If Lucan isn't taking the energy to survive from these women, how can he have enough strength to fight them?"

"Primal rage," Sabelle supplied. "When the surrogates come, it's as if he's defending an attack. It's a delusion, and we can't explain otherwise to him. All his senses, except smell, have shut down. Surrogates bring the smells of their other clients along unwittingly. Lucan fights back."

"Maybe . . . it's time to consider that he wants death," Bram murmured behind him.

Fury slashed through Caden. What kind of friend even thought that? Caden had held the hands of fallen comrades in Iraq and prayed for their recovery . . . even as some rattled their last breath.

"My brother will *not* die like this! I *will* find Anka and bring her back."

"It may be too late. Let the witch go," Bram demanded.

"Please," the scared blonde pleaded.

Caden shook with rage. He wanted to crush something, punch a wall, lash out at magic, which had again screwed up his life. But the sobbing witch in his grasp shrank back in fear, like he, too, was a monster.

For about the two hundredth time since returning to England a fortnight ago, Caden cursed magic. To a human male, the loss of a beloved wife could be emotionally devastating. But as a wizard, Lucan's loss had reduced a perfectly sane person to a rabid animal. The man upstairs wasn't the older brother Caden had idolized as a child.

Though he'd left his childhood home a dozen years ago, and disavowed anything or anyone associated with magic, now that tragedy had struck, and he might lose his only remaining brother, a guilt seared Caden. The thought of never speaking to Lucan again? Unthinkable.

He must restore Lucan's mental health. To do that, he had to find Anka and return her to his brother's arms—quickly. And clearly, the witch Caden currently detained couldn't help.

With a sigh, he released her. "Go."

She sprinted out and closed the door. Silence reverberated.

"Come back to my office," Bram said.

Caden whirled on the wizard. "I won't give up on my brother, damn you!"

With a twitch of Bram's finger, Caden was magically hauled back into the office. Caden seethed with resentment as Bram slammed the door behind them. He opened his mouth to give the wizard a furious earful, but Bram held up a hand.

"I understand your frustration. But our difficulties aren't merely about you and your family. These problems affect us all." He gestured to the other three men in the room. "And the rest of magickind."

"My brother is chained to a bed like a lunatic, Anka is missing, and we haven't a single clue where she's gone. We cannot make Lucan whole without her return. Nothing is more important."

"I wish. Our other problems are many and grave."

Ice Rykard, another of the warriors, was a big man, but when annoyance stamped his square, hollow-cheeked face, like now, sane people backed away. "You summoned me here to tell me what I already know?"

As Ice rose to leave, Bram blocked his path. "Something new has arisen. Prudence requires that we attend to it. All of us."

Bram refused to help his brother, then sought his assistance? Caden would have laughed if he weren't so furious. "I came only to find my brother's missing mate—"

"Former mate," Bram corrected. "Their bond is broken."

"Involuntarily," Caden stressed. "I've no doubt Lucan still regards Anka as his, and they were in love. Why would she not welcome him back? I'm here to find her so they can bond again, not solve your problems."

Bram sighed. "Lucan is my best friend, and I want more than anything to make him whole again. But that is a mission of mercy. The other matters are of life and death."

"If you do not help me find Anka, Lucan will die!"

"If we fail to act on this new problem, thousands, maybe millions, will die. Including Lucan."

Sacrificing one for many. Bram had shoved this "necessity" down Caden's throat before. His patience was wearing thin. Exhaling, he rubbed gritty eyes. Every day, worrying. Every night, not sleeping—he often paced, Lucan's mad countenance swimming in his mind. Meanwhile his brother's "friends" worried about everyone else.

"Please." Simon Northam, or Duke, the youngest of the Doomsday Brethren, drilled him with a stare. "We need you as much as Lucan. The sooner we tend to these issues, the sooner we can help him."

Caden felt four pairs of eyes locked on him. Except for the fact Bram had kept a roof over Lucan's head, he owed these men nothing. He'd known them a mere fortnight, wanted nothing to do with magickind and their problems. But their stares accused him of abandoning them . . . and Lucan's cause. Guilt twisted in his gut.

Blast them! He merely wanted peace and solitude since witnessing half his friends dying in Iraq. Of the few who had survived, two had returned home, only to commit suicide. Another was in prison, unable to make the transition from shooting terrorists in a desert shithole to walking the dog in suburbia. The last had gone missing following a training exercise at his home base. The tragic death of Caden's younger brother nearly two decades ago had proved that magic's body count was even more shocking and heartbreaking. He'd had enough of loss, of death. As soon as Lucan recovered, Caden would return to his sedate life as a staff photographer for a Dallas newspaper. No one died taking pictures of city council meetings.

"The Doomsday Brethren means a great deal to Lucan," Bram reminded.

Manipulative bastard.

"Besides, you may soon need us. Your magic is coming . . ."

Caden prayed that his sleeplessness was merely anxiety, stress, and not a harbinger of his own coming transition into magic. But there was no denying the electrical surges and flashes of emotion racing through his body of late. He feared that the witching hour—in this case, his thirtieth birthday—was approaching. "Not if I can help it."

"You can't." Bram shrugged. "If you have the magic gene, it's coming."

Marrok, the human warrior-giant who looked every inch a medieval knight, from the slash of straight hair that reached his shoulders to the sword strapped to his hip, frowned at Bram. "Does this new problem concern Shock? Have we yet heard from the varlet?"

The shadiest member of the Doomsday Brethren had been MIA since their battle two weeks ago with the evil wizard Mathias, who sought to control magickind with the help of his minions, the Anarki. During that skirmish, Shock had suddenly appeared to switch his loyalties to the other side. No surprise there, given the man's dark background. Because Shock was both Anka's previous suitor and cozy with Mathias, Bram thought he might be willing to divulge Anka's whereabouts. Caden disagreed. Mathias had brutalized Anka after abducting her and forcing her to break her mate bond with Lucan. Shock had apparently done nothing to help her.

Bram, Ice, and Duke all shook their heads.

"Nothing? That is vexing," Marrok snarled. "Surely he has told Mathias much about us."

"It's Mathias's quiet that disturbs me," Ice cut in. "Two weeks of it . . . Right dodgy. Makes me itch."

If Caden cared about magickind, he'd agree. But his only

mission was to determine what Mathias had done with Anka and return her in the hopes of restoring Lucan's sanity.

"During our last battle, Olivia laid a bolt of power on Mathias that should have flattened the bastard," drawled Duke. Clad head to toe in designer everything, he looked perfectly urbane and wealthy, the artful muss of his dark hair cut perfectly, just like his aristocratic features, all the way down to his cleft chin. "It appeared to deplete his magic and should have prevented him from rising again, but . . ."

"This *is* Mathias," Ice finished.

Exactly. If Mathias regained even half his power, the small but determined cabal of warriors assembled under Bram's direction were screwed, and every man in the room knew it. How could the Doomsday Brethren kill a wizard who had already returned from the dead once? He had an army of slaves at his disposal. Caden could count the Doomsday Brethren on one hand.

Bram winced. "I'm afraid, gentlemen, our problems are worse than that."

Marrok muttered, "Would that we knew from whence Mathias found so many disposable recruits."

Those were troubling, indeed. Mathias had stripped the souls from human bodies to create walking dead Anarki, for the purpose of helping Mathias enslave magickind and destroy the Doomsday Brethren. During their last battle, the black-blooded zombies had been plentiful—and immune to magic.

"All true," Bram conceded. "But I called you here to discuss something even more critical."

Ice cast him a cutting stare. "Your magical signature tells me you took a human mate last night? A problem, indeed."

Caden's jaw dropped. Bram, one of the most pedigreed wizards today, had taken a *human* mate?

"Wouldn't your grandfather be proud?" Ice sneered. "Merlin prized that pure bloodline. Pity."

Bram charged toward Ice. "Shut your bloody mouth, you fu—"

"Cease!" Marrok grabbed him and held him back.

Caden was inclined to help. Bram and Ice were always at each other's throats. If Bram needed wizards loyal to him for the Doomsday Brethren, why the devil had he picked Ice to join?

"Piss off!" Bram growled.

"We can fight no enemy if we are too busy fighting one another," Marrok advised.

"Beating in the tosser's skull would make me feel better."

"What has you on edge?" Duke asked.

Caden wondered the same thing. Bram was usually the voice of sanity amidst all this magical muck. At the moment, he behaved as if he was crawling out of his skin, one step away from the mental ward.

"Where is your mate?" Ice added fuel to the fire. "I'd like to offer her my condolences."

"*My* mate is none of your concern. However, the Book of Doomsday is." Bram hesitated, then rolled his shoulders. "Last night, while I slept, she found it."

"Found it? Lying about?" Duke demanded.

"It was hidden." Bram rubbed the back of his neck. "She must have searched for it."

An ominous gong clanged in Caden's gut. Magickind wasn't his issue, but if that book disappeared . . . everyone, magical and human, was at risk.

"She cozied up to you to find the book?" Ice looked ready to laugh.

Bram didn't have to answer; the humiliation on his face did it for him.

"Shut up!" Caden glared at the stubble-headed wizard, then turned back to Bram. "What happened? Where is the diary?"

"She took it and disappeared."

Bram's quiet admission resounded through the room.

"Fuck," Ice muttered.

"You have no idea where it is?" Caden struggled to pick his jaw off the floor. "Where she is?"

"None."

"Double fuck," came Ice again.

The Doomsday Diary was the ultimate weapon in the magical war. Used properly, it was rumored to grant any wish, up to and including the world's annihilation. People had died in Mathias's quest to obtain it. Lucan's life was in shambles because of it. The Doomsday Brethren had formed and were fighting a war to protect it. If Mathias obtained the book and used it to bring about doomsday—well, that *was* everyone's problem.

"I second what Ice said," Caden muttered.

"You had no magical protections on the book?" Duke asked.

"Of course. Against anyone *magical*. I never imagined a human would know of the book's existence, much less that I had it. The only way she could know is if she's Mathias's pawn. I worry . . . What if he has the diary now? What will he do to her?" Bram paced, raking a frantic hand through his golden hair.

Marrok planted a friendly hand on Bram's shoulder. "Use your bond to find her."

With a shake of his golden hair, Bram sighed in frustration. "I can't and I don't understand why. I should be able to . . . It's confounding me."

"You touched her, aye?" Marrok asked. "Did you not use your powers to read her mind?"

"Yes . . . and no. I could read her body with my touch, but not her thoughts. I've never encountered such a woman before."

Duke sighed. "What the devil should we do now?"

Panic? Caden kept the thought to himself.

"Not to add to our problems, but have you seen this?" Duke slid a newspaper in the middle of Bram's desk. The bold black headline screamed *Supernatural Forces Battle in South London Tunnel.*

Bram glanced at the paper. "*Out of This Realm?* It's a rag. No one takes that rubbish seriously."

Not true. Back home, several of the reporters at the *Dallas Morning News* were addicted to the paper's imaginative stories. They were more creative than *The National Enquirer*'s.

"That may change after this issue's lead article. The byline belongs to a reporter named Sydney Blair. She's disturbingly close to the truth. Most news outlets wrote off the battle with Mathias as a foiled terrorist act, a gang initiation, or the work of a madman. Ms. Blair calls it 'an ongoing clash between powerful factions within magickind.' "

Bram's eyes bulged. "How the bloody hell does she even know there's a magickind, much less an ongoing battle? Few in magickind know of Mathias's return."

Though Caden had eschewed magic long ago, even he knew the necessity of keeping magickind's existence a secret from humans. Witch hunts, trials for heresy, and burnings at the stake weren't distant memories for a society whose citizens often lived to be one thousand. The seventeenth century was, relatively speaking, last year. No one was naïve enough to think that technology was any insurance policy against genocide. People still killed what they didn't understand.

"I consulted *Peers and People of Magickind* before coming here. I found no mention of her," Duke said. "She is no witch, nor is she mated to a wizard."

"Human? Mayhap she's one of Mathias's soulless minions," Marrok suggested.

"If Mathias wanted to influence humanity, he wouldn't take over a tabloid reporter's mind to do it," Bram assured. "Besides, if she's still leading a human life, she could not do so looking like an undead Anarki. The other humans notice walking cadavers."

"So she's fully human," Duke surmised. "And frightfully well informed."

"Or perhaps . . ." Ice glared at him. "She's getting her information from someone who rejected magickind and would celebrate its end."

"Me?" Caden jumped in the big wizard's face. "I've no love for magic, true, but I would never advocate mass murder. Besides, ending you all would mean my brother's death. Would I be here saving him if I was willing to kill magickind?"

Duke nodded, the cooler head prevailing. "He's right."

Muttering, Ice backed away. Barely.

Turning back to the newspaper, Duke went on, "Whoever she is, she's dangerous. The rest of the article is equally disturbing. 'The bodies discovered in the tunnel are decomposed far beyond expected, given their recent deaths.' "

"This is no secret." Marrok waved his words away. "The media has been scratching over that like a mongrel with fleas."

"Listen further," Duke barked. " '*Out of This Realm* has learned the bodies bear new wounds and fresh traces of gunpowder, suggesting they somehow fought in the battle, rather than merely being left behind as a macabre message. It appears as if they were actually more dead than alive prior to the battle, but able to fight due to evil magic.' "

"She's guessing," said Bram.

But even he didn't sound convinced. Caden winced.

Duke shook his head. "Here's more: 'According to an anonymous source, there's a mad wizard on the loose once more, allegedly fighting social injustice in the magical world. He'll stop at nothing to tear down the establishment and replace it with his version of anarchy.'"

Caden shook his head. *Poor magical bastards.*

"Who *is* this anonymous source?" Bram demanded.

Duke laced his fingers together with quiet concern. "Ms. Blair claims it's 'a witch who recently found herself tangled in this magical war.'"

"A witch?" Ice spat. "Who knows so much?"

Caden's heart stuttered and adrenaline charged. "Anka."

"Or perhaps any of the other missing women, like Craddock's daughter," Ice pointed out. "But what witch in her right mind would spill sensitive secrets to a bloody reporter?"

Who knew? Still . . . "It could be Anka," Caden insisted.

And possibly the first clue Caden had discovered to her whereabouts in a fortnight.

"Whoever her source, Sydney Blair knows there's a magickind, that we're at war, and that Mathias is supposedly fighting the Social Order," Duke insisted.

"The moment anyone actually listens, humanity will hunt us. It'll make the Inquisition seem like a bloody holiday." Bram raked a hand through his disheveled golden hair and continued to pace. "And if Mathias reads this, her life may well be in danger. We must handle this situation immediately."

Bram leaned back against his desk. The morning sun slanted through the office's open shutters, showing just how much strain the wizard was enduring. He swallowed, then pinned a wily gaze on Caden that made his blood freeze. "I know how we can deal with Ms. Blair. You've worked at a newspaper."

Caden sent him a wary glance. "So?"

"Offer your services as a photographer and shut her up, before she reveals anything more about magickind."

He didn't want to get involved. "Why don't you visit her and do that wizard mind-reading trick of yours?"

"Only works if I'm touching a woman—deeply. Now that I'm mated . . . well, I can no longer get that close to Sydney Blair, or any woman except mine. So you'll have to go and pry information from her the human way."

Caden's thoughts raced. Perhaps he could placate them *and* help his brother. If he worked for Ms. Blair, he could discern if her anonymous source was Anka.

Bram smiled tightly. Bloody bastard had Caden by the balls and he knew it. In order to make Lucan whole, he must find his brother's mate. At the moment, the reporter was his best—and only—lead.

"Have we come to the part yet where I spank you?"

Sydney Blair closed her eyes as the last notes of "Happy Birthday" echoed through the small conference room. Had her perpetually randy coworker, Jamie, actually suggested a little light S&M with the entire staff of *Out of This Realm* looking on?

A dozen of the newspaper's employees twittered with nervous laughter, except her yummy new photographer, Caden MacTavish. Mortified, Sydney risked a glance at him. The taut arms bunched over his wide chest and the chilly blue of his watchful eyes made her wince.

Sydney slowly turned to the office lothario with a glare that let him know how little she appreciated his comment. He merely wagged his brows at her and grinned from ear to ear.

"Have we come to the part yet where you leave?" Caden countered.

The words somehow sounded polite. Caden had that upper crust Londoner sound, though muted by time elsewhere. But he could still say most anything and sound civilized. His current expression, on the other hand, rivaled Attila the Hun's on a bad day.

"You think you should be first to have a go at her?" Jamie challenged Caden. "I've seen how you stare."

Sydney went hot all over—from more than simple embarrassment. Caden lit her up like a millennium fireworks show. She'd be thrilled if the man had sexual thoughts of her. But in the few days she'd worked with him, he had not appeared to notice her more than professionally, despite Jamie's delusions to the contrary.

"Bad karma!" Aquarius, her flower-child assistant, scolded. "Mellow!"

Neither spared a glance for the little waif. Silver bracelets tinkling, Aquarius reached out to Caden. Whether she intended to soothe him or test his aura, Sydney didn't know. She shot a warning glance at her assistant. Now was not a good time for her healing-crystal/save-the-world routine.

"You may find this concept hard to grasp," Caden asserted, "but some men are capable of admiring more about a woman than what's in her knickers."

Jamie scoffed. "If he's a nancy boy."

Sydney smothered a laugh. Caden was definitely not gay. Despite that, she felt certain he'd never considered what went in her knickers. "Stop it, both of you! This is a birthday party, not a brawl."

"What's your wish?" asked Leslie from Circulation, trying to smooth the tension.

A romping shag with Caden, but since that wasn't likely to happen . . . head reporter had a lovely ring to it. Sure, she worked for a paranormal tabloid that few took seriously, but it paid the bills. Soon, she hoped to make a name for herself writing stories that traditional journalists eschewed. And people everywhere would recognize her once she found proof of the supernatural. Until then she would write about the world she believed *must* exist—and her parents had utterly rejected. Besides, *Out of This Realm* was a scream to work at. Where else could she collect a salary for chasing Ripper ghosts and conducting interviews at the London Psychic Centre?

Her personal life, on the other hand? Disaster. How did one manage to become a sad spinster at twenty-eight? The endless string of dates from her uni days had been replaced with deadlines and staff meetings. Her last boyfriend . . . his pretty face had failed to compensate for the fact he had the IQ of a dead houseplant and the emotional range of a pea. Perhaps she *should* wish for a man.

For Caden.

Yummy waves of chocolate hair with caramel streaks, fathomless blue eyes, a body that belonged in magazines—and a reserved exterior that made her long to know the man beneath. Too bad the attraction didn't run both ways. She sighed.

"She can't tell us her wish or it won't come true," Holly, her editor, pointed out, then faced Sydney. "Now stop fannying about and open your gifts."

Sydney looked at the gifts on the table, but her gaze strayed to Caden, who continued glaring at Jamie.

He was a puzzle, that one.

From the moment Caden had walked in the door, he'd been fixated on that battle in the South London tunnel a few weeks back. He'd said her story about the magical war was utter rubbish . . . but asked a load of questions, especially about her source. Not that Sydney would tell him—or anyone else—the woman's name. Impossible, anyway. She didn't know it.

Aquarius distracted the tense crowd by shoving a bright pink floral-wrapped box into Sydney's hands. From the number of packages stacked on the small round table in the conference room, it looked as if everyone had brought her something.

"You shouldn't have gone to such trouble."

"We want to show you how much we appreciate you," said Leslie.

Aquarius started pouring cups of her infamous home-blended herbal tea as Sydney unwrapped gifts. A pair of delicate silver earrings, a relaxing massage at a local day spa, and a sumptuous Italian silk scarf trimmed in blue crushed velvet. Jamie gave her a gift certificate for a large pizza and a Blockbuster card—both of which he'd likely insist on sharing. Caden had given her a somewhat impersonal card and a small box of nice chocolates. She would have preferred a hungry kiss.

Wrapping paper and greeting cards littered the table when Sydney at last got to Aquarius's package. The young woman was practically vibrating with excitement. "Open this! It's from me."

"You baked and organized and still got me something? You shouldn't have."

With the butterfly tattoo on her shoulder and her mesh and lace top, Aquarius didn't dress like a *normal* assistant and refused to make coffee—too full of chemicals and caffeine. She wasn't good with a computer . . . yet. But Aquarius had a knack for stories, for juggling Sydney's hectic schedule, fielding the editor-in-chief, soothing paranoid readers and keeping internal chaos at a minimum. And despite being total opposites, she and Aquarius had become good friends. Sydney smiled at the thought.

"Are you two going to start snogging or are you going to open that?" Jamie hollered.

After tossing another glare at Jamie, Sydney turned to the gift. It was square and slightly heavy. Aquarius had wrapped it in buttery yellow linen and an over layer of white lace—different from her usual recycled choice.

"Open it. Go on," she whispered.

An odd anticipation revved through Sydney as she plucked at the silky white bow and tore open the wrapping to reveal . . . a book. An old-fashioned book. A red leather cover with gilt framing and some sort of scripty-looking symbol on the front. Sydney tried to hide her confusion.

Caden elbowed in and gave the book a very hard stare.

Aquarius laughed and urged her, "Read the card inside."

With a shrug, she opened the cover to reveal. *Hmm* . . . An empty book with ever-so-slightly yellowed pages and a little white square of paper with a formal-looking script that read:

> *On these magical pages, spill your sensual fantasy,*
> *In a mere day's time, your wishes will become reality.*
> *A kiss, a touch, a whisper, whatever you most desire,*
> *In the arms of your lover, pleasure will burn hotter than fire.*

What? Aquarius believed this book could make sexual fantasies a reality? Sydney would *love* that, and she believed in magic, but this little unassuming book? In *her* hands?

Caden prowled close beside her, elbowing in for yet a closer look. He stared hard at the little journal, and she could smell that musky, woodsy scent of his that drove her mad.

"May I see that?" he demanded more than asked, reaching for the book.

"Certainly," Sydney murmured, handing it over. The low-cut black jumper she'd worn yesterday had done nothing to snag his attention. This book? He was enraptured.

Aquarius sent her a secretive smile. "Syd, do you understand? It's—"

"An old book," Jamie hollered, edging in behind her. "What good is that?"

"I appreciate each gift. Thank you, everyone," Sydney said through clenched teeth. "I suspect we should get back to work now." Maybe that would make Jamie shove off.

Around her, the small crowd began to file out. Unfortunately, Jamie lingered. Sydney, her assistant, and Caden, still studying the book, also occupied the dusk-shadowed room.

"If you want something special for your birthday, I'll make time for you this weekend," Jamie offered with a leer as he dropped a hand on her hip and slid it toward her backside.

Sydney eased away and opened her mouth to defer to the mountain of work on her desk when Caden grabbed Jamie's wrist and squeezed—hard.

"Bloody hell!" He jerked away and glared at Caden.

Normally, such high-handed tactics would annoy Sydney. She was a grown woman and knew how to fend off male octopi like Jamie. But if Caden's unexpected caveman impression put the lazy sod off until she found a more private moment to tell him to get lost, splendid. If Caden was just the slightest bit jealous, even better.

"What the devil?" Jamie cried. "Let go!"

"As soon as you do." Caden tightened his grip.

Jamie released her immediately. "Ring me this weekend if you want company."

As Caden watched Jamie's retreating back, he scowled. The waves of his silent disapproval towered over Sydney like a tsunami. She bit her lip.

"Would you mind speaking to me in your office for a few minutes?" he said.

As always, the tone was polite. She wondered if he thought to warn her about the evils of Jamie. *Like an overprotective brother lecturing his adolescent sister?* Depressing thought. Did she have to jump on Caden while naked before he understood?

"Fine." Might as well get it over with.

Caden raised a dark brow at her sharp tone and gestured to the door. "After you."

"Wait!" Aquarius snatched the book from Caden and gave it to Sydney. "Your gift! I should tell you about it."

Oh, the "magical diary." She couldn't leave without hurting Aquarius's feelings. Her confrontation with Caden would have to wait.

"I'll be there in a minute."

After a long glance at her, then the book, Caden nodded and slipped from the room.

Sydney dug her fingernails out of her palms, so frustrated she feared she would draw blood. Being a petite redhead, she didn't have a centerfold's breasts and wasn't one of those model-like creatures men got all in a froth about. But Caden treated her almost asexually.

"You want him," Aquarius whispered. It wasn't a question.

"I couldn't want him any more than if I'd shot myself with Cupid's arrow." She tossed her hands up in the air. "He doesn't reciprocate."

"You don't know that," Aquarius argued.

"Perhaps. He's impossible to read. So bloody private."

"I don't think he's as immune to you as you imagine."

She shook her head glumly. "I'd love to believe that. No, I'd love to *experience* it."

"You can." Aquarius tapped the cover of the old book. "He can be yours for the night."

Caden could have his pick of women. Besides being good-looking, intelligent, and polite, he had proven dependable thus far. He wasn't lazy and seemed to truly listen. What woman wouldn't want a total package? Yesterday's snug shirt had outlined a positively yummy chest. And he was probably devastatingly good in bed—not that she'd ever know personally.

Or could she?

Sydney frowned. The idea tempted her. Could this journal possibly be magical? It sounded awfully fantastical—not that such a book existed, but that it had dropped into *her* lap. Supposing it had . . . would Caden truly be hers for the night after she jotted down a few ideas that involved scented massage oil, a big bed, and his naked body?

She cast a gentle glance at her assistant. "You believe this book is real?"

"It made one of my fantasies come true," Aquarius blurted. "Remember Alex, that yummy neighbor I told you about? He asked me out when I wrote down exactly what I wanted."

"Aquarius, he had an itch for you, so when his calendar opened up, he rang."

"And read my mind?" Aquarius challenged. "Until last

week, I never knew making love under a waterfall would be so . . . invigorating."

"A waterfall? Where did you find—"

"I'll never tell." She smiled coyly.

"Let me get this straight: This hunky bloke suddenly appeared and whisked you away to fulfill your fantasy, exactly as you wrote it?"

Dreamy didn't begin to describe Aquarius's faraway expression. "It was fantastic."

Sydney groped around for a chair. "Maybe you need a holiday. You're past due."

"I'm completely sane. Though I enjoyed Alex, he wasn't right for me—"

"No man ever is."

Aquarius frowned. "There's a man out there. Somewhere. I'll know when I meet him."

Sydney had heard this before.

"Point is, I don't need this journal." Aquarius shoved it at to her. "But you . . ."

"But me . . . what?" Sydney fisted her hands on her hips.

"Well, if you want Caden, write your fantasy in here."

The idea was tempting. With her luck, Caden would find the fantasy she'd written. Since she didn't think he wanted her, mortified wouldn't begin to cover how bad she'd want to crawl into a hole and wait for a new millennium.

"I don't think that's a good idea."

"Neither is pining away. Look," her voice dropped to a whisper, "take the diary with you this weekend and write your deepest desire about Caden. Wait a day or two. If it doesn't come true, what have you lost? When I return from holiday, I'm sure you'll have loads to tell me."

* * *

Caden marched into Sydney's office and barely refrained from slamming the door. The fiery sun setting over the jagged London skyline matched his mood. The Doomsday Diary, here? In human hands? He must steal it from Sydney, remove her from danger. He needed a plan. Now.

But he was besieged by an equally strong urge to punch both Bram Rion and Jamie What's-his-name.

Wanting to beat Bram to a pulp? Caden understood that well. Bram embodied so much of what he despised about magic: the blithe assumption of supremacy, unpredictability, the utter inability to compromise, and the total lack of awareness that it might be required. Magic's inequality chafed as well. In a human world, anyone could learn to defend themselves and grow stronger each day—or buy a better weapon. In the magical world, a witch or wizard never had more power than they were born with, and if they found themselves at the mercy of someone more evil and powerful than themselves . . . God help them.

But Caden's reaction to Jamie he didn't understand. Nor could he grasp his own drive to possess Sydney so completely that she was unaware another male even existed. He'd done his best to ignore it, hide it, but she'd become a fever in his blood. The urge defied logic. He was on a mission. He was good at those, thanks to the U.S. Marine Corps. Focus. Get in, get out, get the job done, end of story. Don't do anything stupid.

Falling in life-altering lust with Sydney, particularly now, fell into the stupid category. Yet he couldn't stop. His assignment was to prevent Sydney from revealing more about magickind—a move that would protect her too—and discover if Anka was her source of information. Unfortunately, he was finding it difficult to focus on more than pushing the saucy reporter against a wall, kissing her senseless, then shagging her into sighing bliss.

Damn it all! He hadn't been naïve enough to believe that his assignment at *Out of This Realm* would be easy, but he'd had little success tracking down Sydney's source of information while stifling her stories. She was infuriatingly and admirably determined. Throw in the sudden and unexpected appearance of the Doomsday Diary? This had become what his platoon buddies called a cluster-fuck.

Cursing, he pulled his mobile phone from his belt and dialed an increasingly familiar number.

Bram answered immediately. "You have news?"

Did he ever, but first things first. "How is my brother?"

Bram hesitated. "Weak. We're doing our best, but we're running out of options."

The wizard's words were a stab in the chest. "Don't you dare let him die while I'm in London doing your dirty work."

"Believe me, if I had anyone else suited to this task, you would still be gnashing your teeth here at Lucan's bedside. Matters are too critical for me to be there. Duke can pass as a human, but who would believe that the Duke of Hurstgrove wants a job at a tabloid? That leaves a fifteen-hundred-year-old warrior, an attitude-challenged wizard, and you. You alone have both experience in photography and the human world."

"Your problem is mine only as long as my brother is alive. If he dies, I cease to care. Are you clear?"

"As if you'd drawn me a picture." Bram shot back. "Believe me, as desperately as we need wizards for this fight, I'll happily release you when I can. I want only those committed to the cause."

Bram's intimation that he wasn't good enough annoyed Caden. He shrugged it off. What did he care if Bram didn't see him as a member of the team he hadn't wished to join?

He'd wanted nothing to do with magic since his younger brother's death—by his own mother's magic. An accident, yes. But he'd been just twelve when Westin, barely toddling, had been stricken.

Since leaving home at eighteen, he'd lived happily among humanity. Their ways seemed normal, comfortable. Being back among magickind now merely reminded Caden of all the reasons he loathed it. This gut-wrenching madness of Lucan's merely underscored everything.

"Rion, do you honestly believe that you and a handful of wizards can defeat the most powerful magical creature in a millennium *and* his growing army?"

"Perhaps not, but we'll certainly fail if we don't try. Why do you care as long as Lucan stays alive?"

"He'd better."

"I'm against this, but Sabelle insists on being his surrogate. Or attempting."

Brilliant! Though Bram's protective attitude was hardly a surprise. But Sabelle was a tough, courageous witch with the unusual ability to make others feel whatever she wanted with a touch. If anyone besides Anka could provide Lucan energy, it was Sabelle.

"Tell your sister I appreciate her more than she can know."

"No guarantee it will work."

It had to. "Thank her anyway."

"All right, then. What news have you to report?"

"I've learned little about Sydney's source of information. She's guarding the name like a national secret."

"Seduce her. Charm her."

Bram's suggestion made Caden grit his teeth. He didn't have Bram's easy way—and he was completely enthralled with the woman he was supposed to bamboozle. He wanted her more than his next breath—and was desperate to bury the feeling.

"Her secret is the least of our issues at the moment. I'm having a devil of a time stalling her next story. Before the bodies were removed from the tunnel, Sydney's previous photographer took a few pictures. Grainy and fuzzy, which works in our favor, but we know of no one else who arrived in time to snap any, so she's still scooped every other news source. People will pick up *Out of This Realm* in droves, I fear, if she prints it with a proposed story that these men comprise Mathias's unwilling Anarki army, out to dissolve the Social Order and eradicate the Doomsday Brethren."

Bram sounded ready to hit the ceiling. "She knows about *us?* Where *is* she getting this information?"

"I'd like to know that myself and have no clue. Unfortunately, it gets worse."

"Worse?"

"Indeed. I found the Doomsday Diary. Sydney Blair acquired it fifteen minutes ago."

Bram cursed a stream of loud, ugly words.

"On that, we're agreed," Caden supplied.

"You're absolutely certain?"

"There can't be many old red books bearing Morganna le Fay's symbol."

"Send me a picture."

Bram didn't trust him. Whatever.

"Bloody hell. Better yet, steal it from her."

"She won't let it loose soon. It was a birthday gift from a dear friend."

"Who?" Bram snapped.

"Aquarius."

"The astrological sign?"

"Sydney's assistant," Caden corrected. "Is she your mate?"

"That wasn't the name—describe her. Perhaps my missing 'wife' uses aliases."

"Short, almost fey looking. Brown wavy hair to her waist, green eyes—"

"Not even close. Which raises the question, if Sydney acquired the book from this woman who is definitely not my mate, how did she get her hands on it?"

"I was hoping you could shed some light."

"None. Ask her. Maybe she'll know how to locate my mate." Frustration oozed from every syllable. "But we must recover that diary. Now."

"I have good news and bad news about that. The bad news is that Sydney is a smart, tenacious reporter who's determined to keep writing 'fresh paranormal stories,' in her words."

"Which means she may choose to write about the diary." He groaned. "How can there possibly be good news?"

"She doesn't know its purpose. Yet. She's been told that writing in the book will grant her sexual fantasies. And I'm not sure she's convinced it's real."

"Pray it stays that way, at least long enough for you to do whatever you must—steal, sweet talk, or seduce her away from that book."

"I'll work on that while determining the name of her source. You're coming to help, right? Use a bit of magic and . . ."

"Can't. There was another Anarki attack two hours ago. I've just left what was the Pullmans' estate. Burned to the ground. Their newly transitioned daughter is missing. Everyone else is dead. I have to report to the Council."

That wasn't good news. If the Anarki were attacking again, that meant Mathias was on the mend and his power rising once more. Caden didn't want to care, but . . . he rubbed his tired eyes with his fingers. After seeing so much war and death in his life, attacks on families, on women, troubled him.

"What will you do next?"

Bram sighed. "What we have been: keep searching for Mathias, not to mention Shock and his brother, Zain, who appears to be the evil bastard's right-hand lackey."

"Have you considered telling other magical families about this attack? They have to start protecting themselves."

"So you're going to pretend you care about magickind now?"

Caden restrained a growl. "I would not wish what's happened to my family on another."

"Rumors are beginning to spread about Mathias's return, but the decision to officially tell magickind falls with the Council. They approve transcasts and issue edicts."

"Certainly a few words on how best to defend yourself—"

"Which is why no such edict will be created any time soon. No one knows how to defend against Mathias, and the Council would rather err on the side of silence than inaccuracy. Bloody stupid bastards."

"You're one of them," Caden pointed out.

"The lone voice of reason, I assure you. I've long argued that we should communicate magical news via transcasts or the like frequently. But by the time the Council agrees to the verbiage . . ." Bram scoffed. "It's old news."

That didn't surprise Caden. Dawdling old fools, Lucan had long said, even their Uncle Sterling at times.

Caden was curious why Bram stayed on the Council, likely enduring one frustration after another. But it was none of Caden's affair. He didn't want to become more entangled in the magical world. Already, he was in too deep.

"You'll come to assist with the diary once you've helped the victims of the latest attack?"

"As soon as I can," Bram said. "Keep working on Sydney Blair."

Caden could think of any number of ways in which he'd like to work on Sydney. Completely naked with her on her back, came immediately to mind. But that couldn't happen. Now he needed to focus on his brother. "I will."

CHAPTER TWO

CADEN RANG OFF WITH BRAM just before Sydney's door burst open. In walked the source of his frustrations and fantasies, carrying the little red book.

A fresh wave of lust blazed across his senses. An electric pulse revved down his spine, shuddered across his skin. He burned with need. What the devil was wrong with him? Lately, he'd felt . . . off. Tired one minute, wired the next. His senses quickened, his fingertips tingled. The odd sweating out of nowhere . . . bloody awful, but it fit with his libido being ever ready.

What ailed him? A frustrating mission? The redheaded dynamo who drove him beyond sanity? Yes to both. The stress wasn't helping. And he missed his job and his adopted home in Dallas, away from all this hocus-pocus. But he feared the problem's true cause was magic. The urge to flee before it ripped away another loved one loomed large.

"What is it, MacTavish?" She thrust one hand on her hip. The other held the Doomsday Diary casually. God, if she had any idea what that book could do . . . he had to wrest it from her as quickly as possible.

Surreptitiously, he withdrew his mobile phone from his belt, pretending to sort through the menus. Quickly, he snapped a picture.

"Hey!" she protested.

"Sorry. New phone. Was trying to silence it. Still learning."

She paused. "What do you want? If you've no need to talk, I have a pub stool and a pint waiting for me."

She was in a snit. Caden hoped she wasn't angry that he'd dismissed Jamie. The thought that she might have any interest in that knuckle-dragger made him grind his teeth.

"Right, then. I have some questions."

"Shocking." She crossed the room, slim hips swaying.

A caustic Sydney was a dazzling sight. He shouldn't stare, but she'd snared him from the first, dug under his skin. Pink tinged her fair face, and her auburn hair tumbled across her shoulders. Those flashing brown eyes were a sucker punch to his gut.

Don't think about her. Think smart. Think mission.

He'd rather think about having her naked underneath him.

"I'll get to the point."

"Lovely."

Sydney stood her ground and stared back with admirable moxie for someone who didn't reach his chin. She defended her stories with considerable passion and wit, fighting back when things got rough. The fact she was also smart and sexy made her damn near impossible to resist.

"But let me first say," she went on. "If you're going to warn me about the evils of Jamie, I'm a big girl."

He hadn't planned on it, but since she'd brought it up. . . . "Are you actually interested in him?"

She shrugged defensively. "Why do you care?"

The possibility drove him mad. He'd never been jealous of such a wanker. He'd never been jealous, period. Splendid, a new low for him. And if the truth slipped out, she would know he wanted her in his bed, her nails in his back, screaming his name. She'd given off clues that she felt similarly, so revealing his desire would be a match on kindling. Still, he must have latent masochistic tendencies because the urge to tell Sydney in excruciating detail exactly how he wanted her bombarded him. But if he let himself be distracted, he might never find Anka. And his brother could pass to his nextlife.

"It's none of my business, I grant you. We've been working together just a few days, and I don't know you well. But I think you can do better."

Sydney cocked her head. "Are you offering?"

Caden's heart skipped a beat before blasting into a furious rhythm. Though every muscle in his body tensed at her suggestion, he doubted Sydney knew how close she was to feeling her desk against her back.

"I'm merely saying that you're a beautiful, talented woman. You deserve more."

Sydney looked at him from beneath the veil of her ginger-shaded lashes. Cunning shone in those brown eyes. And desire. The seductive sight was a blow to his gut. Bloody hell, that was the kind of look that made him ache to give her everything she desired.

"Why do you care?"

The truth would land them both in trouble. "If Jamie turns out to be an ax murderer, I'm out of a job."

Sydney rolled her eyes. "Prat. I'm leaving. On Monday, we'll continue with the magical battle story. I might have the needed facts by then."

He tensed, but did his best to act casually. "You'll be talking to your source over the weekend?"

"Perhaps. It depends on how willing she is to talk."

Not only did Caden need to find out if Anka was her source, he feared that Syndey's stories made her a target for Mathias. Now that she had the Doomsday Diary, he worried even more.

"I have a great deal of experience at extracting information from interview subjects. If you brought me along—"

"Nice try, but no. Besides, I'm not certain she'll emerge from hiding."

"I'll protect her, if that's her concern." *And you.*

She waved his suggestion away. "You can't, not against magic. But this conversation leads me to wonder . . . if you have so much experience back in the States working for a 'reputable' paper, why have you chosen to work for *Out of This Realm*?"

Clever. Caden wasn't surprised she was questioning his cover. Maddened . . . but not surprised.

"As I mentioned when I started Monday, my brother is ill and requires my care. I don't know how long he'll need me, and a man has to make a living."

"Indeed. What ails him again?"

Explaining mate mourning to a human? A definite no-no. "His physicians aren't certain, so I may be here for some time. While here, I could be very beneficial to you."

Beneficial, indeed. Sydney could picture it. Craved it, in fact. But if he was interested in anything beyond a platonic working relationship, he was doing a bloody good job of hiding it.

"I'll keep that in mind," she said finally. "I'm off for the weekend. Ta ta."

She turned to go, but he grabbed her arm. His hand felt warm, large. Real honest-to-goodness tingles shot through her body as he swung her around.

"Wait! The continuation of the battle in the tunnel, will you run that story next week?"

She drew in a shaky breath. "If my source talks more over the weekend, I might have enough information. If not, I have a list of related stories I may be able to flesh out. Holly says circulation is up, and readers are eager for more about magickind."

"Let me help you. Please."

"Because . . . ?"

"Your work is fascinating."

Really? He usually seemed annoyed. "Why aren't you interested in my other stories?"

"Cheeseburger-addicted alien attacks London McDonald's? Stonehenge vandalized by ghosts? A vicar's conversation with Kurt Cobain?"

"The first story wasn't mine originally. I only followed up, as ordered. The other two might be perfectly legitimate. Who knows Stonehenge's secrets, and the vicar might have connections to the other side. How are those less credible than a magical war?"

He hesitated, rubbing that square chin she'd spent hours looking at of late. "You have an information source who isn't in an asylum, for one. At least you haven't mentioned that she is. But given that she's a recluse. . . ."

"She's not mad, but she fears she's in danger," Sydney replied tartly. "Her fear may be nothing more than a punchline to you, but this poor woman has been terrorized—"

"I'm not laughing. If she's afraid, I'm a former U.S. Marine, skilled at hand-to-hand combat and trained as a sniper. I could lend a sense of security, which might persuade her to open up."

Truly? Sydney hadn't known any of that, but he had a military sharpness about him. "Your shoulders are as wide as a mountain and you smile as often as a mortician. The woman was repeatedly raped. You'll scare the piss out of her, more like. You're not going. Anything else?"

Caden clenched his jaw. "You're making a mistake."

"It's mine to make. Arguments aside, a few of my friends are waiting for me at the pub 'round the corner. Join us?"

Sydney held her breath. Spending the evening with Caden, knocking back a few, flirting . . . seeing where it led, would be one of the best birthday presents ever. Yes, he worked with her, and she knew she shouldn't shit where she ate, as the saying went. But something about him had her positively giddy.

He shook his head. "I need to visit my brother. Enjoy your birthday."

Without him? It wouldn't be nearly as much fun. His refusal hurt more than it should. She wanted him. Short of stripping off and dancing naked for the man, how else could she show it? This conversation only proved that he wasn't interested.

But she'd sure love to change his mind.

Sydney shooed him out and exited the room, Doomsday Diary in hand. Damn!

Still, he could ask Aquarius how she'd acquired it and look for clues about the identity of Sydney's source. Since the redheaded reporter worked quite late usually, he hadn't yet had the chance.

Five minutes. He'd give her that long to visit the loo, collect her things, and leave the old building.

While waiting, he sent the picture of the book to Bram. In moments, the wizard answered: *Bingo! Grab it.* Caden sighed. As if it were that simple . . .

While waiting for Sydney's departure, he popped by Aquarius's cubicle. Gone, damn it. Lights out, hippie tie-dye coat off its hook. He'd never thought to ask where Aquarius was taking her holiday or when she'd return. Caden winced against an oncoming headache. Well, he'd simply focus on

Sydney until the other woman returned. He could think of plenty of ways to keep busy with her.

Four minutes and fifty-eight seconds later, Caden moved nonchalantly down the hallway. Sydney's office was clear, thank goodness. Laptop shut down, lights off. Good.

If the woman wasn't going to take him along when she talked to her source, he had to find some way to learn the woman's identity. That was top priority. Bram would disagree . . . but so bloody what. Caden prayed Sydney knew Anka's location and was helping her. This might be his only chance to find his brother's mate, bring her home, and restore his brother's sanity.

Easing into Sydney's office, he shut the door. Total darkness enveloped him. The November sun set much earlier in London than in his adopted home, Texas. Though he'd grown up in the UK, he'd forgotten its long nights. It was past five and pitch black out, so he didn't dare turn the lights on. At least a faint glow from the streetlamps filtered in. He took out a pocket flashlight and flicked it on.

Sydney often jotted thoughts on little pieces of paper. *Now, where would she keep those notes?*

He opened a few drawers. Plastic spoons, snack crackers, chewing gum, a calculator, lots of red pens, and paper clips by the dozens. Some old news articles, now yellowing, about nothing of importance, but nothing in her handwriting, no addresses, nor anything that might lead him to Anka.

Caden shut the drawers with a quiet sigh. Damn! Where else would she hide notes? He spun around to a short filing cabinet. Locked, both drawers. He reached behind him for a paper clip. This wasn't the first time he'd broken into a filing cabinet. But as he shaped the little scrap of metal for his purposes, a burst of energy flooded his senses. His fingertips tingled. A wave of dizziness and a cold sweat followed. Then a distinct urge to pass his fingers in front of the cabinet and focus on mentally unlocking it.

Biting back a curse, Caden resisted the magical impulse. He'd been having them for the better part of a year. Hated them, too. Ignored them and hoped that if he never succumbed to such urges, they'd dissipate. But they were getting stronger.

Leaning against Sydney's desk, Caden focused on twisting the paper clip in the near dark. Despite a fumble or two, he managed to bend it into the shape he needed. Thirty seconds later, the filing cabinet was open. A quick prowl proved her files absent of information about Sydney's source. Damn, the little firecracker must keep her notes closer to her.

Pushing the drawer shut silently, he locked it up, then cast his desperate gaze at her laptop. Maybe she kept information there? He booted the machine up, only to be confronted with a prompt for a password. He had no idea what that might be.

Again, instinct screamed at him to grip the machine, connect to it with his mind, coax it to tell him Sydney's secrets. Again, he refused. Instead, he began searching under her desk, inside drawers, for scraps of papers with passwords lying about. But as always, Sydney was sharp and organized, and kept her secrets hidden.

Time to guess. What did he know about her, besides the fact she was gorgeous, smart, and determined? He typed in her birthday, and the system rejected his attempt. Only two more attempts before the system locked him out, so he'd better think smart.

Had she mentioned upcoming travel? Was she excited about Christmas? Did she have any pets? What was favorite color? Favorite food? All common fodder for passwords, but

Caden found himself genuinely interested in the answers. Christ, he had it bad for her.

He'd picked up an anonymous blonde a mere three days ago. And a well-curved brunette the night before that. And still he was hungry, crawling out of his skin for sex. But since meeting Sydney, he was utterly fixated on her. This intense attraction had to be magically enhanced. He didn't dare scratch the itch.

Focusing on the business at hand, Caden hovered his fingers over the keyboard again. *Think, think.* As his fingertips touched down, a wave of energy rolled through him, tingles drifted up his arms. Then knowledge burst across his brain. *Cadensexy1.* That was her password? Impossible.

But in the absence of other ideas, he typed it in. Her desktop appeared a few moments later.

Sydney found him sexy. Knowing that notched up his arousal. Not good. His fire didn't need more fuel. He couldn't jeopardize this job. He needed it to complete his mission. Sex with her would have to remain a fantasy.

Even worse, his unintentional magic had revealed her password to him. He'd never performed such an act before and feared it meant his transition from man to wizard was looming.

He scowled when he searched her computer from top to bottom and found nothing but old stories, months-old letters, and dull e-mails.

Caden extinguished the flashlight with a sigh. Now what? Figures that Sydney was too smart to leave important information unsecured. Waiting until Monday to move on this mission wasn't an option. Anka was alone, possibly in pain or danger. His favorite redhead would be crafting more stories over the weekend. Lucan was sliding closer to death. That damned diary of Morganna's . . . thank God she was no longer around to wield it, but the book in a human reporter's hands spelled disaster.

He had to talk to Sydney. Charm her, Bram had said. He'd rather not use Sydney that way. He liked her too much. But time was short, and he didn't have enough of it to gain her trust.

After a quick stop by the office manager's desk, Caden had the information he needed. Time to turn on the charm . . . he hoped.

The next morning, Sydney sipped tea, still fixated on Caden.

She fingered the spine of the little red book Aquarius had given her. Would it really make her sexual fantasies come true? Even if it did, she'd be a pretty sad sack to magically coerce a man into bed who hadn't shown the slightest interest in her.

With a shrug, she tucked the book away in her nightstand and returned to the kitchen. Halfway there, she heard a knock at her door.

"Who is it?"

"Caden."

Truly?

She couldn't run to the door fast enough. After fumbling with the locks, she jerked the door open and stared in surprise.

Caden was there, in the flesh . . . and what incredible flesh it was. Tight black T-shirt, faded crotch-hugging jeans, and an expression that said he had more on his mind than business.

He swallowed. And stared. "Is now a bad time?"

"N-no," she stuttered.

After a lingering glance down her body, he swallowed again. "Glad to hear it."

Sydney frowned at his odd behavior, then looked down at herself—and gasped.

Her one indulgence was lingerie, of which she was wearing her latest . . . and skimpiest. Pale and silky, the lace-edged straps of the camisole hugged her shoulders. More lace tipped the low-cut V and hugged the swells of her breasts. Silk cupped her beneath their curves, just as she'd like his palms to do. The faint outline of her nipples showed through the flesh-colored fabric. His gaze, his stance, hardened as he stared. She wondered what else did, and fought the urge to look down.

He had no such hesitation, his gaze traveling over the sheer boy shorts that showed off every inch of her legs. Sydney suspected he could see a hint of the fiery hair between, as well.

Blast! The sound of Caden's voice had made her utterly forget she was more than half naked before she answered the door.

"Wait here." Sydney jogged away and returned a moment later wearing a matching dressing gown. Frowning, she belted the flowing garment around her waist. It didn't cover everything, but enough to make her decent.

"Do you want to come in or stare at me like a mutant in a circus freak show?"

He swallowed. "You don't look like a freak. At all."

That voice of his poured over her like melted chocolate, rich, warm, tempting. Sydney drank it in, though she wondered if he truly meant it. First, a look. Now, a compliment. Uncharacteristic, to say the least.

"Is this a bad time?" he asked. "Too early to talk?"

She stepped aside and let him in. "I'm surprised you're here at all. Is something wrong?"

"Must something be wrong for me to want to talk to you?"

On a Saturday morning? *Yes.* "How did you find me?"

Caden merely smiled. What the blazes did that smoldering look mean?

"Why not simply call?" she rephrased.

"You never gave me your number."

"I never gave you my address, either. How did you get it?"

"I have my ways."

Very cryptic. But since he was here, maybe she could work his unexpected visit to her advantage, see if he had a bit more interest in her than she'd suspected.

He shut the door and approached, standing close, almost touching . . . but not quite.

"I want to talk to you," he murmured. "Say things I couldn't at the office."

Her belly fluttered. It sounded sexual. Until five minutes ago, she would have chided herself for wishful thinking. Now . . . ?

She remained close, and his warm breath hit her lips. His eyes locked onto her as if she was the only woman in the world. Forget flutters, her belly plunged to her knees.

Suddenly, he wanted to be cozy? They hadn't worked together long. It was possible he'd simply been cautious. Maybe it was the reporter in her, but she needed to ask questions, get to the bottom of this.

"Sit down and say whatever you've come to say. Tea?"

"No, thanks." He settled himself on her sofa and stretched his arms clear across the back.

The wide span of his arms, coupled with those amazing shoulders, made her salivate in a way she shouldn't about a colleague. But he wasn't helping, drat him, by looking so sexy—and staring as if she was edible.

"Come sit beside me." He patted the sofa cushion.

Sydney looked between the two empty chairs in the room, then again at the sofa. Gingerly, she settled in next to him. "I'm listening and I like having you here, but if your visit has anything to do with my source for the articles, I'm not taking you with me to our meeting—"

"No, nothing to do with that. But it's important and better said outside the office."

Right, then. Well, that made her curious, especially when his gaze skimmed down her body, lingering. Though she wasn't naked, his gaze made her she felt like it. "Go on."

Caden hesitated. "Maybe you should change."

He was suggesting that she put on more clothes after thoroughly looking his fill? Odd . . . his burning stare said he was two seconds from ravishing her; his behavior was cagey. Sydney prided herself on being able to read people, but Caden had her baffled.

Instinct told her that something was off. That same instinct told her she wasn't going to solve this mystery unless she played along.

Finally, Sydney left the room, sashayed down the hall, and shut her bedroom door. Caden lamented losing the stunning view. The woman revved his body thoroughly into overdrive. But he was here to find clues to Anka's whereabouts and the book—and to make this magical nightmare go away.

Caden raced into action and began searching. If Sydney had an appointment to see the woman this weekend maybe he could find an address, a phone number, a name that would prove this goose chase worthwhile.

With the clock ticking, he started with a nearby antique secretary propped against the wall between her living area and her kitchen. Immediately he could see she hadn't stashed the little red diary here. Bills, pictures, a list of things to do, a little calendar with various dates written inside . . . like Aquarius being on holiday. No mention of where she was headed.

He sighed, righted everything, then dashed to the kitchen. Next to the phone he found a shopping list and a neat row of phone numbers for restaurants that delivered. Gads, the woman lived by lists.

Meanwhile, the damn clock was ticking, and he didn't care that she needed milk from the market and had a local pizzeria on speed dial. Ignoring an odd tingle and a cold sweat, he scanned the room and saw her handbag sitting on a little table near the front door. No time to be squeamish about invading her privacy.

He unzipped the flap, pushed aside her coin purse, keys, and lipstick. A notepad with a pen attached. He flipped it open. *Eureka!* It was littered with notes. Some large, some sideways, some in an odd shorthand he couldn't decipher. He lifted one page, another, a third . . . at the seventh, he paused. A whole page dedicated to the story of magickind she was slowly, foolishly revealing.

Saturday @ 4, A's place, one of her notes said. This Saturday? Who was A? Anka or someone else, like Aquarius? Had Anka been free long enough to have her own place? If she had, why hadn't she returned home? Where was this place? Was it possible that Mathias knew who she was and where she lived? Nothing else on the little scrap of paper answered any of those questions. Damn!

Just below that was a list of seemingly random thoughts under the heading POSSIBILITIES. She had written yet another list with items like "decomposition of bodies," "magickind living among humans," "magical war/other battles," and "origin of the magical diary."

Caden took a moment to absorb those horrific possible stories. Sydney had already written about the battle in the tunnel. Any of these would seem like natural follow-up. And if she wrote a single word of the Doomsday Diary in *Out of This Realm*, Mathias and the Anarki would hunt her down within hours. Mathias ate sweet morsels like Sydney for snacks. The thought made his blood freeze.

His reaction made little sense; he barely knew the woman, but Caden's first instinct was to protect her with his life. He knew he'd die before letting Mathias hurt her. And he didn't want to question why.

Caden heard fumbling from the end of the hall. With a curse, he shoved the little notepad back into place, then crept to the living room, planting himself on the sofa before Sydney stepped in, wearing a pair of long, flowing pants and a curve-hugging sweater. He liked the lingerie better. But this outfit emphasized how small she was. If he was to lay her down and cover her body with his, he would completely envelop her and mold every lush little curve to him. . . .

Not a smart train of thought. He was losing what little spare room he had in his jeans, and Sydney's quizzical expression told him that she'd done some thinking while she was changing. That was never good.

"What's so urgent that you had to hunt me down over the weekend? That you couldn't say in the office?"

She always got to the point. All the women he had dated who chatted endlessly and never really had a point—they drove him mad. The one woman he wished would prattle and simply let him lead the conversation was having none of it. He sighed.

"Sit beside me." He patted the sofa cushion beside him once more. *Charm her*, he reminded himself.

She settled in, studying him as if she could read his thoughts. He tamped down on the urge to squirm.

"The office is always hectic," he commented.

"We're in a deadline-driven business."

"True, but that doesn't leave us much time to get acquainted."

"And you think that will improve our working relationship?"

"Perhaps, but that's not why I'm here, Sydney." He purposely dropped his voice an octave and leaned closer.

She raised a skeptical brow. "Out with it."

"I want to get to know you, as a person. As a woman. Not as a reporter."

She cocked her head and stared at him, the wheels in her mind obviously turning. "For what purpose?"

Bloody hell, was this woman immune to seduction? "Are you always this direct?"

"Are you always this vague?" she countered.

This was becoming a proper mess. He was ill-prepared for pretending interest in a woman while he was actually mad for her—yet hiding his desire. He had to be flirtatious, but no more. But his fierce desire was interfering with his mission. He knew how magical men instinctively found their mates, and he suspected that one kiss would be his doom.

"I'm trying to say that you interest me without you filing a harassment complaint."

That made her laugh. "I'll tell you if you cross the line. Interesting how?"

"In just about every way imaginable." That, he didn't have to lie about. The lingerie she'd had on earlier told him without a doubt that she'd have a gorgeous body he'd kill to devour. She fascinated him with the wicked sweep of those little auburn brows over sharp brown eyes. The woman brimmed intelligence. The way she asked questions, deduced the truth quickly, but carried herself with undeniable sensuality, all dazzled him, along with her zest. Had he ever attacked each day with such passion? Certainly not since Iraq and being one of the few survivors of his platoon. Perhaps not even since Westin's death.

"You sound as if you mean more than professionally," she remarked.

He shrugged, hating the need to be coy. "We work together, so the situation requires caution. I hoped we could . . . get to know each other first, then see if we wanted to pursue more."

Her eyes narrowed. "This is the first I've heard or seen of any interest beyond the professional."

"I've tried to keep unprofessional thoughts to myself at the office." That was the truth, and hopefully enough for her curiosity.

"You've had them?"

Caden chastised himself for underestimating her tenacity. "You're a beautiful woman."

"Thank you." His flattery only sharpened her gaze. "But this seems . . . sudden."

"I could tell you my first thought after meeting you, but it's definitely not fit for the office, nor terribly polite."

Sydney turned sideways, tucking one leg under her and anchoring her arm across the back of the sofa, her fingers so close to his shoulder. If he leaned toward her just a bit, she'd be touching him. The thought blasted heat to his cock.

Then she smiled. "That so? All right, I'll play. I've had similar thoughts."

"I thought so yesterday. In your office. It was in your eyes."

"So that's why you decided to say something?"

"Yes." It sounded reasonable, though he'd sensed her interest a few days ago.

"What do you think should happen next?"

"We should take it slow," he murmured. "Get to know each other, then decide if we want to proceed, so we don't jeopardize our working relationship."

"Hmm. Very wise and gentlemanly."

Caden exhaled, hoping she believed him. But one look at her, and he resisted the urge to wince. Something was going on in that head of hers.

"But let me make certain I understand. I'm to believe that you've had lascivious thoughts since meeting me, but hid them until you . . . either broke into someone's filing cabinet to find my address or followed me home, which shows an amazing dedication to seducing me. Then you knocked on my door on a Saturday and looked at me as if you'd like to strip me bare in the foyer. And you did all this so that we could take our relationship slowly? Have I got that right?"

Well, damn. Caden clenched his fists as his brain went into overdrive. Now that she'd seen through his ruse, how did he repair the damage and salvage his mission—without risking their working relationship and his future?

"What I'd like to do and what's prudent are two different things."

"Often, yes. But let me tell you what I think is happening here: You insulted Jamie because he's a slacker, and you object to them as a rule. Very against your military background. You want to be a part of the magickind war story for some reason, and are fixated on my source, and when I refused to let you tag along, you decided to resort to a half-hearted seduction in an attempt to hoodwink me into changing my mind. Is that closer to the truth?"

Dear God. He'd had undercover missions easier than this.

Too smart, she was. "No. What's happening is that I'm far more attracted to a colleague than I'm proud of, and the things I want to do with you would make even your pert little freckles blush. I tried to keep quiet because I need this job, but when I saw it was mutual, I couldn't hold my desire in. I didn't mention it at the office because it's inappropriate there. And as much as I'd like to get you naked in the next three minutes, I don't want to simply shag you. That wouldn't help me to know you better. Yes, I'm interested in your source about the magical war story because I understand war, and let's face it, a woman claiming such things is intriguing. But I'm also not trying to rush you to bed because I don't want to build artificial intimacy simply to get my way. I want you to choose to make me your partner at the office, regardless of our personal relationship."

That sounded logical. And a bit too close to the truth.

Sydney sent him a considering stare. "What do you recommend next?"

Caden released the breath he'd been holding. Maybe she believed him. Perhaps. He had to keep to his role. "Lunch?"

"Actually, I was about to toss together a sandwich. You're welcome to join me."

"I meant to take you out."

"Wouldn't staying here allow for more privacy? If we're going to get to know each other, that's much harder in public."

And much easier for him to put his hands all over her, as he was dying to now. "Whatever you like."

"Perfect." She rose to her feet and headed for the kitchen, grabbing ingredients as she dashed about. "Tell me about your parents. Are they still alive?"

He was supposed to be getting to know her, finding ways to make her trust him, not the other way around. "They are, but I was a late-in-life baby. They're quite elderly. Yours? I want to hear about you."

"Later." She waved off his question. "So you're caring for your brother because your parents can't?"

"Precisely."

"Other siblings?"

Not anymore, and not for anything would he drag up that terrible story. "None. You? Any siblings?"

"Only child. Stop changing the subject," she admonished, opening a jar. "Mustard?"

"Please. I really want—"

"How much older is your brother?"

Three hundred sixty-seven years. He suspected she wouldn't take that well. "Upwards of a decade."

"Significant, then. Tell me more about his illness."

"Lucan is unconscious, they have little idea how to help him, and this isn't the Inquisition."

He rose and entered the kitchen. Sydney stood against the counter, spreading mustard on brown bread. He eased up behind her, placed his hands on her hips and whispered against her neck, "I'm here to get to know *you*."

With a saucy tilt of her head, she shot him a glance over her shoulder. "As I've said, no siblings. My parents are both professors. My mother teaches history at Oxford. My father once taught, but now conducts very important research to help create a purely artificial fuel source."

Caden winced, and Sydney laughed. "You asked."

"They sound very serious, indeed."

"They're even more so in person, I assure you."

Something on her face gave Caden pause. "And are they supportive of your career?"

She hesitated. "I'm a bitter disappointment, and I'm reminded of that every time I see them."

Though Sydney said it laughingly, he could read the pain on her face. She was hurt by their lack of support. It was foolish and stupid and dangerous, but he eased his arms around her. "I think you're brilliant, and I have no doubt that someday you're going to be wildly famous for doing exactly what you love."

"Hmm. Flattery." She didn't sound impressed.

But this, he truly meant. She'd wowed him with her very first story. Though she knew nothing about magickind, she'd somehow caught onto the nuances, what was important to the warring factions. "Honesty."

He longed to kiss her mouth, mere inches from his, taste her, bring her closer to him, ease her pain. Inside, he damned his magical impulses for dangling this temptation in front of him and making her so forbidden. If she was, as he suspected, the mate magic intended for him—no, he couldn't think about what could be or he'd go mad.

The reality was, he was deep in this magical war. Not only did he want to avoid Lucan's fate, but he didn't want to place Sydney in danger. If he kissed her and succumbed to the need to Call to her as his mate . . . he couldn't bear the thought that, instead of reporting about a woman who had been repeatedly raped by Mathias, she might actually *become* one.

"Are you going to stare at my mouth or kiss me?"

Caden backed away. "I'm reminding myself to take it slowly. Perhaps I should help with lunch."

She sighed. "There's some clementines and crisps in the cupboard."

After retrieving them, he turned to find Sydney setting up the little bistro-style table in her kitchen. She turned and grabbed two plates piled high with lettuce and fresh tomato. He held the chair for her. Sydney sent a raised brow at him, but sat.

"So," he said before she could start interrogating him again. "Your parents don't love what you've chosen to do with your life. My guess is that you work very hard to be the best and hope they will someday recognize your genius."

"Thank you, Dr. Freud." She sent him a quelling glance. "Something like that. Though I know I can't live to please them."

"No adult does, but you hate to disappoint them, right?"

She swallowed her bite of sandwich and peered across the table at him. "You came to get to know me, yet clearly you already do. Perhaps we skip the rest of this silly 'getting to know you' crap and go straight to bed?"

CHAPTER THREE

AN HOUR LATER, SYDNEY knew for certain that Caden was following her when she ducked into a little jewelry shop—and he peeked in the window moments later. Not for an instant did she believe that he had window-shopped for a lovely pair of earrings or a belly stud.

In fact, today he had a hidden agenda. After professing his infatuation, what unattached, red-blooded man turned down sex so blatantly offered? Only the kind trying to dupe her. His sneaking after her now merely confirmed her suspicions. The only thing he'd shown genuine interest in since coming to work with her? The magical war story. She suspected that he meant to steal it.

After she'd refused to let him accompany her to visit her source, he turned up on her doorstep and suddenly professed romantic interest. How stupid did he think she was? She'd called his bluff over lunch by inviting him to her bed, figuring she'd determine whether he was feeding her crap or genuinely interested in her. She'd personally hoped for the latter. Though he was a deceitful wanker, he was a sexy one.

His stuttered refusal was his loss. Caden lying about desiring her didn't hurt. All right, perhaps a bit. But she had to stop thinking with her emotions and get smart. He sought to scoop her, after all.

Over her dead body.

She was going—alone, thank you—to meet the battered witch, listen to more of the woeful tale that tore at her heart, and gather more information for her story. She shoved thoughts of her gorgeous, deceitful photographer aside.

Exiting to the street again, Sydney walked half a block. She'd give Caden credit; she couldn't see him behind her, but she sensed him. As she rounded a bend in the road, she caught a glimpse of him, pretending interest in a street vendor who shivered in the November chill. He didn't look her way, but Sydney felt his attention.

Nonchalantly, she proceeded south, hunkering down into her coat until she found the right place. Once spotted, she dodged traffic and crossed the road, then entered a crowded, smoky pub. She sat on a stool near the back, far from the barkeep.

A dozen seconds later, Caden and a stiff breeze blew in. Sydney grabbed a discarded menu and pretended to read.

He wandered along the front of the pub, looking out the windows at the sidewalk, presumably not noticing her. Finally he sat at an empty table in the corner, grabbed a menu—and peered at her over the top. She made a great show of checking her watch and her mobile, fidgeting and squirming.

Finally, a waitress popped by his table. What he ordered Sydney didn't know or care. Now was her chance.

She rose and headed conspicuously for the toilet. She wished she could see the look on Caden's face when he realized she wasn't coming back out. As the door to the loo shut behind her, the thought made her smile.

She'd vanished. Out the window of the loo, he'd guess. Brilliant.

He'd underestimated both her cleverness and determination. Again.

Frustration crept in, and Caden raked a hand through

his hair. How the devil could he find her source if she didn't trust him? But he was also concerned about Sydney. Didn't the girl realize that she was potentially in danger?

The mobile at his side rang. A glance at the display had him cursing not so softly.

"What?" he snapped.

"Your delightful mood means things aren't going well, I take it?" Bram drawled.

"Not exactly. The woman is too smart by half and knows everything I say is shit."

"You're not being charming enough."

Caden gritted his teeth. "Deception isn't my style."

"It's *charm*. Do you need me to demonstrate?"

Though Bram was mated, the thought of him anywhere near Sydney made Caden feel uncomfortably homicidal. "The same charm you showed your now-missing mate?"

"Leave my mate out of this," Bram snarled.

If you return the favor.

As soon as the words blazed across Caden's mind, he sucked in a breath. Damn, he had to stop thinking about Sydney like that. He didn't want a magical mate. And now he had to distract Bram. "Likewise, leave Sydney alone."

"Are you having the urge to Call to this reporter?"

Every time he neared her, his temperature spiked. She was a fever, and if he kissed her, he feared he'd blurt the words that could bind them together. Not good signs.

Her proposition at lunch had boiled his blood. A hearty "yes" had hovered on the tip of his tongue. Yes, he wanted her naked. Yes, he wanted to taste every inch of her fair skin, possess that sweet body. Yes, he wanted all that intelligence and sass. Yes, he wanted to be the one to protect her. But giving in to his urges would spell disaster. Too bad no one had given his instincts the memo.

"Can we focus on the mission?" Caden unleashed his annoyance. "She knows I've scarcely said a true word to her since we met. She's seeing her contact this afternoon, knew I was following her, and intentionally lost me. Now, she's thinking of writing an article about the Doomsday Diary. What do you think will happen if she does?"

Bram cursed. "She'll get a very unpleasant, firsthand look at magic, Mathias-style."

"Exactly." Caden gripped the phone, the thought too terrible to contemplate. He would protect Sydney at any cost, do anything to silence that story. Keep her safe. As much as it chafed him to ask for Bram's help, he must.

"You need to step in," he went on. "I'm compromised. Sydney knows I'm interested in the magical war story and that my seduction wasn't real."

"I can't." Suddenly, Bram sighed, sounding frustrated. "Another attack last night. Nearly everyone dead, two women missing. One transitioned just last week. Gossip and panic is beginning to spread around magickind about Mathias's return. The Council elders have their thumbs up their arses, as usual. They want me to quell the rumors. I'm trying to be the voice of reason, but they don't wish to hear logic. Duke and I are visiting Privileged households likely to be attacked and preaching caution, but . . . it's frustrating to be forced to lie. I dare not leave the Council to their own devices for long. I'd insist on transcasting the truth to magickind, but I don't have enough of the other Councilmen's votes behind me. In the meantime, Marrok is ferociously training us for the war we all know is coming. If I sent Ice to help you, he would simply flatten *Out of This Realm*. Besides, magic isn't a cure-all. I can't just wave my wand and have Sydney forget about the book and her story ideas."

Bram painted a bleak picture, and Caden nearly felt sorry

for the bastard. What the hell good was magic? Oh, that's right, none. He'd had proof enough of that early in life. Caden gripped the back of his neck and massaged at the tension gripping him. The damn tingles had returned. He was exhausted, yet his body craved sex. Lots of lovelies in the pub, several looking in his direction. But a glance south proved his cock was having none of them. It was fixated on Sydney. He sighed.

"You're going to have to fix this," Bram said. "Get closer to Sydney, however you must. Convince her with whatever necessary. Get that bloody diary out of her hands. Stop those stories. Nothing about the Doomsday Diary can appear in print."

Caden sighed. How the devil was he to do all that?

"I'll talk to her tonight," he told Bram. "I'll be waiting for her when she gets home. Until then, I should visit my brother for a bit."

"I can't spare any of the warriors to transport you, but I can send my sister."

"Sabelle's company is always a delight."

Bram snorted. "Spoken like someone who does not have to live with the minx."

They rang off, and Caden waited. Sure enough, within moments Sabelle walked into the pub. Every male head turned. Jaws dropped. One man even rose to his feet, looking as if he was in a trance. She held up a hand, and he wandered back to his stool instantly, looking a bit confused.

"Do you get that reaction from men everywhere you go?"

She shrugged. "It's my grandmother's siren blood, not me. I could be the ugliest hag in creation and they'd still respond that way."

But she wasn't. Far from it. Sabelle was truly stunning. Wars had been started over faces half so lovely. Centerfolds would kill for her body. The first time he'd seen her standing in the middle of his living room in Texas, explaining that his brother was suffering, he'd had to truly focus on her words, not his shock at her utter beauty.

But he'd quickly learned that she wasn't just beautiful on the outside. Caden genuinely liked her. But he didn't *want* her.

"If Bram hasn't passed the message to you, thank you for helping Lucan."

"I've known him all my life, Caden. He's a dear friend. I'm not about to let him die senselessly."

A brave soul. "Every other surrogate we've sent has been terrified."

She shrugged. "I believe, deep down, he would recognize *me* before he did any serious harm."

"Sabelle, he doesn't know himself."

With a nod, she conceded. "Yes, well . . . it hasn't been going as well as I would like. The energy he's derived from my fear simply isn't enough. He expends it all thrashing and calling Anka's name. Lucan needs more."

"Meaning?"

"With the previous surrogates, he growled that he scented another man, then tried to attack them. I think I might have a solution. You're welcome to observe."

Something in the witch's tone made him pause. "Perhaps we should discuss this."

Sabelle shook her head, golden curls brushing her slender arms. "I need to do this my way."

"I don't want you risking your safety."

She patted his arm. "I'm fine. Why don't we meander outside and round the back? We'll attract less attention when we teleport."

Caden knew a firm change of subject when he heard one

and gave up, for now. He nodded, and they made their way into the windy evening chill.

Once they were out of sight, Sabelle positioned them away from people, out of the light, wrapped her hand in his and *poof*! One minute he was standing in a dark alley, the next he fought a black, stomach-turning void. Bloody magic! Then he stood in Bram's foyer. And the man himself was there waiting.

"Glad to see you're here. I was getting worried," he visually inspected his sister, clearly reassuring himself that no harm had come to her.

She sighed. "I'm *eighty*-four, not four. I'm perfectly capable of finding someone and bringing them here."

"But not necessarily without avoiding trouble."

Sabelle rolled her eyes. "If you'll excuse me, I have important things to do." She clapped Caden on the shoulder. "Entertain him for a bit, will you? I'm worn out."

With that parting shot, she disappeared.

Bram cast him a rueful glance. "I'll trade you a brother in mate mourning for a mischievous sister."

Caden almost laughed. "Thanks, but no. Honestly, I don't want either problem."

"I know."

"You look exhausted." Caden knew he shouldn't ask, lest he find himself deeper in magical muck. But as much as he disliked some of Bram's tactics, the wizard had taken his brother in, offered his home, his assistance, and now, his sister. "Any luck finding your mate?"

Bram winced, and the strain showed on the tired lines around his eyes and mouth. "No, it's as if she's vanished. I feel . . . nothing except her absence."

"But she has not broken your bond?" The last thing he needed was for Bram to be in Lucan's condition. Making his brother whole would be impossible.

"No, thank God. She is still mine, yet all my attempts to trace her lead nowhere."

Odd, but then that was magic, difficult, baffling, and frustratingly cryptic. "Do you know anything about her? Where she lives, her phone number, relatives' names?"

"As far as I can tell, everything she told me is a lie." He scrubbed a hand over his tense expression. "I'm going to have to call one of those damn surrogates for energy. Mating is certainly effective; I don't want any woman but her. Somehow——" Bram broke off with a shake of his head. "Never mind. I'll work it out. Go see your brother."

"If I haven't said thanks already——" Caden choked out. He disliked being beholden to Bram, but the words needed saying.

"Don't. Lucan is like family to me, as is Anka. I only hope we can bring them back together."

Beginning to fear that was impossible, Caden turned to the giant staircase on his left. One step at a time, he trudged up, dread pulsing through him as he climbed to the top, then marched to the end of the hall where Lucan lay.

God, he'd rather be anywhere but here.

Taking a deep breath, he lifted his hand to the knob of the closed door, wondering how his life had become hellish so quickly. What must Lucan's be like?

Caden opened the door. Inside, the drapes were drawn, shutting out the weak twilight sun. The shadowed room smelled of sweat and rage and desperation. Lucan reeked of all three. He was a terrible, panting example of magic's cruelty.

Bracing his forearm against the doorjamb, Caden hesitated. Though their sibling bond dictated that he care for Lucan, he didn't want to walk in. When he'd been a boy himself, he'd helplessly watched Westin die. Laughing toddler one moment, corpse the next. A stab in the heart. The possibility of reliving the trauma of a sibling's death terrified him.

A growl sounded from the bed, and Caden took a cautious step into the dark bedroom. There Lucan lay still and chained, naked except for a pair of white briefs. He stared in horror at his brother's gaunt cheeks and pallid complexion. In the past days, his brother had deteriorated.

Swallowing his horror, Caden vowed that when he saw Sydney again, he'd focus on nothing but his mission. He *must* find Anka and make Lucan whole again.

An adjoining door opened to his right, and Sabelle exited the bathroom in a cloud of humid, perfumed air. She wore a simple white dressing gown, damp hair pinned to the top of her head, water droplets still clinging to her golden skin. Determination stamped her regal features and movements as she strode to a chair beside the bed. When she glanced Caden's way and saw him staring at Lucan, regret softened her face.

"It's not always this way."

Her whisper was like a blade to his chest. She meant to be comforting, reassuring. Instead, her words only angered him more.

"Caden," Sabelle tried again. "I believe his bond with Anka was true and deep. He's hurting now, but he had over a century of joy with a woman he loved. Any of us should be half so lucky."

"To be reduced to an animal? You would feel lucky to endure this?"

"Mate mourning for a woman works differently, so I can't say for certain. Males undergo a period of intense . . . adjustment. A witch suddenly alone is often compelled to seek out another wizard for comfort, protection, and energy. She doesn't remember her former mate, but there's a sense of loss, and she pines. Just not in this way." Sabelle gestured to his brother.

Meaning that Anka could be anywhere, her memory of Lucan completely gone, and shagging someone else. If the mate mourning didn't finish Lucan off, that knowledge might.

Sabelle placed a gentle hand on his shoulder. "I know this is unpleasant to you—"

"Horrific," Caden corrected. "He—he's a lunatic and he's a burden to you. Will he ever again be himself?"

Regret tightened her mouth, shadowed her eyes. "His mate mourning is severe. We're trying. Honestly. I'm—"

"Please don't think I'm faulting you," he said gently. "I don't blame you or your brother in the least. I'm . . . frustrated. He's gotten worse."

"Until he takes energy, he cannot stabilize."

Caden paced. "I feel helpless. I know I can't do anything to help except find Anka. Without her, is there any end in sight other than his death?"

"One day at a time. You're trying. We all are. Don't discount Lucan. He's strong. It's not uncommon for a wizard's mate mourning to end abruptly. Tomorrow, he could awaken perfectly fine."

Or this condition could kill him. Caden snorted. "Magic could never be so kind."

"Then give up on him." She tossed her hands in the air. "But I won't. Lucan is our friend. His death would kill my brother."

She didn't wait for a reply before she approached the bed and raised her hands to Lucan, lingering at one ankle, then the other. Then she made her way to the top corners of the bed, murmured a few words, and passed her fingers over each of Lucan's hands.

Suddenly, the chains binding him loosened a bit, allowing him limited movement.

With a roar, Lucan thrashed about, eyes wild. The whites were gone, his pupils mere dots in a sea of tumultuous blue.

"Dear God, what are you doing?" He rushed forward to tighten Lucan's restraints again.

Sabelle stayed him with a raised hand. "I'm serving him."

Caden wished that didn't mean what he feared. "Lucan could kill you. He nearly did the others because they weren't Anka."

"With the surrogates, he smelled other men on them. He assumed they were enemies, come to kill him. So he attacked. I'm attempting a new tactic. I'm completely clean and washed with Anka's soap and shampoo, for good measure."

"But allowing him so much slack in the chains . . . isn't that dangerous?"

"When others have been feral, they've had a need to dominate, according to my Aunt Millie. In this state, Lucan will require any woman he beds to be beneath him. Besides, I hope that having some freedom of movement will signal to him that he's not under attack and enable him to take me. He'll derive more energy if he does."

Caden swallowed. "And you'll just let him . . ."

She stared back at Caden over her shoulder. "My body is a small thing to give to keep a dear friend alive. If embracing another eases him past his mourning, why would I not help him?"

Her selfless words hit Caden in the gut. This wonderful woman was risking herself. He adored her, yet was scared for her, all at once.

"Does Bram know what you're about?"

She shook her head. "He'd only be a hindrance."

Caden shook his head. Foolish, brave, amazing woman. "What if Lucan attacks you?"

She smiled sadly. "You're here."

He bit back a scream that he wanted no part of this, but Sabelle's courage made him feel like a coward. Lucan needed this to stay alive, and the witch was willing to risk her life and body to heal him. Though there was no risk to himself, Caden wanted no part of watching his brother siphon sexual energy from Sabelle. He railed against being here at all. The response shamed him.

"Back way to the farthest corner of the room. If he smells you . . ." She winced.

No telling what Lucan would do, except that it wouldn't be good. Ridiculously grateful for that small reprieve, he shut the door and leaned against it, watching his brother and waiting.

Sabelle nodded, then dropped her robe. She wasn't wearing a stitch.

His jaw dropped. The witch wasn't just a pretty face; she had curves stacked everywhere, long legs, a lush backside, a long, narrow torso with a flat belly. Her breasts . . . the stuff of wet dreams.

Still, Caden had no urge to touch her. He couldn't when he had so much to fear. And such tumultuous feelings for Sydney.

Kicking the robe away, Sabelle edged onto the bed and lay beside Lucan.

Immediately, he lunged for her, his eyes wide and frenetic and sightless. He sniffed at her, growled, and rolled her body beneath his, flattening her against the mattress, overwhelming her with his taut body.

"Sabelle?" Caden called and darted for her.

"I'm fine," she vowed. "Stay back."

Caden managed to do as instructed—barely.

"Female," Lucan purred as he buried his face in her neck. His mouth devoured her skin as he panted, and his chest rumbled with sounds of approval. His nose began to roam her body. He used the slack in his chains to squeeze a breast, then cupped between her legs. "Anka?"

When Lucan panted and bit at her neck, she shuddered. Her eyes slid shut. Caden flinched and resisted the urge to rescue her. He gripped the edges of the portal behind him, fingers digging into the wood. Watching his brother sexually dominate her was both horrifying and repelling. If Caden had been against magical mating before, seeing this nightmare sealed the deal.

Sabelle wrapped her arms around him and encouraged, "That's it. More."

Lucan didn't respond; he could not hear. So she communicated by stroking his shoulders, filtering her fingers through his hair. She glided one palm down Lucan's back and arched toward him. With that urging, Lucan unleashed more of his inner beast, and his hands roamed her pale flesh. He tried to claim her mouth, but Sabelle dodged him, offering her neck. Finally, Lucan gave up, and dropped his mouth to her breasts, ravishing them. Caden winced, fighting his instinct to protect Sabelle, as Lucan pinned her down for his pleasure.

"Anka," he breathed against Sabelle's skin, fisted his hand in her wet hair. "My Anka!"

Lucan pressed against Sabelle intimately, thrusting his hips at her. Caden recoiled, yet he couldn't turn away for Sabelle's safety. For Lucan's sake, he wanted this to work, but watching his brother take from Sabelle utterly disturbed him.

"Stop," Caden demanded. "You don't have to do this."

Sabelle opened her eyes and turned her head to meet his stare. "I do, but if you can't stay, I understand."

The offer was tempting, but . . . "Who will be your safety net?"

"He's chained. Go on. It's all right."

"I won't leave you to face this alone. We neither of us know what he's capable of."

Her expression was like a shrug as she stripped away Lucan's briefs.

With an animal growl, Lucan completely covered her, his much bigger body all but swallowing her up. Chains rattling, he gripped her hips in his hands and lunged for her mouth, intent on fusing them together. Again, she dodged him.

"Give me!" Lucan roared.

Caden lunged toward the bed again, but a glance from Sabelle stopped him in his tracks. His fingers, still gripping the door frame, turned numb. The witch was determined, and his brother needed her. But, oh God . . . this was terrible, painful. He could only imagine what Sabelle endured.

When Lucan could not kiss her, he grew more agitated, his hands clutching her cheeks and forcing her mouth under his. Sabelle pressed her lips together.

Panic crossed her face.

Frustration and fear gnawed at Caden's gut. "Will kissing him turn him more feral?"

Sabelle raised her head over Lucan's shoulder, dodging him again. "If he tastes me, he'll know I'm not Anka."

Of course. Every wizard knew his mate instinctively by taste. Their kiss, their tears, their cream—whatever he tasted, it would carry the flavor of his mate. Lucan would sense it, or rather its absence, in Sabelle.

She distracted him by spreading her thighs beneath him, and arching her hips in invitation. Lucan hesitated. As he loosed a feral howl, he invaded her body.

Wincing, she cried out.

That was it. Caden could not stand about and do nothing. He ripped away from the door.

"Stay back!" Sabelle shouted. "If he smells you, he will assume we're attacking him and try to kill me."

Since Sabelle's position under Lucan made her vulnerable, he could kill her instantly.

Swallowing bile and his pride, Caden eased back. "Work free of him, and I'll help you tighten the chains."

Lucan nudged her neck with his face, braced his hands on her hips, prepared to fuck her like a madman. But he paused.

Sabelle caressed his back and lifted to him again in encouragement.

Without warning, Lucan thrust forward savagely, sinking deep. He plundered her like a jackhammer on asphalt, pistoning into her in a non-stop rhythm. Sabelle cried out as she absorbed his onslaught.

"Please let me stop him." Caden would have begged if he thought Sabelle would listen.

"No."

Caden closed his eyes, then forced them open. He was Sabelle's safety net, no matter how ugly this was, how angry the destructive forces of magic made him, he must watch.

At that moment, Lucan pressed his advantage. Grabbing her chin, he forced his plundering mouth over hers. It took only an instant before he lifted his head, let out a mighty roar, and wrapped his hand around Sabelle's throat and squeezed.

More than ready, Caden darted toward them. Lucan's arms flexed with muscle and fury as he tried to wring the life out of the witch. Her legs flailed, and she raised her arms, clearly trying to summon magic.

They did not need to compound one tragedy with another. There must be another way to help his brother. He'd step up his efforts with Sydney—anything but this.

With his own shout, Caden threw a forearm around his brother's neck and braced his knees on the mattress. Yanking at Lucan, he tugged his brother away from Sabelle. She gasped, and he was relieved to hear her catch her breath. But the relief was short-lived when Lucan broke loose, turned on him with the wild blue eyes of a madman, and attacked.

When riled, his brother had the strength of ten men, and Caden knew as soon as Lucan pinned him to the bed and grabbed his throat that, despite superior training, he was in for the fight of his life. He pushed at Lucan's chest and writhed, struggling against his brother's hold. But Lucan held a tight grip, nearly crushing his windpipe, cutting off his air. He choked, gasped, barely registering a shuffling beside him. While he didn't want to die, he prayed Sabelle got help, rather than putting herself in harm's path again.

Suddenly, Lucan went slack and collapsed in a heap over Caden like dead weight. He pushed his brother off him, then looked around for Sabelle, who was belting her robe around her waist, looking somewhere between embarrassed and contrite.

"I'm so sorry," she murmured, looking ready to tear up.

Caden shoved his brother away, then rose and held her awkwardly. "For not succeeding? How could you have known?"

"No, for being naïve. I didn't believe he would actually hurt a loved one." She dropped her gaze, bit her lip. "He would have killed us both if we hadn't worked together."

"How did you do stop him?"

"A quick spell. You intervened enough for me to use my hands and cast it. Lucan is not just asleep but unconscious. I hope that, in my panic, my spell didn't hit him too hard." She winced.

Another instance of magic potentially backfiring, and he still had the original problem to tackle. "You did what was necessary to save us both."

"It wouldn't have happened if I hadn't loosened his chains, had kept him from kissing me. I . . ."

Sabelle began to sob. Caden wrapped his arms around her gently and let her cry. He didn't want magic in his life, didn't want to be here, but the least he could do was help the woman who had bravely put herself in harm's path to aid Lucan.

Caden held her tighter, swearing that he would never have a mate to mourn, never put others through this magical torture. He wanted to ask her what they could do next to care for Lucan, but now wasn't the time. The burden sat squarely on his shoulders. Caden had to find Anka and not rely on Sabelle's sacrifices.

"Never again." He took her face in his hands and wiped her tears away. Guilt crashed into him. He should have said no from the start. "Ever. We'll find another way."

"This may be the only way to keep him alive."

"That can't be true. You did your best, but—"

"*What* is going on here?"

Caden's gaze zipped to the door and the sound of the growl. Ice filled up the portal, wearing an unpleasant scowl that said he hadn't yet decided whether to offer help or rip Caden's head off. The big, skull-shaved warrior prowled into the room, his green gaze settling on Sabelle—and getting more furious by the instant. He looked like a man about to pound flesh first and ask questions later. He also radiated a territorial vibe Caden couldn't miss.

Caden backed away from Sabelle. No need to compound the problems already swirling in the room.

"What the fuck is this?" If patience and politeness were virtues, Ice possessed not an iota of either.

Sabelle raised her chin. "I was caring for Lucan."

Ice looked between Lucan on the floor, then Sabelle with her wild, tangled hair, the hem of her short robe, and the blue imprint of fingers on her neck.

Fury roared across Ice's face as the menacing warrior turned on him. "Your prick of a brother did this to her? Did you stand and watch, you motherfucking pervert, while he hurt her?"

Before Caden could think of an explanation, Ice clobbered him with a right cross, then followed up with a mean uppercut to the abdomen. Caden doubled over and nearly vomited. He could fight the warrior in hand-to-hand and, being better trained, could probably win. But Caden remained still. Why defend his actions?

"Were you hoping to have a go at her next? I'm going to rip your throat out with my bare hands. Neither you nor your brother will touch her again."

"Ice, stop!" Sabelle demanded.

To his surprise, the big warrior whipped his fists to his sides, despite looking ready to pulverize any who touched Sabelle again.

"It was my choice to serve Lucan and have Caden stay."

Clenched jaw, Ice cursed. "He hurt you. I won't allow that."

"I don't need your approval. Lucan is not in his right mind, and he's my friend." She turned to Caden, who rubbed his assaulted gut. "Go. I need to gather myself, clean up before I face my brother."

She swallowed and, for the first time, looked genuinely nervous.

Caden grabbed her hand. "I cannot thank you enough for your effort. On behalf of my brother, I'm sorry . . . for what he put you through. I will talk to Bram—"

Ice shouldered his way between them and shoved Caden back. "Do *not* touch her."

Rather than tempt fate, Caden stepped away.

Sabelle sighed. "I'll talk to my brother. Tell him I'll be down shortly."

With a sigh, Caden turned away. At the portal, he glanced back to see Sabelle send Ice a fiery glare. No one said a word, but he had a feeling that the possessive male was about to get a serious dressing down. Caden's guess? Sabelle wanted plenty of distance between her and Ice. His other guess? Ice wasn't about to let that stop him.

Long after dark, Sydney finished her interview and reached home, completely drained physically. Emotionally, she was wired. So much food for thought. That poor woman remembered so little of her adulthood, and Sydney could only imagine how horrific her torture had been. Despite being victimized, the self-professed witch knew that she'd left loved ones behind. The woman had sobbed about the open wound inside her, about the guilt and incompleteness that hollowed her.

Being unmoved by such a soul-baring was impossible. It made Sydney question everything in her life. She'd put men and dating on the back burner to concentrate on her career. But at times, like tonight, she felt so alone. Her body and heart ached. But now, sitting in her darkened living room, not just any man would fill up the empty place inside her.

Only Caden.

Why? She barely knew him. A few days shouldn't be enough to make her crave him. But she wanted him in a way that was beyond both her experience and her ability to describe. She didn't just want, she *needed* to feel his mouth demanding carnal pleasure from her, to see desire in his eyes, to have him wrap her in his arms afterward and hold her tenderly. The thought of taking him in her hands, watching his pleasure build, then sharing herself with him and revealing how much he meant to her, made her ache. What the bloody hell was it about the man? They shared good chemistry . . . but this was more.

Sighing, she uncurled herself from the sofa and meandered back to her bedroom. She might as well tuck herself in early, catch up on sleep. Maybe this odd need would go away.

Good advice, but Sydney gravitated straight to the picture window in her bedroom. The night danced across the moonlit skyline, a vision of urban romance with St. Paul and the London Eye lit up. The sight magnified her loneliness. In the silent blue dark, with faint sounds of humanity below, she admitted that she didn't want anyone but Caden.

If he wanted her, it wasn't with the same passion.

As she turned away from the window to her bed, heavy tears filled her eyes again. Swallowing, she stared up at the ceiling and willed them away. Not now. Later, she would give in to her loneliness and her need for chocolate. If she started now, she feared she'd cry until her nose turned bunny red and her eyes swelled for days.

Determined to leave the pity party behind, Sydney went through her bedtime ritual. If she felt sorry for anyone, it should be that poor witch, who was haunted by a man she couldn't remember—and wanted to so desperately. Her plight had touched something inside Sydney. Though her own parents were happy, she'd always been unlucky in love. And now she wanted no one but Caden.

Sydney crawled into bed. She closed her eyes and pictured him lying beside her, touching her, rolling over and demanding her body with just one look from those piercing blue eyes. In her mind, he murmured how much he wanted her, how much she meant to him, and she melted.

Foolish. She shook her head to clear away the fantasy. He wanted her story, her sources, her information, much more than he wanted her. She must dislodge the fantasy and get to sleep.

A distraction. She needed one now to take her mind off the melodrama of her own PMS-induced depression or whatever it was.

A good book would do the trick. Or maybe she should spend a little time with her new "magical" diary. She snorted, but she opened her nightstand drawer and glanced at it.

She'd expected Aquarius to fix her office in a Feng Shui-friendly arrangement or give her a half-hour session with an astrological counselor. But a magical journal that granted fantasies? The concept was intriguing and unexpected, but a bit far out—even for Aquarius.

What do you have to lose? her assistant had asked. Her dignity. Her sanity. Her hunky photographer when he laughed in her face if he ever saw what she wrote.

But how would he? She kept the book in her bedroom—a place he'd likely never enter. Besides, the possibility that she actually held a magical diary was as likely as little green men taking over Britain next week. So how *would* he ever know?

As she snuggled down into her blankets, she wondered what Caden would be like as a lover. Soft? Dominating? A challenge? Intense—she'd bet that much. Caden didn't seem the type to do anything halfway.

At the thought, need gripped Sydney low in her belly. She felt hot and cold, light-headed and heavy-limbed as a new vision gripped her imagination. What if, yesterday morning, he hadn't come to her flat to search for information, but to ravish her? What if, when she answered the door in her lingerie, he'd been overcome with passion and taken her right there? *Mmm, heaven.* Sinking into the vision, she imagined them breathing together—a sharp inhalation at the end of each plunging thrust. With strong fingers, he'd grip her hips as if he couldn't get deep enough, wouldn't be satisfied until he claimed her completely. She closed her eyes and let the fantasy consume her. A drop of sweat trickled down his brow, onto her chest. Jaw set, he threw his head back and moaned that no other woman affected him this way.

Yes, she knew he'd turned her down and been more interested in the contents of her stories than her knickers. But it was *her* fantasy.

Maybe . . . writing her wishes about Caden would be cathartic. If she got them out of her system, perhaps she could sleep and wake tomorrow with this odd obsession gone.

Sydney peeked at the diary. Flushed and tingling, she picked up the red book. To hell with caution. She would worry later about what would happen if Caden ever read her wishes. Or the unlikely chance that she could actually compel him to her bed magically. If that happened, she'd deal with the damage to her heart then. Plus, she'd earmarked the book as a potential story. If she was considering writing about the little volume, shouldn't she research it?

Impulsively, she grabbed the little book and wrote:

> *Dear Magical Diary,*
> *I have this fantasy. Mad, really. But*
> *I dream of Caden MacTavish storming*
> *my door, ordering me naked, ravishing my*
> *body . . .*

An hour later, Sydney sighed as she put her pen aside and closed the book. Desire dampened her palms, the valley between her breasts, the cleft between her thighs. Oh, now she *really* ached for Caden and the delicious fantasy she'd just written.

Imagination was a powerful aphrodisiac. As the words flowed from her mind onto the page, Sydney felt as if she'd slipped into a trance. She could nearly feel Caden's mouth caressing her nape, his fingers rolling her nipples, his erection sliding a burning path deep inside her. She could almost hear him say that he could not resist her for another minute, look at her like she alone mattered to him.

The compelling fantasy left her with an urgent need for satisfaction. And while she wanted Caden to sate her, he wasn't here. Nor was he likely to suddenly appear and make this all a reality, despite Aquarius's claims.

Sydney reached for the light, intent on dousing it so she could find her own relief. But she happened to glance at the book first. There, in script that was not hers, were two lines she had not written:

> *Sleep, dream, anticipate . . .*
> *The fantasy you imagine will soon be your fate.*

CHAPTER FOUR

SUNDAY MORNING CAME, AND though his head throbbed after drowning images of last night with whiskey, Caden knew he must ask someone to teleport him to London. He hated relying on magic, but without a clear idea where he was or how to get back to London, he was stuck.

"You look like hell," Bram offered.

No shit. Caden pried open one eye, wincing at the sunlight, and stared back at the Doomsday Brethren's leader. The wizard looked surprisingly disheveled and exhausted.

"You're unlikely to win any bloody pageants, either." Caden snorted, then sobered as he remembered Sabelle and her sacrifice. "Bram, about your sister . . . she's taking a great deal of risk to help my brother and . . ."

He didn't want anything tragic to befall Sabelle, but how could he tell Bram to make her stop when she might be the only person separating Lucan from death?

"You're worried." Bram sighed. "I'm not surprised. She's always been too brave."

"Helping Lucan is very dangerous."

Bram frowned. "She's your last recourse. I understand your discomfort. Even Ice had words with me last night about the matter. But, in truth, she'll heed none of us and do exactly as she likes."

Before Caden could argue, a series of gongs and whistles sounded, startling him.

Bram stiffened and swore. "What the hell does he want?"

"Who?" Caden scanned the room in confusion. There was no one about but the two of them.

"Shock Denzell. That sound is his magical calling card."

Instead of mentally easing the barriers around the estate, Bram stomped down the stairs and darted out the open door. There, in the distance, stood a cross between a bodybuilder and a Mack truck. Something out of a Terminator movie. Big, bad, and hiding behind dark sunglasses, Shock stood with arms crossed over his leather-clad chest, wearing an unapologetic fuck-off glare.

"Why are you here?" Bram stalked out to meet him. Caden followed in curiosity.

"Let me in."

Caden stiffened. The man had been Lucan's rival for Anka. Since Caden had been avoiding everyone magical for years, he didn't know the intimate details of his brother's life. He hadn't seen Lucan's mate since he was a young boy. But one thing he *knew:* His brother hated Shock.

"After the way you supported your old chum Mathias a few short weeks ago?" Bram stopped before the wizard, arms crossed. "I think not."

"Are you bloody stupid?" Shock whispered. "Who put the Doomsday Diary back in Olivia's hands that night? Who helped her focus her magic so she could blast Mathias with her power?"

"Trying to convince me you're a hero?" Bram drawled, skeptical brow raised.

"Pull your head out of your arse, Rion. Think."

"Right now, I simply can't. Your boss is making my life hell and I would rather fry your brain and be done with you."

"You're a stubborn sod, you know that? I'm being cautious in case I've been followed. Zain is suspicious and eager to please Mathias. Let me in so we can't be overheard, and I'll explain."

"Are you alone?"

Caden whirled on Bram. Trust Shock? "Are you mad?"

The wizard ignored him.

Shock threw his arms wide as if to illustrate his solitude. "Yes. If I weren't, I know you'd try to kill me."

"There would be no *try* about it." Then Bram closed his eyes, frowning in concentration. A minute later, he pierced Shock with a cold stare. "You have three minutes to explain where the bloody hell you've been. If you pull anything, nearly every Doomsday warrior is here and would be glad to help me off you. If I dislike your answer, I'll shut you in a room with Lucan, and God help you then."

Shock scowled, looking puzzled, but began hiking through the foggy morning, toward the house. Caden wondered how the devil Shock could possibly be confused.

"I say we skip his explanation and let Lucan take him apart. I'll help."

"The option has appeal, but I want to hear this."

"Honestly," Caden whispered, holding him back. "Who benefited most when Anka disappeared?"

"Shock, clearly. But Olivia herself saw Anka with Mathias."

"And who does Shock likely work for? Perhaps I've been chasing Sydney's source foolishly. Maybe Shock has Anka under our noses and in his bed."

Bram paused. "I don't think he'd advocate a scheme that allowed Mathias to abuse her. Shock Called to Anka. A wizard's first instinct is to protect the woman he sees as his mate. Besides, during the battle in the tunnel, Shock delivered the Book of Doomsday to Olivia, not Mathias. The big question is, why?"

Likely for his own purposes. Caden gritted his teeth. Bram was going to think whatever he wished until something convinced him otherwise; he'd learned that much about the wizard in the last few weeks. Fine. Shock would show his true colors soon enough.

A few moments later, they entered the foyer, the click of Shock's boots surprisingly quiet for someone who so nearly qualified as a giant. Caden sized him up, hate poisoning his blood. Shock must know something about Anka's whereabouts. He was likely hoping Lucan would die and leave behind a grieving widow looking for someone to cling to.

"What the fuck are you staring at?" Shock challenged him.

"Trash."

The big wizard set his jaw, mouth tight. "I haven't come here to fight with you."

In a way, Caden wished he would. If it weren't for the magic thing, Caden believed that he could take Shock and teach him a lesson or two, despite the fact Shock was big and mean. Caden had fast reflexes, good training, and fury on his side.

"You can't beat me. I could crush you without magic. Learn to mask your thoughts, neophyte."

That was it; Caden had had enough. A part of him wanted to avenge his brother. He'd done precious little else for Lucan in years. What if he died before Caden could make amends? The other part of him simply hated his leather-clad swagger.

As he lunged for Shock, Bram stuck out an arm, blocking his chest and, using some sort of damn magic, pushed him against the wall.

"You two aren't doing this now." Then he turned to Shock. "Say what you came to."

"I want everyone to hear, Ice, Marrok, Duke, Lucan."

"Ice and Marrok are here. I'll call for Duke." Bram paused. "I'll play along that you know nothing about Anka."

"Anka?" Shock's face lost the challenging sneer. "What about her?"

"Your boss took her from my brother," Caden spat, frustration at the last few weeks boiling up. "He broke their bond, raped her, and now she's missing."

Shock froze. Violence filled the air as his mouth thinned into a white line. *"What?"*

"Terriforz," Bram supplied. "It appears Mathias overtook Anka's mind and forced her body to crave what she mentally rejected. Now, we can't locate her."

Shock looked at the ceiling, drew in a deep, noisy breath. Caden had the distinct impression the wizard was collecting himself.

When he looked back at them, rage had transformed his face. Even with the sunglasses, Caden discerned horror and anger—and bloodlust.

He whirled on Bram. "How is this fucking possible? How did I not hear about this?"

"Actually, that's our question for you. After all, you and Mathias are chummy these days."

Shock shook his head. "We're playing bloody head games. Don't you know that he became the most feared wizard of our time because he's damned devious? He's suspicious and keeps many secrets. Do you have any leads on Anka's whereabouts? Can Lucan help?"

Bram shrugged. "No. Lucan is mad with mate mourning, Anka was with Mathias . . . then disappeared."

"So you don't even know if she's alive?"

Caden hadn't wanted to entertain the notion that she might be otherwise. But deep down, in a sick region of his stomach, he worried. She had been alive a few days following

Mathais's abduction, but since . . . the ruthless bastard may have killed her and disposed of her body.

Bram shook his head.

"What's been done to recover her?" Shock barked.

Not a word about Lucan or what he'd endured. *Prick.* "I'm looking. She belongs to my brother, and I will—"

"Piss off," Shock shouted. "If your brother hadn't stolen her away, she would have been *my* mate, safe in *my* house. *I* will find her."

Over his dead body. He must find Anka before Shock did.

"How?" Bram challenged. "Can you ask Mathias?"

"Call the others. I'll explain."

Within a few minutes, Ice and Marrok crowded into Bram's office. Arguments ensued. Accusations were hurled. Shock didn't have many fans among the Doomsday Brethren. In fact, he was generally regarded as a traitor. Caden smiled in grim satisfaction.

It took a few moments more, but Duke arrived, looking more than a bit disinterested in Shock's excuses.

Once everyone was seated, Shock brushed everyone's attitudes aside and paced at the front of the room, excess energy rolling off of him.

"First, I had no notion about Anka." Shock looked up and speared Caden with a glance. "I will do everything I can to find her. You have my word."

The word of a wizard, especially this one, meant little to Caden, but arguing that point would only belabor the conversation.

"You all assumed the worst of me," Shock began. "Given my family name, I'm not surprised. But I never imagined that the lot of you would be that thick."

"Meaning?" Bram raised a haughty brow to let Shock know he was treading thin ice.

"Do you daft fools really believe you're going to defeat Mathias in a fair fight? We're five; seven if we count junior and the lunatic."

Again, Caden gnashed his teeth to restrain the urge to pound Shock.

"Mathias," he went on, "has a growing army we barely know how to fight. A handful of able-bodied fighters against a sea of willing suicide killers. Did you honestly believe we could win without a spy? Without someone to rot the Anarki from the inside out?"

Damn it all. Caden really hated this bastard. But he made sense.

Bram raised a sharp brow. "So you abandoned us abruptly because you saw an opportunity to pretend to join Mathias's cause, earn his trust, and eventually stab him in the back?"

"Exactly. I visited my brother in your holding cell after Lucan and Duke captured him at Marrok's cottage. I got an earful of Zain's hero worship for Mathias and a load of alarming information that made me realize we cannot win without being one step ahead. The only way to do that is to have a mole on the inside."

Marrok crossed his enormous arms across his chest. "If that is so, why did you not warn us that Mathias had killed my mate's father, then masqueraded as Gray so he could lure her to bring the diary to him? Or that he planned to attack in the tunnel?"

"Or have any bloody clue what had happened to Anka or where she is now?" Caden challenged.

He cursed. "Mathias knows I've never backed others with his views, so he's leery of my support. Trust will take time to build. I'm making progress. Be patient."

Be patient . . . while the Doomsday Brethren were left to wonder whether Shock was being honest or using these words as a ploy so he could betray them. A quick glance around proved warriors' attitudes were anywhere from considering to accusatory.

"Let's pretend for a moment that any of us believe you," Bram said. "The first thing I would say is—"

"Pretend you believe? Piss off. The lot of you!" He pinned Bram with a narrow-eyed glare. "In case you've forgotten, you asked *me* to join the Doomsday Brethren. I don't need your distrust."

Shock charged toward the door. Marrok blocked it.

"Out of my way, human."

Marrok leveled him with a stare that would make a normal man shiver. "I will let you leave when Bram tells me you can pass. Not before."

"I can zap the life out of you," he sneered.

Marrok drew his broadsword. "Not before I sever your head from your body."

"Gentlemen," Bram placated. "Enough. As you always say, Marrok, we cannot defeat Mathias if we are too busy fighting one another. Because I have no better option and you know it, we will continue with your 'plan,' Shock. For now. I want *regular* reports, and they'd best be useful. Provide me ideas about the means necessary to defeat Mathias, information like the size of his army and any vulnerabilities. And do it quickly. If you do, we'll get on just fine. Betray me, and I will find you, then kill you slowly and without mercy."

Caden smiled. "With that I'll be happy to help."

Monday morning arrived, as did Caden at nine sharp, sticking his head inside Sydney's office. He looked generally out of sorts and agitated. Pity for him. If Caden liked doormats, they weren't going to get on very well.

Since he couldn't read her lascivious thoughts or know what she'd written in her "magical" diary, his visit must be about the magickind story again. She sighed.

Even so, one glance at him was like a punch to her stomach. He looked incredible in charcoal slacks, a crisp white collar, and a burgundy sweater that accentuated his outdoorsman's coloring and deep-blue eyes. She must stop mooning like an adolescent. The man was trying to steal from her, no matter how gorgeous he looked. Wanting someone who sought to use her was both stupid and self-destructive.

She sent him a bland expression, then looked back to her computer screen. "What is it MacTavish? Angry that I lost you at the pub?"

He shook his head. "No. I want to talk to you. I have since Saturday, but prefer not to talk in the office."

"Well, I've work to do, so if you've something to say, speak up now. And this best be good."

"I came to see you last night." His stare was hot, direct. It nearly melted her.

The thought of Caden in her flat again, as she'd written in the diary, made her shiver with longing. Stupid. She'd best keep her head with this one—or she'd find herself out of a story.

"Did you? I fell asleep early. But after feeding me a load of shit about having inappropriate feelings for me, I'm shocked that you dared to knock on my door again."

"That wasn't a load of shit."

"So you stopped by to . . . what? Proposition me after you'd already refused sex?"

"No. To apologize for trying to force you to take me to your contact. If I want your trust as a partner, that wasn't the way to earn it."

The sincerity in his words pried her gaze away from her

e-mails and back to Caden. Granted, this could be another ruse to earn her trust, but he looked earnest.

"All right, then. Tell me, why are you pursuing this story so hard?"

"I've no wish to steal it. I know you think I do. I swear, I'm not working for a rival or hoping to plaster it across the Internet with my byline."

She propped her chin on her hand. "Really? Then why is your curiosity insatiable?"

He shrugged. "I'm not alone. According to our last staff meeting, so is your readers'."

"True, but your interest seems a bit more intense."

He sighed, looking reluctant. "I'm worried. Mathias sounds powerful. If you print this story, will he or his army be able to track your source down? How do you know she isn't critical to Mathias's success and that he won't come after her again if you even hint at this woman's location? Who or what will keep her safe? Is she going with Aquarius on holiday or staying at Aquarius's place? Will she be safe? If he can't find her, what about you? Won't he pursue you to lead him to her?"

"I can't imagine that anyone magical reads—" Sydney stopped and scanned her memory. "Aquarius's place? I never said that."

Instantly, Caden stiffened. "You did. The other day."

Sydney thought again. "No. I had something like that written down, though. On the notes in my handbag. You snooped." *Oh, the lying snake!* "You came to my flat Saturday, not because you're interested in me, but because you were prying through my notes. See, you merely want to talk to my source so you can scoop me."

"That's not true."

"You turned down a blatant invitation for sex and repeated things I wrote only in my notes. You apologized to get back in my good graces. It's clear what you're after."

Instead of guilt, desire ripped across his expression. He raked his hands through his hair, practically oozing frustration. Sydney had never seen him so agitated.

"You're wrong." Through clenched teeth, he vowed, "If I had been less of a gentleman, I would have very gladly taken you up on your offer, fucked you like mad, and shown you not just that I want you, but precisely how."

That low-voiced growl, the way his stare seemed to burn the clothes from her body . . . The man made her a walking hormone. Her knickers suddenly went damp, and the way he stared at her, Sydney wouldn't be surprised if he knew it. She fought to shake off the insane need that scalded her blood, but no such luck. Too bad. She wasn't about to let him use her desire against her.

"I challenged you to a game of chicken, and you flinched. Now I know what you're really about, you poacher. I won't fall for your manufactured lust and let you steal my story."

Caden stormed around her desk and towered over her. His gorgeous body put off heat like an oven, and a scent that made her melt into a puddle of lust. His mouth hovered bare inches above her own, and against her better judgment, Sydney trembled.

"Manufactured?" he growled. "What I feel is very real. If I was on top of you, plunged deep, while you were screaming my name, you'd know better."

Her insides trembled, and she resisted the urge to fan herself. "Prove it."

Caden cursed, something low and ugly. "I can't. I want to. God, but it's beyond complicated."

Ah, the excuses. "I'm a smart girl. I think I can keep up."

* * *

Caden swallowed. How much of the truth did he dare tell? Nothing about his quest for Anka, clearly, but the rest. . . . Honesty would be best—or Sydney would see right through him.

"Desire roils in my gut for you. I've never known anything like it. Sometimes, it's all I can do to stay away." His voice shook. He was hard as steel, but she wasn't looking there. Instead, Caden realized he'd grabbed the arms of her chair, and his face hovered just above hers. She blinked. Her rosy lips parted. He gripped the plastic armrests until he thought they'd break. Damn it, the urge to kiss her nearly overpowered him.

When had he ever bared such personal feelings to a woman? The question rattled him because he knew the answer was never.

Sydney rolled her eyes. "C'mon, MacTavish. I handed you sex on a silver platter—twice—and you refused."

It had been one of the most difficult things he'd ever done.

Being this close to Sydney was revving up his libido. If he didn't get some distance between them, he'd take her up on her offer here and now. God help her if he ever unleashed all this want on her.

He took a deep breath and a step back. "Not from lack of desire, but a sense of responsibility. We work together. My life now, with Lucan's illness, is beyond complex. Once he recovers, I'll be returning to Texas, so beginning anything with you—that would only be temporary and unfair."

She frowned. "You'd hardly be my first fling. Or my last. I didn't ask for commitment."

Caden ground his jaw as he imagined another man's hands on her. The more time he spent with her, the more homicidal that thought made him feel. "If I touched you, I would want more. Need it. That, I know."

She sucked in a shocked breath. "What does this have to do with your behavior Saturday? It's not as if you tried to follow me to my contact because you want to shag me."

He looked down at his boots and weighed his answer. Again, he stuck as close to the truth as he dared. "No. I followed you because I worry about you."

"Me? Not the contact?"

God, this woman was blazingly tenacious and determined to pry every bit of truth out of him she could. "I don't want to see anyone hurt, but I'm most concerned about you."

"Because I'm crossing town or talking to a woman who fears her own shadow?"

That ever-logical side that drew him to her also proved to make her a stubborn pain in his arse. "Not just a woman, a *witch*. You don't know what she's capable of or if Mathias is still after her. Or could pursue you, simply for writing this story."

"Perhaps. But I won't let that stand in the way of the truth."

"I know," he said honestly. If he knew one thing about Sydney, it was that her dedication was unquestionable. "Which is exactly why I didn't say it sooner. I want to protect you. This may offend your feminist sensibilities, but it's the soldier in me."

Sydney sent him a skeptical glare, but it wasn't untrue. While protecting her hadn't been Caden's primary motive, it had been on his mind.

She snorted. "I admit, you're oozing macho."

"I didn't want to tell you because I knew you'd reject the need for a bodyguard."

"Indeed. Let's say I believe that you're merely concerned about me because you have feelings for me that you think would be unfair to act on. What next?"

"Save my sanity, please. Let me protect you—at least a bit. Tell me what's happening with the magical war story, so I can be prepared."

She hesitated, sent him a long measuring glance. "All right."

Caden wasn't sure she truly believed him, but at least she was talking. He let out a huge sigh of relief. Yes, he wanted to find Anka, right Lucan's life, return to Dallas. But he did feel the urge to protect Sydney. He would miss her—worry about her—once he'd gone.

"Did your source give you more information?" he asked, sitting in the office's guest chair once more.

"A bit."

"Enough for another article?"

"Not certain yet."

She was holding back . . . and he didn't blame her. He'd handled things badly before. Today hadn't been loads better, but a least she no longer looked hostile. "Will you share what you know? Please."

For a long moment, Sydney did nothing but stare, as if trying to read his thoughts. Finally, she shrugged. "Since you're my photographer and assigned partner, I'm supposed to work with you. And you'll read the details when they're printed.

"According to my source, the magical war is escalating. Mathias rose from an exile that was supposed to be like death and last forever. Apparently, no one knows how he did it, but everyone knows he wants to overthrow a terrible class system that oppresses the poor. His goal is to help them rise up."

Caden had never heard such a load of tripe. "Or so he says."

"Indeed. But it makes for a juicy story. Holly wants me to

play the angle that since he's arisen like a savior, magickind will embrace him. The battle in the tunnel a few weeks ago was one of many to throw off the oppressors, and stay tuned for more details."

He couldn't let her print any of that, though he couldn't tell her why without revealing too much. Besides, Sydney was an independent creature. The minute he told her to do one thing, she'd do the opposite.

"So you're glorifying the man who raped this poor woman?" he asked.

She paused, then wrinkled her nose. "That's been my objection, but Holly likes the angle that this witch was an enemy of his utopia and he dealt harshly with her. I couldn't see another slant."

"Mathias is no hero. You know bollocks about combat."

"Admittedly."

"The psychological game is more than half the battle. The aggressor needs the masses on his side, and if he's in the wrong, he must lie. What if Mathias is bamboozling these magical people? What if he's claiming to be their savior, but merely wants power for his own gain? What if he's convinced the poor that he can lift them up, but it's a huge ruse?" He clenched his fists, and his shoulders tensed, as if he was barely restraining himself from pounding on the desk. "And what if he raped that poor woman because she belonged to someone fighting on the right side, and Mathias knew he could crush that man by brutalizing his woman?"

Sydney's jaw dropped, then she scrambled for a notepad. "You're bloody good at this. Much more interesting than Holly's suggestion."

"If I talked to your source, in addition to protecting you, perhaps we could craft a better story together."

"Can't." Sydney didn't miss a beat, just continued jotting down notes. "I've told you, the poor witch is terrified. A man, especially one like you, would send her scurrying to dig her own grave. She'd never talk again."

"Tell me about her. Maybe I can find some way to ease her fears," he went on. "You could assure her that I would never harm her. She trusts you."

"Very little. She jumps at a shadow. No offense, but you wear that soldier mien a bit too well. You could never soothe her."

"Perhaps I should talk to her on the phone first, allay her worries, and pave the way for a face-to-face meeting. For your safety, I'd rather you not meet with her again unless I'm there."

Pausing, Sydney looked up from her notes. "She doesn't want her picture taken."

Caden couldn't tell if she believed him or would delay meeting with her source without him. And he could neither lose his only possible lead to Anka nor allow Sydney to risk herself.

"So I won't take it."

Sydney shrugged. "Convincing her will be a challenge. Besides, she's gone for a bit."

"With Aquarius on holiday? Where?"

"I don't know. Their plans weren't set. Said something about Paris, perhaps."

Damn! Aquarius and Anka, if she was indeed Sydney's source, could be anywhere.

"I have a bad feeling about this story," he murmured. "I beg you to hold off unless I can be certain you're safe."

"I think you're worried more than necessary. It's . . . sweet of you, but Holly wants another story now. I'm a big girl and I can take care of myself."

Tamping down his frustration, he reached for logic. He

had to get through to this woman, stop this story. "Where is the picture your previous photographer took of the battle aftermath? Can I have a look?"

Sydney frowned, then rifled through one of the folders on her desk. When she found the photo, she slid it across the desk to him. "Here."

He slid it back in front of her. "How many dead bodies do you see?"

She glanced at the picture, then away. "It's too dark and grainy to tell."

"More than a few?" he challenged.

She hesitated, as if sensing his point before he made it and already looking for a way to refute it. "Yes."

"Dozens, in fact. Wouldn't you say?"

"Perhaps." She shrugged.

"No. Obviously. These were men. Judging from their uniforms, many were soldiers, which means they were trained in combat. And they are dead in droves." He paused, letting the words sink in. "If Mathias wanted this story hushed, do you think he'd have any compunction about killing you?"

Sydney didn't answer, but Caden knew by the look on her face that she understood his point.

"By all accounts, there was blood everywhere. Severed heads and limbs, multiple gunshots, and a lot of death. What do you know about avoiding those?"

Looking about, she fiddled with a pen, tapped her toes. She didn't like the truth.

"Sydney?"

"All right. Nothing. But you can't fight off magic."

"I know how to use a gun. Before you do anything for this story, especially visit the madman's victim, take me with you. That's all I ask."

"I'll . . . think about it."

CHAPTER FIVE

TOWARD THE END OF the day, Holly stomped into Sydney's office, brows and hands both raised in an expectant expression. People often underestimated her because of her Kewpie doll looks—and always paid the price.

"Where is the latest installment in the magical war saga?" Holly asked. "I've got loads of e-mails. You won't believe how interested readers are."

Wrong. Seems everyone was, especially her hunky freelance photographer. But this morning, he'd conveyed interest in more than the story with his body taut and passionate words. Whether that interest was a scam remained to be seen. God knows, it had nearly melted her on the spot. She wanted to believe him.

"I have a draft of the story," Sydney said. "Maybe by tomorrow or Wednesday."

"What? No, I need it now. It has to be to copy editing no later than tomorrow morning to make the next issue."

"I know. It's . . . well, I'm not happy with it, actually. The angle troubles me."

"We've been over this. I gave you a perfectly good angle."

Sydney grimaced. "And I still don't like glorifying a rapist."

"Most people who read us think we're total rubbish or are lunatics themselves. It's not as if they're going to be questioning your journalistic integrity."

Sydney felt compelled to get this right. Some of the stories she wrote she knew weren't real. This felt not only real but critical. "But it's got *my* name on the byline. And I know this angle is wrong. Then there's safety, both the source's and mine. What if this Mathias character really is real? What if he's not a savior but a villain?"

Holly shrugged. "Whatever his reason, would a wizard trying to take magickind in hand really be spending his time reading human tabloids and compiling his hit list?" Holly frowned. "What's made you change your mind? After our conversation last night, you seemed set with the story."

"Well, I talked to Caden. He made me look at the story in a new light."

"His version won't sell more copies of the paper."

Sydney disagreed, not that no one expected accurate reporting from them. Many believed all their stories were fabricated. But Sydney had a different feeling about this one.

"This poor witch makes me want to print the truth. With it, maybe her family will find her. Or we can prevent more women from being raped, even if Mathias leads a good cause, he's got a terrible human rights policy. And Caden's angle sounded interesting, even plausible."

"If Caden's thoughts are causing you to hesitate on turning in an already good story, then he's given you crap. Why are you letting that man crawl into your head?"

Good question. She should be focused on her story, told from her perspective. But his concerns for her safety were valid. His insistence was compelling. She felt in those moments as if she'd seen the *real* Caden, not necessarily his words, but a caring side he usually hid from others. "Something about him isn't spot on, yet—"

"You mean besides trying to talk you out of fine stories? Is he doing his job properly?"

"He is. Amazing pictures. Crisp. Beautiful angles, even

on terrible subjects. His work is like art. That's not what troubles me. It's the man himself."

Holly frowned, her blond hair falling from her ponytail. "Meaning? Oh hell, you two aren't having an office shag, are you?"

Sydney lowered her head to hide the flush she felt crawling up her face. Shagged him, no. Like to? Absolutely. "No. I just need pointers on working with him more effectively."

Her editor raised an arched brow. "If you can't get on with a man that dishy, I'm not certain there's any hope for you. Smile, flirt, if you must. But tell him what pictures you need. Get the job done."

"It's not that simple. His behavior . . . I wondered for a bit if he took this job to scoop me on the magical war story."

Holly stood up straighter. "Why do you think that?"

"I'm not certain anymore, but at first, he literally talked of nothing else and showed no interest in any of my other stories. He forever asked questions and hounded me about my source. I told him to bugger off."

Holly smiled. "How did he take that?"

Sydney grimaced. She didn't mean to put Caden in a bad light, but Holly was more than a boss; she was a mentor too. Perhaps Holly could help her put this mess into perspective. She couldn't get her editor's opinion without being honest.

"Over the weekend, he came to my flat, expressing interest in me romantically, but I assumed he was lying and threw him out. So he waited for me to leave my flat and tried to follow me to my meeting."

"Prat. I ought to sack him now."

"I thought the same thing. I particularly doubted his reason for returning to the UK. I'm still suspicious of his brother's mystery illness. Do you know anything about it?"

"No, since that's personal, I didn't ask."

"I did. He said next to nothing except that it was his reason for returning here after over a dozen years away. He went on sabbatical from a prestigious job to work here, but never talks about his brother. He doesn't sneak away to call or visit the hospital. He's reluctant to talk about his brother's ailment. It's odd."

"He's quiet, that one. So you fear he's trying to scoop you and made up an ill brother to explain why he's working here? Tried to get romantic with you so you'd share your source?"

"Though it sounds far-fetched, I thought so, but now I wonder. Maybe I've been tired and paranoid. But he says he's concerned for my safety, that Mathias could be dangerous. And why help me find a better angle for my story if he only wanted to steal it? Bloody puzzle. Just in case, I'm doing my best to keep him at bay. I don't want the man getting my information and selling it elsewhere."

Holly nodded. "Good thinking. Does he behave guiltily?"

"Oddly, yes. Guiltily . . . hard to say. Still waters run deep. Until he suddenly became agitated today, I don't think I've ever seen a man more still."

"Agitated? Do you think he's violent?"

"No. But I can't shake the feeling that something isn't right. I can't prove he wants my story. He argued very passionately that he doesn't, but I can't fathom another reason for his odd behavior."

Her editor frowned. "This story is too important to us. Keep your notes to yourself. Lock everything up. Don't leave your computer untended without password protecting it. And drop off the current one to copy editing tonight."

Sydney hesitated, then nodded.

"Good. Other papers are starting to get interested. In fact, I had a call from a rival today, feeling me out on the same thing. Which reminds me! I've also had a ring from another bloke, claiming to have pictures of the tunnel and the bodies no one else has. Odd name . . ." Holly's brow furrowed as the wheels in her head turned. "Zain Something-or-another!" She shrugged. "I'll chat with him, see what he's got and if we want to acquire it."

That should have made Sydney feel better, but didn't. The fact remained, Caden worked beside her for a cause she could only guess at, while her interest in him had grown. "Brilliant."

"What's next?"

"In the magical war story? I don't know. This trail is starting to get cold. I don't think my source can tell me much more. And if I told her I was a reporter, I think she'd stop talking altogether. So unless there's another magical battle, I'll have to try some related stories. I have the supposed 'magical diary' that Aquarius gave me for my birthday. When she returns from holiday, I'll ask about its origins."

"Have you tested it out?"

A mental image of a naked Caden pressing her body to a wall and taking everything he wanted from her burned across her brain. She'd written that nearly forty-eight hours ago.

Sydney sighed in disappointment. "Yeah. I don't think it works."

With a gasp, Caden sat up in his darkened room, bathed in sweat. *Oh dear God.* That had been the most vivid dream of his life. Of all the times to have X-rated dreams, why now? And why about Sydney Blair?

Closing his eyes, he relived her greeting at the door wearing a wisp of lace hardly worth mentioning. What happened next—wild against the wall after she stripped slowly for him—was straight out of his fantasies.

He could have that tonight, have her. Now. She'd offered

a mere two days ago and would have gotten naked with him that moment if he had accepted her proposition. There were a thousand reasons he shouldn't and only one that compelled him: that bloody mating instinct that told him he'd found his "the one" and screamed at him to take her.

Exhaling, still trying to recover his heartbeat, he looked down at his erection in the shadowy dark. Insistent. Painful. Fueled by the oldest magic there was.

Bloody hell.

He wouldn't sleep again tonight, not while he ached and his blood was on fire and visions of Sydney against him burned into his thoughts. He could endure a sleepless night; it wouldn't be his first. But tomorrow, he'd have to face Sydney at the office, his brain continually tripping over all the delicious ways in which she'd clawed his back as he thrust deep into her in his dream. He knew the musky scent of her arousal, the faint tang of her skin, the throaty groan she made when she came, and the peace of being with her and knowing she was safe and whole. And his.

Closing his eyes, he lay back in his empty bed. Thinking about Sydney this way wasn't going to help him get back to sleep or deal with her tomorrow. He turned to the clock. Eleven p.m.? He sighed, frustration cutting him like a razor.

Bloody hellacious day. After verbally boxing with Sydney, he'd come home exhausted yet thrumming with sexual energy. All day, thoughts of stripping Sydney of her evil little skirt and finding out exactly what she had beneath plagued him. Once at home, however, the need for sleep had pulled him under. He'd crashed into bed around seven. The previous two nights, he'd slept nearly twelve hours. Very unlike him. So was having erotic dreams and waking up after a mere four hours of sleep because his body demanded her.

Go to Sydney, something in his head whispered. *You ache for her. She wants you.*

"And then what?" he muttered to the empty room. He still had to work with her. And after what Lucan had endured, he didn't want a magical mate, especially one intent on exposing Mathias.

But Sydney haunted him. He wanted—needed—to feel her naked under him, to know she was his. He was bloody obsessed. To make matters worse, his transition was coming.

Obviously, magic wasn't going to leave him alone. His change from man to wizard wasn't coming tonight, but it *was* coming soon. There wasn't a damn thing he could do to stop it. If male and born with the magical gene, somewhere around thirty, you transitioned and you endured. His birthday was in eight days.

Caden shivered in the November chill, despite his overheated body. He reached for the blankets and groaned when they brushed his naked cock. The sensation made him grit his teeth and fist the blankets. The ache nearly flattened him with need for Sydney.

Madness. He had to stop this. Had to put her out of his mind, douse his sex drive, get some sleep so he could function tomorrow.

Reaching beneath the covers, he took himself in hand and stroked his turgid length once. Again. Again, rapidly picking up speed and pleasure. After his dream, it didn't take much, and he soon felt ready to burst. A vision of Sydney, bare and wanton, blazed across his mind as his muscles tensed. His breathing ratcheted up; his hand moved faster. He dug his heels into the mattress and arched as the need detonated into a bliss that had him shouting at his peak.

As the orgasm subsided, he cursed, still panting. He was

every bit as hard and needy as he had been before masturbating. Visions of Sydney still gyrated in his head. Yet he was so damn tired. Drained.

He closed his eyes, and the dream came back.

"Touch me," she whispered in his slumber. "Here." She guided his hand over her breast, inviting him to toy with her hard nipple. "And here." She brought his hand all the way between her legs, to where she was moist and burning and ready.

Again, he wrapped his fingers around his erection. Like steel, as if his orgasm had never happened. Jerking his hand away, Caden cursed. He didn't want more self-pleasure; it wouldn't help, not when he craved a certain redheaded reporter and her honest, intelligent grit.

Damn magic for ensuring he couldn't ignore his feelings for Sydney.

He rose and took a quick shower, tossed on a T-shirt, jog pants, and trainers. Then he hesitated.

He couldn't just cross town in the middle of the night, pound on Sydney's door, and demand sex. It made no sense, especially after he'd raised her suspicions. She might even refuse to let him in her flat.

If he made love to her . . . well, the whole event was fraught with personal danger, magical landmines. He refused to take a mate and risk Lucan's fate. So he couldn't kiss Sydney, taste her at all. Nor could he risk this job. He needed this job too badly for his mission to fail merely for a shag.

But what he felt for sassy, smart Sydney was more than sex. Far more. He connected with her in a way he couldn't explain, and Caden feared that, once he had her, the random women at the pubs he'd been using to balance his sexual energy would no longer do. Already, his fixation on Sydney frightened him.

Definitely, he should stay home. Undress, go back to sleep, stop thinking about the sharp, sexy redhead. He raced to the kitchen of his little rented flat near the paper's offices. Shadows darkened the room, faintly illuminated by London's lights. There, on the counter, were his keys. He needed to leave them there, refuse temptation.

In his dream, Caden had been unable to resist Sydney. What he felt now was ten times stronger.

With a curse, he grabbed the keys, shoved them in his pocket, then stormed out the door.

After midnight, Sydney unfolded herself from the couch and stretched. Lace and silk cupped her torso, the ribbon laces of her mini-corset rubbing the soft flesh between her breasts. The tiny sheer thong hugged her hips. She adored the feel of soft, feminine things against her skin. But her exposed cheeks 'round back were a bit nippy. Time for bed, anyway.

Grabbing her robe from the arm of the sofa, she made for the hallway with a yawn. Her next installment of the magical war story would run later this week. She hoped she'd taken the right approach in rewriting it as Caden suggested before turning it in. Contrary to Holly's opinion, Sydney did think the angle made a difference.

All night, she'd thought of Caden. She'd half-expected the diary to work. Hoping that tonight was the night, she'd donned her sexiest lingerie, but as she'd told Holly, Aquarius's claims that the diary was magical seemed to be crap.

She took two steps down the hallway, before someone banged a fist on her door. Frowning, she darted for the foyer. Her telly was off and she didn't have a yappy dog, so whoever stood at her door couldn't be complaining about noise. Maybe someone needed help?

Racing the last few steps to the door, she called, "Who is it?"

"Caden. Open the door, Sydney. Now."

Her surprise was quickly washed away by that voice. A bit angry. Insistent. And dripping sex. She shivered.

Her jittery fingers closed around the lock and unlatched it, then fumbled to grab the knob. Before she could turn it, the cold metal rotated in her palm and the door flew open.

Caden filled the doorway, breathing hard, his entire body tense. Those blue eyes lit on her mouth like a laser. Hot. Sydney tingled.

Clearing her throat, she struggled to find her voice. "Why—"

He kicked the door closed. The crash boomed in her little foyer, resounding in her ears, echoing her racing heart as he reached behind his head, gathered his baggy white shirt in his fist, and yanked it over his head. Tossing it to the floor, he stood silently. Watching. Primed. His muscled chest and shoulders rose and fell with each hard breath. His abdomen rippled. Veins and tendons stood out across his forearms and hands.

Her mouth was agape, and she couldn't stop staring. Oh my Lord, she'd known he was gorgeous, suspected he was well put together. But this male animal was far more than she bargained for. Dangerous. Pushed to the edge.

Sydney had never wanted any man more. She swallowed.

"You know why I've come."

If she hadn't guessed by now, his sexual growl told her everything.

Had he reconsidered her proposition? Or was it even possible the magical book had persuaded him?

"What about a fling being unfair to me because you're returning to Dallas?"

Those burning eyes of his lit a path of fire from her face to her breasts, then . . . between her legs. She felt his stare like a physical caress, as if he'd reached out and rubbed his fingers over her flesh. Sydney steadied herself on the table beside her. Her robe, once slung over her arm, floated to the floor.

"I . . . can't stay away. God knows I tried. Do you want me?"

She shouldn't. This was mad. Dangerous. "Yes."

His gaze skated over her lingerie once more. "Take it off. All of it."

"Here?" Her voice squeaked, and she cursed herself. She was never meek, never backed down, and rarely showed vulnerability. She also didn't sleep with men she'd never dated. But Caden . . . apparently, she had a whole new set of rules for him.

He lifted a brow, stepped closer, and reached for her. Sydney got the distinct impression that if she didn't get her silky things off fast enough, he'd dispense with them quickly—and without a lot of care, just like the fantasy she'd written in the magical diary. Her womb clenched at the thought.

It took her two tries, but she plucked at the tie between her breasts and loosened the soft corset. Breathing ragged, she shimmied it over her hips, exposing her breasts to the cool night air and his rapt gaze.

He zeroed in on the hard tips. Usually a pale peach, tonight, for Caden, they were a deep coral. His possessive stare made her ache.

With a new lover, she often worried they'd find her smallish breasts disappointing. The way Caden's gaze latched onto her, and he clenched his fists as he stepped closer made her insecurity evaporate. The worry was replaced by pure heat—a wall of it as his chest loomed close and his temperature rivaled an inferno.

"The rest," he growled, eyeing the nearly transparent thong with malice.

A thrill zipped up her spine as she hooked her thumbs in the waistband of her little panties and lowered them down her thighs, over her calves, until she kicked them away, leaving her entirely exposed.

He took a step closer, then another, and placed his palm flat against the wall beside her head. His chest brushed hers, scalding hot. Sydney gasped.

"Touch me," she whispered. "Here."

Trembling, she guided his hand over her breast. A moment later, his thumb and forefinger put delicious pressure on her nipple. Her breath caught as the cascade of hot tingles sizzled through her body, lighting her up. Her head slipped back to lean against the wall. She closed her eyes. This was her fantasy, only better.

"Look at me." His voice was a rumble in the shadows. He stood, brightened only by the little lamp on her foyer table, just enough to highlight his serious six-pack and the molten demand in his eyes.

Caden nodded his approval, and a fresh wave of delighted surprise swept over her. Until today, she'd always thought of him as controlled, of having his emotions buried. Now, he strained against his own leash, the edges of his restraint frayed. One unexpected move, and he might unchain a whole mountain of alpha male on her. Goodie.

"And touch me here." Latching onto his wrist, she ushered his hand between her legs, where she was moist and burning and needy.

He seemed more than happy to accommodate her, his fingers dipping into her slit to gather moisture, then rub it over her clit. Their gazes locked as an aching ball of tension clenched low in her belly. Awareness of him lapped at her as the sensations he gave overwhelmed her. She gripped his arms, reveling in the taut, solid feel of him as his fingers filled the aching emptiness inside her. Yes, she needed this. Needed *him*.

He pumped his fingers into her, catching that spot high and inside that had her clawing his back, panting his name, hoping she never had to let him go. How could he do that in two minutes or less? And could he please do it again?

"If you don't want me to fuck you now, you have three seconds to say no."

Sydney didn't hesitate. "I said yes when you walked in the door."

He took a deep breath, air filling his chest, his massive shoulders rising like he was preparing for something big. Then, in a few short movements, he plucked at the drawstring of his pants and toed off his trainers. No boxers or tightie whities for him. Everything about the sight was impressive.

While she was still staring, he crouched in front of her and placed a hot, open-mouthed kiss on the flat of her abdomen, then wound up her body to suck and nip at the hard tips of her breasts. He gripped her thighs in his large hands as his mouth marched up to the column of her neck. She arched to give him better access, and he laved her with hot kisses that feathered a shiver all down her spine.

Sydney hadn't finished processing the thrill of his mouth on her skin and the knee-melting male scent of him when he lifted her against him and braced her back against the wall.

"The bedroom is just down the hall," she whispered, though secretly thrilled that he wanted to take her rough and urgent against the wall, just as she'd written.

"Here. Now."

He lowered her to his upthrust erection, probing until he found the creamy welcome he'd ensured with his fingers. Then he paused, stared into her eyes. The connection between them locked into place, jolting her. The ticking of her grandfather clock in the next room and his harsh breaths filled her ears. Her belly tightened; her heart knocked against her ribs.

Roaring through clenched teeth, he pushed her down onto his shaft, arching up to meet her, driving deep. She gasped, long and astounded, as he filled her completely, stretching her nearly to the point of pain. But that pain quickly turned to pleasure. The feel of him, hot and large, clasped deep in her body, overwhelmed her.

She drew in a shuddering breath. "More."

No need to ask him twice. With his chest, he kept her pinned in place as he brushed his mouth across her shoulder and impaled her again. His arms and shoulders flexed as he lifted her up and pushed her back down, leaving a trail of fire. The veins and tendons rose in his biceps and neck. And the pleasure was unlike anything she'd ever imagined. Like opening a door and finding infinity, bright and endless and stunning.

He established a hard rhythm, holding her wide open with her legs over his arms. Her arms curled around him, her nails in the hard flesh of his back, as she moved with him.

Soon, her thighs trembled as she approached orgasm again, this one far bigger. Breathing? Impossible, and she didn't care, not when her entire body rushed headlong to the kind of fulfillment she'd only read about. Again, he filled her, sliding deep, the slick friction of his stroke driving her quickly to a point from which she could not hold back.

Sydney moaned, and she felt Caden's mouth near her ear.

His labored breathing sent a fresh bolt of shivers down her spine.

"I feel you," he whispered between thrusts. "So tight." Another surge deep inside her that had her clawing him again. "So ready."

"Yes. Yes!"

His pace was nearly violent as he pumped again. More incredible than her fantasy even. And Sydney couldn't stand it anymore.

"Let go," he roared.

Those two words were all she needed to see stars behind her eyes, to fall off the cliff into a drugging release. He cried out, his fingers digging into her backside, his mouth clamped on her shoulder as a warm spray jetted inside her.

"Oh, shit," she panted. "We forgot a condom."

"I'm clean."

"I am, as well. But not on birth control."

He hesitated, and something regretful crossed his face. "With me, pregnancy is not an issue."

Sydney opened her mouth to ask what that meant. Was he sterile? Had a vasectomy? Before she could voice her questions, he brushed erotic kisses down her neck until she shivered.

When he finally came up for air, he murmured, "Where's the bed?"

Caden woke in the predawn, wrapped around a warm raspberry-scented body. Silky hair like fire streamed down a narrow feminine back. Soft. Everything about her felt that way as she lay against him, sleeping peacefully. Sydney.

Despite taking her against the wall earlier, then twice again in the bed, he awoke full of energy and ready for more of her. She was no longer a craving, but an addiction.

He'd been so bloody careful with her. No kissing of that sweet, lush mouth or tasting of the wet flesh between her thighs—no matter how badly he'd ached to or how loud the voice in his head screamed at him. But it didn't matter. Everything in him cried out to take her again. And again. And he feared that if he kissed her, the dangerous, ancient words swirling in his head would fly out of his mouth. If they did . . . presto chango. He'd be mated in the blink of an eye, bound his entire life only to her, only able to derive his energy, obtain sex, and feel love with her. And if she didn't accept his Mating Call, or chose to break their bond someday . . . well, his brother was a living, breathing example of the result.

He wanted no part of magical anything, but seeing what Lucan had endured, Caden wanted no part of mating, in particular. Quick shags from random beauties suited him. Putting himself in a position to be feral and out of his mind without Sydney? Unthinkable.

Deep in slumber, she shifted, stretching against him with a sigh, her firm little backside brushing him in dangerous places. He hissed as a fresh jolt of lust pounded him. Then she settled back against him, her body limp and trusting. His temperature rose. She was definitely not helping his restraint.

Cripes, he had to get out of here. That bloody dream, a stupid whim, had brought him to Sydney's flat. He wanted to exit stage left immediately. But this was a prime opportunity to search her place again, find something useful to his mission, then retreat, before he did something *really* foolish, like succumb to the screaming need to kiss her and prove all his instincts right.

Gently, he rose, moving away from Sydney by degrees, careful not to wake her. Then he edged off the bed, onto his feet. He'd start with her notes—and that bloody magical diary, if he could find it. Something he could take and call this fiasco a success.

On his feet, he padded across the hardwood floors and found his clothes where he'd left them in the foyer last night wadded on the floor. With a curse for his unusually impulsive behavior, he donned everything, then began searching.

A quick inventory of the front rooms proved that she hadn't brought her laptop home. No notes, no scraps of paper with handy information, no Doomsday Diary. *Bugger!*

That meant he was going to have to return to Sydney's bedroom and risk waking her. He debated leaving now, forgetting the mission for the moment. But if he was smart and avoided more personal contact with Sydney, he would not have another opportunity to search her flat.

In the bedroom, he ignored the voice in his head asking if disregarding Sydney was even possible and worked methodically. Nothing in her wardrobe except a neat row of clothes on hangers arranged in outfits. Her sexy chocolate skirt and soft cream blouse were wrapped in plastic from the dry cleaners, hung beside the bold black and white dress that clung to her small, curved frame like a dream and always made him wonder exactly what she had beneath. Now that he knew, how would he ever stay away?

Drawing in a bracing breath, he forged on. A scan of her bathroom made him smile, despite the less than optimal situation. Orderly rows of lotions and perfume bottles. Sticky notes of lists stuck to her mirror, reminding her to buy toothpaste and return a DVD rental. Always organized.

Focus, he warned himself. Notes, names, Doomsday Diary.

With no place left to search except the area immediately around the bed, he walked toward her like a man on a death march. He wasn't quite convinced that he wouldn't shed his clothes again, slide back into her bed and into her body.

Swallowing, he approached her side of the bed. *Don't look at her*, he warned himself. Too late.

Her pale skin glowed in the moonlight streaming through the window. A burst of that glorious red hair covered her shoulder, and few of her pale freckles peeked from between the shining strands.

Damn, he sounded like a bloody poet. He was dying to kiss her—and didn't dare.

Caden performed a cursory check of her dresser and found nothing except more lingerie in all types and colors that weren't contributing to his ability to focus. But nothing more.

A few steps closer and he reached her small night table, on which he saw a stack of books. The top one was a book about paranormal research, the one beneath about the ghosts of Jack the Ripper's victims. But he was most interested in the little red volume at the bottom.

Quietly, he shuffled the top two books to the side, then lifted the last. Small, red, gilt-edged, graced with an entwined ML symbol on the front. *Bingo!*

He didn't open it. No time. No need. It wasn't as if he wanted the bloody thing. He would return it to Bram so he could focus on finding Anka.

The night table had a little drawer, and he opened it, hoping to find something about Anka there.

The drawer contained some little reading glasses, a decorative bookmark, and an ambitious reading list. But that was Sydney. Unfortunately, the little drawer held nothing about her source, and he resisted the urge to slam it shut.

Sydney moaned, stirred, leaned across the bed, her arm outstretched as if she was searching for him. A little crease of a frown appeared between her eyes. Was she awake enough to realize he was gone?

Time to go. Leave now. He found nothing here in her apartment that would lead him to Anka. He'd try again at the office in a bit. A quick glance at the clock on her night table told him it was nearly six in the morning. He'd arrive early at *Out of This Realm*'s offices and search there.

But now he had to grab the book and go before she woke up and started asking questions that he couldn't answer.

With a last lingering glance, Caden turned and ducked out of Sydney's bedroom, Doomsday Diary clutched in his hand. A few more steps to the front door, then he'd ride the Tube home and call Bram. Recovering this bloody book ought to make the wizard happy, even if it didn't help Lucan.

Caden was playing that conversation in his head as he opened Sydney's front door and stepped over the threshold, into the foggy London morn.

An instant later, the book dissolved in his hands.

CHAPTER SIX

POOF! THE BOOK WAS gone. Disappeared.

What the devil! He patted his shirt, his pants' pockets, but . . . nothing. The Doomsday Diary was gone.

Stepping inside and easing the door shut, he scanned the house and made his way to Sydney's room. He spotted the familiar red volume on her night table, stacked once more under the other two books. And he cursed.

Grabbing the book once again, he hoped more than believed that some magic would permit him to leave with the volume this time. But as he stepped over her threshold, it dissipated once more. A quick glance in Sydney's room again revealed the book had found its way back to the bedside table.

He raked a hand through his hair. Bloody magic. Illogical, unpredictable crap. Why the devil couldn't he remove the book from Sydney's flat? No doubt there was some vexing magical reason. Caden hoped Bram could explain it, but couldn't spare time to call the wizard now.

As he turned to leave Sydney's flat again, the rustling of sheets nabbed his attention. He glanced over his shoulder in time to see her sit up and halfheartedly hold the sheet over her breasts. "Going somewhere so early?"

Sydney could be tough as nails, but after last night, she looked vulnerable to him. All that moxie of hers protected a sensitive inner core. Suddenly he could see that she wanted to be cared for, wanted a man to find her worthy, be the center of his universe. In that moment, he wanted to be that man for her.

Instead, he was ducking out, and she knew it. Pain lanced deep in his chest when the dawn light illuminated the tension in her soft brown eyes. Lying to her, though necessary, felt like a bomb detonating in his belly.

"Of course you are," she answered herself, and drew the sheet higher over her breasts. "You've had your night with me. Curiosity fulfilled. Another notch in your bedpost. It's not as if you made me any promises." She hung her head, looking very much like she'd berate herself for giving in to him the moment he'd gone. "Go."

"Syd—"

"Don't say anything. No doubt I'll find someone else and forget last night, and that will be that."

Like hell she would! His reaction was instant, undeniable, and violent.

Caden backtracked and cupped her cheek, aching inside. Staying wasn't smart; it would only tempt him to claim the lifelong mate magic intended for him—one he feared would be his undoing. Yet seeing her dejected was agonizing. But making her his for always had consequences he couldn't handle—and she may loathe. Staying with her would change their lives forever—not necessarily for the better.

If he left her without a word now, their relationship would be over. He'd rather give himself a lobotomy with a rusty knife before crushing her, as her expression said his departure would. To complicate matters, every bit of ground he had gained, the little bit of trust he had managed to resurrect, would disappear as quickly as the Doomsday Diary had if he simply walked out.

If he wanted to find Anka, escape this magical freak show, and avoid hurting Sydney, he must stay a bit longer, reassure her, get the necessary information, then devise a way to leave that would not crush her heart—or leave a hole in his.

"Sydney, I'm not some lothario sneaking off the morning after. I need to change clothes for work, and I'd like to call and check on my brother before I go in."

Her face softened a bit. She'd never worn her emotions so openly, and it was disarming. Could he read her now because he knew her better? Or even more, because he felt connected to her?

"I'm not stopping you. Go."

Damn it! He should, but he couldn't.

He sank onto the bed, sitting beside her half-supine form. He couldn't resist holding her hand. "It would be better if I did not smell like sex at work. Our boss may not appreciate it."

"It doesn't take long for Holly to catch on." Sydney sent him a halfhearted smile.

"Not only do we not want her angry, we have important work to do." Caden took a deep breath and plunged in. "This magical war story could be quite dangerous. Let me protect you. *Please.* Don't meet your source again without me. I'll find a way to set her at ease and—"

"Caden," she chided. "Leave work at the office. Any time alone we spend should be about us. I've just spent the night with a man I want to know better. If this isn't a one-off, shouldn't we be getting to know each other? Tell me something about you."

I'm going to be magical soon, and I'm fairly certain that if I kissed you I would issue you a Mating Call that would shock you to your pretty toes. How do you feel about being a wizard's mate and living a thousand years?

Caden cleared his throat. If he said too much . . . it would only connect them further. Their eventual separation would hurt more later. "I want to move back to Texas. I miss Mexican food."

A reluctant smile spread across her face. "We Brits don't make it well?"

"I've seen dog food with more appeal."

Sydney laughed. "That's harsh."

"The truth often is."

Some of the uncertainty left her eyes, and he saw that flash of the Sydney he knew. "That's not personal. You've never spoken of your parents, while you know all about mine."

"As I said, my parents are elderly and frail. They live outside of York."

"Are they able to come visit Lucan?"

"They don't know about his condition." That was another thing that made him feel like shit. "I don't dare tell them. I fear them knowing their elder son is . . . unwell would be too much to bear at their age."

She nodded sympathetically. "What will you do if the worst happens?"

"Lucan is receiving good care from experts. He's strong, and I'm by his side. I must believe he will pull through."

"Thank you for sharing that. I'm sorry about your brother. What can you tell me about his condition?"

Nothing. Some part of him wanted to open up to Sydney, share his burden with her. The urge was nearly as compelling as his need to make love to her last night. Damn, that was a dangerous sign, especially since that sort of sharing would only lead to heartbreak—on both sides.

Finally, Caden said, "His disorder is mental. He's a danger to himself and others now."

"Oh my God." Empathy softened her dark eyes.

"Certainly you see why I didn't want to admit something like that the day we met."

"I'm sorry. I have a nasty habit of prying. The curse of being a reporter."

"I understand."

"While I'm prying, I wonder if you'd answer another question for me."

He stiffened. Already he'd said more than he should. With Sydney, he was walking a tightrope. He had to seem engaged, but not invest so much that he couldn't leave later. It was already going to hurt like hell. Using her left a bad taste in his mouth, but staying by her side until he got the information needed to get his brother's life back was critical. Adoring her as he wanted would only mean a broken promise later.

"I'll try."

Sydney seemed to sense the change in his tone and bit her lip. "Why move to the States? Why leave for so long if your parents are elderly? Why join the U.S. Marines? Why—"

"One at a time." He held up a hand to stay her with an indulgent glance. "I moved away at eighteen. Went to school for a bit, met some Marines and decided I wanted to join them. I obtained a green card, quit school, went to basic." He shrugged. "My parents and I . . . didn't see eye-to-eye about my future, and a decade ago, putting distance between us seemed like a good idea."

A huge understatement. Caden's mother, once a gifted seer like many women in her line, kept insisting that Caden would someday embrace his considerable magic and distinguish himself as a champion. Rubbish!

By the time she'd started making such predictions, Westin was dead, and Caden wanted nothing to do with magic, especially not hers. After leaving home, he'd judiciously avoided magickind, lurking in the States and lived among humans, seen life through their eyes—and he'd never wanted life another way since.

"So you moved to another country?"

Put like that, it sounded extreme. "They had Lucan to carry on the family traditions. I wasn't interested."

"A family business?"

"Ah, something like that," he hedged. "Anyway, I joined the Marines because it was far, far from home, and I wanted to fight—something my parents had always been against." At least in the human sense. "I made some great friends."

With the Marines, he'd fit in for the first time in his life. Sure, his platoon had ribbed him about being British and having a teacup up his ass and the like. He missed them like hell.

But no one in his platoon had known about his magical family or had expectations of him becoming any sort of wand-waving Superman. He was great with automatic weapons, could wipe the floor with most in hand-to-hand, and was without peer in explosives. He'd been happy to help Bram and the Doomsday Brethren learn some of those skills. But lending his magic . . . hell, he didn't have any. Nor did he want to.

"Are you still friends today?"

Caden sucked a fresh breath of pain. "Most all are gone. Many died in Iraq. Some committed suicide after coming home. Another went to prison. One is missing. I'm one of the few left standing."

She was the first person he'd told. No one else had asked or cared. Sharing his sorrow with her was dangerous, but felt good. Sydney threw her arms around him, as if she knew exactly how much pain it had cost him to lose friends like Walt, who everyone called T-Rex because he'd been huge and his footsteps lumbering. Or Brian, the prankster with the weird tattoos. Damn hard to believe that Brian went missing under mysterious circumstances two months ago and was presumed dead.

"I'm sorry," Sydney murmured. "I never meant to bring up something painful."

Gently, Caden pulled away—though he desperately wanted to stay. For a brief moment in her arms, the hurt of the past and the worries about tomorrow had been absent. He'd simply lived in the peaceful moment. But now it was time for reality.

"I won't ask if that satisfies your curiosity, since I know better. But I should get going," he said, unable to resist filtering his fingers through her soft hair one last time. His fingers trailed away with regret.

Sydney grabbed his wrist. "Kiss me. We never got to that last night."

So tempting. He craved her taste, but the increasing sweats, sex drive, and tingles told him that he'd soon be a wizard. Like any wizard, he'd have the ability to sense his mate by taste—if he didn't already have that "gift." Unless he wanted to tie himself to Sydney forever, kissing her was forbidden. And mating aside, if he kissed her when he had no intention of staying, it would be more cruel, not less.

He put a hand over his mouth. "Not before I find a toothbrush. You'll thank me later."

A frown wrinkled her brow. "You say the right things, but why do I get the feeling that once you walk out the door, you'll never be like this with me again?"

Caden tried like hell to keep his expression neutral, but when she stared back in distress, he guessed he'd failed Subterfuge 101. How the hell could he answer her?

"It's . . . um, a complicated time in my life now, with my brother, my parents, and there's more. If it weren't for all that, everything between us would be different. I would choose to be with you and never let you go."

He forcibly pressed his mouth shut. *Stop. There. Now.* The

canned response he should have given her about being interested and taking it one day at a time? Not in his vocabulary at that moment. What had possessed him to be so honest?

Despite not lying—or perhaps because of it—she looked ready to cry. She clutched the sheet tight against her breasts. "Are you turning away because I won't give up my source? Did you hope to shag it out of me?"

Regret sliced him to the bone. "No, but mixing business and pleasure wasn't wise."

"Then go. We'll forget last night ever happened."

Impossible.

Her expression was a kick to the heart. He was heartily sick of playing this wretched game with her. "Sydney, later, if my life becomes less complicated . . ."

Sydney shut her eyes and shook her head. "Just go."

Reluctantly, he turned and left her bedroom with a last glance over his shoulder at her pale curves barely concealed in the white sheet, surrounded by a halo of that fiery hair. He nearly couldn't find the fortitude to leave, knowing his chances of ever holding her again were slim.

But he forced himself to put one foot in front of the other and disappear down her hall.

Halfway to the door, he heard her murmur, "We both know there's no 'later' for us."

The truth was like an upper cut to his abdomen. Caden braced himself against the wall and, fists clenched, fought the urge to return to her.

Damn it! Leaving was for the best. Still, if he'd wanted to escape with his heart intact, he was about twelve hours too late.

Sydney sat behind her desk that morning, struggling to focus. At the moment, weak sunlight barely leaked through her office windows, and it was an ungodly seven in the morning. But it wouldn't be long before Caden arrived, and she had to look at him. Work with him. Not touch him.

Last night had been, in a word, incredible. Passionate, giving her one jolt of pleasure after another, keeping her trembling and needy, Caden had been the lover she'd always wanted and never had. Well, except for the fact he hadn't kissed her. Odd, that. Then again, they'd been so busy doing other amazingly luscious things.

But they were done now, she feared. And the sense of rightness that had sparked last night was gone. Whatever was going on with his brother, in his life, he was letting it come between them.

Then again, maybe it wasn't him. Maybe last night had only happened because she'd *wished* it into reality, a byproduct of the fact she'd written her fantasy about him in that damned red book. Right down to the connection that had made her heart leap. If that was true, how ridiculous and pathetic. She deserved her heartache.

Penning her wish in the book and having it come true seemed fantastic, but then, she wrote of such things all day. And believed more than a few. She'd never imagined something amazing would happen to her, but maybe this had.

Sydney covered her face and tried to fight tears. Damn it, even knowing he had some hidden agenda, she had still written of her desire for him, then succumbed to his touch completely. Stupid! And no matter what he said, her refusal to give up the name of her source played a role in his abrupt departure. Every part of their conversation this morning—except the brief moments he'd discussed his brother and his platoon—had felt off somehow.

Work. She had to focus on that. Her fling with Caden had been brief, perhaps even manufactured. Just because they'd clicked surprisingly well didn't mean it was some spectacular affair of the heart. They'd shagged. She'd never allowed any man to break her heart, and he wouldn't earn that distinction after a single night.

Launching her e-mail, Sydney vowed to focus. She perked up right away when she received an e-mail from her informant at the Coroner's Office, a friend from her uni days. The woman finally had news regarding the bodies of the partially decomposed soldiers in the tunnel discovered just over two weeks ago. The e-mail simply read *Call me before nine.*

Heart pounding, palms sweating, Sydney rang Chloe's mobile phone.

" 'lo," answered a groggy man.

"Is Chloe there? Sorry to ring so early."

After a moment of shuffling and a giggle, Chloe answered, "Syd?"

Chloe had been happily married for nearly four years to a handsome devil named Blake. Sydney would be jealous if she hadn't always regarded Blake as the big brother she'd never had.

"What's your news?" Sydney asked, dispensing with pleasantries.

"Good morning to you, too." Chloe laughed. "*Very* unofficially, here's what I know about the bodies discovered in the tunnel."

"Following the November fourteenth skirmish I've been writing about? The magic thing?"

"Exactly," Chloe confirmed. "Tests have identified all the bodies. Are you sitting?"

"Yes. On with it, you tease!"

"You know me too well." Chloe shot back, then sobered. "All the bodies were of servicemen—from all over the world, including seven of the eight *American* soldiers who mysteriously disappeared on September nineteenth from a training exercise at Camp Lejeune, North Carolina. They were all part of the Marines Special Operations Command."

Sydney's jaw dropped. As the surreal words sunk in, she muttered, "Bugger! Special Forces . . . I remember hearing about the disappearance of those soldiers!"

"The higher-ups at the office are all being very hush-hush. But that in itself says something. Next of kin are being notified now, but their identities aren't being released to the media yet, so I can't give you that or my boss would be suspicious."

Chloe had already delivered more than expected. She owed her old friend a pint or two at least. "Of course. Anything else you can give me?"

"You know from our previous conversation that the bodies were decomposed weeks beyond what their battle wounds suggested. Your grainy photos showed that several were decapitated, a few others shot or stabbed. But they bled as profusely as if they were alive. And they bled black."

"Black?"

"Indeed. It's a complete mystery. There's no blood type. Everyone was identified by fingerprints, distinguishing marks, or dental records."

Sydney paused. What would cause such a thing? New disease? Black blood sounded crazy, but working at *Out of This Realm*, she'd quickly learned that nothing was impossible. "Odd."

"Very," Chloe agreed. "Assuming your story is real, do you have any theories about which side the poor bastards fought for?"

"No. I've heard little about the other side, this Doomsday Brethren. My source says they're good, but they're fighting Mathias, who claims to be battling for equality. Yet he raped a woman until she was little more than a broken shell. But does his evil automatically make the Doomsday Brethren good? If I had to guess, I'd say the soldiers were Mathias's. If he cares so little as to repeatedly rape a woman, I doubt he's above kidnapping a few well-trained soldiers and using them in his army."

Chloe hesitated. "Do you really think this is all true, not merely this terrorized woman's hallucinations?"

"It's possible, I suppose. But there's enough fact here to make me pause. Call me if you hear any more."

They rang off, and Sydney jotted down a few notes—which quickly grew frustrating. She had another story to crank out this week on the magical war, and she wanted it to be about Chloe's information, slanted accurately, but she had so many questions. How did these soldiers fit into the grand scheme of the war? Had they been used for magical purposes? How were they persuaded or forced to fight and give their lives for this cause? Perhaps she could run with the facts as they were, but the pieces of the puzzle didn't fit. She needed to talk to her source again and see what else the witch might know.

Sydney placed a quick call to Aquarius. When her assistant didn't answer, she left a voicemail, apologizing for the interruption of her holiday and asking for a ring back indicating whether Aquarius's guest would talk again.

Not long after she placed the phone back in the cradle, she felt a presence in the doorway.

Caden.

"Good morning," she said, forcing a businesslike tone. "Did you need something? I'm off to a busy start, so spit it out."

He stepped in and shut the door behind him, planting his fists on her desk and leaning closer. "Sydney, I'm—"

"Stop." She put up a hand, refusing to reveal that the sight of him had her blood pumping and her heart aching. If they talked about last night, she'd risk tears. "I just have one question: Why did you come over last night? What made you leave your flat in the middle of the night and come all the way crosstown to mine? Was it the sex or something else?"

He paused, scrubbing a hand over his face. A weariness she'd never seen dragged down his eyes, mouth, shoulders. For a moment, Sydney's heart went out to him, until she reminded herself that she couldn't feel for him and keep her heart unscathed. Something about Caden called to her, and she wasn't certain he suffered the same affliction. He'd risen from her bed, dressed, left, and as far as she could see, suffered no side effects other than lack of sleep. It wasn't as if she was looking for a down-on-one-knee proposal, just the truth.

"Pure impulse. I was attracted to you from the first. I tried to keep to myself because we work together, my life is complicated now, and I can't give you a tomorrow. But I came over last night because I could no longer stay away. I tried to talk myself out of going to your flat, but every moment I was away from you, I became more obsessed with making love to you."

Had that been the magical diary compelling him to come to my door? Sydney swallowed. *No. It was just an old red book, right?* This had to be about her story. She believed in magic, yes. But not involving her.

"Did you come because you wanted to persuade me to divulge my magical source?"

"No, but if you'd like to make me a full partner in this story, I'd love that."

"And what, you thought being my partner in the bedroom would help you get there faster?"

"Damn it! I dreamed of you, literally, in the precise linge-rie you wore for me last night. I dreamed of tearing it off, of the sweet taste of your breasts, of your body clutching my cock, of the groans you made when you came for me. How the bloody hell was I supposed to stay away from you after that?"

Oh God. Sydney sat back with a gulp. "Would you . . . um, say you felt compelled?"

"Yes. But I take responsibility for mucking up every-thing." Caden stopped, leaned closer, peering at her as if trying to unravel a puzzle. "Wait. Did you write about me in that bloody book Aquarius gave you?"

She wanted to crawl under the desk and stay for a decade. "Don't be absurd."

How had he guessed so quickly? Had her words really brought him to her door? God, she felt like an idiot!

"Forget I asked about last night. Let's focus on work."

His eyes narrowed. "What made you open the door and let me in?"

"It's no secret I wanted you. But as you said earlier, itch scratched. Moving on."

"I said no such thing," he growled.

Hadn't he, just hours ago? Hadn't he said repeatedly they had no future? Of course. He hadn't been there of his own free will in the first place. "Don't play games."

"Which is exactly what you've done by cheapening last night."

He was right; she had cheapened last night, most likely. In a way she hoped he never discovered. "Sorry."

She couldn't expect an emotional response from Caden when she'd used a magical diary to break his natural reti-cence. He'd come to her flat and shagged her because that had been her wish, not because he felt any eternal devotion.

"Forget I mentioned it. Work is piling up this morning, and I'm stressed."

Caden gnashed his teeth and looked away. "Is it going to start another fight if I ask if there's anything I can do to help?"

"No." Because if he stayed with her in this small office, she was in grave danger of wrapping her arms around him and pleading for his affection.

Before he could respond, Sydney's phone rang. The caller ID had her sighing in relief. Aquarius.

Sydney picked it up and answered, "Thank God you've called. Can you meet me?"

Caden wasn't certain who Sydney was talking to and, at the moment, didn't much care. Frustration ate at him. Everything about this situation was wrong, and he had no idea how to fix it. And now Sydney was on the bloody phone with God knew who, discussing God knew what. For all he knew, she was making a date.

On second thought, he did care who she talked to; he needed to know who to kill.

Quickly, Sydney covered her earpiece, "Can you give me a moment?"

With an angry jerk, he turned to leave. But he couldn't make himself walk away. If Sydney was in the process of replacing him in her bed mere hours later . . . well, he wasn't a masochist by nature, but something in him needed to know. He couldn't keep her, but he couldn't stand the thought of losing her.

With a distracted push, Sydney eased the door nearly shut. Caden leaned closer to the slightly ajar door and listened.

"I'm here," she said. "Lunch sounds great. Can you meet

me at eleven-thirty at that um . . . Blue whatever the name was?" She paused. "Perfect. I'll see both of you then."

Both of them? Was she contemplating dating more than one man?

"Work is fine. I know you're supposed to be on holiday. I don't want to bog you down, but I need help with this week's story. It's still developing. I also need to ask you about that magical diary you gave me for my birthday."

Oh, so she was talking to Aquarius and going to meet her—and a friend?—for lunch. Caden sighed with relief. Not only because Aquarius was in town, but because Sydney was still single. He couldn't stomach the thought of her with another man, and it would be wise to refrain from violence before eight a.m.

"What can you tell me about that book? Its origins? Does it have any ties to the magical world I've been writing about?" She spoke in low tones.

Caden closed his eyes and concentrated very hard, hoping to hear both sides of Sydney's conversation. Aquarius loudly answered yes to Sydney's last question, then her voice dropped again. He picked up a word or two about someone named Emma, whoever the bloody hell that was.

Then Sydney spoke again, "Perfect. I'm still working on the ongoing war angle of this story, but would you mind if I wrote this week's article about the book?"

Her words jolted Caden, as if someone had put ten thousand volts through his body. Damn and blast, he couldn't let Sydney write that. The danger to her if Mathias read the article. . . . Caden's blood chilled and his breath stopped as he imagined everything the terrible wizard would force her to endure. Hadn't he convinced her yet that this angle was dangerous? That she could be a target?

Hand on the knob to her door, Caden prepared to charge

in. He could not let her write about that bloody book. Not this week, not ever.

Before he could push the door open, someone tapped his shoulder. Caden whirled to see Holly, Sydney's editor. Well, damn. This looked bad.

"I was just going to ask her a question."

"And it's taken the last two minutes of intense eavesdropping to decide what to say?"

"No. Well, she . . . I don't think—"

Holly held up a hand to stop him. "Come with me."

Caden looked back at Sydney's closed door. He didn't have much choice. Later, before Sydney left for lunch, he'd talk to her, make her see reason, convince her not to run that story.

With a sigh, he followed Holly.

"Do you have anything personal in your cubicle?"

"Just my camera. Why?"

"Get it." She walked him to his desk, where he retrieved his camera and keys. Other than that, he'd brought nothing.

"That's all, then? I'll walk you to the door."

A chill went up his spine. "The door?"

Holly sent him a glare that said the jig was more than up as she escorted him to the front. "C'mon, MacTavish. You've used every angle to learn her source. Hitting on her, going to her apartment, eavesdropping. It's clear you want to scoop her and—"

"No! God, no. I swear. Holly—"

"Save it. You're sacked." Holly opened the paper's front door. Weak morning sun glared in his eyes, blinding him. "Get out. Now."

CHAPTER SEVEN

CADEN MADE IT BACK to his flat, rage barely in check. The minute the door slammed behind him, he shouted a string of curses. He'd been sacked and he had no idea where to find the mystery "Blue" restaurant at which Sydney, Aquarius and whoever would have lunch. Translation: Mission failed. He'd never learned if Sydney's source was Anka. Damn it all, no Anka meant no return to sanity for Lucan, and no going back to Texas for him. Sydney was going to pursue a dangerous story, and he was no longer there to protect her.

As a Marine, failure wasn't something he tolerated well. Logically, he knew he should be glad. Now that he was no longer employed at *Out of This Realm*, Bram would have to assign the mission to someone else. Eliminating lies and subterfuge thrilled him. But not completing a mission rankled. He'd continue searching for Anka another way, of course. He didn't recall any magical detectives from his childhood, and he knew from his own mother that seers could be notoriously unreliable. He needed another plan, one that removed Sydney from danger.

He reached into his pocket and picked out one of the white summoning rocks Bram had given him, then thrust it back. Like anything magical, Caden had come to hate these after Westin's death. Once he'd been old enough to learn to bewitch one, he'd been completely against it, despite Lucan offering to teach him. Having lived among humankind for so long, tossing a pebble in the air, calling someone's name, and having them appear moments later seemed creepy and abnormal.

He knew his magic was coming. Today, he'd awakened energized and refreshed for the first time in weeks. Within hours, the shakes, the sweats, and the never-ending sex drive had kicked in again. Signs of his coming change. But until magic forced unwanted powers upon him, by God, he was still a man.

Grabbing his mobile phone, he punched in Bram's number. He'd tell the sod to assign someone else to this errand. He was out of the James Bond business.

But being sacked also meant he had no more reason to see Sydney each day. After the way he'd left her this morning, she was angry and hurt. That made him wince.

Had her anger been strong enough to sabotage his job? Sydney had long suspected he was trying to scoop her story. Holly had reiterated the same suspicion, and he'd seen precious little of the editor. The woman couldn't have fabricated that worry by herself. Sydney had likely helped her reach that conclusion. Because of his abrupt departure this morning?

Caden didn't lament the loss of the job. The loss of the woman? God help him, that was a stab in the heart.

If he kissed her and opened his burgeoning magical senses to Sydney, he was certain they would demand he speak the Call. And given his complete lack of restraint with Sydney, he would have blurted the words, caution be damned. That quickly, magic would have forced a mate on him.

Caden required self-control, and Sydney stripped him of it more easily than he liked. Losing her after mating himself to her would only leave him ripe for the kind of lunacy that could kill him. Worse, magickind was fast becoming a dangerous place—one in which she didn't belong. She would be safer if she stayed away from him. And stopped writing stories likely to catch Mathias's notice.

"MacTavish?" Bram answered, sounding irritable. "It's nine a.m. on a Tuesday, and you're ringing me? Tell me—"

"I've been sacked."

"*What?!*"

Caden reiterated the morning's events, leaving out the fact he had spent the night in Sydney's arms and bed.

After he was finished, Bram sighed. "We didn't need this setback."

"As some of my American friends say, I screwed the pooch." And that burned his hide. "Damage done. Now you're free to send someone else in to snuff the stories. I just ask that whomever you send protect Sydney."

"We've discussed this. My options are limited."

"Send Sabelle. She and Sydney would get on well."

"Impossible. My sister is tied up with Council business."

Caden frowned. "She's not a member of the Council."

"But she does have a certain charm for the old codgers who sit beside me that I apparently lack."

Despite the gravity of the situation, Caden laughed at the image. "She is far prettier."

"She smiles and flatters and makes them feel young again. It's a needed skill. Word of all the Anarki attacks is leaking out and the rest of the Council is demanding I stop them."

"The rumors or the attacks?"

"The former, but I know that can't happen until I stop the latter, which they're still refusing to publicly acknowledge."

"And you're trying to persuade the Council to make a statement to magickind at large, explaining the real danger, correct?" Caden grunted. "Good luck."

The group of elders had never moved quickly or advocated

a less-than-traditional path. It could take them months, even years or decades, to reach a consensus on a public statement about Mathias's return. By then, Mathias may have already taken over magickind. Stupid sods.

"I need it. And Sabelle." Bram sighed. "I could send Shock, I suppose. He can skim Sydney's thoughts—"

"Absolutely not! How do I know he won't deliver her to Mathias? I will not have that turncoat anywhere near my . . ." *Mate.* The word nearly rolled off his tongue. "Former coworker." There, that sounded better.

And like a pitiful lie.

Though Shock was bound to Anka, despite the fact she'd rejected his Call and he could, therefore, not touch Sydney sexually, the thought of Shock anywhere in the same postal-code still made him murderous.

"Do you think Sydney is your mate?" Bram asked pointedly.

"I haven't tasted her."

Bram hesitated. "For everyone's sake, I hope she isn't. You're preparing for transition. I sense it. You're irritable and tense. You've been tired a great deal, haven't you? And the urge for sex is overwhelming, right?"

Caden didn't answer. Why tell Bram he'd hit a bull's-eye? The sod likely knew it anyway.

"You'll need to find a witch to transition with. You're going to need sexual energy to power your coming magic."

Grinding his teeth, Caden turned away. Yes, he knew he needed sex—and a lot of it—to create the energy necessary to transition. If he had issued the Call to Sydney, only she would do. But he hadn't. If he could restrain himself a bit longer, he wouldn't. Problem was, he didn't want some nameless witch.

"I have not issued the Call to mate," Caden reiterated.

"Unless that changes, you have no problem."

Wrong. "She believes in this story and is suspicious of everyone. No one is more suspect than Shock. You come," Caden suggested.

The thought of Bram charming Sydney made him want to grind his teeth into powder, but the wizard was newly mated. He couldn't woo Sydney. And he wouldn't turn her over to Mathias.

"I told you, I can't, not until I complete the Council's demand for magickind to stop spreading rumors—even if they're the truth." Bram snorted. "This assignment also allows me to quietly warn Privileged families that Mathias is likely to target them and demonstrate to his Deprived followers that he embraces their bid for equality."

"It's shit."

"But I cannot defer this duty. There have been four Anarki attacks in the last three weeks. If the Council won't send a transcast, I must warn people unofficially. I am spending what little free time I have trying to locate my errant mate."

In Bram's shoes, he'd be doing the same. "Keep Shock away from Sydney."

"Then stop her from writing articles."

"I've been sacked. How do you propose I do that? Sydney may very well write an article about the Doomsday Diary. Just this morning, she was inquiring about its origins."

"For the last bloody time, charm the woman!"

"I tried. It's . . . complicated." And he wasn't spilling a single detail.

"Uncomplicate it," Bram snapped.

"This was your fucking mission to start with. I did my best and, as much as I hate failure, I admit to it. This morning, I tried to steal the Doomsday Diary from Sydney, but

when I attempted to leave her flat with it, the book dissolved
in my hands. Twice. Why?"

"Dissolved?"

"Completely. Moments later, it appeared again on the
nightstand from which I took it."

"In other words, it would not leave Sydney's flat with you.
Interesting . . . but I think I might know why. You're male.
You've heard me say the book is an object of feminine rever-
ence? That means the book responds only to women."

"I didn't try to use it."

Bram hesitated. "Stealing it may work the same way.
We're learning as we go, but it makes sense. Eons ago, Marrok paid a woman to steal it from Morganna. After she did,
she *gave* it to him. Marrok kept it in the same cottage for
centuries. Then came Olivia. She brought the book to my
estate and hid it. I assumed at the time that anyone could
transport the book, but, given your experience, clearly not.
Neither Marrok nor I could write in it when Mathias abducted Olivia. Sabelle, however, could. A wish to fix a button
was granted instantly. Her wish to save Olivia was not, and
we discerned that whoever uses the book must have both
great power and great desire to fulfill the wish. My mate
stole it from me. Somehow, it fell into this Aquarius's hands,
and she gave it to Sydney. Female to female to female. When
you tried to steal it from Sydney—"

"I'm not female."

"Exactly."

Caden sighed. Interesting, but . . . "I've barely met
Aquarius, so I don't know about her, but Sydney is definitely
human, not magical."

"Apparently having two X chromosomes is more important than having a magical one."

"Even more reason you should send someone else in my

place, Olivia, perhaps, and let me look for Anka elsewhere."

Bram huffed. "Is giving up what the Marines taught you? Last I heard, failure wasn't an option."

Blast it, the wizard was right. Caden hadn't asked for this mission, but the guilt of failure ate at him. Nor did he want to leave Sydney unprotected. But what else could he do? So, like any good tactician, he resorted to a diversionary tactic.

"I may have some information about the book and how Aquarius acquired it."

"I'm listening."

Caden gripped the phone. "I don't know how she fits into the equation, but Aquarius mentioned someone named Emma."

"*What* did you say?"

The violence of Bram's question took him aback. "E-Emma?"

"You're certain?"

"I overheard a telephone conversation, but reasonably so, yes."

The wizard didn't hesitate. "You have a new mission: Besides getting that book away from Sydney, make her tell you more about Emma. Immediately."

Bram's sudden command was somewhere between stunning and what-the-hell?

"You don't have time to help me when you're throwing me to the wolves, but when I mention some woman—"

A loud chirp, a flap of wings, followed by a woman's panicked voice interrupted the beginnings of Caden's tirade. Some witch had compelled a bird to deliver a message to Bram. And from the sound of it, the message was urgent.

"I must go. I'll send you help to obtain the book since you're not female. But get all the information you can about Emma, then call me."

"Damn it, I'm not your errand boy." Caden shouted. "Who is Emma?"

"My mate. That's the first clue I've had of her since she disappeared. And I'm going to find that woman if it's the last bloody thing I do."

After the worst Tuesday ever, Sydney was more than happy to escape back to her flat. She shed her clothes as she headed back to her bedroom. She shed tears just as easily.

Dear Lord, her careless words had gotten Caden sacked. Granted, he had been eavesdropping, and suspicion that he'd been trying to scoop her still lingered. She'd tried to talk Holly into taking him back. No luck. And Caden had likely assumed that she'd tattled to her editor because he'd hurt her by leaving her bed this morning. He'd think her spiteful and never want to see her again.

That possibility crushed her. She must find Caden, set matters straight. Already she missed him with a yearning she didn't understand. It was impossible to fall in love in a few days with a man who had begrudgingly shared himself. Blast, he had never even kissed her.

Even if the man wanted nothing more to do with her, she couldn't tolerate the thought that he might believe that she'd had him sacked in a scorned woman's act of vengeance. Under normal circumstances, she would ring him up and explain and apologize. But she had no means of getting in touch with Caden—no idea where he lived, no mobile number . . . nothing.

Sydney bit her lip. Well, except that magical diary.

Had the fact she had written in it previously brought Caden to her door? Or had it been mere coincidence?

She couldn't know for certain unless she experimented.

With a sigh, Sydney reached for her mobile and called Aquarius.

As soon as her friend and assistant picked up, Sydney blurted, "Did the book work for you?"

"Mellow, boss lady. Like I said at lunch, it works. From what you said, you discovered that yourself."

"Maybe it was coincidence."

Aquarius laughed. "Though I love magic, I was skeptical at first. I wrote about Alex a few times before I truly believed."

This morning, she'd felt wretched and unintentionally manipulative. Had she made a man who didn't truly want her come to her flat and have sex with her? She still winced at the possibility.

"It seems like such a pathetic thing to do, write a fantasy so it will come true, regardless of what he wants."

"I understand being worried about bad karma."

That wasn't exactly her issue, but close enough. "But if I'm going to report about the book, I should test it again. Caden is the only man I fantasize about. I can't move forward with the story about the identities of the bodies in the tunnel yet. I need to shore up a few facts. I didn't have the heart to ask your cousin any more questions after she broke down at lunch today. She looked so pale and tired. Is she all right?"

"As well as can be expected, but she won't talk anymore, Sydney. When she asked me if you were a journalist, I couldn't lie. She knows she's said too much, and when I admitted you'd written stories based on her information, she became terrified that Mathias will find her."

"I promise, I've never given details about her identity."

"She says it's too risky for her, for magickind, and for you. Mathias is ruthless."

Damn it! Sydney gripped the phone. She *needed* that source . . . yet the witch's fragile physical and mental state not only raised Sydney's pity, but concern. Aquarius's cousin was one shock away from a breakdown. Sydney would have to find another means of researching this magical war.

As soon as she made this week's deadline—and got in touch with Caden.

Sydney and Aquarius rang off. She sank onto the edge of her bed, unstacked the books on her desk, and lifted the one at the bottom. The little red one. She turned to the page where she'd written her previous fantasy about Caden making love to her.

Last night when she'd arrived home from work, the words had been on the page, mocking her for her stupidity in believing that magic would ever fall into her lap. Tonight, the page was blank. The words were gone. Disappeared. She peered at the spine, but no signs of a ripped page. No erasure marks. Just one perfect, pristine page after another.

What did that mean? That her fantasy had come true so the words had . . . vanished?

No. There must be some logical explanation. The pages were stuck together or she wasn't seeing the ink right in this light or, heaven forbid, Caden had found the page while he was here last night and carefully removed it.

Sydney bit her lip. Whatever was going on here, she wanted to talk to Caden, and hoped that he wanted her beyond what she'd written.

Before she could lose her nerve, Sydney grabbed a pen, then carefully crafted a "sexual fantasy." That is, if a fantasy of Caden darkening her door to have an honest conversation with her counted as sexual. She couldn't resist adding a line wishing that he'd make love to her if he genuinely desired and cared about her.

Sighing, Sydney put the pen down. Moments later, fresh ink appeared on the next page:

Sleep, dream, anticipate . . .
  The fantasy you imagine will soon be
your fate.

Twice now, the book had responded. Sydney shivered. Apparently something paranormal *had* happened to her . . . and might happen again. As she closed the book, her thoughts spun.

What if the diary was unable to make emotional fantasies come true? What if it didn't grant conversation, just sexual wishes? She had asked for honesty, not pillow talk.

Crap! She'd written in pen, and couldn't erase the words. But honestly, she didn't want to. If it brought Caden here so they could talk—and she could apologize—she'd put the brakes on anything else until she was certain it was truly mutual.

The question was, how long would she have to wait before she saw him? And what would happen once she did?

After a basically sleepless night, Sydney trudged into the office the following morning, lugging her briefcase in one hand and her extra enormous coffee in the other. Wednesday. Technically, only one more day before her next story was due to copy editing. Bloody hell, she hadn't even started it. She was waiting. On Caden. Would the magical book work?

"Morning, Syd!" Holly popped her head in her office, blond curls framing her face in a way many women paid hundreds of pounds to reproduce, her cupid's bow mouth painted an eye-catching red.

"Morning, Holly."

Sydney wanted to be angry at Holly for Caden's dismissal,

but after her description of his eavesdropping, she understood Holly's position. Even if Caden had done it because he wanted to protect her, it looked fishy.

"You look like shit. Sleep more. If you're losing some over Caden's sacking, problem solved. Meet Zain Denzell."

As if Caden could be replaced with any warm body . . .

In the doorway, Holly stepped back. A man edged forward, tall, lanky, and scruffy. He sported inky black hair, a goatee, a crooked nose, and an office-inappropriate T-shirt that said "Wanted: Meaningful Overnight Relationship." But the eyes . . . those were sharp, almost dissecting. Sydney had the immediate impression that Zain was used to people underestimating him, and he preferred it that way.

"Hello." She walked around the desk and stuck out her hand.

Zain approached, something between a walk and a swagger, then took her hand. She had a brief impression of slightly damp palms. He didn't give off the demeanor of someone with large stature, but still hit her square in the chest, as if he was important somehow.

"Nice to meet you," he said with a nod, then backed away.

"Likewise."

Biting her lip, Sydney studied him. Not as easy on the eyes as the last one, but he'd be less distracting. Zain's deference seemed a bit practiced, but she supposed anyone young trying to succeed in the news business learned to bow and scrape in a hurry.

Suddenly, he smiled. "Too awkward? Sorry. I'm a loner and not used to mingling with others, especially before noon."

"You're fine."

Holly clapped her hands. "Great, now that the introductions are over, why don't you and Zain spend thirty seconds forming a meaningful work bond, then start making me money?"

With that cheerful demand, Holly left, shutting the door behind her. Sydney rolled her eyes, and Zain laughed.

"Is she always that . . ."

"Brash? Absolutely. If you hear people talk about Cruella, you know who they mean."

Zain rubbed his hands together. "We still have a few moments; tell me about you."

Sydney perched herself on the edge of her desk. "I'm a reporter with deadlines who doesn't have time for crap. You may not believe my stories, but if so, I don't want to hear it."

"No. I believe. Especially the magical war story."

"That's right. You're the one Holly told me had pictures of the bodies in the tunnel. How did you get them?"

Zain hesitated. "I have a source who claims to be involved. That's why I wanted to work here. I think we can blow the doors off this story and make big names for ourselves."

She stood up straight, her interest in Zain zooming. "A source involved in the magical war? And you don't think he or she is mental? Tell me more."

"Can't, really. He didn't meet with me. I got a note, you see, that basically said, 'be here at this time.' I was, and found the bodies just after the battle." Zain shrugged.

Odd. "Was this note delivered to your home?"

He winced, looking a bit sheepish. "It just . . . appeared in my flat."

Like poof, as in magic? "Has it happened again?"

Nodding, Zain explained, "The last one said something big was coming and he'd let me know."

"Why you?" Sydney asked. "Why not someone already working on this story?"

Zain lifted a shoulder. "I don't know. Maybe because I've always been interested in magic."

Possible, but it sounded convenient. Sydney's guess was that Zain wanted this job, and had invented a reclusive source to get it. The pictures in the tunnel? For all Sydney knew, he could have Photoshopped them. Time would tell.

Repressing a smile, she sank back to the edge of the desk. "I'm working on a new angle about the battle in the tunnel. You know, where you took the pictures of the bodies? I'm having some difficulty. The last article I wrote—"

"Was rubbish," he blurted, then looked sheepish. "No disrespect intended. But you got it all wrong. Mathias is the good guy in the magical world. He wants to end oppression."

Sydney slanted him a considering stare. "I have a source, too, who claims Mathias repeatedly raped her. He doesn't sound like a great bloke."

"Energy," Zain said. "Powerful emotions, commonly sex, fuels their magic, or so I've been told. They *must* have it frequently. She may have called it rape to win sympathy, but these people shag like mad to keep themselves charged up."

Talk about rubbish. First, Aquarius's cousin had an abused demeanor, not a satisfied one. She'd seen nothing to suggest the woman had engaged in mutually consensual sex. The rest sounded like a tall tale. If it was true, why would his source have confided this sort of information, when it had nothing to do with the war?

"Interesting." She gave him a tight smile. "For my next story . . ."

The words *I'll just need a few pictures of this red book that grants sexual fantasies* stuck in her throat. He might wonder how she'd acquired such a thing. And if he was the sort who would lie about his inside information, maybe he would try to steal the book from her. After Caden's words of caution and everything that had befallen Aquarius's cousin, it made sense to be cautious.

He sat forward, attentive, focused on her. Now she knew how an animal at the zoo felt.

"I've got it under control," she said finally.

He frowned. "You don't need me this week?"

"My last photographer already took pictures," she lied. "But bring your snapshots of the bodies. I'll look at those for my next piece. This week, I've got another story. Oh, and if you can, ask your source why, if Mathias is the good sort, abducted foreign soldiers were found among the dead in that tunnel. And what does he make of the Doomsday Brethren?"

The afternoon both flew and dragged by. Sydney crafted a story about the magical diary. Googling turned up sites about Aleister Crowley, Harry Potter—even a supposedly magical cat. The book she possessed couldn't belong to any of these people. Finally, buried a few pages down, she found some scholar's works about a supposed magical diary dating back to King Arthur's time. She was no expert, but the markings on the book were too old to belong to Crowley, Potter was fictional, and as much as she loved the fantastical, the cat was beyond even her belief. The Arthurian angle fit best.

A grueling seven hours and a missed lunch later, Sydney submitted her story about the book. She hoped she'd gotten it right. If not, she had until tomorrow to retract it and invent another, in case Caden failed to appear.

She dug her keys from her handbag and unlocked the door to her flat, her mind on the story and Zain. Had she done the right thing by submitting that story and not accepting Zain's help? Odd that the man hadn't seemed at all puzzled when she'd mentioned the Doomsday Brethren. Then again, maybe he'd been following her stories.

Deep in thought, she turned to shut the door. There Caden stood in the shadowed portico, looming large.

Sydney gasped, hand over her chest. He looked out of sorts, sweating, agitated. She might have wondered if he was taking drugs, but he hated losing control too much for that.

"You scared me." She lowered her hand and gestured to him. "Come in. Thank God, you came. I—I'm so sorry about Holly and—"

"I don't bloody care about the job." He took a step in, shed his coat, then shut the door behind him, his eyes boring into hers. "I couldn't stay away from you."

Chapter Eight

CADEN FISTED HIS HANDS at his sides, trying to keep them to himself. Sydney looked gorgeous and fiery in a short black skirt and a shiny, coppery blouse. The former clung lovingly to her hips; the latter provided a mouthwatering glimpse of cleavage. She'd swept her long hair back into some feminine knot that made his fingers itch to unravel it as he unraveled her. The remnants of reddish gloss stained her plump lips.

Without thinking, he found himself crossing the room to taste her lush mouth—and any other part of her she'd let him.

No! Down that path lay disaster. Damn it, he was here to end this mission, for Sydney's safety—and his own heart. He could not do something irresponsible. Already, this was going to hurt.

Blast Bram and his grand schemes. Caden had only agreed to this one because it would keep Sydney safe. But she would also hate him forever.

"We should talk."

She nodded and locked the door behind him, then headed for the kitchen, casting a nervous glance over her shoulder as she went. Damn. Caden wanted to be rational in her presence. A gentleman. But the urge to fuck her until she screamed his name, coupled with the gut-wrenching fear this was the last time he'd see her, made that impossible.

"Tea?" she asked.

"No," he scratched out.

"Something stronger?" She reached to the top of a cabinet and pulled out a bottle of whiskey.

Very dangerous. If he clouded his judgment with alcohol, no telling how little conversation and how much sex they'd have. He owed her his best behavior.

He shook his head. "Sit down."

Sydney bit her lip, then crossed the room. She settled on the sofa, and he sat beside her, intentionally keeping space between them. Bloody hell, she smelled like peaches and jasmine and softness. He swallowed as need clawed at him. Everything about her called to him. It was sharper tonight, painful almost. His body shook. As hot as he felt, he would have sworn it was July during a swelter, not late November.

"Why are you here?" she whispered. "If it's to pick up where we left off—"

"No." He would restrain himself, talk to her. Keep her safe. "I came to explain."

She raised a ginger brow.

"I swear, I haven't tried to steal your magical war story. Who would I sell it to?"

"We have competitors who are ruthless and not picky about ethics."

Though he'd known she suspected he plotted to steal from her, her suspicions still hurt. "I'm not one of them. *Please* trust me on that."

"Holly caught you eavesdropping. What were you doing?"

Bloody hell, Sydney proved over and over how sharp and direct she was. As always, he admired—no, desired her—for it. "I wasn't planning to steal your story. I wanted to know what was happening with you. If . . . you were seeing another man."

Another man? Had he been jealous? "There's no one else.

For the record, I did not ask Holly to release you. In fact, I spoke to her before we ever . . ." Sydney scrubbed her hand across her face. "Holly is my trusted mentor, so I asked for advice. Whatever you believe, I never thought she'd sack you. I asked her to take you back, but after she caught you eavesdropping, she refused."

"I understand. It's all right."

"If you weren't stealing, then why all the questions about my story? Why romance me?" Sydney bit her lip and hesitated. "Was any of it real?"

God, he wanted to avoid answering that telling question and just ask her if Anka was her source. But that was impossible. Sydney would ask too many questions. And the first would be, how did he know Anka, a magical woman? If he was honest and said that she was his brother's former "wife," Sydney would know he was close to magic. She would want more information about magickind that wasn't his to give or safe for her to know. Or she could think he was one of Mathias's minions, looking to torture Anka again. If Sydney thought that, she would shut him out completely. But he owed her as much of the truth as he dare give.

"Everything I felt, every touch, every concern, was real. Being with you . . . was incredible. This is a terrible time in my life for romance. I should've stayed away. But you're damned hard to resist."

She flushed, and he smiled.

Then he sobered. How the devil could he answer her questions about his interest in the story? Damn. He felt rotten. Tired, hot, and aroused, his thoughts were sluggish and his body demanding. Worse today than yesterday by far. Bloody transition.

Sydney still looked at him expectantly, and the more information he gave her, the stickier the explanation. Lies upon lies upon lies, and he hated them. The truth was no better. The more he gave her, the more she'd put in another story, further jeopardizing her.

Finally, an idea hit him like a bolt. A godsend. He sighed in relief.

"I'm looking for a witch named Anka." He watched Sydney's face, but it remained impassive. If she knew Anka, she hid it well. "Nothing has helped my brother's condition, and I spoke with a . . . healer who believed that Anka had magical powers that could help Lucan. I've tried everything else to make my brother whole, to no avail. Anka disappeared recently, and when I started reading your stories in the paper, I wondered if she was your source."

Not a lie . . . just not the whole truth.

Regret and sadness crossed her face. "I can't tell you if the woman you're seeking is my source. As much as I want to help your brother . . ." She grimaced. "I can't."

Caden nodded. "I know. Working with you under false pretenses was wrong. I didn't mean to be dodgy. I was desperate."

He refused to coerce her into compromising her ethics and giving him her source's name. She'd resent him, and he couldn't tolerate adding more fuel to the anger she'd feel after tonight. Already he felt guilty for doing his best to stop the story that could help her prove her merit to the world and her stodgy parents.

Somehow, he must devise another way to locate Anka, and he could barely think beyond his exhaustion and need to touch Sydney. But now he must deceive her again. The knowledge burned, though this was for her own safety—and that of magickind.

"The other reason I came was to prove I have no designs on your story. I've found two people who are experts on that old book Aquarius got you, the one you want to write about." He nearly choked on the lie.

"You *told* people about it?" She rolled her eyes. "Doesn't matter. They can't beat me to press."

"I told people who can help you understand the book. I swear, no one has designs on your story."

She hesitated. "All right, but everything I've written is conjecture. If you brought me experts . . . I've already turned the story in, but I've got a bit of time—"

"A story about the book?" At her nod, his stomach lurched. *Dear God.* With that article, she was painting a huge red target on her forehead for Mathias. He forced himself to relax. "Well, you have until tomorrow afternoon to change it, right?"

"Unless Holly puts it up as a web story first. She'll let me know in the morning."

"Call her and tell her to hold it. You'll want to, once you talk to my connections. Olivia Gray owns a local art gallery and is an expert in antiquities. She's handled something remarkably similar before."

Sydney's face softened and excitement bloomed. "Really?"

Feeling guilt sear him again, he managed to nod. "I also spoke with Simon Northam. He's—"

"*The* Simon Northam? The Duke of Hurstgrove?"

"You know him?"

"I know *of* him. Who doesn't? *Hello! Magazine* named him England's sexiest bachelor. He's filthy rich and intelligent and . . . he knows about this book and is willing to talk to *me?*"

"Indeed. Antique books are a passion of his. They both need to examine the book. In your presence, of course." *Right before they take it.* "Will you let them? They can either come here or meet you at the pub 'round the corner. I told them I would call if you were willing."

Sydney hesitated, biting her lip. The sight distracted Caden, who restrained the urge to lean across and kiss her. Giving into that impulse? Disaster. He didn't want to be magically compelled to mate. Sydney was human. She didn't belong in the middle of this magical war. And if she accepted his Call, her lifespan would match his. Who would want to live centuries fraught with danger, surrounded by people who could kill her in the blink of an eye when she had no way to fight back? And did he want to risk losing her and winding up like Lucan? No and no.

"I want to talk to them. But no pictures. The book doesn't leave my sight. No one writes anything down."

Caden nodded, even as the pain of deceiving her again lanced him. Though it was for her own good, it ripped his insides. "And you'll call Holly?"

A heartbeat passed, another. He'd do anything to keep that article out of the paper and keep her safe.

"If I like what Olivia and Hurstgrove say, I'll call and tell her to hold the story so I can make some modifications. If I don't hear anything interesting, it'll run as is."

Caden released a shaky breath. He hoped that gave them enough time to take the book and somehow convince her to pull the story. He'd have to devise a new way to find Anka. Because he refused to keep hurting his pretty redheaded firecracker.

"Thank you. I hope you find Olivia and Duke's information helpful."

"Duke?"

"Simon's nickname."

"*Simon*, is it? How well do you know him?"

Well enough to have fought a battle by his side. Well

enough to have endured Marrok's physical training with Duke until they nearly dropped. Of all the Doomsday Brethren, Caden liked Duke most. He didn't bark orders, like Marrok. He wasn't half mad, like Ice. Or a manipulative sod, like Bram. He was reliable, unlike Shock. Duke was quiet, shrewd, and tough when necessary. Having a bazillion pounds hadn't made him pretentious at all.

"We met a few weeks ago," he hedged. "He's a friend of my brother's."

Sydney shook her head. "This is surreal. I appreciate you introducing me to Olivia and 'Duke.' But regardless of what they say, I still can't give you the name of my source."

Caden wished otherwise, but he respected her loyalty. "I know."

"If you want me to meet these people, why come here alone?"

Because he wanted to see her. Talk to her. Touch her one last time.

Her lips parted expectantly, and he tensed, stepped closer. It would be so easy. . . . Lean in, close his eyes, press his mouth to hers, let magic and fate take over. He'd have someone who would be his 'til death parted them.

What if she didn't want that? Or want to live a millennium? Committing to him wouldn't be for a typical fifty years, after all. What if they discovered they didn't like each other in a few hundred years, or for that matter, two decades, or two months? Or what if the war took her from him tomorrow and he slid into mate mourning madness?

"Caden?" she prompted.

Impossible to be totally honest with her, but he had to be as honest as he could and leave with the cleanest conscience possible.

"As I said, I can't stay away from you. You're an amazing woman."

She swallowed. The moment pulsed between them, thick, tense. Caden leaned in farther, drawn by her fruity jasmine scent, by those chocolate eyes that were melting him by the second. *No, no, no!* His internal temperature kicked up—right along with his amped-up sex drive. He hadn't touched her and already he felt unbearably aroused. He cupped her cheek with shaking hand, trailed his thumb over her lips. Her mouth looked like heaven.

"This isn't a good idea," she breathed raggedly.

She was affected, too. The knowledge seared him.

Caden caressed his way from her shoulder to her nape. "Stop me."

Her breathing picked up speed. "Why do you want this?"

"I think of you. Constantly. For once in my life, I'm not in control. I shouldn't do this. I know it. Yet, I can't stop."

That was the complete truth.

Sydney breathed hard. "This is a terrible idea."

Agreed, but that didn't douse his need.

When she paced nervously to her little dining room, he followed. "I never meant to hurt you. I wanted to help my brother, but then I got caught up in you. I wasn't always honest. I apologize. But I can't tell you I don't want you. That would be the biggest lie of all."

Sydney pressed her lips together and looked at him over her shoulder. Her expression said she was staving off tears. "I have never had serious feelings for any man. But in less than a week, you've changed everything. Letting you leave here Tuesday morning was one of the most difficult things I've done, but I refused to fight for something you didn't want. Now you're back. What's changed?"

Even in matters of the heart, she whittled away the crap

and asked the tough questions. But it was a fair question. Something *had* changed inside him. More dreams of Sydney, his magical instincts and admiration growing stronger, that damn persistent ache in his chest, fear he'd never see her again—none of it was letting him leave her.

"What I feel is too strong to ignore. I tried, God knows. It's such a difficult time in my life, and a pull this strong can't be natural."

Caden edged closer, pressing his body against her back, his erection against the taut curves of her backside. He gritted his teeth, trying to stay focused. His energy, which had been lagging all day, shot up the moment he pressed himself to her. Unfortunately, so did his need.

"I can't fight it," he murmured.

Her breath hitched on a sob. "Me, either."

"I've known you to be smart, sexy, ambitious, tough, compassionate . . . and brutally honest. I appreciate you for it."

He cupped her chin in his hand and turned her face in his direction. When she stared over her shoulder, he saw her eyes glossed with tears. Her cheeks were red, her lips a swollen invitation to paradise.

"But I don't want to hurt you," he murmured.

"You will, if you spend the night and leave again in the morning without a backward glance."

"I don't think I can leave you again. My connection to you is stronger than my will."

God, if he was going to confess that, why not just kiss her? Issue the Call that was instinctually bred down into every wizard's bones and be done? He'd never known or paid attention to the words of the Call until meeting Sydney. Now, they slid through his head with frightening regularity.

"You truly want to be here?" Her voice trembled.

Yes and no . . . but more yes. "I don't think I could leave, even if you tossed me out."

His mobile phone, tucked in his pocket, rang. He glanced at the display and cursed. Duke.

"Don't answer that," Sydney said, startling him.

Want darkened her eyes. His body tightened, leapt in response. He shouldn't do this. She deserved better. But he'd likely never again touch her, and the knowledge was killing him.

"You're certain?"

After a slight pause, she gave him a shaky nod. "I may regret this tomorrow, but you're right. I'm honest and I want you."

With a press of his thumb, he silenced the phone's ring, then set it on the table.

Bloody hell, he wanted to kiss Sydney. So damn badly. Those parted rosy lips were mere inches under his, moist and enticing. Somehow, for both of them, he had to resist. Otherwise, he'd blurt the Call. The words were a constant chanting in his head. *Become a part of me . . .*

He pressed his mouth to her jaw, the side of her neck. She scooted around, trying to inch her mouth under his again.

A distraction. They both needed one before things got out of hand.

Caden nibbled at the shell of her ear, breath harsh. She shivered. But her body trembled harder when he reached around her other shoulder and his fingers found the buttons to her little attention-getting blouse. He undid the first, the second, none too gently, then slid his hand inside, beneath her bra, to cup her breast. Under his palm, her heart beat like a wild drum. She pressed her backside against him and moaned. Beautiful, sweet woman.

As I become a part of you . . . the Call continued in his head.

He shoved the words from his mind and focused on the rest of the buttons. They parted for him in a fluid unveiling of skin, sighs, and desire. When he peeled the garment away, he couldn't keep his hands from devouring all the soft cinnamon-freckled skin on her soft abdomen, until he molded his palms over her lace-covered breasts.

She threw her head back onto his shoulder and gasped. He smelled her fruity-jasmine scent, which had haunted him for two days. But now there was more. Musk. Desire. He could *smell* her arousal. Because of his coming transition? Was he simply more attuned to her? Didn't matter. It kicked blood straight to his cock, and he pressed against her, dying to fill her up and be one with her.

Sydney reached up between his hands and he heard a little *click*. Suddenly her bra eased away from her breasts.

Grabbing one strap, he tore it off and tossed it across the room. Then he filled his hands with her bare breasts, the little beaded nipples scorching his palms. God help him. He'd always adored women, but this . . .this was more. Beyond control. Sydney set him on fire, pushed him past restraint. Amazed him.

Soft, feminine arms reached around him to clasp at the back of his neck, which pressed her breasts even deeper into his hands. Words kept popping into his head.

And ever after, I promise myself to thee.

He rolled her nipples between her fingers, and she moaned. His body shook. Fire raged inside him, barely in control. He wanted—no, needed—more from Sydney. Everything. Now.

Lowering his hands to the curve of her waist, over her hips, he encountered the side release of her skirt. He could have easily lifted it, but he liked the idea of her being bare for him.

He yanked the zip down, then shoved the garment over her hips. What she wore beneath—black, lacy, small—easy to shred with his hands.

Now she was naked, all warm flesh and breathy sighs, arched, exposed. *His.*

Caden had his shirt off in a moment. Sydney tilted her head, giving him the naked flesh of her neck and the soft curve of her shoulder. He put his mouth to her, dying for any taste of her he could afford.

He ripped into his jeans, discarding them and everything beneath, laving his tongue across her skin. He savored her addicting salty honey flavor. He moaned into her ear, and she shivered against him.

"Sydney?"

"Yes," she breathed as his lips trailed across her shoulder blade. "Now."

That was all Caden had to hear.

Taking her hip in one hand, he guided his erection to her slick sex with the other and pressed in slowly. Tight, like an amazing glove fit just for him. So perfect.

Each day we share, I will be honest, good, and true.

Caden shook his head, trying to dislodge the words that kept circling in his brain. This was about savoring their last touch, not claiming her forever. But Sydney's hot grip short-circuited him. Instead, he sank in, gave himself over, let pleasure take him dangerously higher.

Beneath him, Sydney panted. Her body softened. The smell of her arousal grew stronger, so strong he swore he could almost taste her. Every instinct he possessed urged him to kiss her—her mouth, her sex—any part of her, every part.

He fought the urge, clenching her hip in one hand and wrapping the other around her body until his fingers found her clit. Draped over her back, Caden worked the delicate bud of nerves. Grazing, circling, slow caresses designed to drive her mad, while he filled her with deep, possessive strokes.

Soon, she tightened on him. Her fingernails dug into his wrist. Her pants became groans, then wails. And his body tensed, dying to feel everything about her, release himself into her completely, give himself, body and soul.

If this you seek, heed my Call.

The words no sooner crossed his mind when Sydney clamped down, cried out, and her body surrendered to his completely. God, he wanted to see her face, watch her expressive dark eyes as pleasure overtook her, kiss her mouth, and claim her as he came.

Even the thought sent him straight over the edge, into a white-light abyss that burned into his brain brighter than anything he'd ever experienced. Ecstasy jolted him, an unrelenting vise of need he'd strangled since he'd last been inside her. Now freed, the pleasure clawed down his spine, up his cock. He shouted, mesmerized by her feel, her smell. He drank her in, as if he was destined to know her above all others. Remember her only.

From this moment on, there is no other for me but you.

"That was . . ." Sydney didn't finish the thought.

Straight from his heart.

"It was," he panted, afraid to speak his thought aloud.

Now that the time to part had come, he wondered if he could keep her, tell her the truth, let her decide if she wanted to deal with magickind and the war. Or should he let her go, try desperately to forget her and know he'd likely never mate?

He didn't want to think of such things while still buried within her. Not while he had his arms about her. But that wasn't reality. The phone vibrating on the table beside them was. Duke, again. No doubt wondering where the hell they were.

His breathing had not yet recovered when he withdrew from Sydney with a curse, then picked up the phone. He didn't bother with pleasantries. "We'll be there in ten."

Caden didn't wait for a reply, but simply hung up.

"Are you all right?" He caressed her shoulder, down the line of her spine, admiring the sleek curve of her waist, then pulled her body against his, front to her back.

She gave him a shaky nod. "What happens after this meeting? With us?"

Though a fair question, it stabbed him. Putting distance between them would be best for her, but could he stay away?

"After this meeting, we'll talk."

Caden guided Sydney into the crowded pub with a hand at the small of her back. Pathetic. Twenty minutes after one of the most amazing sexual experiences in his life and the only thing it had done was make him greedy for more. Now was the time for business.

He hoped he could focus.

The walls of the crowded pub seemed to close in, pressed with tables and bodies and the smell of ale. He started to sweat again, shake. His energy waned with every step. He'd like to think he'd simply needed a bit of a nap after an orgasm that had nearly blown his head off. Given his urge to hold Sydney close and drown in her again, he knew better.

"Where the hell have you been?" Duke grabbed his elbow and barked in his ear.

Sluggishly, Caden turned his head. The wizard looked incredibly brassed off. Splendid.

A few feet in front of him, he was vaguely aware of Olivia introducing herself to Sydney and smiles being exchanged. Olivia led Sydney to another table. He barely let her go with a growl. The women began chatting.

"Sit down," Duke commanded.

Perhaps he should and rest his head. He needed sleep. Badly.

He swayed on his feet, the room spinning. Duke peered into his face, then sniffed. "Never mind. I know what you've been about. Sex at a time this critical?"

"Piss off," he growled, then collapsed onto a stool.

"Damn it!" Duke hissed. "Look at me."

Caden slowly opened unfocused eyes. "Wha . . . ?"

Duke pinched the bridge of his nose. "Have you been sweating all day? Shaking?"

He nodded.

"Craving sex?"

A snort punctuated Caden's answer. "Last two weeks."

"You just shagged her and you're already exhausted?"

In the battle between Caden and his heavy eyelids, the eyelids won. "Watch your mouth."

"Answer me."

Somehow, Caden found the energy to nod.

"Fuck."

Usually, the titled wizard was every bit a gentleman. Caden winced at Duke's curse.

"Your magical signature is beginning to take shape. Black, blue, and gray. But there's something yellow and white trying to merge with it." Duke turned his attention toward Sydney. "Is she your mate? I know you haven't spoken the words but . . ."

Caden nodded. He'd finally admitted what his body had been telling him since virtually the moment he'd met her. It wasn't a happy admission.

"Your transition from human to wizard is upon you. We've got to find a female to go through it with you. You'll need great amounts of sexual energy."

"Sydney—"

"Is a reporter! If you transition with her, you'll bed her like a madman for the next few days, then emerge as a wizard involuntarily displaying your special power, which will likely be impossible to hide. How do you know she won't print it in her human newspaper? You cannot choose her."

"Want her."

"I know," he soothed. "But you can't have her for your transition. Not for your mate, either. She'll learn too much and expose us to humanity. I'll call Bram. Certainly, he'll know a witch who will help you." Duke reached for his mobile.

Caden's sluggish brain took in Duke's words. Everything inside him rebelled. Drudging up all his energy, he grabbed Duke's phone and banged it against the table. It chirped and broke into a dozen little pieces of plastic and wires.

Duke recoiled, looking around to see who had noticed. "Have you gone mental?"

"I want Sydney."

Duke clenched his jaw tight, but then a fresh tremor overtook Caden's body, rocking every muscle. The wizard closed the short distance between them and draped an arm around his shoulders. "Let's go."

"What's wrong with him?" Olivia. Caden knew that voice.

"Guess," Duke barked. "Mr. Hormones destroyed my mobile. Use yours to call Bram. Tell him I'll be babysitting for a few days."

"Get him out of here quickly," Olivia said to Duke. "People are staring. They probably think he's having a seizure." She turned to Sydney. "Perhaps we can continue our discussion—"

"Sydney comes with me." Caden raised his head and glared daggers at Olivia. Marrok would kill him for it later, but now all that mattered was keeping Sydney at his side. He turned his heavy stare on Olivia, willing her to understand.

"What's wrong with him?" Sydney looked stunned and concerned.

"If you'll go with Caden and help him, I'd like to take the book and examine it overnight," Olivia said.

"No." Sydney's refusal was a crisp syllable that didn't surprise Caden at all. "Ring me tomorrow. We'll meet again. Tell me what's ailing him."

Duke and Olivia shared a glance. No way to answer her. Caden didn't care what they said. He only knew that he was burning up from the inside and that he needed these clothes off and Sydney under him. Immediately. She would soothe him. Only she would do.

He lifted his head and sent a burning gaze to her. "Need you."

"I'm here."

Olivia edged Sydney away. Caden lurched across the feet separating them. Duke dragged him back with a yank and got in his face.

"You do not, under *any* circumstances, kiss her. Or get oral with her. No tasting at all. No speaking the Call. Is that clear?"

CHAPTER NINE

"BUGGER OFF," CADEN SNEERED, then staggered toward Sydney.

She steadied him with an arm about his shoulders. Dear God, he was an inferno. She gasped. Fear knotted her gut. What the devil was wrong with him?

"He needs a hospital!" she barked at Duke and Olivia.

Duke sighed, and Sydney recognized his expression; she'd seen it on other male faces prior to conversation: dread.

"No. He needs a bed with you beside him."

"*What?* If he's ill, the last thing he needs is sex!"

She opened her mouth to argue the virtues of modern medicine, but Caden nuzzled her neck. She shivered and momentarily lost focus, until a cultured voice brought her back.

"That, my dear, is the very thing he needs."

She could *not* have heard Hurstgrove right. "I don't understand. Is this what his brother has? Some sexual compulsion?"

"No."

A horrible thought skittered through her head. What if she had done this to him by writing the latest fantasy in the book?

"We can't talk here," Hurstgrove went on. "I'll explain when we reach your flat. Can you . . . care for him?"

If Caden needed her, Sydney wanted to be there for him. She owed him, really, in case her midnight fantasies had put him in this state. But he was more than an obligation to her.

Though Caden hadn't always been honest with her, she understood his reasons for subterfuge. If she'd had a sibling and a few lies could save their life . . . she would likely have done the same. Besides, she sensed Caden needed her on a deeper level. Maybe helping him through this ailment would enable her to see all the way to his core and bring them closer.

"Yes," she said finally.

"Thank you." His eyes closed in relief. "Very much. Let's go."

She didn't understand what was happening, but now wasn't the time for a lot of chatter. After Caden had recovered, absolutely. She'd want every detail.

"I'll come along, in case you need help."

From curious to bizarre. Help in bed? "I've got sex covered, thank you."

Despite her confusion, when Caden nibbled on her ear, Sydney shivered. He was insistent, almost feral. The female in her basked at the intensity of his desire, though she didn't fully understand.

"I need you," Caden breathed, caressing a palm up her hip, under her shirt, to cup her breast. "With me . . ."

As his touch burned her sensitive skin, Sydney met his gaze. Blistering blue supplication radiated from him, along with anxiety. Whatever ailed him, he wasn't in complete control—and that terrified him. Never had Caden seemed vulnerable, and even if her writings had nothing to do with it, she wouldn't deny him.

"I'll be in the next room to make sure he doesn't get . . . out of control." Hurstgrove yanked Caden's hand off her, then pushed them toward the door.

Sydney risked a glance around. People were staring— loads of them. Her cheeks heated up as if she flushed twenty shades of red. How many had seen Caden's intimate display of public affection? Duke didn't have to push her again; she dashed out of the pub, dragging Caden along. Olivia held the door open.

Outside, Sydney halted in the stinging November wind. She and Caden had walked to the pub. How the devil was she going to get him to stroll back to her flat when he was solely focused on unbuttoning her shirt?

A moment later, Duke provided a solution, sprinting toward a very posh black SUV and opening the door. Sydney climbed into the backseat, and Caden followed with a growl, his predatory blue eyes glowing in shadow. Those eyes told her that he wanted her in every way possible. Though his condition concerned her, Sydney's belly flipped with desire.

With a feral smile, Caden grabbed her legs and swung her sideways until she reclined across the seat. She gasped as he covered her until most of her body lay beneath him. Then he lifted her skirt.

"Caden," she whispered, trying not to surrender entirely to the delicious feel of him and the fact he needed her. "Wait! My flat is five minutes—"

"Can't wait." His voice was rough. "Need you."

There again, that vulnerability. She wouldn't abandon him. Somehow, she had to make him understand that she was only putting him off until they were alone.

"Just a few minutes longer."

Caden growled and wrapped his body around hers. Sydney supposed she should be mortified, but desire, both to hold and heal him, trampled her modesty. He'd never insulted her intellect or her profession—she couldn't say as much for her last date, let alone her parents. And given her brief conversation with Olivia, she knew Caden had truly brought her experts to talk about the unusual book she possessed. And how many men would move across an ocean and go to such lengths to help a brother? She'd been suspicious and judged him without really knowing him or understanding his behavior.

The fear she'd seen earlier on his face resurfaced, and he reached for her. His expression confessed his need for her—body and heart. "Help me."

"Of course. Five minutes."

He growled.

Two slams penetrated her consciousness, and she turned her head to see Duke and Olivia settle in the front seat, resolutely not looking their way.

"Did you call Bram?" Duke asked Olivia.

Who? Sydney wondered. The thought dashed away when Caden took her blouse in hand and ripped it in two. She gasped as the remnants of her top drifted to the floorboard.

"Not here!"

He didn't listen. His mouth latched onto her breast through her bra. Her nipples, still tender from their last encounter, leapt to full, aching attention. She stifled a moan. God, she hoped no one was watching, but couldn't tear herself away to check.

"I left him a message," Olivia whispered.

Duke cursed softly. "Damn. This is going to take a while." He glanced in the rearview mirror, then looked away. "Where do you live?"

With the feel of Caden, the smell of his musk and desire, she didn't worry what Duke saw. Then Caden planted soft, open-mouthed kisses all over her abdomen and began edging lower.

With an impatient roar, he pushed her skirt up around her waist. Cripes, she was wet. Caden latched onto her breast again and his fingers dove under the silk between her thighs.

Peeling out and away from the curb, Duke cursed again. "Quickly. Where do you live?"

Moaning between a kiss and a touch, Sydney rattled off her address, and he darted away, programming his GPS accordingly. Three minutes later, he reached her building. Caden was trying to work her knickers off with one hand, her bra off with the other, kissing the flat of her belly in between. She was trying not to help him along, only because she couldn't walk to her flat naked.

"Car park?" Duke barked.

"No," Sydney managed to croak out.

Duke pulled close to the walk, then turned to Olivia. "Can you park this? Call Marrok and tell him your location. Suggest that Sabelle fetch you as soon as possible. I hate to leave you alone, even for a moment."

Olivia laid a soft hand on his shoulder. "I'm fine."

"Bad people still want their bloody hands on you, my little le Fay. You're in danger. Be *careful*."

Le Fay? Like Morganna le Fay?

A smile curved the beauty's mouth. "You're like the annoying big brother I never had."

"Big brothers know best. Now go."

At Olivia's nod, Duke exited the vehicle, doffing his sweater. When, the back door opened, he leaned in. Sydney wriggled to lower her skirt, which earned her a growl from Caden. Hurstgrove never looked her way.

"Come with me." Duke grabbed Caden by the neck and yanked him to his feet. Caden fought, hitting his head on the top of the door.

"Careful!" she insisted.

As soon as he cleared the vehicle, Caden snarled and whirled, throwing wicked punches in the air.

Duke spun him around, then clamped his arms around

Caden's middle. "Put this on." He tossed her his sweater. "Go. Open your door. We'll follow."

Sydney skipped the lift and headed for the stairs, uncertain that Duke could contain Caden during the ancient machine's long ascent.

Behind her, Caden grunted, straining to be free. She swallowed. His desire was contagious. Want hiked up her breathing, cramped her sex. But terror crept in. What if she couldn't help him? What if her efforts to reach his heart didn't heal him? What if this was all due to that damn book?

Suddenly, Duke huffed. "Bloody hell!"

Glancing over her shoulder, Sydney found Duke doubled over—and Caden charging for her. He pinned her to the wall a moment later, grabbing her thigh in one hand and nipping at her throat with his lips. She felt his erection pressed against her. Her anticipation skyrocketed, and she palmed her way under his shirt, eager to feel the hot, bare skin of his back.

"Not in the hall," Duke admonished. "Let's get behind closed doors, shall we?"

Oops! No matter how badly she wanted Caden, Hurstgrove was right. Admittedly, it was odd to be nearly ravished in front of a stranger, and she was hardly in the humor to provide a peep show for her neighbors. But caring at the moment was bloody hard. What woman didn't have a fantasy or two about a man being so overcome with passion he was hardly himself? Even more, the fact Caden had asked her to be the anchor in his storm added to her thrill.

So when Caden pressed against her and whispered that he couldn't wait to be alone with her, inside her, she melted all over again.

With a curse, Duke managed to pry Caden away and push him up the stairs. They trudged toward her door.

As they reached it, Duke tried to soothe her by patting her shoulder. "After you're inside and together, all will be well."

Suddenly, Caden shoved her behind his big, hot body, then whirled to face Hurstgrove, then clasped his hand around the duke's throat. "You will not touch her."

"Right." Duke held up both hands in surrender. "Won't do that."

Caden growled and let go, then turned back to Sydney. Possessiveness? Yes, it was in his eyes. She'd always been certain that this relationship meant more to her heart than his, but now . . . now she questioned that. Was she finally seeing the emotions he'd kept hidden behind his barriers?

Hoping yes, she raced for her door, inserting her key with trembling fingers. He was right behind her, pressing her to the wood, breathing hot and hard in her ear.

"Don't leave me, Sydney."

She finally managed to turn the key, and they spilled inside the little flat. Caden roared in after her, his expression a pledge that he meant to have her. Heart trumpeting, she drew in a ragged breath. Duke followed them in, shutting and locking the door, his gaze discreetly focused elsewhere.

Hurstgrove spotted the hallway leading to her bedroom and gestured to her. "Take him."

"Be with me," Caden murmured. "Now. I need you."

Sydney wanted that more than anything, but needed some information about his condition first. "We're here. Explain. Why is he suddenly a randy octopus and why does he want *my* help?"

Duke mussed his expensively coiffed hair by raking a hand through it. He cursed something ugly. Then he glanced at Caden, feverish and sliding his hands over her arms, across her abdomen, burning her up with his touch.

"This is off the record. If one word of this appears in your tabloid, I will use all my wealth and connections to shut it down and unemploy you permanently."

His intimidation tactics startled Sydney—and annoyed her. If he hadn't been Caden's friend and she hadn't seen his concern in action, she'd have tossed him out on his ear. Yes, he was wealthy and powerful, but if she stumbled upon a hidden truth, she wanted to tell it. Still, she had no doubt Duke could make good on his threats.

"I don't like being bullied." She glared at Duke.

"Understood. But you're dealing with something very dangerous you can't possibly understand."

Her heart stopped. "Caden's condition is that serious?"

Duke hesitated. "Not exactly. It's everything you've been writing about."

Caden had warned her of that repeatedly, seemed gravely concerned about her safety. "In what way? What does magic have to do with him?"

At that moment, Caden planted his mouth on her neck, hand under the sweater, and whispered of his need. She shivered, her mind whirling and her body aching. But Duke's words demanded a few moments of attention before she lost herself in Caden's touch.

"We're out of time. All I can say now is that Caden has been touched by magic and he's chosen you, and you alone, to provide a healing touch. He'll reject all others, I suspect."

The fact he'd chosen her was both thrilling and surprising, but . . . "Touched by magic? Cursed?"

Sydney thought again of the book and all she'd written and winced.

"I'm certain that's how he sees it. By joining with you, he can convert the energy you generate together into something that heals him."

"How do you know?" Sydney managed to gasp out as Caden gripped her hips and pressed into her, clearly ready for a night of sin. She wasn't at all immune to the idea.

"I've been through this. He needs you now. Please," Duke cajoled. "He's going to require everything you're willing to give. Just don't kiss him. It would be catastrophic."

"To his health?"

Caden's hands maneuvered up her belly, to the sweater and began lifting it. Sydney tried to wriggle away, but his grip was like iron. He wanted her. Now.

Duke nodded. "And perhaps yours."

"Does this have anything to do with the book?" Sydney hated to think she'd done this to him. He'd be furious and hate her—and rightfully so.

Caden had apparently tired of talking. He tore Duke's sweater from her body and urged her down the hall. When she resisted, he scooped her up and carried her.

"What the—Caden!"

With a grunt, he kept going.

"Give him what he needs for as long as you can," Duke called out.

"I will!"

Now her only questions were: How long would that be? And did she have everything necessary to heal him?

"So what happens now?"

Duke whirled toward the voice. Olivia. He hadn't heard her come in the door.

"That was locked." He frowned.

She shrugged. "I've been working on my simple magic. Locks are a breeze for me now."

Despite the tense situation, he smiled. "Marrok always says you're mischievous. I see why. Is Sabelle coming for you?"

A thud reverberated through the room, like something—or someone—had hit the wall. Moments later, a murmur, a rip, then a sigh. Clearly, they weren't wasting any time. Duke winced.

"Soon," Olivia answered, flushing a pretty shade of pink. "She's helping Bram elsewhere now. Marrok asked me to wait with you for a bit."

With a nod, Duke sat on the sofa. Olivia followed suit.

On the other side of the wall, sighs turned to moans.

He hesitated. "I suppose you won't settle for the short version of upcoming events."

"You know better."

Duke settled his elbows on his knees and peered over at the violet-eyed beauty. She was striking and soon would be a powerful witch once she went through Caden's current plight.

"He's transitioning, and I suspect he's been fighting the need for some weeks, so he'll need a tremendous amount of energy. It's going to be long and difficult. And dangerous. It's made worse because he's fighting the urge to Call to her."

Olivia's eyes threatened to pop from her head. "A human reporter? Has he completely lost it?"

Her American expressions often amused Duke, but now wasn't the time. "I've warned him. I also placed a secret repelling spell over her mouth. It's not foolproof and won't hold for more than a few days, but it's all I can do for now. My biggest concern is whether she'll be strong enough to pull him through this transition."

"It doesn't take a lot of physical strength for a female to have sex," she pointed out.

"Perhaps stamina is a better word."

Olivia frowned. "How long will they be at this?"

A loud feminine moan penetrated the walls, followed by a male voice muttering in encouraging tones.

Duke managed to hide his grimace. "The average is two days."

"But it can be longer?"

"Yes." He scrubbed a hand over his face. Frightening the girl who had yet to undergo her own transition was something he wanted to avoid, but being dishonest benefitted no one. "My transition came two years early. In my ignorance, I fought it. My parents knew little about magic, since mine came from my grandmother, who had long since disappeared. So when I transitioned, it was harsh, as I suspect Caden's will be."

"And yours took longer?"

Before he could answer, a thumping against the wall startled him. The sound echoed through Sydney's little living room once, twice, again, then settled into a rhythmic pace. Bloody hell.

"Three days," he confessed. It was one of the few times his body and magic had completely overridden his decorum. For those few days, no amount of sex had been enough, no act too wicked. He'd rejected food, water, family.

"The poor woman must have been exhausted after three days. I can see why you're worried for Sydney."

When Duke had transitioned, his emotions had not been engaged with a woman, as Caden's were. He'd started with a woman he'd been casually dating. When she fell into an exhausted sleep, he hadn't thought twice about opening the door to growl for another.

But he said nothing. Still, something on his face must have shown his discomfort.

"More than one woman?" Olivia choked.

He closed his eyes. "Four." And the last had nearly had to be replaced.

A good thing, he thought in retrospect. At the end of every transition, each witch's or wizard's special power, unique to them, emerged—without any warning when or what would manifest. When his special power had emerged, if the woman he'd been with hadn't been mostly unconscious, she would have screamed in utter terror.

"What happens if Sydney isn't strong enough to pull him through?"

"Let's hope for the best, shall we?"

Olivia didn't look comforted. "Are you trying to avoid telling me that he could die?"

He patted her hand to reassure her. "You will be better prepared. Bram will tell Marrok well in advance what's to come and how to behave. My family was not so lucky. Do not fear; your transition will come off splendidly."

"I'm not worried about me. Marrok will do everything in his power to get me through. But I'm worried about Caden. What if Sydney can't? Who will—"

"Replacing her doesn't seem to be an option. Caden is dangerously attached, and I can only hope we find some way to separate them before he cements the bond by issuing the Call or—"

"Yes. Yes!" Sydney wailed on the other side of the wall.

"We won't ever be able to part them," Olivia finished.

"He'll kill anyone who tries. A wizard will fight for his mate to the death."

"But she's a reporter who could spill every one of our secrets. Caden says she's ambitious and plans to use her current job as a stepping stone to something big. Blowing the magickind story open is disaster for us. She already knows too much about the war and Mathias and—"

"Could make genocide of our kind a terrible reality. But the way he looks at her, I fear it won't be long after this transition before they form a mate bond."

She grimaced. "Well, there must be something productive we can do while we wait. We need the Diary. Shouldn't we look for it while Sydney is . . . busy? If we find it, I'll be able to grab it and go."

"Good thought. In the past you've been able to feel its power. Do you sense it here?"

With a scowl, Olivia rose and wandered around the little flat. "I don't feel it in this room." She meandered into the kitchen, the foyer, into every corner of the apartment on the near side of Sydney's bedroom door, then sighed. "If it's in this flat, Sydney is keeping it in her bedroom. I can't feel the surge of the book's power unless it's close, and definitely not through the door."

Duke pinched the bridge of his nose. "If you go into the bedroom to search while Caden is transitioning, he may perceive you as a threat."

"And try to kill me. Spectacular."

He patted her shoulder. "And if I let anything happen to you, Marrok would kill me. Why don't we return to the sofa and wait . . . and hope disaster isn't around the corner?"

Caden rolled away from Sydney and immediately fell into a deep sleep. She cracked open an eye. The sun was setting. Again. She hadn't left this room in two days—she'd scarcely left the bed. Every muscle in her body ached beyond description. She'd never questioned how many orgasms a woman could have in a day, but Sydney wondered idly if the Guinness people would be interested in chatting with her.

Joking aside, this time with Caden was no laughing matter. Besides his unusual affliction, her feelings for her sexy former photographer had grown each minute they shared. She'd soothed his fear, and he'd rewarded her with a treasure trove of sparking smiles and sumptuous touches. She still didn't understand this sex marathon and planned to question Duke about this "curse" later. Now, she was too exhausted to care. She needed to use the toilet, eat, bathe, and sleep—in that order. Unfortunately, she wasn't sure she was capable of moving a muscle.

At a soft knock on the door, she grabbed the sheet to cover her nakedness. Truth be told, she'd been naked for nearly forty-eight hours. Even the sheet felt unnatural and abrasive against her. Caden's skin, however . . . she could get used to waking beside him every morning.

The knock sounded again, jarring her out of her reverie. She covered Caden's bare backside and murmured, "Come in."

Not surprising, Hurstgrove peeked inside her bedroom.

"It got quiet. I thought I should check on you."

He looked nearly as tired as she. He wore the same clothes and needed a shave. He'd stripped off his tie, unbuttoned his shirt at the collar and wrists, turned the cuffs back to reveal capable hands and strong forearms. He couldn't be comfortable snoozing on her small sofa, yet he, a real duke, was inquiring after her.

"Tired," she whispered. "I need food and a bath, a few days' sleep, then I'll be fine."

Duke cast a sidelong glance at Caden. "Has anything unusual happened yet?"

Besides shagging a caveman on aphrodisiacs and losing my heart? "If you don't count his incredible stamina as unusual, no."

He stepped in the room, regret shaping his features. "He's not going to tire for some time."

Sydney hadn't needed Mr. Pedigree to tell her that. "If anything, he's gaining momentum."

That was an understatement. The first night, Caden had made love to her every few hours. The following day, every other hour. Tonight, every hour on the hour. She could nearly set a watch by him. Currently, it was three forty-nine. Bugger.

"If you can no longer cope, I wouldn't blame you. I can find a replacement—"

"No!" Vehemence rocketed through her body. Very obviously, Caden was no novice in the bedroom, but while she was with him, Sydney intended to be his only woman. "I'm not certain what's happening, but I won't have any other woman near him. I have very few minutes to see to my needs before Caden awakens. Give me a moment, will you?"

Duke hesitated. "Has he kissed you?"

She stopped and sorted through the jumble of the last two days. "No."

"Or tasted you in any other way?"

What did he mean? Oh. Oral sex. She flushed. "He's been far too busy."

Relief crossed Duke's face. "I hope this runs its course in the next few hours. If you're certain you don't want help—"

"No!" And never again if she could help it. "If there's time before he awakens again, you're going to explain this to me in detail."

"Agreed. I'll grab you some protein bars and water. You bathe. Quickly." Duke cast a glance at Caden. "He's stirring."

Sydney peered at the man beside her. He rolled closer, an absent hand feeling its way for her side. If she wanted any creature comforts, now was the time.

Rising as quickly as her protesting muscles allowed, she grabbed her robe from the back of her door and ambled down the hall to her little bath. She ran a hot tub to soak away sore muscles and brushed her teeth. A moment later, Hurstgrove knocked, then brought in protein bars and an energy drink.

"Where did you get this?"

He paused. "Olivia brought them by. I hope you don't mind."

At the moment, she could hug him. She was famished. Sydney didn't have a lot of weight on her bones anyway, and since she could scarcely remember her last meal, she figured that she had lost at least half a stone.

"Wonderful. Thank you."

Conscious of the ticking clock, she shut the door in his face and locked it, shedding her dressing gown with one hand and tearing into the protein bar with the other. She scarfed the first one down. It was little better than coated cardboard, but she lunged for the second and grabbed the energy drink, chugging it down in less than a minute.

After a quick visit to the toilet, she sank into the hot bath, savoring her last few bites of the second protein bar. She noticed he'd also brought a plastic container. When Sydney ripped into it, she practically inhaled the baby carrots and apple slices she found within.

Belly not exactly sated but no longer rumbling, she grabbed the shampoo and scrubbed her hair. Soap next. She attacked her body with it, scouring until her sensitive skin glowed.

A glance at the clock she kept on her counter told her it was three fifty-seven. Not much time before Caden awoke and demanded her body again. And she gave a bit more of her heart.

Feeling marginally revived, she rinsed and unplugged the drain, then reached for a towel. She never got it.

A thump at the door made her pause. "Hurstgrove?"

Not a word. Instead, another thump. A grunt. Then the slam of a body and the crash of the door striking the wall.

Caden filled the doorway, naked, magnificent. With hungry eyes and an erection only a blind woman could miss, Sydney had no doubt what he wanted.

Despite her exhaustion, her wobbly legs, and the tenderness in places she'd never been sore before, she wanted him again. To touch him in this moment and know he was all hers. It was pure insanity, but pointless to deny.

He took a huge step into the little bathroom and grabbed her hand, hauling her out of the tub and into his arms. "Sydney."

Her damp skin made contact with his hot, dry flesh, and she sizzled—inside and out. What was it about this man? Intelligence, yes. Loads of it. Good looks, naturally. But she sensed his soldier's core of honor. Even when he'd lied to her, he'd done it for a good cause. He been uncomfortable with the subterfuge, which explained why she'd seen through him. Despite his mission, he'd done his best not to hurt her, even refusing the sex she'd so blithely offered and he so clearly wanted. The fact he'd endured this fever of heat and sex had likely been her fault. An aftereffect of writing in that blasted book.

To make matters worse, when this ailment of Caden's was over, he would likely resume life without her. He still had his brother's illness to deal with, and they no longer worked together. But at least she could enjoy the moment with Caden, savor every last touch. Yes, she was exhausted. But damned if she was going to let another woman finish what she'd started.

"I'm here for you," she whispered in his ear.

The words set him in motion. He secured his hands under her arms and lifted her straight up, demonstrating incredible strength in his flexing forearms and biceps. Then he brought her against his body. Automatically, she curled her legs around his waist, her arms clinging to his shoulders. The tip of his penis probed her swollen folds.

He began to sink into her. Slowly at first, like honey drizzling across something warm and sugary. He eased his way in, grazing sensitive tissues as he filled her. Sydney gasped, digging her nails into his hard shoulders.

Finally, she sank down to the hilt, then he lifted her up, up until the tip of his erection was barely tucked inside her. She wriggled, trying to bring him inside again. He resisted.

Then he stepped forward and pushed down. *Bam!* The electric sensation jolted every nerve in her body. God, in this position, Caden felt enormous and more intent than the many times he had made love to her in the past two days. This time, there *was* something different about him, more concentrated, compelling, certain.

Another step and he lifted her, only to shove her down with his next stride. The amazing sensations ricocheted through her body again. After days of sex, she should be completely desensitized. Instead, she was more sensitive with each touch.

Once back in her room, Caden kicked her door shut and lowered her to the bed, still buried deep inside her. Then he grabbed the far side of the mattress and used the leverage to impale her with long, broad strokes.

"Feel me," he entreated with a growl.

How could she not? *Oh. My. God.* Pleasure soared in seconds under his unrelenting demand. Sydney thrust against him, feeling passion catch fire in her blood. In response, Caden wrapped one arm around her, grabbing her backside and canting her hips up to his even more. And on his next thrust—she screamed.

"That's it," he growled in her ear. "So tight, so perfect." Then he picked up the pace, going from frenzied to frantic.

The *bam, bam, bam* of the headboard against the wall was like a chant in her ears. "Damn it, it's near."

Orgasm? The answer didn't matter when pleasure began to overtake her. The burning ache that had been brewing deep in her womb raced in a hot flood to her clit. It built—bigger than anything she had yet experienced. She clawed at him, bit his hard shoulder, felt her passage tighten on his erection. Which only ramped up the friction and sent her closer to the edge.

The bed shook, as did her body. Every nerve ending sat on the edge of a huge precipice. Suddenly, she was holding her breath, anticipating, needing. She lost her breath, the edges of her vision went dark.

And then it hit her, mowing her down in a burst of ecstasy and emotion, red-hot pleasure piercing her entire body. As a buzzing wound through her head and her vision tilted, a starburst of every feeling inside her seeped into her embrace. She rained kisses across Caden's shoulder, his neck. And knew that, even if he left her, she would belong to him forever.

The thought slammed her beleaguered brain just as Caden wrapped both arms around her as if she was his life jacket in a storm-tossed sea. His grunts became a shout of completion that made her ears ring as he pounded into her, one breath-stealing thrust after the other. As he did, Sydney felt the heat of his release inside her.

The shouts turned to sobs, and his body shuddered as he rolled onto his side, taking her with him, arching his back, his face wrenched up in pain.

"Oh God! No! Oh my—" Then he screamed.

When Sydney realized why, she followed suit at the top of her lungs.

CHAPTER TEN

"**WHAT IN THE BLOODY** hell is going on here?" Sydney screeched as she leapt from the bed, clutching the sheet against her bare breasts.

Her voice brought Caden back from the blackness and through the fog. His thoughts swam through exhaustion and confusion. *What was she screaming about?*

"Do you have a kinky twin fantasy?" she demanded.

What the devil? He frowned. "No."

Her gaze bounced between him and some point in the room just beyond him. Her words rattled around in his head, but figuring them out wasn't nearly as appealing as a twelve-hour nap.

"Really?" she demanded. "When did he get here?"

"Who?"

"Him!" She pointed behind him.

With a sinking feeling that cut into his mellow haze, Caden looked over his shoulder. On the far side of the bed sat another man. It was like looking in a mirror. Except when Caden moved, his mirror image merely sent him a questioning stare.

A corporeal clone. Caden's heart stopped in his chest. *Welcome to magickind.*

"Fuck!" he muttered. Creating another self explained the feeling of being torn in half.

"Is this how you've managed to shag me senseless these past few days? Did you two take turns popping in and out of my bedroom, snickering at me behind my back and high-fiving each other as you passed in the hall?"

Ugly picture. But what else would she think? And how could he answer? He shook his head, straining for an explanation he could give, but his fuzzy thoughts would not cooperate.

What other explanation did he have? *Gee, I transitioned into my magic and duplication is my unique power.* Not only would that freak her out, but all the associated explanations he'd owe her. . . . He winced. Still, he had to say something. She looked so scared, clutching that white sheet to her as if it would save her. Caden hated to hurt or frighten her more. Nor could he afford to give her more fodder for the paper.

"Take a deep breath. Sit beside me."

"I don't want to sit! I want a bloody explanation now!"

No doubt. But what? He looked over his shoulder again, and the other him shrugged.

"She deserves that much."

Not only did he look like a real man, but was apparently capable of his own thoughts and speech. Brilliant. "What are you, my bloody conscience? I know she deserves an explanation. Can you think of one that makes sense?"

"Sydney gave you one . . . brother."

Conscience? More like the bloody devil on his shoulder.

Caden gritted his teeth. Fun. His mirror blithely said things he'd contemplated himself, but then censored. The other him had yet to master that skill, it seemed.

"Piss about if you like, but I'm telling the truth."

"I want the truth," Sydney demanded.

Perhaps, but the truth was dangerous for him, for her, and for magickind.

He scowled at his clone. "How do I make you go away?"

The other him shrugged, then regarded Sydney. "I'm sorry, sweetheart. I know this is a shock." He rose and wrapped the bed's little throw around his waist, approaching Sydney with the kind of caution one would when approaching a wounded lion. "But no one meant to hurt you."

"Ha! You probably laughed as you shared me, like it's some bloody joke." Her posture screamed anger, but that vulnerable crack in her voice went straight to Caden's heart.

"I promise," Caden said. "That isn't so."

The other him stepped closer and cupped Sydney's shoulder. The sight of any male hand on her, even a duplicate of his own, was an unwelcome sight.

"Don't touch her," Caden warned with a growl.

"He's already had it all. Why be squeamish now?" she shot back tartly. Then she turned to the other him. "Get your bloody hand off me."

Sydney clasped his wrist and shoved him away. When he tried to hold on, her fingernails raked his forearm, drawing blood. The clone hissed.

"Ouch!" Caden looked down at his own wrist, and though he didn't see the scratch that appeared on his clone's skin, he felt the pain. *Very odd.*

She zipped her gaze over to him. "I don't know what's going on here, you wanker. *Wankers,*" she corrected. "Bloody circus. Explain or get the hell out."

Caden pressed his lips together, still minus a plausible explanation he was at liberty to divulge. Instead, he leaned closer and cupped her shoulder. "It's . . . complicated."

"No, it's easy. You shared me with your twin, you bastard!" Sydney slapped him.

Face stinging, Caden reared back, wincing. He whirled, shocked to see an angry palm print on his clone's cheek that likely mirrored his own.

He felt his clone's pain, but did not sustain injury. The clone, however, suffered both. Confounding, but then, magic always was. Westin's death alone proved that.

"Say something." Tears began to seep from her eyes.

Nothing he said would make sense. Caden sighed. "I'm sorry."

Bloody lame answer, his clone sneered inside his head.

Splendid. Now he could converse mentally with the unwanted prat.

She stomped her foot and grabbed a dressing gown littered on the floor near the bed. With angry movements, she thrust it on. "Piss off—both of you!"

As she marched from the bedroom, Caden's mind reeled. Sydney would quickly find Duke, who was likely still loitering on Sydney's sofa, and say she saw two Cadens. News of his ability to clone would go straight to Bram, who would find a use for him in this bloody war. No, thank you.

Squeezing his eyes shut, he tried to remember everything he'd learned of magic as a young boy. He'd blocked out most, but bits, especially when Lucan had visited, returned.

Power and passion. Both were important in magic. A wizard had to have the magical ability to cast the spell they sought. Equally important was the desire for the outcome. In this case, he hoped that magic wouldn't be so cruel as to saddle him with a power he couldn't control. As much as he hated magic, he needed the clone gone.

Forearms straining with the tight clench of his fists, he focused on merging himself back into one essence, visualized his clone assimilating into his form. He heard a sucking noise, felt a slam against his back, followed by a pounding in his head. Bloody hell, every muscle hurt worse than before, and he felt slightly nauseous. But when he looked around, the blanket about his clone's waist was in a heap on the ground and the being was gone.

So was Sydney.

He stumbled into his pants and raced out of her bedroom, calling her name. To his relief, she hadn't gone far.

Duke had caught her after no more than a few steps and blocked her from escaping down the shadowed hallway.

The other man looked up when Caden raced out of the bedroom. "What the devil is going on here? She's babbling something about kinky twin tricks."

"Exhaustion." Caden said the first thing that came to his belabored brain.

He hated hurting Sydney or making her look foolish. When would this magical nightmare end? Now that he'd transitioned, would it?

"Liar!" She wrested free of Duke's grip and turned on him. "I saw two of you."

Duke shot him an arch look.

Caden ignored him. "Sweetheart, you've had a busy time of it. We're both tired—"

"I may be tired after two days of shagging, but I'm not daft."

Caden shook his head. "Sydney, we should—" Two days? If he'd been busy that long—so had *Out of This Realm*.

"Damn!" Caden turned to Sydney in horror, fearing the answer before he asked the question. "Did you ring Holly and tell her to pull the story about the book?"

Sydney blinked. "No. Don't change the subject."

"Fuck! It's Saturday?" Caden demanded of the other man.

"Yes."

The latest edition of *Out of This Realm* had come out that morning.

"Did the article print?" Duke asked with a wince.

"I'm certain it did," she snapped back. "I'm not saying another word until you explain your twin."

Duke repeated the curse as well, embellishing it with several creative accompaniments.

Wiping a hand across his tired face, Caden wondered what else could go wrong. He'd already transitioned into magic he didn't want. Sydney had seen his clone and knew damn well she hadn't been hallucinating. He was exhausted and wanted to sleep for the next week. Instead, he had to deal with the fact the public—including Mathias—could now read about the Doomsday Diary.

"What did the article say?"

"Why were there two of you?"

"Damn it, woman!" Duke thundered. "Answer him. This is life or death."

Sydney looked like she wanted to argue, but Duke's face deterred her. "I wrote that it's red and reputed to be the creation of Morganna le Fay. That it has the ability to grant people's . . . wishes."

A more than adequate description for Mathias to identify the diary. Caden renewed his F-bombs. Duke followed suit.

"What? It's all true," Sydney spat.

Bram would be furious. Sydney would be in danger. Things were going to hell fast. And he feared matters would only get worse.

He had to fix this or he'd likely get eternal rest because either Bram or Mathias would put him six feet under. And the latter would make certain Sydney joined him.

"Where is the book now?"

Sydney narrowed her eyes and crossed her arms over her chest. "Why?"

Caden looked at Duke, who stared back. He knew exactly

what the other man was thinking: How the bloody hell should they answer that?

"Remember that curse I told you about?" Duke asked.

"Yes?" She arched a brow.

"No!" Caden stepped closer to her, his manner gentle. "This isn't about a curse, but a madman who would do anything to obtain that book, even kill you."

With a step back and a considering frown, Sydney regarded him. "How would you know this? From Scotland Yard, are you? What about that curse?"

"Nothing." Caden risked another glance at Duke, who nodded almost imperceptibly. "We've simply had some experience with these affairs."

"Madmen in general or ones after my book? The average person isn't going to believe the article. Likely, they'll all think I'm mad. *I* know better. And why should I believe a word you say when you've yet to explain my unexpected houseguest?"

"Dear God, spare me such a woman," Duke muttered.

Caden and Sydney both shot him a glare, then he took her by the shoulders. "I know you're angry and uncertain, but have I ever put your life in danger?"

She hesitated. "No."

"Now is not the time to explain. Grab your book. We'll need to find Aquarius. She knows where it came from, how it came to be unprotected."

"Why would a book need protecting?"

"Do you think it's a normal book?" Caden shot back.

Sydney flushed. So she knew it wasn't. Had she written in it about him? She'd said no when he had asked before, but now he wondered.

"Go get it," Duke barked. "We're wasting time. Even now, we're in jeopardy."

Duke was right. Mathias could be breathing down their necks at any moment. He brought Sydney closer for a moment, terrified at the thought of the evil wizard after her. How much good would Duke and an exhausted, newly transitioned wizard do in fighting off an Anarki army? Highly unlikely that he'd be able to conjure a duplicate on purpose. And damn it, he didn't want to use magic to fight. He'd rather stick with the training he'd received in the Marines.

Sydney broke his hold. "Until you explain everything, I am not budging an inch."

"Pick her up and throw her over your shoulder, or by God, I will," Duke ordered.

As much as it pained him to force Sydney, it was for her own good. With a curse, he bent at the knees and hoisted her onto his shoulder in a fireman's carry, careful to keep her dressing gown over her pert little ass.

"Put me down, you bloody bastard! I'm going to string you up by your stones, then take a rusty knife to you."

Wincing, Caden turned to Duke. "The book is on her night table. Grab it and put it in her hands."

With a sharp nod, Duke turned and disappeared. A moment later, he reappeared, holding the Doomsday Diary, then shoved it into Sydney's grasp.

They made their way toward her front door, Caden pinning Sydney's struggling form onto his shoulder, Duke following in silent solidarity. Sydney more than broke the silence with a string of wretched curses. He hated to hurt her, but better she be angry than dead.

Three feet from the door, someone on the other side banged. Adrenaline burst into his blood stream. Caden paused, clutching Sydney. Duke drew his wand.

"Caden, are you bloody in there? If you're not dead, I'll kill you myself."

Bram. *Shit!*

Heaving a sigh, Duke swerved around him and wrested open the door. Sure enough, the Doomsday Brethren's leader stood on the other side, holding a newspaper in one hand. His other was clenched in a fist.

"Does someone want to tell me what the devil is going on here?" His gaze bounced back and forth between Caden and Duke.

"Who the blazes are you?" Sydney lifted her head and looked at Bram.

"Bram Rion. I'd say it's a pleasure, but you've been nothing but a thorn in my side since you started writing about those bodies in the tunnel." Clenching his teeth, he slapped the newspaper on a nearby table and tore his attention away from Sydney to glare at Caden. "One small mission. Keep her quiet. And you failed miserably."

"He's just transitioned," Duke cut in.

"Transitioned?" Sydney asked.

No one answered. Bram hesitated, cast another glance at Caden, then nodded before turning back to Duke. "Why did you stay all this time?"

Duke set his jaw. "Babysitting hasn't been fun. I still need Marrok's training—"

"Exactly."

"I have no doubt other crises have erupted in the past two days. It's been damn difficult to hold my impatience while nature took its course. But if she'd been unable to finish the task . . ."

Bram nodded in resignation.

"What are you blathering about?" Sydney wriggled and screamed until Caden let her down—right in the middle of the three. But she didn't back down. Not his Sydney.

For a foolish moment, Caden was actually proud of his

little firecracker. Even in the face of three large men and an incredibly bizarre situation, she didn't cower or stop asking questions.

"Later," he said. "We have to get out of here now."

Sydney crossed her arms over her chest and shook her head. "You've promised answers. I've yet to receive them. I refuse to leave until I do. And the next one who tries to lift me over their shoulder will lose an arm."

"We've no time for this." Bram cursed. "You're inexorably in the thick of things, so I'm going to give you the condensed version and trust that you want to save your own backside enough to keep quiet. There *is* a magickind, the three of us are all wizards, and every bloody one of those stories you've been writing has put us in danger. We don't need exposure to humans so they can unleash a witch hunt. Nor do you want Mathias coming after you. But that's exactly what will happen now that you were stupid enough to write this." Bram held the paper up again. "As if that isn't enough, you shared a byline in another story with Mathias's second in command." At her incredulous gasp, he went on. "Zain is loyal to the very villain you've reviled. Didn't tell you that, did he?"

"Zain?" Caden whirled on Sydney. "Zain Denzell?"

Slowly, Sydney nodded. "Holly hired him as your replacement. He said he had photos of the magical war, information . . ."

"I'll bet he did." The thought of Zain anywhere near Sydney froze Caden's blood.

"No doubt he also had nefarious plans for you," Bram interjected. "I understand that Mathias repeatedly raped your source for these articles. If he finds you, he'll do the same to you. Then kill you for the sport of it. When you were writing this, did you wonder if any of it was real? It is. Welcome to the war, cupcake."

"Piss off!" Caden demanded. "She didn't know."

Bram grunted, but thankfully shut up.

Bloody hell. Reeling with a mixture of fatigue and shock, Caden thrust out an arm to steady himself. Holly had hired Zain as his replacement? And Bram telling Sydney virtually everything?

"Congratulations. You've just put her in even more danger," Caden spat.

Bram raised a pale brow. "Don't start. All you had to do was shut her up and get the book before every bloody *Out of This Realm* reader discovered our secrets and magickind's greatest weapon. You failed."

Caden reared back. He'd done his best to help. He knew it had been inadequate. But he *had* tried. Bram's disdain felt like a slap in the face.

"Let's cease this ridiculous sparring and get out of here before Mathias looks up your girlfriend and fries us all," Duke suggested, his voice on edge.

His admonishment broke the tension between Bram and Caden. Sydney didn't catch on—or didn't want to.

"This is really real? I'd wondered. Believed. But . . . magickind and Mathias and this book, it's all connected and not a by-product of a tortured woman's mind?"

Bram rolled his eyes. "Someone get the girl a prize."

Sydney stared at Bram. "Prove it."

"As soon as we're no longer sitting here like targets at a practice range, certainly."

"Don't patronize her," Caden growled. "She's had three minutes to adjust to magickind. You've had four hundred years."

"Four hundred!" Sydney's jaw dropped.

Everyone ignored her.

Frustration pouring off him, Bram cocked his head, pulling at tense muscles in his shoulders. "Bugger off. I'm only three hundred ninety-eight. And Duke is right; we need to get out of here. I'll yell at you once we're safe."

"I'm not leaving," Sydney protested. "It's my book and my flat and my article. I'm not going anywhere without answers."

Duke rolled his eyes. "You're certain about this one? Seems more trouble than she's worth."

Caden pulled Sydney against him. "I won't leave her here."

"God, no. She'll be dead by noon if you do—after she's told Mathias all she knows." Bram elbowed Caden aside and grabbed Sydney's wrist. "If you want to live, come with us."

Sydney hesitated, then looked back at Caden.

"Please," he cajoled, extricating her from Bram's grip. "If you've ever believed a single word I've said, believe that I would die if Mathias hurt you. And he will, given the chance."

She bit her lower lip, then nodded. "All right."

Caden exhaled the tense breath he'd been holding. It would be all right. *She* would be all right. Whatever else happened, he'd have the assurance of knowing she was safe from the clutches of a madman who would use her in the cruelest way possible until she broke, then discard her without a backward glance.

"Thank you." He enfolded her against his chest, resisting the urge to press his mouth to hers. Need burned him like a fever, and the words of the Call were echoing in his brain. Instead, he buried his face in that fiery mane of hers and resisted—barely.

"Enough. Let's go," Bram said.

Collectively, they turned for the door and Sydney found a familiar elfin-looking flower child standing there, crying.

"Aquarius!" Sydney broke free from Caden's hold and ran for her friend.

The other woman welcomed Sydney, then clutched her as if in pain.

"Poppet, what's the matter?"

Bram lifted Sydney away from Aquarius and grabbed the other woman, who reared back with watery eyes.

"Mellow," she suggested. "Your aura is full of anger and—"

"I don't give a bloody damn." Bram grabbed the book from Sydney's hand, then barked at Aquarius, "Who gave this to you?"

"I can't say."

Bram clenched his teeth and fists. "Is this the day for difficult females?"

"Bring her with us," Duke suggested. "Question her later, but we're burning daylight."

"Indeed." He grabbed Aquarius by the wrist. "Come along."

Aquarius wriggled free. "Forcing me . . . bad karma."

"I've had a run of it lately. A bit more won't matter." Bram shoved her toward the door again.

The small woman planted her heels. "I came to see Sydney." She cast fearful green eyes at the other woman. "My cousin, have you seen her?"

"No." Sydney tensed.

Aquarius gulped. "I popped out earlier. When I returned she was gone. I hoped perhaps she'd come here."

Caden's heart stopped. *Gone?*

"Was she your source?" Caden demanded.

Sydney hesitated, and he could practically hear her thoughts churning until she finally nodded.

Caden leapt to life and grabbed Aquarius by the shoulders. "What is your cousin's name?"

The little brunette pressed her lips together in a silent protest.

"Please!" Caden implored. "I think—I'm almost certain she's my brother's missing wife."

God, it finally felt good to ask a direct question. Now that Bram had spilled the truth, he no longer had to think of an angle that wouldn't arouse suspicion or give away magickind's existence.

At his side, Sydney gasped. He looked her way, not sure what reaction he might find. The compassion softening her face hit him in the chest. Seeing that side of her now, when he needed it, only added to his need to keep her by his side.

Aquarius cocked her head. "If she's your brother's wife, what is her name?"

"Anka. Anka MacTavish. Please."

Tearing up, Aquarius nodded. "She couldn't recall her last name. We hadn't seen each other since childhood. A few weeks ago, she came to me near death, shortly after—"

"Mathias raped her."

Dread swelled inside him. He'd never met Anka, but felt terrible for all she'd endured, and what that knowledge would do to Lucan, if he lived. Knowing that she was alone again, where Mathias might find her. . . . He shuddered. Why had she left relative safety?

Aquarius nodded. Sydney enfolded her friend in her arms. Fresh tears ensued. "It was awful. Took her over a week to heal enough to stand. She could remember little beyond her first name and girlhood memories. That's why she came to me. That, and the fact Mathias has no idea I exist."

"Any chance she'll return?" Caden grilled.

"Not certain. She's never left alone before. Too frightened. But I think she left of her own free will. Nothing in my flat was disturbed. The air didn't feel violent or scary. Lately, she's been having dreams of a happier past. I offered to help her find the parts of her she'd lost, but she was afraid of Mathias harming me and the loved ones she'd left behind."

"She left no note?" Caden asked.

Aquarius eased back from Sydney's embrace and shook her head. "She communicated most with Sydney, as if telling her everything was cathartic." The petite woman clung to Sydney's hands. "Though she never told you her name, you helped her merely by listening."

Caden's stomach plummeted and he tasted the bile of fear and failure as he stared at the ceiling. Dear God, to have come so close to Anka only to lose her again. Then there was the fact he'd failed Lucan and everyone else.

"How long has she been gone?" he asked Aquarius. "An hour? Two?"

"No more than that," she assured. "She's weak and hurting, so she can't have gone far. I don't know why she'd leave."

Bitter disappointment pounded into Caden. So bloody close. He'd known, *known*, Sydney's source of information was Anka. And he hadn't been able to reach her fast enough, build trust with Sydney. He'd been too fixated on fighting his feelings for his little firecracker reporter. Then too consumed by his transition. If they didn't find Anka soon, she and Lucan would pay the price.

"She can go far, very quickly." A fact Caden mourned, even as he spoke the words.

"A pop here, a pop there." Duke sighed. "With proper energy, she could have teleported to India by now."

Or she could have already been captured by Mathias, and they all knew it.

"Teleported?"

"Later," Bram growled.

Sydney turned back to Caden. "You were trying to save her all this time?"

Caden turned to her. "Yes. I told you all I could. I know I gave you no reason to believe me."

"I'm sorry." Her voice shook. "I'm so sorry. Lucan must be beside himself."

An understatement. Caden raked a tired hand across his face. There was no time to rest now. He had to keep moving forward and hope they found Anka before her trail went cold.

He squeezed Sydney's hand, and turned to Anka. "Did she leave anything behind?"

"She brought nothing with her. The clothes on her back were bloodied shreds. I burned them."

Duke clapped him on the back, startling Caden. "We'll find her. We'll all help. I know what this means to you. But now we must go."

The other wizard's words moved him. Perhaps he was overwrought and exhausted from the past two days, but Duke had stayed by his side, no matter what. Like one of his platoon buddies would have.

"Agreed," Bram said to the group. "Mathias is many things, but not stupid. It won't take him long to track you down, Sydney. And then—"

"And then, we'll take the Doomsday Diary and kill her," said a frighteningly familiar voice.

CHAPTER ELEVEN

AQUARIUS GASPED. SYDNEY AND the men whirled, and her eyes opened wide when she spotted a familiar man and a dozen vicious berobed figures behind him. "Zain!"

Before Sydney could process why he was standing at her doorstep with a bunch of blokes in robes behind him, their faces in shadow, he reached through the crowd and grabbed her hair. With a firm fist, Zain yanked her back against his front, positioning her like a human shield. He was wiry and deceptively strong. She struggled, fighting both the hold and the sudden pain. In mere seconds, he wrapped his other hand around her throat and squeezed.

"Let her go!" Caden demanded, lunging for her, fury carved into his face.

Constricting her throat, Zain dragged her out of Caden's reach and surrounded himself with the cluster of hooded figures he'd arrived with. The pressure on her windpipe raked her with panic and her eyes stung with tears. Sydney wished like the devil that she'd been more cautious when Caden had warned her of the danger.

Zain clutched her throat tighter, burying his face in her neck. He inhaled long and loud. Then he growled, the sound ripe with disgust.

"You smell like him." He tossed his head at Caden. "Every pore. Everywhere. The stench of integrity."

"What the hell do you want?" Bram demanded.

"As if you have no notion." Zain's laugh was humorless. "Give me that book you're holding, or the bitch dies."

Sydney went cold. What would Zain do to her? At the office she'd gotten an odd vibe from him, but was he a killer? Apparently so, given his implacable voice and cruel grip. Why would he kill her for a little journal that granted sexual fantasies?

Or was the book capable of more?

"Seriously evil aura," Aquarius murmured to Caden.

Ignoring the flower child, he reached for Sydney, fear for her in his fierce expression. His efforts to save her went straight to her heart, even as she worried Zain would hurt him, as well. Sydney wheezed, gasped for air. She flailed, feeling as if he would crush her throat and kill her at any moment.

Barreling past two of the freaks in robes, Caden charged to her rescue, elbowing one in the temple, punching the other in the nose. They crashed to the ground in a heap. Caden stepped over them and lunged for her. Bram and Duke were right behind him, felling more of what must be Anarki.

With a curse, Zain flicked his wrist and opened his free hand. Caden slammed into an invisible wall between them. Again he tried, and again, he crashed against it.

How the devil had Zain done that?

Bram flicked a wrist and a burst of light headed toward Zain—before stopping abruptly. Sydney blinked twice. Definitely magic.

She'd been right all these years. The paranormal existed! Now she had to stay alive long enough to write about it.

"Oh, you can block magic now. Been learning parlor tricks from Mathias?" Bram taunted.

Zain tensed. "I'm learning from a master. And learning well."

Caden roared, trying to shove his way past the force field once more, his face mottled red with rage. His blue eyes drilled into Zain's, vowing retribution.

"Let her go!" Caden insisted. "She knows nothing."

"She wrote the article. Your master is holding the book in his hand," he said, then turned to Bram. "It's a simple trans- action: the book for the girl."

"Give it to him," Caden barked at Bram.

The blond wizard shot him a long-suffering expression that demanded he be reasonable. "Zain may have trained up a bit, but he's a snot-nosed tot compared to me, inferior in both bloodline and ability. Isn't that right?"

"I know the newly transitioned whelp is two seconds from losing his shag if you don't cooperate." Zain squeezed her neck a fraction tighter, and she choked, clawing for air. "Did you know I have the ability to heat a human up from the inside, boil their blood, cook their organs? I'm a human microwave oven."

Sydney would have gasped, if she had the air. Unwelcome gray danced at the edge of her vision. She didn't know if Zain could follow through on such a threat, but that death sounded too horrific to tempt fate. Caden looked somewhere between panicked and nuclear. And Bram was dangling the damn book just beyond Zain's reach.

"There's something to be proud of," Bram quipped.

Finally, clawing at his skin, Sydney managed to loosen Zain's grip on her a fraction. She gasped in a huge breath, then rasped at Bram, "Shut up! It's my book. Bloody give it to him."

Zain loosed his grip a bit more. "Good girl."

Bram rolled his eyes. "Sorry. If he wants it, he's going to have to fight me first. If he's stupid enough to try to kill you, I'll take the book, disappear forever, and his boss will flay him alive for failing. Again. So, are you feeling stupid?" he asked Zain.

"You holier-than-thou fuck!" Zain snarled. "If you leave here with the book, you'll disappear forever, no matter what I do. If I kill Little Red, however, the younger MacTavish could turn completely mental, like the elder, which reduces the able ranks of your Doomsday Brethren even more. You're the stupid one. You have three warriors, one of them unable to fight after I kill Red, and I've got ten Anarki remaining. Do you really think you can defeat us?"

Bram's confidence didn't slip an inch. Sydney began to suspect he was off his trolley. Zain had a *very* good point; they were totally outnumbered. The fact Zain was talking about her death as if it was a fait accompli hardly comforted her.

"For God's sake, give him the bloody book!" she snapped at Bram.

He merely raised a superior golden brow at her. Duke's expression was no less assured. Were they utterly mad?

Now that she could breathe, Sydney stomped her foot on Zain's instep at the same time she rammed her elbow into his abdomen, grateful for the self-defense class she'd taken last year. Zain grunted in pain. In the ensuing moment of surprise, she darted away and ran toward Bram, hand outstretched for the book.

The wizard held it away from her, then shot Caden a glare. "Control your woman or I will."

"You'll pay, bitch!" Zain shouted as he worked to stand upright and charged Bram.

As Caden restrained her, Sydney railed at him. But something inside her savored his touch. His arm around her, holding her close, breath in her ear, made her feel alive. Safe.

Quickly, he shoved her behind him. The blond wizard

tossed the book at Duke, who caught it in an efficient grab. Before she could blink, Bram waved his hand. Something that looked like a magic wand appeared.

A wand, seriously? How Harry Potter.

Sydney had barely completed the thought when Bram brandished the wooden stick, jolting Zain with a burst of energy that hit him like a live wire, making the other man jerk and sizzle. Some of his minions rushed toward Bram and Duke, wands suddenly in some upraised hands. The others . . . Oh, God! Now that they stepped into the light, she saw they were little more than skeletons with rotting flesh dripping from gray bones, staring out from under their hoods. Their eyes promised pain.

"Retreat!" Bram demanded, waving his wand with an efficient flourish that made two of the robed figures crumple into unconscious heaps next to those Caden had subdued earlier.

Someone dragged Sydney close with an arm about her waist while Caden clung to her. She screamed until she turned and saw that the second arm belonged to Duke. Bram reached out for Aquarius, who'd been watching in wide-eyed, uncharacteristic silence.

Before Bram could secure Aquarius against his side, one of the mutants in robes grabbed the little woman and tossed her in Zain's direction, waves of her light brown hair streaming behind her like a flag. She shrieked, the terrified sound making the hair on the back of Sydney's neck stand up.

"No one is leaving!" Zain insisted as Aquarius landed against him.

He absorbed her smaller body with a grunt, then trapped her in his arms, gripping her below the breasts. Aquarius jerked, gasped, green eyes popping wide. Suddenly, she loosed a bloodcurdling scream. A moment later, her face turned red, then purple, then swelled into something terrible.

Sydney wriggled against the arms holding her back, struggling to reach her friend. Between Caden and Duke, their grips were unyielding.

"Do something. Save her!" Sydney screeched.

As her words pinged off the walls, Aquarius's eyes rolled into the back of her head and she fell limp in Zain's arms, her entire body bloated, skin blistered. Was she even breathing?

"No!" Sydney flailed and cursed, redoubling her efforts to get free.

Neither man budged an inch.

Retaining his grip on her, Caden kicked one of the corpse-like attackers, delivering some martial arts trick that snapped the minion's spine in half. Blood spurted everywhere. *Black* blood, just like Chloe had described. Sydney gaped on in horror.

"Humans converted to magical zombies, just like the dead soldiers in the tunnel. Oh. My. God," she whispered.

"Yes, Anarki. Conscripted men minus a soul." Caden kicked another half-dead creature who tried to sneak up on Bram. Again, the body broke apart and bled black as he collapsed.

Bram, who had been fighting off the others in robes, rushed to her side again. All around was a pile of unconscious Mathias followers, some rotting, some not, littering the ground. Now, only Zain and two of his robed peers stood.

"Put the girl down," Bram said. "Call off what's left of your lackeys. They're no match. Let's fight this fairly, you and I."

Zain scoffed. "I don't give two fucks about fighting fairly. The girl is alive." He jostled Aquarius in his grip, and she bounced like a rag doll, making Sydney cry out. "But only just. Give me the book and I'll let her live. If not . . ."

Sydney's heart nearly stopped.

"Give it to him!" she screamed at Bram.

Bram huffed, rolled his eyes. He wasn't budging.

The book must be more powerful than Aquarius had indicated. In her head, she knew that putting it in Zain's hands would be as good as putting it into Mathias's, but her friend . . . if Bram didn't comply, Zain would kill her.

To her surprise, he eased the book toward Zain, who reached for it while retaining his hold on Aquarius. Sydney cast an anxious glance at her friend. *God, she looks so still, so dead.* Sydney held in a cry.

At the last second, Bram pulled the book back into his protective clutch and slung the tip of his wand toward Aquarius. The little woman was suddenly caught up in a sweep of wind, like a giant vacuum that sucked her toward Bram.

But Zain was having none of that. He brandished his wand at Aquarius, too, and her body jolted as she stopped, jerking in midair. She keened, the sound rife with pain.

Around her, Duke dispatched the final two Anarki with a pair of spells, both normal looking men who clutched wands in their frozen fists.

"Your Anarki are all unconscious. You're alone," Bram pointed out. "Give up or fight me."

Suddenly, he shoved the book into Sydney's hand. Startled, she grasped it. Her eyes met Bram's blue ones, sharp with warning. *Do not give it to Zain.* He'd described it as a weapon of some sort, but what about Aquarius?

Zain paused, looking uncertain for the first time. Bram

took advantage of the opening and lunged, hooking one arm around the other man. With his free hand, he grabbed Aquarius.

"Go!" he shouted at Duke.

Instantly, Duke's arm tightened around Sydney. A sense of falling assailed her. Like being in a dark, endless well. She thrashed about, looking for escape, but Duke and Caden both held her tight. She squeezed her eyes shut.

Long moments later, the sensation stopped. Cautiously, Sydney opened her eyes to a stunning office, filled with weak afternoon sunlight, pricy artwork—and a roomful of men so menacing, she took a step back.

"Who the hell are these people, where am I, and how did I get here?"

"The Doomsday Brethren," Caden whispered in her ear.

Truly? "Anka has spoken of them. Only a bit, but . . ." She hadn't been sure of their role earlier, but now? These imposing wizards fought on the side of right.

"I teleported you here," Duke said quietly. "This is Bram's office."

"Good. How am I getting home?" She put a hand on her hip.

The blokes all looked at one another, then Caden sighed. "We'll work it out."

Oh. She got the feeling that her concept of home had just changed. If the Anarki knew where she lived and believed that she had possession of a magic book . . . no "if" anymore, really. There *was* danger, just as Caden had said. She'd landed in the middle of it. Caden had tried to talk her out of running the story on the book. Though he'd given her no substantial reasons, she wished she'd listened. But now that danger wasn't imminent, her inner journalist was thrilled to be embroiled in the paranormal.

Her next story for *Out of This Realm* would turn heads and win awards!

First, she had to help Aquarius and get the information she needed, then make haste to somewhere safe. Then perhaps once the article printed and she brought forth proof this magickind existed, her parents would have to look outside their academic box and take her seriously. Dare she even hope they'd be proud for bringing in a story no other journalist had?

Holding Zain in one arm, Bram appeared a few meters away and dropped the unconscious wizard on the ground. In the other arm, he held her friend cradled against his chest, the little woman so heartbreakingly still.

"Aquarius!" She dashed for her friend.

As soon as she drew close, the big blond wizard snatched the red diary from her hands.

"That's mine!" she protested.

"No." Bram's tone didn't invite argument. "It was stolen from us. Thank you for returning it. We will keep it safe."

"But—"

"After what you saw today, do you honestly believe you can defend yourself against the kind of garbage who will hunt you for this?" He held up the journal.

The wizard had a point. She might be able to fend off a normal man, but Zain wasn't normal. None of the wizards she'd seen today were, Caden included.

She had been making love with someone magical. *Oh. My. God.*

As if the thought had conjured him by her side, Caden took her by the hand and led her to a love seat. "Let him have it, firecracker. Please."

What would she do with it? Coerce Caden into bed again? Be a target for Mathias? Sydney nodded.

Bram accepted with a smile, then nodded to all the men in the room. "You're all here. Excellent."

"Waiting for news of the book," said another, a big bloke with a goatee, a sword at his side, and the look of a battle-hardened warrior. "Thank God you recaptured it."

"Indeed." Then he stuck his head out the door and yelled, "Sabelle!"

A moment later, a breathtaking blonde appeared—literally out of nowhere—looking tired and disheveled.

Bram narrowed his eyes. "Where have you been?"

"Nowhere you'd disapprove of, big brother. Merely helping Lucan."

Caden's brother? Bram's sister knew him?

"You had assistance, yes?" Bram prompted.

"Yes," Sabelle assured.

"Did he take your energy?" Caden asked, sounding choked and desperate.

Sydney's heart went out to him. Then she realized . . . Zain had been telling the truth about Caden's magical people shagging to rev themselves up. Which explained a lot about his stamina with her. And why his brother was bedding Bram's sister. His wife was the missing Anka.

"Some. He's a bit stronger than the last time you saw him. I'm trying." Sabelle laid a soft hand on Caden's forearm.

Sydney didn't like the gorgeous woman touching him. At all.

Gritting her teeth, she said, "Could someone explain to me how we're going to help Aquarius?"

"Aquarius?" Sabelle asked.

"Sydney's friend." Bram held up the limp figure in his arms.

She wanted to cry. They desperately needed to get

Aquarius some medical care, or . . . no, she wouldn't think the worst.

Suddenly, Bram handed the book back to her. Sydney stared at him as she took it cautiously. Was he mad? Hadn't Caden just pleaded with her to let Bram keep it?

"Give this to my sister." His tone didn't invite argument.

She held the little book to her chest. "You just told me I couldn't handle it, now you give it back, then ask me to hand it to another woman who doesn't look equipped for battle either?"

"Do. It," he ordered through clenched teeth. "The book must pass from female to female. The sooner you cooperate, the sooner we can focus on helping your friend."

If she didn't, would they withhold care? Sydney didn't want to learn the answer the hard way. Not understanding Bram's female-to-female comment, Sydney glared at the beautiful woman and slapped the book into her hands.

Sabelle gripped it tightly. "I will guard it with my life."

"Hopefully, that will not be necessary," Bram said grimly. "Just hide it until I'm free. For now, call for Aunt Millie. Have her meet you upstairs."

Bram glanced at Zain on the floor, then kicked him aside. When he stepped away, Sydney could see another big bloke on the sofa, shrouded in sunglasses, leather, and bad attitude.

"Shock." Bram sounded almost surprised to see him. "You've returned, then?"

What kind of name is that?

"As of a few minutes ago. I have news." The man took up the whole sofa.

Bram nodded. "Good. Will you take the injured woman upstairs? Ice, take Zain to our lovely barred accommodations below. And filch his wand."

"Can't we just kill him?" asked a menacing figure with hair trimmed nearly to his skull.

Shock growled in response. Bram raised a hand. "No, Ice, we can't. He has useful information."

With a sigh, Ice picked the unconscious Zain up as if he was holding a big pile of refuse, slammed the body over his shoulder, then disappeared.

The big man on the couch finally rose to his feet. Holy cow! Shock was enormous, easily topping every other man in the room, except perhaps the one with the goatee and sword. Gingerly, he took Aquarius in his arms. He dwarfed Sydney's friend, but his gentle grip reassured her. The man's gravelly voice didn't.

"I'll do your bidding this once, but kick Zain again, and I'll cut off your bloody stones."

Sydney didn't care how big and bad Shock was. If he was going to defend Zain, he was going to hear from her. "Zain nearly murdered my best friend. A swift kick is the very least he deserves."

Shock whipped his head around to face her. She couldn't see his eyes behind the dark sunglasses, but she had an impression of cold fury.

"He may be a shit, but he's my brother. Who the hell are you?"

Caden came to her rescue, putting an arm around her shoulder and sending the other man a challenging glare. "She's not to be harmed." Shock raised a questioning brow, black above the rim of his glasses. "Do you think you're a big, menacing wizard now that you transitioned all of ten minutes ago?"

Transitioned? From a man to a wizard. Was that why he'd needed so much energy? Why there'd been two of them afterward, his new and old self? What had happened to the other Caden?

"You two." Bram pointed to Caden and Shock. "Bury the animosity. We've no time for it."

"You're simply going to trust him and hope he doesn't fuck you over?" Caden challenged.

"That's my problem. Marrok has warned us repeatedly about these rows. If we're too busy fighting one another, how will we ever unite against our common enemy?"

"Agreed." Caden nodded. "Only because focusing on Mathias, Zain, and the Anarki will better help me find Anka and keep Sydney safe."

"Fine." Shock rolled his eyes.

"Good." Bram nodded. "Shock, take Aquarius upstairs. Please. We haven't much time to save her."

If it's not already too late. The unspoken words hung in the air.

Bram sighed. "When that's done, return here. Sabelle, follow and wait for Aunt Millie. Sydney, you'll want to stay with your friend, I presume? Go with them."

With that, she was dismissed. She cast a gaze toward Caden, feeling lost in Wonderland without a map or any bleeding clue what to do next. He squeezed her hand and nodded.

"I'll find you soon. I promise."

What choice did she have? Aquarius's life hung in the balance, and her friend might need her if she had any hope of pulling through. But the reporter in her wanted to stay behind. Something told her the men were about to have a conversation she'd kill to hear. But as the door to that museum-quality office closed behind her, Sydney knew she wouldn't get that chance. At least not today.

The giant, Shock, laid Aquarius on an enormous four-poster bed with a sumptuous beige silk coverlet. He took a half step back, still staring. His expression seemed to ask the same question tearing through Sydney's mind: Would she live? The worry was like an awl gouging out her composure.

For Aquarius, she had to be strong.

Sydney grabbed her friend's hand, edging Shock aside. He adjusted his sunglasses on his face, then glanced her way. "Need anything more?"

How would she know? Sydney could barely comprehend that this giant's brother had nearly fried her friend's insides. But Shock looked at Aquarius with something like compassion.

Olivia, the woman she'd met in the pub, entered the room and grabbed Sydney's hand while answering Shock. "If we do, we'll let you know. We're fine for now."

Shock hesitated, brushed a knuckle down Aquarius's arm, then turned away. Staring after him as he left, Sydney wondered what that was all about.

The question must have shown on her face because Olivia said, "Don't try to figure him out. You'll give yourself a headache. I've been living here with my mate Marrok for about six weeks, so I see the guys often. Except Shock. He completely baffles me."

She *lived* here? "Marrok?"

"Yeah. Big, bossy warrior, carries a sword."

Indeed. Sydney remembered him vividly. Imposing bloke. Hard to imagine that the tiny, violet-eyed beauty belonged with such a man. But lately she'd seen far more unusual things.

"Smashing." Sabelle breezed into the room, rubbing her hands together—the only indication of her nervousness. "Aunt Millie will be here shortly."

"She's got heart magic and can do a bit of healing," Olivia whispered to her.

"Precisely. Sorry." Sabelle sent her a rueful grin. "Ask me questions when I don't explain. I'm a bit topsy-turvy at the moment."

Sabelle might regret that offer someday, but Sydney intended to take advantage of it.

"How long until this aunt shows up?"

"I'm here, dear," a spry voice said from behind her.

Sydney whirled to see a little woman with lively blue eyes wearing a dotty lace dress and a straw bonnet. *This* was Aquarius's savior?

"No offense, but wouldn't a doctor be more effective?"

"Not with a magical malady." Millie took Sydney's hand in hers. "Let me have a look, then."

The lady with the thick, pale bun ambled past Sydney and put bony hands across Aquarius's chest. Then frowned. "Does the girl have any magic?"

Olivia and Sabelle both turned to her. Sydney shrugged. "I-I don't know. Does it matter for her healing?"

"A bit."

Sydney blew out a breath, then realized that Aquarius had rarely talked about her family. She mentioned friends and lovers, her failed uni days, karma, and her hopes for the future. But the family, she'd carefully danced around that.

"It's possible. Caden's brother's wife is her cousin, and Anka is a witch, right?"

"Yes, but your friend may not be magical. It isn't automatic. I'll just have to hope I get it right." Millie sighed, then closed her eyes.

Long, agonizing moments of silence passed. The woman skimmed her hands above Aquarius's belly and chest, making only occasional murmurs. Sydney had no idea what the devil they meant. And in the meantime, her friend's breathing had grown more labored. The purple, swollen color remained.

Her lips were blistered, her lids nearly swollen shut, her skin cracking.

"Can you help her?" Sydney finally asked, losing patience.

The older woman looked up with regret in her eyes. "I'm sorry. I've never seen anything like this. The damage is extensive."

The little woman's answer slammed Sydney's composure. She covered her mouth with her hand as the little woman left. Somehow, Millie's poise had made her hope that she could solve Aquarius's crisis. To hear otherwise crushed her.

"I think I know someone who might be able to," Olivia said. "A moment, please."

She disappeared. Sydney had no notion what to do or say, so merely grabbed her friend's hand and held it tightly in her own.

"Fight," she whispered to Aquarius. "It's bad karma for you to leave me all alone."

Her breath caught in her throat, and tears stung her eyes. Guilt stabbed her. If Sydney had listened to Bram when he'd said to get out, Aquarius would be well. *If I hadn't struggled to escape Zain or if I'd found some way to protect my friend, no harm would have befallen her.* But Sydney couldn't change any of it now. All she could do was hope.

"It's not your fault," Sabelle offered, stroking her shoulder.

Sydney blinked. "How—how did you know?"

"I can read your thoughts. Sorry. Thought I should give you fair warning. But I've delved into your friend's mind. Deep. She's worried about you."

The tears started flowing in earnest. Only a friend like Aquarius would be near death and still worry about someone else.

"I feel so helpless. Aquarius would at least have some

healing crystal, sacred chant, herbal tea. All I've got is my hand."

"And the power of your friendship. She feels it."

Sabelle's understanding sank into Sydney. Even if she thought the gorgeous blonde was full of rubbish and trying to soothe her, Sydney appreciated the gesture. *Perhaps Sabelle wasn't so bad after all—as long as she kept her hands off Caden.*

"In the future, I will. He's all yours, I promise."

Sydney hiccuped, smiling despite her tears. "You're not intimidated by me surely?"

"Caden and Bram both said you're tough, but no. My attentions are . . . engaged elsewhere."

"Olivia said you wanted to see me," a voice growled from the door.

Sydney turned, along with the other two women. Ice stood there. His behemoth shoulders bulged out of a black tank. An expressive mouth and the dark stubble dusting his otherwise sleek head, along with the faded fatigues, made him an intimidating figure. And when Sydney looked at him, the hunger in his expression, directed purely at Sabelle, blasted her like a heat wave.

The blonde merely blushed and cast a demure glance down. Then she sent Ice a nervous smile. "I think Olivia believed you might be able to help."

He frowned as he glanced at Aquarius. "I know blast and damn about her condition."

"Zain cooked her from the inside out," Sydney blurted.

"I'm not a healer." His craggy face gentled in apology.

"But Olivia sent you." Sydney couldn't understand why she had if Ice couldn't help.

He shrugged uncomfortably. "To stand guard?"

Sabelle edged around Sydney and approached Ice, drawing

in a bracing breath. "Your nickname, does it imply ability? Maybe . . ."

At his scowl, Sabelle broke off. Sydney's thoughts raced. Did Ice have some ability to cool down Aquarius's insides?

He swallowed, hesitated, then nodded. "But I don't know how to heal."

Ice turned away, and Sydney moved to chase him down, anger flashing through her. *He's giving up, just like that?* Aquarius may not mean anything to him, but her friend meant the world to her. Sabelle pulled her back and held up a steadying palm. Then she stopped Ice herself, wrapping her hand around his huge biceps.

"Please . . ."

Sabelle looked up at Ice, beseeching blue eyes wide open. Renewed hunger stormed his face. The wizard wanted her. Badly. And he was letting her see it. Sabelle didn't back down; she gripped him tighter, though Sydney sensed that the witch was overwhelmed by Ice. Yet she held her ground for Aquarius's sake, a woman she did not know.

Initial impressions be damned. Sabelle had just earned herself a new friend.

Ice huffed, then groused, "I need a conduit. I can create objects of ice, but transferring it to something living is beyond me."

"I can try," Sabelle assured, her hands dropping from his biceps.

"How?"

The blond witch licked her lips. "I'm part siren. I can often influence people's feelings by touching them. If you can pass the feeling onto me . . ."

Part siren? There was such a thing? And they could change other's feelings? Wow, the material she'd have to put in her next article.

Ice retreated. "Your brother will object."

"Bram can't always have his way."

He clenched his jaw. "Sabelle, I have to *touch* you to use you as a conduit."

She drew in a shaky breath, clearly nervous. And excited. She stared at Ice as if he was the forbidden fruit. "Touch me how?"

Desire leapt in his gaze again. "As much as you'll let me. The more contact, the more successful I'm likely to be."

The witch paused.

"Worried my insanity is contagious, princess?" Ice challenged with a dark raised brow.

"No," Sabelle snapped, then glanced at Aquarius, who labored for each breath. The witch bit her lip. Something about Sabelle's demeanor told Sydney that her reticence wasn't about Ice's intimidating demeanor, but the sexual vibes floating between them.

"I'll do it." Sabelle said in a voice that cracked and wobbled.

"Relax and trust me. You can't be afraid, no matter what."

Sabelle gave a shaky nod. Sydney suspected that Ice's request was easier said than done. Either way, she wished they'd hurry. Aquarius's clock was ticking down.

"Do we need anything else?" the blond witch asked.

"Just put your hands on her and concentrate. Whatever happens, don't move away from me."

The gorgeous witch positioned herself at the side of the bed, arms out so that her hands rested on Aquarius's torso. She drew in a deep breath, as if bracing herself.

Ice moved in behind her, stopping a mere breath away. "Ready?"

She nodded, but her body tensed. And no wonder, the sexual tension between them was thick and undeniable.

Closing the last bit between them, Ice wrapped his arms around Sabelle's middle, just beneath her breasts. His legs shadowed hers, thighs to thighs, shins to calves, his feet braced around hers. The woman's breath caught when Ice dropped his head, resting his cheek against her neck. His breath fanned the little tendrils of hair at her nape. Some of the hair artlessly piled on her head slipped free of its clip, caressing Ice, and she leaned back into him.

Neither moved, yet their bodies seemed to meld together.

"I'm going to blast you with cold, like an inanimate object. Try to pass it through you to her."

Like some sort of energy transfer? It didn't escape Sydney that if Aquarius were awake, she would embrace this holistic energy healing bit and give it two thumbs up on the karma scale. But Sydney herself held her breath, willing this to work.

Sabelle closed her eyes. A moment later, she stiffened, gasped. Then she tried to jerk away from Ice.

"No," he growled. "Stay with me. Pass it through. See where she needs cooling and give it to her."

With chattering teeth, Sabelle tried to nod. Her hands turned white, then blue. Sydney frowned. The chill seemed to be coating Sabelle outside, but not reaching inside her so she could transfer it to Aquarius.

"Please," Sydney cajoled. "Can you . . ." But she didn't know what to tell Sabelle to do.

Olivia rushed back into the room and gave her hand a supportive squeeze.

Ice wrapped his arms around Sabelle tighter, touching his lips against her ear. "Take it in, princess. Send it through."

Sabelle squinted, trying to focus inward, judging from her expression. Ice gripped one hip, pressing himself closer until there wasn't a breath of air between them. The other hand he splayed across the flat of her stomach, fingers stretched from just beneath her breasts, all the way to her navel. Sabelle's head fell against his shoulder, eyes closed.

"Feel me?" he whispered.

"Yes," she gasped raggedly. Within seconds, color pinkened Sabelle's skin and flushed her cheeks.

But Aquarius looked unchanged.

"What the devil?" Sydney perched on the other side of the bed, close to Aquarius. Another look at Sabelle's face shocked her. Face dreamy, lips parted, head tilted back against Ice's shoulder, she looked . . . aroused.

"Fuck!" Ice jumped away from her suddenly, as if scalded. "You sent me a blast of heat."

"I-I don't know why." Sabelle glanced away, but Sydney could see her eyes. They looked unfocused, dilated—and guilty.

She *was* aroused and didn't want to admit it. Understanding dawned on Ice's face. As it did, his expression said that he was mustering all his self-control to resist getting naked with her.

Grabbing her elbow, Ice turned her toward him, and with a finger, he lifted her chin, forcing her to look at him. "Princess, talk to me."

"Leave it be." She tried to jerk away.

He held tighter. "Not until you explain what just happened."

Ice knew that Sabelle's arousal had melted his chill, but he wanted to hear her say it. And it frustrated the hell out of Sydney. Aquarius would not live if they didn't think of something fast.

"It didn't work. That's all." Sabelle turned back to Sydney, all traces of sensuality gone from her expression.

"That's not all," Ice challenged. "I felt more."

Sabelle said nothing for a long moment, then whispered, "You know it's impossible." Her expression turned contrite. "I'm sorry."

With that, the witch all but ran out of the room, Ice looking after her with a need so stark, it was painful. Olivia's gaping mouth told Sydney that she wasn't the only one flabbergasted by what had just happened.

Nor did she think Ice would simply let Sabelle run from him now that he knew the attraction was mutual.

CHAPTER TWELVE

THE MINUTE ICE RETURNED to the room, Bram began pacing in front of his ornate desk, looking at each man. Caden felt the gravity—and disapproval—of that stare. He bristled. Admittedly, if Caden had still been a Marine, and Bram his superior officer, he would have deserved an ass chewing.

But he had his own problems—his transition, Sydney's attack, Lucan's illness. He wanted to shout that he owed Bram nothing. But the situation was no longer that simple. The man's sister was keeping his brother alive at great personal expense.

He also couldn't deny that, without Bram, Zain likely would have killed Sydney. Caden knew little magic—and preferred it that way. Knowing it would be unnecessary once he returned to Texas, but today . . . leaving wasn't an option. Because there was no mistaking the fact Sydney's fate had changed utterly. As long as the Anarki believed she had the diary, true or not, they'd hunt her relentlessly.

Then there was the fact that Anka was alone and unprotected, with little idea where she belonged. As much as Caden despised it, he needed Bram's help now more than ever to find her so they could right Lucan's life.

"Today, many things changed. Caden transitioned. The Anarki began hotly pursuing the book once more. We have a prisoner. Again."

"Unlike last time, we won't let him escape," Ice growled.

Shock ground his teeth and set his jaw, but nodded. "As

long as he's here, I should keep a low profile. If he gets free, he may convince Mathias that I'm on your side."

"Agreed. Caden, tell the others what you learned about the book when you tried to steal it."

Quickly, he explained his failed attempts to steal the book from Sydney, stressing the fact it literally disappeared from his hands when he left her flat.

"This underscores what we've suspected about the Doomsday Diary: It can only be 'owned' by females. Several of us have tried to write in it. Nothing. So it cannot be *utilized* by a man, either. Which begs the question, does Mathias know this little twist?"

"How? That cursed book has scarcely left my sight in fifteen hundred years, and I knew this not until today," Marrok said.

"True. But we don't know if Mathias has other means." Bram turned to Shock. "Does he?"

Every eye in the room turned to stare at their supposed double agent.

"Can't say for certain." He shrugged leather-clad shoulders.

Nice and vague. Naturally. Why would Shock tell the Doomsday Brethren anything useful?

"We'll work on him. Discern what he knows. Perhaps talk to Zain, as long as he's going to be gracing us with his presence below."

Shock nodded. "Zain's capture will hurt the Anarki. Physically, Mathias is still weak from Olivia's blast in the tunnel a few weeks past. He's recovering, mind you, but slowly. Zain has been elevated to acting head fiend, so his absence will be felt."

Ice clenched his fists. "I wish they could feel me blasting them all to hell."

"Me, too," Bram chimed in. "Crippling their operation is a start, but—"

"He's not as crippled as you think," Shock advised. "He's ramping up the Anarki. The ranks of half-dead are swelling enormously. I don't know how. His followers are abducting soldiers from all over the world and converting them very quickly. More arrive, angry and belligerent, each day. It isn't long before their souls are gone and they're sporting robes."

"Why soldiers?" Caden asked.

"Think, you sod. Well trained."

Caden let the insult slide. He was too infuriated about Mathias forcing servicemen into his ranks to respond to Shock's petty shit.

"How many, a few dozen?" Bram asked.

"A few hundred. At least. The speed of the conversions defies logic."

"Each one usually takes days, perhaps weeks." Bram's blue eyes threatened to bulge.

"I've overheard Mathias talking about an object he recently acquired. I've offered to help Zain and the others for appearance's sake." He shrugged. "They haven't taken me up on it yet."

"Mathias isn't converting them?" Bram sounded surprised.

"Too weak."

"Ah. I thought surely he'd be up for some mass torture. He so enjoys others' pain. Nice to know we've deprived him of his fun. Does he stay abed, then?"

"Yes. He is draining women of their energy daily. I can hear their screams." Shock blanched, swallowed.

How could any normal man stand to listen to a woman being brutalized? Then again, Shock wasn't normal. Did those events truly disturb him?

"I hate it, but if I blow my cover many will die," Shock added somberly.

Caden fisted his hands, hating the bastard more every minute. But he was right.

Bram paced, his thoughts clearly racing. "This can't go on. The Council isn't willing to admit that Mathias has returned. Against my best advice, I've been ordered to quell the rumors and I've had some success. But clearly, no one except us will help magickind. It's imperative we devise a game plan to defeat Mathias that bloody works."

"Now that Zain has been captured," said Shock, "the Anarki will be in disarray, even with the new army, if Mathias isn't strong enough to lead them. I can give you all you need to stage an attack on his secret location."

Or all he needed to lead the Doomsday Brethren into a trap.

"If he's weak, and the ranks are in chaos, perhaps the time is right." Bram regarded the others. "Duke? Marrok? Ice?"

Duke crossed his arms over his chest, and despite recently having battled a dozen men, he still looked surprisingly GQ. "We'll need to train a bit more. But the idea sounds reasonable."

"Aye," Marrok added. "The strategy must be sound. I want nothing left to chance."

Ice merely gave a humorless laugh. "I'm always in favor of kicking Anarki arse."

"What if he's leading us into a trap?" Caden couldn't keep his suspicion silent. Bram didn't want dissension. *But good God, could they not see the obvious?*

The men cast measuring glances at Shock. He stood tall, arms crossed, legs akimbo.

"Think what you want. Ignore me if you like." He shrugged. "Just a suggestion."

"A calculated risk I think we must take," Bram replied.

Caden tried not to let his jaw hit the ground. "What about Anka? We can't just leave her alone and afraid, by herself."

"What do you mean?" Shock growled and he grabbed Caden by the arms and shook him.

Caden jerked free, fighting the urge to plow a fist in the man's jaw. "Don't bloody touch me!"

"He means," Duke added, "that we discovered Anka had been staying with her cousin Aquarius all these weeks and apparently left a few hours ago of her own free will."

Relief swept across Shock's face. "She's alive?"

"And belongs with my brother," Caden pointed out.

Shock sent him a tight smile. "Not necessarily."

"Stop bickering!" Bram demanded. "Caden, you, Duke and Ice go out now and search for Anka. Marrok, Shock and I will stay behind to formulate an attack plan. We'll advise you when it's ready."

Exhaustion wound like molten lead through Caden's veins, weighing him down. The adrenaline from the battle was wearing off, and all he wanted to do was lie down and sleep for a week, preferably with Sydney wrapped around him. But Anka needed him.

Suddenly, Bram turned to him. "Now that you've transitioned, your magic will be helpful to the cause. You'll need a wand. Normally, your family would—"

"No one in my family is in any position to give me one." *Thank God.*

"I'll do it," Bram offered. "Give me an hour or two and I'll present it to you."

As much as he hated to admit it, Caden owed Bram, especially now that he'd lent more warriors to the search. He'd even offered to perform this sacred family ritual with him. But Caden wanted as little involvement with magic as possible. Besides, taking a wand from Bram made his position in both magickind and the Doomsday Brethren feel permanent.

"I don't need or want a wand. I still prefer to be a man, not a wizard."

"But you *are* a wizard."

"Only if I choose to exercise my powers. And I don't."

Hours later, Caden woke slowly to an unfamiliar room and an unfamiliar bed, the effects of last night's exhaustion slowly fading. A familiar warmth lay beside him. Sydney. It was reckless, but he snuggled up to her. After spending fruitless hours looking for Anka, he'd returned to Bram's after midnight, fatigued to the core, and found her cozy in a big bed. Wanting her warmth, to reassure himself of her safety, he'd joined her. In the past, he'd talked to Sydney, argued with her, touched her, worried about her. But he really hadn't had the opportunity to simply lie with her and hold her in his arms. Right away, he knew he'd missed something special.

Soft, warm, quiet—at least for her. Burying his face in her hair, he smiled . . . until the noises below woke him. Men's voices. A shout—Bram. The slamming of a door. Then outside the clank of metal on metal, the report of firearms. Marrok was training the others. He frowned.

A moment later, Duke popped his head in the door and said, "Everyone is outside. Well, everyone but Shock."

Typical. The elder Denzell brother claimed to be a double agent, but why would Shock turn against his family, allow his own brother to be captured, and battle the rest of his class to defeat the man who supposedly wanted to uplift them? As far as Caden could see, unless Shock had a hidden altruistic streak his "loyalty" to Bram made no bloody sense.

Briefly, Caden pondered staying beside Sydney. More than once, he'd wanted to tell Bram to shove his request for training. But they'd struck a deal when he first arrived: His help in exchange for theirs in finding Anka.

"I'll be there shortly," he said, then glanced regretfully at Sydney.

He owed her answers—loads of them. Inadvertently, he'd plucked her from her ordinary world and plopped her down in the middle of a war zone. And given that Mathias's minions knew exactly where she lived, she couldn't go back now. Until the threat ended, he'd do whatever necessary to keep her out of harm's way.

Carefully, he rolled away from her, extricating his arm from beneath her neck, unwrapping his legs from hers. Now separate, he sat up, trying not to disturb her. After yesterday's ordeal, she needed rest. Time to adjust.

A feminine hand touched his bare back. "Where are you going?"

"To help with the combat training. Go back to sleep."

He glanced over his shoulder. She looked so sweet and sleep-tousled. Until he stared into her eyes. There a million questions lurked—along with an equal number of worries. The reporter in her was clearly determined to get answers. But the woman in her looked unsettled, and for the first time, afraid.

"Wait. You're in midst of a war." Her voice was raspy and heavy with sleep. "And I've just realized that includes me now." She bit her lip, looking lost and confused.

That expression squeezed his chest. Caden eased back on the bed and took her hand. "I'm sorry. I didn't want this for you."

"What's happening here, really? What is this war truly about? What are you fighting against? Anka spoke of oppression, but Mathias doesn't seem to be the answer."

"Sydney, I only meant to answer your questions about the

past few days at your flat, perhaps the book's real purpose. What you're asking for is very dangerous knowledge."

She huffed in frustration. "Without the larger picture, it's impossible to take in. I wanted the paranormal to be real. *Believed* in it. Part of me is happy to be proven right. The other part . . ."

When her brave face crumpled, Caden couldn't deny her. He opened his arms and folded them around her. "Is scared, I know."

Sydney went to him eagerly, cuddling against his chest. "I never imagined knowing the truth would be so dangerous. I only saw the accolades and Pulitzers. Never the down side."

His first instinct was to tell her that nothing good could come from her knowing all of magickind's secrets. There'd only be more danger.

"But I have to know. If I'm involved now, what good will come from burying my head in the sand and not understanding the danger?"

None. She was up to her pretty neck in magical war. Ignorance could only get her killed.

"The war is about oppression on the surface, but that's bunk. Oppression exists in the magical world, yes. There are two distinct classes, the Privileged and the Deprived, and other than here in Bram's house because the war demands it, they don't mix. It's simply not done, since some long-ago magical Council separated the classes for 'safety's' sake. That has to change. The Council needs to stop being feudal and update their laws. But Mathias uses that division as an excuse to cause chaos. Ultimately, he's just another power-monger."

"Mathias wants that book badly. How does he think it will help? Power-hungry tyrants aren't usually looking to fulfill their sexual fantasies."

She blinked up at him, brown eyes sober and open. He noticed that she wore a little white negligee, likely courtesy of Sabelle or Olivia. It dipped off one shoulder to reveal creamy skin dotted with cinnamon freckles. His unruly libido stood at attention, but he tamped it down. Now was hardly the time.

"The book grants wishes, sexual or otherwise. It's known as the Doomsday Diary because, in the hands of a woman powerful enough, it could bring about doomsday."

Sydney cocked her head. "Woman, not a man?"

Caden shook his head, preparing to launch into a history lesson. "You were right when you wrote in your article that King Arthur's half sister, Morganna le Fay, created the book. She used it as a means to curse people. The theory is that if a witch writes in the book, her wish will come true. A powerful witch could work seriously dangerous magic with it. As with all magic, the one casting it must have the power and the passion to back it up."

Sydney frowned, looking somewhat perturbed. "So it grants wishes only when a witch writes in it?"

"As far as I know. But perhaps any woman can. We don't know everything about it. The diary disappeared a millennium and a half ago, and just a few weeks past, Bram discovered Marrok had been keeping it all that time."

"You mean in his family, right? He-he can't be *that* old."

"Incredible, isn't it? Morganna cursed him with immortality, using the diary. He stole it from her to try to uncurse himself, but nothing worked until he met Olivia. Bram tracked down the book and Marrok when he realized Mathias was returning from exile."

"What did he do to earn his exile?"

"This is not the first time he's tried to control magickind by foul means. If someone doesn't stop him, he'll oppress everyone and likely go on a killing spree that will make Ted Bundy look like an angel."

She gasped as the words sunk in. "Wow. You tried to tell me that Mathias was no savior."

"I couldn't explain exactly why without giving away magickind's secrets to a human. I never meant to drag you into this muck."

"Human? You say that as if you're another species. Though I suppose you are. Those two days we spent in my bed—"

"I transitioned from man to wizard," he admitted the inescapable truth.

"I suspected as much after yesterday's discussion."

"It's not something I asked for or wanted. I spent a lot of years praying the gene would pass me by. If I hurt or upset you as I transitioned, I apologize."

"You were urgent but careful. Tell me the truth." She turned her profile to him and stared at the wall. "Was I bedding more than one of you during those two days?"

Caden winced. This would be a tough admission, but she deserved it. "You weren't. I would never abuse your trust by sneaking a copy of myself into your bed."

"Then why did I see two of you? Did I see your human self and your magical self at once? Can you separate them at will? What happened to your human half?"

"It's not like that. At the end of any magical being's transition, the power that is uniquely theirs materializes, whether they want it or not. Mine is the ability to . . . ah, clone myself."

"Amazing." Sydney sat back against her pillows and drew her knees to her chest. "Yet you seem less than thrilled. If anyone should be rattled about all this, it's me."

"Little firecracker, given where you work and the stories

you've been developing, you were much more prepared for magic's emergence in your life than I. Until Sabelle appeared in my living room to tell me that Lucan was ill, I'd been blissfully ignoring it all."

She frowned. "Until Lucan's illness, you avoided this war. You weren't fighting?"

"No."

Her expression jerked into a frown. "So for weeks—months—the war has been raging, your people dying, and you stayed away?"

Damn, when the woman put it like that, he sounded cowardly. "They aren't my people."

"They are now."

In name only. "I have a life and a job in Texas. I merely stepped into my brother's shoes in the Doomsday Brethren until we find Anka. He's in no condition to fight."

"Any luck finding her last night?"

Regret skittered through him. He didn't know what else he could have done to locate his brother's mate, let alone something that would have rescued her before she'd been thrust alone in a dangerous world. "No."

"I'm sorry. I know you're concerned."

"Thank you." He rose reluctantly from the bed. "I should go. Will you be all right? Sabelle and Olivia should both be about."

"Perhaps they'll help me find a shower and a toothbrush?"

He smiled softly. "I've no doubt. Then they'll direct you to breakfast and keep you company for a bit."

"Hmm. Actually, I think I'd like to work on my next story."

He froze. "You can't write about everything I've just said."

"Not until Mathias is vanquished and all is safe," she assured. "I would never do anything to endanger you or your friends. I want to stay and help them, in fact. But this is amazing material."

He shook his head. "Bram will fight your printing a word."

"I'll be careful, change names and places . . . whatever needed. But a story of oppression and war and heroism is something all humans will relate to, even if it's about magickind. Besides, getting this story into the open may benefit magickind too."

Caden raked a hand through his hair, largely to keep from grabbing her and shaking sense into her. "By inciting panic? How do you think humans will react when they know the bloke next door could be a wizard? Twenty-first century witch hunts aren't that far-fetched."

"You're being paranoid. Hysteria like that hasn't happened in hundreds of years. I'll make certain it doesn't happen. I would never let anything happen to these people."

"You can't write this story."

Why the devil didn't he tell her to work it through Bram, let him be the bad guy? Magickind wasn't where he belonged. Why was he feeling protective?

"You'd have me bury the biggest story of my career?" She crossed her arms over her chest. "The one incredible story that could make me and show my parents that I'm every bit as successful—"

"And even if Mathias is defeated, magickind's story will still be dangerous to tell, for everyone. No."

She sucked in a breath and stood, her small curves outlined in gossamer ivory. "That's not your decision."

Caden wanted to refute that. Since transition, his instincts about Sydney had been clawing at him. Seeing her so passionate stirred his libido. Battling her defiance brought out his every instinct to claim her and make it his decision.

Sydney swept past him, and he grabbed her arm, holding her at his side. At the soft feel of her, his cock stiffened. Instantly. She should not affect him so quickly. He'd had enough sex to be content for a few days, surely. But even the hint of her surrender made heat slide over his skin and pool in his groin. Thick desire muddled his mind until he could only think of possessing her—completely. Duke and Bram and the others could wait.

Caden tumbled her to the bed. She gasped as he rolled her beneath him and positioned himself between her thighs. They wore too many clothes, damn it. His jeans, her wispy little nightgown. But he could fix that.

Lifting the hem of her gown, he stared into Sydney's dark, stormy eyes, down at the parted berry lips luring him like a siren call. They looked sweet and plump and perfect, and could be his so easily.

He lowered his head, then hesitated. He knew, *knew*, that she was his mate. If he kissed her, the words would tumble out. As much as his instincts were screaming *yes!*, if he followed through, he'd tie himself irrevocably to her, to magic, and this place forever, stuck with a destiny he didn't want. And he'd put Sydney in more danger.

With a growled curse, he levered himself up on shaky arms and sat on the edge of the bed, away from her. Bloody hell, if he wasn't breathing hard. His every muscle and nerve urged him to kiss her, spill the words, complete the deed. His head knew better.

"What was that about?" Sydney sat up and was suddenly at his back, melting him with her nearness and the mixed scent of her arousal and anger.

"I should be training with the others."

"You order me about." Her voice hitched. "Tumble me into bed to change the subject, then avoid kissing me, as if I'm diseased."

He whirled and found her earnest face—and temptation—so close. He put distance between them. "Sydney, the more tangled up in you I get, the more dangerous it is for both of us."

"That didn't stop you from spending two days in my bed."

Caden hesitated, hurt tingeing both her words and her expression. Sydney didn't often show her vulnerabilities. Now that she was, he had no good answer to right her smile.

"Witches and wizards require sex during transition. Without it, they will die."

The hurt deepened. "So I could have been anyone? Or was I merely convenient because I happened to have that book you wanted so bloody bad?"

"I wanted you." He grabbed her by the shoulders. "Only you. Duke insisted he bring in someone else to transition with me, and I refused. It is helpful that you had the book, but even if you hadn't, I would have insisted on being with you. I'm not a heartless cad. I care about you. But having a relationship now isn't smart if we want to stay alive."

"Rubbish! Excuses. Every time we've had sex, you've more than hinted it was against your better judgment. I propositioned; you refused. The night you beat down my door, you couldn't run away quickly enough the next morning. The evening you bent me over my kitchen table, *I* asked *you* to make love. Then your transition hit, and I happened to be the only woman handy. All along, you wanted to stop my story more than you wanted *me*."

Caden's jaw dropped. "You're mad. I want you until I can't breathe, until my thoughts are tangled inside out, until I could nearly die for not touching you. But I don't want your death on my conscience. I don't want to hurt you when I leave."

I don't want to meet the same end as my brother.

"Leave?" She blinked, her thoughts clearly working as she fought tears.

He wanted to reassure her. But that was pointless.

"Once your brother is well, you'll go back to Dallas?"

"Yes."

"Alone?"

Saying the word would hurt them both, so he merely nodded.

"Which leaves us nowhere." She tensed, absently plucking at a stray thread on the coverlet.

"It's for the best." He willed her to understand. The sooner she could safely leave, the sooner he could resume his normal life and put magic behind him. They could both live, if not happily-ever-after, at least without constantly looking over their shoulder.

"You're being a coward."

The slur felt like a flaming torch to Caden's chest. She didn't understand how much he feared mating and hated magic. She hadn't been running happily with her laughing younger brother through the grass one moment, then seen him hit by errant magic and fall the next, never to rise again. She couldn't fathom the devastation this war would bring, the growing certainty that, if he mated her, she would be targeted for death. All too clearly, he saw that if he didn't find a way out of this war soon, magic would not only change his life, but ruin it—and hers.

But more explanations would only prolong the inevitable and change nothing.

"I'm sorry you feel that way." Caden straightened his clothes and donned his discarded trainers.

"For the first time in my life, I began to think that I might be falling in love with a man who liked and understood me, didn't think my theories were crazy. Supported me. Even my own parents haven't done that." Her voice was a low thing that throbbed with pain, striking him deep in the chest. "If you're going to kill my hope, help me understand."

Love? She might *love* him? Bloody hell. . . . Surprise washed over him, along with a cold chill in his veins. Yet wasn't the reverse true? If he really considered the situation, wasn't he falling for the stubborn, brave, intelligent, loyal reporter as well?

"They're waiting for me on the training field." He backed away, toward the door. "You likely won't believe me, but I never meant to hurt you."

With that, he cast one last look at Sydney, looking so soft and kissable among the rumpled bedding. Then, before he did something reckless he'd regret, he left, closing the door with a soft click behind him.

CHAPTER THIRTEEN

NIGHT DESCENDED AND MEALTIME arrived. Bram, Ice, and Duke looked sweaty and haggard after a long day of training and a fruitless evening of searching for Anka. The one responsible for their sore muscles, Marrok, ate energetically, seemingly untaxed by the day's hard work as he consumed nearly his body weight in food. How any one man could eat that much, Sydney had no idea. That he sneaked heated glances at his mate, Olivia, didn't escape her notice either.

Everyone else ignored them. Especially Caden.

Seated beside her, he carefully avoided brushing elbows or looking at her. He said absolutely nothing. After Sydney's day of nursing Aquarius in a desperate attempt to cool her down, fending off a hundred questions during a brief phone call to Holly, scribbling her thoughts about her next magickind story, and trying not to feel her heart shattering into a million pieces—the distance he put between them hurt.

It was possible during all the time they'd worked, touched, and fought off the Anarki together that he'd come to care for her. But not enough to cross the chasm between them. He wanted to abandon the very world she'd been seeking her whole life. He had some disliking for magic, and if he ever discovered that she'd written in that book to bring him to her bed, he'd hate her for it.

"Any change in Aquarius?" Bram asked, breaking the heavy silence.

Sydney shook her head and picked at the tender meat on her plate. Guilt and heartache were appetite killers. "No."

She supposed she should be thankful that Zain had left her friend alive. She didn't know if his spell prevented her from dying from her injuries or if Sydney's efforts to keep Aquarius cool with compresses and ice packs had helped. Whatever the cause, thankfully, her resilient friend had hung on.

Bram turned to his sister. "Did you call for Conrad, the healer? He's had more experience than Millie, and he tended Marrok well enough a few weeks past."

The blonde glanced at Ice before she focused on her brother. "He popped by earlier. Said he's never seen anything like it either. He can't help, but suggested the *helbresele* spell."

"A healing spell would be lovely, but until Zain awakens and gives his blessing, that's impossible."

That didn't improve Sydney's mood. She didn't fully understand the spell, but even if Zain was conscious, he certainly wouldn't consent to help Aquarius.

Sabelle turned toward Caden. "He also looked in on Lucan."

"I spoke with Conrad before he left." From Caden's tone she wondered if his brother's condition had worsened.

"He told you that we should try moving him to his own home? That he might improve with exposure to more familiar surroundings?"

"Yes. I'll be preparing his house over the next day or two. Anka put up a quite a fight, and it's in shambles. As soon as it's ready, I'll move him."

"I'll help," she said. "If moving him will help his condition improve."

"I can lend a hand," Sydney offered.

"No," Caden bit out. "But thank you."

His immediate, adamant refusal stung.

Caden leaned closer and murmured, "I don't want to involve you any more than I must. Let me protect you."

Was he simply trying to keep her safe or had that been a lie to soften the blow? *What danger could there be in cleaning up a house?*

Sydney suspected that he simply didn't want her there. Had the tenderness he'd once shown her been manufactured by the Doomsday Diary? After all, it granted wishes, and she'd fantasized about him on the page. What they shared had been more than sex. For her, anyway. Now that the spell was gone, so, it appeared, was his caring.

In some ways, she wished she'd never laid eyes on that book. But had she not, Caden would never have let down that mammoth self-control and become her lover.

He had a lot on his plate, true. But deep down she feared he simply didn't want her for more than a shag, and she had no one to blame but herself. Rather than dwelling on her screwup, she'd be better served by focusing on her story. Once this ordeal was over, releasing it would be safe. With great copy and proof of magickind's existence, she'd be a journalistic sensation.

But right now, her old life seemed a million miles away. Sydney pushed her plate aside.

"Anyone seen Shock?" Duke ventured, more to change the subject than anything she suspected. The man had disappeared again late last night.

"No. I tried to reach him earlier today to coordinate some last minute plans for our—" Bram glanced her way, then pursed his lips together. "He didn't answer."

And whatever he'd been about to say would remain a secret. She understood why Bram didn't trust her, but she wouldn't write a word for *Out of This Realm* when doing so would endanger them. She'd made that clear to Holly. But they had no reason to trust her.

A series of trills and gongs sounded. Bram sat up straight, listening intently. As soon as the last note faded away, he rose and stalked from the room.

"What's that?" Sydney asked.

Sabelle looked puzzled, but explained, "It's a magical calling card. To be polite, we send a distinct sound to another residence when we wish to visit."

"Each person has an individual bell ring?"

"Something like that."

"Do you know who that one belongs to?" she asked.

"Everyone," Bram called from the narrow dining room's portal. "This is Tynan O'Shea."

Mr. O'Shea was, in a word, yummy. Hair as dark and shiny as ink and slightly spiked, as if he were ready for a photo shoot. A rugged face, a strong chin, and bronzed skin all gave the appearance of a hearty outdoorsman. But his flat gray eyes looked as if all life and happiness had been sucked dry.

He held up a large palm by way of greeting, not meeting anyone's eye, then turned an intense gaze back to Bram. Clearly, he wasn't here to be sociable.

"Sit." Bram gestured toward an empty seat at the table. "Hungry?"

O'Shea shook his head. "I came to talk. I want answers."

"Has something happened to your family?"

Slowly, he shook his head, then he swallowed. "I've heard whispers that Mathias has returned."

Sydney frowned. Whispers? Of course Mathias had returned. How could Tynan not know?

Bram shifted in his chair. "Have you asked your grandfather?"

Tynan drilled him with a derisive stare. "Would I be here if I'd gotten answers?"

"Officially, as a Council member, I'm not at liberty to —"

"The devil with the Council!" Tynan erupted suddenly. "Who killed Auropha MacKinnett?"

Clearing his throat, Bram sighed. Sydney got the distinct impression that Bram was stalling for time.

"We haven't yet determined precisely—"

"The truth, damn you!" O'Shea looked ready to burst a blood vessel. His olive complexion flushed red. His eyes flared to furious life, like smoke and danger and determination. "Was it Mathias?"

"There *are* rumors that some rogue vestige of the Anarki are trying to wreak havoc."

"I hear others have been attacked!" O'Shea pointed out. "People claim they've *seen* Mathias. I saw Auropha's body." He choked on the last word.

Sydney's heart went out to him. The man looked genuinely anguished. And furious, as if he had a death wish. As long as he could avenge Auropha first, Tynan O'Shea would die a satisfied man.

"Tell me the bloody truth!" Tynan demanded.

Mathias on the loose should be all over magickind's version of the news. Maybe he'd been living in a fishbowl? Sydney saw confusion and desperate need in his expression. The man fisted his hands, clearly trying to hold back. Tension vibrated in the air, and she had little doubt O'Shea was close to snapping.

"You know I'm not allowed to speak of Council matters," Bram said finally.

"Do not fuck with me," he growled. "I loved Auropha. She was to be my mate after her transition next year. If that Satan's spawn raped her until she found her nextlife, then I want to show him his. The more painful his death, the better."

Sydney held her breath. Ice cursed softly. Duke looked at Bram, seemingly waiting for a cue. Would no one tell this grieving man about the Doomsday Brethren?

"Damn it, have you formed a clandestine army? There are whispers. I visited the Pullman family after they were attacked. One of the neighbors thought you might be gathering warriors to combat Mathias, and doing it under the Council's nose." He rose and growled. "If you're fighting, I want in."

"Mere rumors," Bram said weakly.

Sydney's jaw dropped, then she snapped her mouth shut. *Why would Bram lie?*

Tynan sneered. "Only in dire circumstances would I find a Deprived like Rykard supping at the same table as the ultimate Privileged. You need only your friend Lucan MacTavish to complete the picture. Where is he?"

Dead silence fell across the table. Sydney bit her lip. *Couldn't these people see Tynan O'Shea's anguish? Why wouldn't they help him?* Sydney hurt for the man and his soul searing loss. *How could they refuse this poor man something as simple as the truth? Besides, if the odds were so seriously against Bram, Caden, and the others, wouldn't they want another warrior?*

"Lucan is injured," Sydney finally said, testing the waters.

Every head at the table whipped in her direction, especially O'Shea's. His gaze fixed on her until she felt pinned as surely as if he held her to the ground. *Oops, maybe I shouldn't have said anything.*

"And they're fighting Mathias as a group, human?"

Sydney frowned. *How did he know I was human? Not important now.* Instead, she caught Bram's gaze, silently asking why he wouldn't want to tell O'Shea the truth. Finally, the blond wizard sighed.

"Fine. Unofficially, yes. We have formed a group, the Doomsday Brethren, designed to both keep the Doomsday Diary safe and fight Mathias, who has returned from exile, and the Anarki. If you take the information about the Doomsday Brethren to your grandfather, I will deny it to him and the rest of the Council with my dying breath."

"Why would I end a group that can help me avenge Auropha and prevent this tragedy from befalling another family? I'm relieved you're taking action. I know the Council will do nothing to quell Mathias. They'll merely deny his existence, despite news like this."

O'Shea pulled a scrap of paper from his pocket. Sydney would have recognized it anywhere. It was her article from *Out of This Realm* about the battle in the tunnel. She gasped.

"You read my article?" The words slipped out before she could stop them.

"This and the others in the series." O'Shea crossed the room, grabbed Sydney's shoulders and hauled her out of her chair. *"You're* the reporter? What else do you know?"

Suddenly, Caden stepped between them. "Take your hands off my—the woman."

Tynan pinned him with a contemptuous gaze. "You are a MacTavish, clearly."

"Caden, Lucan's younger brother."

The distraught man held Sydney tighter. "Until someone gives me information, I'm going to keep asking her questions. She's talking, at least."

The murderous look O'Shea tossed at Bram chilled Sydney. He was deadly serious.

"She's already told you all she knows," Bram drawled,

looking totally unconcerned. But she sensed the tenseness in his shoulders, the slight pull of his mouth.

"Let me fight with you."

Caden spoke up then. "Let her go and get lost. There's more here than wand waving."

Tynan raised a dark brow. "Meaning?"

"In for a penny, in for a pound," Bram grumbled. "Mathias is 'recruiting' Anarki involuntarily, using human soldiers for his army once he rips their souls from their body. They don't wield magic and seem impervious to it, so the only way to defeat them is through human methods. Ever punched a man? Fired a gun? Sliced someone in two with a sword?"

The angry intruder looked around the room, seeming to gauge whether everyone else knew these things as well. He released Sydney. "I'll learn."

After pausing, Bram shook his head. "No. I can't risk it."

Duke interjected, "A handful of weeks ago, few of us knew any of those things, either."

"I can teach the lout quickly, should he learn to curb his temper," Marrok added. "An emotional warrior is a sloppy one."

"I'll curb it. Just . . . damn it, let me fight." Tynan curled his hands around the sides of an ornate dining room chair, his knuckles turning white.

"If I let you fight beside us and you're killed, your grandfather would do everything in his power to see me separated from the Council and my head severed from my body. No."

"You need more warriors," Caden argued. "I'm not staying. Lucan . . ." He shrugged painfully. "He may never fight again. Shock comes, Shock goes."

"Shock Denzell?" O'Shea asked, incredulous. "His family has always supported Mathias. Isn't he on the other side?"

Bram didn't answer. He turned to Caden instead. "Your point?"

"Mathias is quickly swelling his ranks with all these soldiers he's conscripting. You have a wizard willing to fight. You allowed everyone else here to fight with the understanding that their safety was on their own head. Why change the rules for him?" Duke pointed to Tynan. "We need him as much as he wants to join. It isn't as if we have more appealing options."

Sydney winced. It was the blunt truth.

"I absolve you of any and all blame if something happens to me," Tynan assured.

"Your family won't."

"Burn the body, then. They'll simply think I disappeared. The great Bram Rion has ways to protect his precious reputation, I have no doubt. But don't exclude me because you're afraid of an old man like my grandfather."

Oh, that was ugly. Animosity was thick in the air.

Marrok stood suddenly, clutching the hilt of his sword, always strapped about his hips. "Have you brought your wand?"

Tynan looked at Marrok as if he'd gone mad. "I never go anywhere without it."

With a quick nod, his long, dark hair brushing his shoulders, Marrok said, "Come with us. I will test your fighting prowess, and Bram, your magical skills. If you have aptitude, mayhap you can join. Bram?"

Bram's face told Sydney that he didn't like being boxed into a corner, but saw the logic. "If you possess skill with a wand and can demonstrate the ability to learn human combat, I'll consider it."

Tynan nodded eagerly. Bram shot Marrok a rancorous glare and followed him. A moment later, the back door slammed. Duke rose next and crossed the room, exiting after them. Then Ice. Olivia and Sabelle followed.

Suddenly, Caden and Sydney found themselves alone. She rose and took a few steps toward the hall—until Caden wrapped his hand around her arm and pulled her back.

She whirled to him, certain that what was about to happen would make a great story. "I want to see what happens next."

"And I don't want you involved any deeper."

She had always been independent, and that would never change. Besides, while this was a story that could make her, it was one people should read as well.

"Unlike you, I'm not one to bury my head in the sand." Sydney jerked her arm free and turned to stomp away.

He grabbed her arm again. "What does that bloody mean?"

"These people need you. And you plan to turn your back on them because you think it's not your fight? I never knew Marines were afraid."

Caden's blue eyes narrowed. "Is that what you think? I'm not afraid of fighting. If I survived two tours in Iraq, I can survive this, I assure you."

"Then explain why you won't fight with your people."

His grip loosened, and he pulled away. "I left England and everyone magical I knew at eighteen. All this wand waving and the like, it isn't normal."

"Normal? You've already transitioned. You can't change that. What magickind can do is so extraordinary . . . amazing. Humans would kill to have your abilities. A gift like yours can help take down a madman. And you want to walk away from it?"

He crossed his arms over his chest, mouth thin with anger. "Why don't you want to follow your parents and join the academic crowd?"

Sydney hesitated. "I just didn't. It didn't fit me."

"Precisely!" Caden threw his hands wide.

If anyone tried to force her into that tediously dull and pretentious academic scene, they'd have to drag her kicking and screaming. She didn't fit there. Square peg, round hole. But this wasn't about a career. This was his heritage! She sensed Caden's reticence was deep.

He wasn't being completely honest with her. Given that, how could he possibly claim she was important? He'd demonstrated that he felt responsible for her, but his unwillingness to truly share himself said he didn't love her. And it hurt.

"They need you," she said quietly.

He shook his head. "They need someone passionate about their cause. That isn't me."

"What's the real reason?" She should bloody stop trying to make him share himself, but she kept hoping.

Caden recoiled. "I don't want to discuss it."

He didn't trust her, not with his story, not with his secrets. Not with his heart. And he didn't care for her enough to try. She had no one to blame but herself. Bloody stupid impulse to write in the book.

"I can't make you. It's simply . . . Bram and the others won't survive without able wizards on their side."

Caden closed his eyes, and Sydney almost regretted her words . . . almost. But she couldn't skirt the truth. Even if he didn't want to hear it, he belonged here. He was a wizard. By virtue of his brother's illness and his sister-in-law's rape, he had a stake in this fight. Heck, she barely knew Anka and had never seen Lucan, but already her heart went out to them. And for the people who had tried to help Aquarius, she resolved to help however she could.

Caden shrugged his shoulders uncomfortably. "More Tynans will appear at Bram's door as word inevitably spreads."

She hoped so. "Why doesn't everyone know about Mathias and the Doomsday Brethren?" Sydney anchored a hand on her hip. "I gather Bram wants to keep the Doomsday Brethren hush-hush from the Council so he can operate without their interference, but Tynan has only heard whispers of Mathias's return. And people are being attacked. What's going on?"

Caden pinched the bridge of his nose. "Bram sits on the magical Council that governs magickind. There are seven councilmen in total. Tynan O'Shea's grandfather is among them. Bram has pushed to advise magickind about Mathias, but the rest of the Council are controlling bastards who prefer to pretend problems don't exist. Bram wants a transcast. It's a television-like broadcast using magical mirrors, for lack of a better description. They were established for just such emergencies."

"And the Council said no?" Sydney's jaw dropped.

"They don't see this as an emergency. Some even write off the 'problem' as pranksters stirring up trouble for the sport of scaring people."

"That's insane! If they had seen Anka's condition . . . the poor woman could barely speak coherently when I first met her. And this Auropha woman; Mathias *killed* her. Hardly a prank!"

"Despite the fact Auropha MacKinnett's father sat on the Council and the girl was murdered by Mathias, the Council won't budge. Bram says they are a traditional lot. I think they're afraid."

"Magickind should know. This is censorship! And very dangerous to people caught unaware. I want to talk to Bram." The first item on her agenda was the thing she excelled at most. "Everyone must know about Mathias so they can protect themselves."

He frowned. "Why do you want to talk to Bram?"

"I've never done a . . . what did you call it? Transcast. But I *am* a reporter. In an emergency, I don't have to be magical or entertaining, just informational."

He leaned in with a scowl. "You want to transcast to magickind?"

"It's the only way I can help. I'll never learn to fight or be able to wave a wand. But by God, I can keep people informed."

Caden knew his mouth gaped open. *Did Sydney have any notion of the target she'd be painting on herself if she transcasted?* All of magickind would see her face. Especially Mathias. No one he attacked put up a fight, because they were unprepared. And for breaking that secrecy, he'd want her dead. Caden couldn't help but admire her courage and willingness but . . .

"No. Absolutely not."

"It's not your choice, Caden. You'll be returning to Dallas alone, remember?"

She brushed past him out the dining room and into the hall. She was headed to the back door, where she'd join all the others and embroil herself deeper into this morass. He'd failed Lucan with his inability to return Anka. He'd failed Anka by letting her slip through his fingers. He would not fail Sydney by letting her place herself in mortal danger. Even if he couldn't mate with her, the thought of her dying . . . it flattened his soul.

Caden stalked into the hall, then grabbed her arm. "You cannot do this. The fact I'm not staying doesn't bloody mean I don't care."

"No, the fact you won't be honest about your reasons for avoiding magic tells me you don't."

Damn, the woman was too bloody smart by half. He grabbed her shoulders and brought her against him. "I won't see you hurt or worse."

"You may be comfortable retreating, but I'm not. I can help. There's nothing I can do for Aquarius, but I can try to make certain no one else suffers her fate. Or Anka's. Since you and I are through, and you're unwilling to stay and fight Mathias or fight for us, we have nothing to say."

A tennis-ball–sized lump of apprehension stuck in his throat. After a few days here, she didn't have a proper grasp on magickind's real peril. He had to stop her. If he failed . . . the thought of Mathias hurting her was so painful, he nearly staggered to his knees.

"The hell we don't!"

She glanced at him over her shoulder, those arrow-sharp eyes of hers piercing him with fire. Her red hair floated around her shoulders, curled halfway down her back. Even in anger, she was a beauty. He couldn't let her talk Bram into a transcast. It would mean her death.

Pumped full of protective fury, Caden charged after Sydney and scooped her up against him, lifting her off her feet to carry her into the nearest room with a closed door, the library.

Sydney wriggled and grunted in frustration. "Put me down, damn you!"

Lightning tore through him as she moved against him. But despite his hunger for her, they had to talk. She had to see reason, damn it.

He plopped her on Bram's plush sofa, and she sprawled out beneath him, eyes spitting fury. Desire sparked in his veins. Everything inside him tensed as he tried to ignore it.

"Let me be very clear, Sydney: You are not transcasting."

She scoffed. "I'm a grown woman who makes her own decisions. Besides, how will you stop me once you're gone?"

Her challenge hit him like a hammer. She was right. If he found Anka and righted Lucan's life and departed, Sydney would be left to her own devices.

Not bloody likely.

"Until you realize the folly of your idea, I'm not going anywhere. In fact, I'll be staying very close to you."

Sydney raised a ginger brow. "Go away."

Her dismissal riled his mating instinct and urge to protect. The human signs of her arousal exploded across his brain—her peachy-floral scent, peaked nipples, the heat in her eyes.

Caden shook his head. "I'll remain so close you'll feel my breath on the back of your neck. Constantly."

She stilled, her breath turning rougher. "I don't need a babysitter."

"No, you need a keeper, and I'm him."

With an outraged gasp, she began squirming, trying to worm free. Her arching and bucking inflamed already sizzling nerves.

"Stop it!" He clamped his hands on her hips to still her.

"Make me."

Her dare went straight to his core. Heat bolted through him, and instinct overruled logic. *Mine. Take. Now!*

Breathing hard, he fitted his body completely over hers until their lips were inches apart. The temptation of her little red mouth was right under his, and the urge to taste it for the first time nearly consumed him. *Just once . . .*

One kiss would be the nail in his coffin. *Would it be so bad?* A needling voice in his head asked the insidious question. What if they mated and she transcasted and he lost her? He would become a carbon copy of his brother. She was so intent on slaying the evil she didn't understand, it would kill her.

The thought made him grab her tighter, as if he could take every part of her into him and keep her safe. His body pulsed, electric. She was so warm and vital and female, and he needed her with a desperation that bordered insanity.

Trailing kisses across her cheek, he dared to brush the corner of her mouth. The sweet scent of her nearly overcame him. He grabbed the edge of the sofa in one hand, her hip in the other, barely restraining the urge to devour every part of her with his mouth. Determined to distract them both, he kissed his way down her throat, down to the soft skin above her breasts, rising and falling rapidly.

"Caden, this is insane. We should talk." Smart words, but her voice was breathy.

"We did."

Shoving her T-shirt aside, he inhaled deeply. Since transition, his sense of smell was keener. Though he knew she'd showered since they'd last made love, he smelled himself on her, and it aroused him out of his mind. Skin. He needed her bare skin—against his hands and his tongue.

"But—"

Caden wrapped his fingers around the clasp of her bra and yanked. It snapped into pieces. When he laved her nipple with his tongue, Sydney moaned, and he smiled in satisfaction. She couldn't deny that she wanted him. Her breathing, accelerated heartbeat, alluring smell, fingernails in his shoulders—all told him the truth.

"Damn it, how do you reduce me to a puddle in moments?" she panted.

"You do the same to me."

With a quick yank, he doffed his shirt, then tugged hers over her head. Thank God she was wearing a flowing skirt, which was blessedly easy to flip up. The knickers beneath provided no barrier for his insistent hands. Next thing he knew, he had his fingers buried between her slick folds, counting the seconds until his cock could replace them.

The feel of her enticed him—her little pebbled coral-pink nipples, the way she wrapped her fists in his hair and looked at him as if his touch was her whole world. Wriggling his fingers inside her, he felt her sweet spot, massaged it. She gasped, climbing closer, closer to the edge of pleasure.

Extracting his fingers, he brushed the wet tip of her clit gently, a slow, maddening caress that had her whimpering and calling his name. And he loved it, needing her to need him. As he needed her.

After making quick work of his button and zip, he shoved his jeans past his hips and spread her thighs wider.

"Caden, wait," she panted. "We haven't settled the matter."

"Do you truly want to stop?" If she said yes, it would kill him, but he would get up. Zip up. Walk away.

Time ceased. Sydney hesitated. A dozen seconds or more passed in silence. That answered his question . . . not that he blamed her. Caden caressed her cheek, smoothed his thumb over her brow, then made to rise.

She tightened her arms around him. "I'll likely regret this later, but stay."

Caden smiled. Even while his logical mind was screaming that he was playing with fire, the reckless side of him was looking forward to the burn.

Wrapping his arms around Sydney, he gathered her up, lifting her hips to him. He paused to worship one breast with his mouth, then the other. She wrapped her legs around him and tried to urge him higher up her body, inside her. She didn't have to invite him twice.

"Are you still sore?" When he'd touched her, she'd felt swollen.

"A bit . . . but not enough to stop you."

Resolving to be gentle, he positioned himself at her entrance and pressed slowly. Beneath him, she tensed by degrees, and he withdrew slightly. When she relaxed, he edged forward, deeper, then back out when her body objected. Back and forth, back and forth. Seconds turned to minutes, and still he wasn't completely inside her. His eyes were about to cross from the tight, wet friction of her around him—along with the mingling of their scents.

There. Finally, he was as deep as possible. Sydney was heaven, and he intended to enjoy every inch of her now, while she was all his.

She laid a series of kisses on his cheek, his throat, his shoulder, as he buried his face in her fragrant neck and gently thrust. Immediately, he groaned. Something was happening here; something new, more intense. Amazing.

A deep breath in, out, as he pushed deeper, easing inside her again. Another need, a dangerous one, rose up. He bit his tongue, squinting hard against the urge, but once the words scorched his brain, he couldn't stop.

"Become a part of me, as I become a part of you . . ."

Sydney, flushed and damp, looked up at him with those big chocolate eyes. A coy smile curved her lips. "I think you have."

He tried to clamp his jaw shut, keep the other words in.

"In fact, I know you are," she murmured, moving with him. "And I love it."

Damn, that wasn't helping his restraint. Caden picked up the pace, sliding inside her with more urgency. The desire and the need to speak the Call were gaining steam, colliding in his head, coiling together in his belly. The need swelled, more than pleasure, more than emotion. Belonging. A desire to claim.

The next words slipped out. "Ever after, I promise—"

Before he could finish the sentence, Sydney moaned, tightening around him, her sex beginning to pulse in a way no man, wizard or otherwise, could resist.

I promise myself to thee.

With a guttural shout, ecstasy congealed deep inside him. He roared as pleasure shot through his body like a supernova.

Each day we share, I will be honest, good, and true. If this you seek, heed my call . . .

As he held her against him, the sense that she was meant for him clogged his throat, filled his chest. Frightening. Intense. Impossible.

Inevitable? Magic wasn't choosing a mate for him. It wasn't going to rule him or ruin her. Still, this felt like more than magic. Instinct aside, he liked her grit and determination, respected her intelligence. Her sassy mouth made him hard. If he'd remained human and been choosing a wife, he suspected he'd pursue Sydney to the ends of the earth.

Now, he couldn't think about that. He had another objective: to prevent her from transcasting. Once accomplished and Lucan's life was fixed, he'd be back in Texas with the Doomsday Brethren in his proverbial rearview mirror.

But what do I have to return to? Disturbed by the question, Caden withdrew, stood, righted his jeans, then looked at Sydney, all flushed and disheveled and gorgeous.

He found himself saying, "I promise . . ."

The Mating Call clogged his throat. Instead, he shook his head, then took a step back. "I promise to do everything in my power to keep you from transcasting. And to protect you. I can't let you get more involved with magickind. I'll be watching."

CHAPTER FOURTEEN

A HALF HOUR LATER, Bram crashed through the back door. Tynan came next, with Marrok following behind, slapping him on the back and smiling. Just like that, the new bloke had been accepted. The lot of them looked *smug*.

Already on edge from his encounter with Sydney in the library, Caden stared, anger he didn't understand slicing through his gut. So Bram had found a new warrior with no battle experience or training. Caden crossed his arms over his chest. He wasn't one of the Doomsday Brethren, so he shouldn't care that Bram had chosen someone so untried. In fact, he should be thrilled that Bram had already added his replacement to the ranks. Or he would be, once his mood improved.

Olivia filed in next, then Sabelle, the wind tugging at her blond curls. Ice followed close behind, his green eyes glued to the gorgeous witch like he wanted to swallow her whole. She tossed a long glance over her shoulder, until Duke entered and shut the door behind him.

Behind Caden, Sydney marched down the stairs. When he'd been changing into all black to resume his search for Anka, Sydney had gone upstairs, likely checked on Aquarius, and showered.

Now, she walked past him, a siren to his senses. He wanted her again—and not just sexually. Being near her soothed and fired him at once.

Denying her and his feelings would be much easier if he didn't suspect that he loved every stubborn, passionate inch of her. So he could not continue this . . . thing with Sydney. He could only stop her plans to transcast before she entangled herself more deeply in magickind, keep his mouth shut and his trousers zipped.

At the moment, she was clearly avoiding him, hovering in the doorway to the library, never looking in his direction. Not that he was surprised. He'd seen the hurt on her face, and he hated himself for it. But he simply wasn't the crusader she was. He'd been burned by magic as a kid, suffered loss after loss as a Marine. Staying here, taking the chance to get close to her—everyone, really—in the middle of this war was a recipe for insanity. He refused to drink the Kool-Aid.

Grasping her arm, he stopped her and murmured, "Please drop this transcasting idea."

She yanked free of his grip and crossed her arms over her chest. "Please stop hiding from me and yourself."

Direct never worked with Sydney. She gave as good as she got. *Maybe another tactic.* "I know you're frustrated with me for many reasons. I'm sorry. But you can't protect yourself during this war, and I don't want to see you hurt."

The uber-bitch façade dropped, and she looked at him as if he was ripping her heart out. Seeing her hold back tears was a pick axe to his chest.

"I can't sit about and do nothing. If you cared for me at all, you'd understand that."

"Firecracker, it's because I care that I can't let you," he said, voice low.

She arched an auburn brow at him. "You never asked me what *I* wanted. What *I* was willing to risk? You assumed that, like you, I shouldn't risk anything. You're not even being honest about why you won't permanently join Bram. So I'm not surprised that you can't be honest with me about your feelings."

Before he could reply, Bram and the others spilled into the hallway. Caden bit his tongue, wanting to tell her there was so much she didn't understand. But even if she did, Sydney still wouldn't comprehend not diving in with total passion. Despite what had happened to Anka, she still insisted on doing what she believed was right. He'd known soldiers who prayed for such courage. She both amazed and terrified him.

"We're going to brief Tynan on Mathias's attacks and any other relevant information. Joining us?" Bram asked.

Caden shook his head. "I'm searching for Anka. My brother isn't improving, despite Sabelle's efforts."

Bram hesitated. "Yet."

"Can you spare anyone to help me?" He glanced over to Tynan, who was still wearing an eternal glower. Something inside him twinged when he saw how naturally the O'Shea bloke fit in with the others. Even after weeks, Caden almost always felt like an outsider. But Tynan had melded with the group after less than an hour. "Or do you no longer need me now that you have someone new?"

Bram frowned. "We need every hand we can get. You and I have had our differences, but we share a common goal: doing what's best for Lucan."

"As long as that doesn't interfere with your war."

Nodding, Bram didn't make any apologies. "It can't. Will you stay and fight? I'll send the others out with you tonight, regardless. After that I have to devote all the resources I can to defeating Mathias if you won't remain."

They had planned the attack on Mathias's compound. As soon as Shock surfaced again, they'd finish their plans and implement. He didn't want to tie himself any closer to magic than necessary, but what if Anka had been recaptured? Could he let this opportunity pass?

"Yes," he muttered.

Bram smiled. "Until then."

"In the meantime, she has nothing to say that you should hear." Caden pointed at Sydney. "Are we clear?"

"Damn you!" Sydney spat.

Bram fought a smile. "Indeed."

Then the wizard turned away, gesturing to Tynan to enter his office. Marrok followed, closing the door behind them. The feeling that they were shutting him out intensified. Foolish, since he hadn't wished to join in the first place.

"Where to?" Ice asked, slipping on a pair of leather gloves to ward off the November chill.

Caden had no idea.

Standing alone in the hall, Sydney huffed at the closed doors. All the men were now gone. Not only had Caden cut off her access to Bram, he'd abandoned her again—after trying to tell her what to do. Bloody prat!

It was stupid that magickind knew nothing of their worst enemy returning from exile to wreak havoc on them all. They should be informed not only of the truth, but of safety precautions, ways to reach out in case they were attacked, who to contact in the event of a Mathias sighting. Something.

Thinking about that almost kept her mind off Caden and the fact he wanted her body and sought to protect her, but held back from truly being with her. *What was in his head?* She'd chalk it up to a typical fear of commitment, but he wasn't entirely immune to her emotionally. There was some . . . tug between them. Or had her entries in the diary created some artificial emotions in him?

With a sigh, she left Aquarius lying amid fresh ice packs and meandered into the library. It looked different with the lights blazing. Sabelle and Olivia now occupied the sofa. Did they have any notion what she and Caden had been doing there an hour ago?

"I didn't until you thought about it," Sabelle said with a teasing smile. "Join us?"

Aquarius was resting, and Sydney had set aside the loads of notes about her story. She could do something now if she could talk to Bram or his sister. "Thank you."

With a nod and a smile, Sabelle gestured to Sydney to sit in a nearby chair. As she did, the witch said, "Talk to me about what?"

"A way I can help magickind. Caden is furious, and may . . . I don't know, paralyze my mouth if I say this, but—"

She burst out laughing. "Caden is out, so he can't overhear."

True, but that worried Sydney as well. For all anyone knew, Mathias could be searching for Anka. If he was, if Caden found both of them and there was trouble. . . . She worried about him, too. But she hadn't tried to prohibit *him* from doing what he must.

"Caden, Ice, and Duke are large wizards. Experienced fighters. Mathias is currently weak," Sabelle said.

"But they're all helping." Even if Caden didn't want to. "Caden expects me to do nothing but cower in the name of safety."

"Wizards can be overprotective," Sabelle added. "My brother epitomizes that."

"Amen," Olivia added. "I love Marrok—most days. Then he brings on the 'me big warrior, you little woman' attitude. I have to remind him that I'm not playing that game."

Sydney smiled. She could actually see the little brunette standing up to her massive husband, and him backing down . . . eventually. He loved her to distraction; even Sydney had noticed. And she was green with envy.

Caden had his moments. While making love to her earlier today, he said something more romantic and poetic than any man had ever said to her. *Become a part of me, as I become a part of you . . .*

"He said *what*?" Sabelle demanded.

Wincing, Sydney flushed red. "Sorry. I need to keep my thoughts to myself."

Sabelle waved away her apology. "He said, 'Become a part of me, as I become a part of you'?"

"Yes."

The blond witch and Olivia exchanged a glance. Uh oh, something was afoot.

"Is that a problem?"

Sabelle hesitated. "Did he say anything after that?"

Sydney scanned her memory. " 'Ever after, I promise—' then he stopped and turned into an overbearing lout."

Sabelle's raised brow and another look at Olivia said she understood. Good. Perhaps the witch could enlighten her.

"Indeed," Sabelle said. "When a wizard takes a mate—a wife, in human terms—he speaks words. A Mating Call. What Caden said begins the wizard's vow to his mate. Not the overbearing lout bit, though that comes with the territory."

Heart beating in triple time, Sydney gasped. "So he speaks those words and poof, we're mated? For life?"

"Not quite that simple, no. You have to answer his Call."

"And then?"

"You're mates for up to a thousand years. No worrying about picking the right china pattern."

A proposal and a wedding all at once. Efficient. Had Caden really meant to "propose" to her, or had that been the diary's influence?

"I'm confused. Human males can take an annoyingly long

time to decide if they're in love and want to marry. Caden
and I have known each other just over a week. I love him,
but . . . is a wizard any different than a regular man?"

Olivia snorted. "Want a list?"

Sabelle giggled. "Indeed. Magic cuts through a great
many human mating rituals. A wizard knows his mate by
taste. Instantly. One kiss, one taste of her—any fluid—and
he knows. Often, her taste compels the words immediately."
She looked behind her, ensured the door was shut, then whispered, "It happened to my brother just before Caden came
to work with you. He met a woman in a pub and brought her
here—most unlike him. By morning, they were mated, and
she had run off. Bram told me, one kiss and he could hardly
keep the words to himself."

One kiss? That explained so much. And it nearly crushed
her. "Caden has never kissed me. I thought maybe he wasn't
the kissing sort or something. So often, we were rushed or
he was frenzied." Sydney flushed, realizing how much of her
personal life she was spilling. "But he never tasted me in any
way. Why would he think I'm his mate?"

"Instinct. It would tell him eventually. A kiss would tell
him more quickly."

From the first, he'd been avoiding locking lips with her. Pain
stabbed her chest, shattered her heart. She couldn't breathe,
couldn't swallow. Tears were an ice pick in the back of her eyes.
She tried to keep them in, but they fell anyway. Caden had
squashed his instinct once he'd suspected she was his mate.

Or was she? Maybe writing her sexual fantasies of him
in that bloody book had wrought some lust cloud that
prompted those mating words. Maybe he hadn't finished
them because he hadn't meant them.

"If he spoke even a few of the words, he knows," Sabelle
assured.

"That *I'm* his mate?"

"Yep," Olivia added. "No doubt that scares the crap out of him. In case you haven't clued in, he doesn't want to be here and doesn't want anything to do with magic."

"I gathered." And it was tearing them apart.

"Sorry." Sympathy softened Sabelle's face.

Sydney bit her lip, but knew she had to ask the question. "Is there any chance he feels this way because I wrote about him in that red book? Twice?"

Sabelle and Olivia both stilled.

"What did you write?" Olivia asked.

How to put this delicately without sounding sex starved?

With a smile, Sabelle said, "Did you ask to be his mate forever or for the night?"

"Just the night," she assured.

"We really don't know," Olivia finally said. "But probably not. Our theory is that the diary grants one's true desire if you write it, and that you must have enough passion and power to make it come true. But it's only a theory."

She sniffed at her tears, wishing she had more answers. "Do you have a book that describes this mating ritual?"

"Absolutely. Feel free to take anything in the library you want. Bram and I have been adding to the family collection like mad of late. Fiction is in that corner." She pointed to the far left. "The rest is nonfiction. Human history, science, technology, et cetera, on the near left. The right and back wall are all magical tomes. What you want will be there. Let me know if you need help."

Sydney's ears perked up. She'd wandered the library once, but the number of books had been overwhelming. She could arm herself with information and occupy her maudlin thoughts by tackling the article about magickind once it was safe—but more information would help.

"Bram will never let you print such an article," Sabelle vowed. "But as long as you're going to stay among us, you should have more information." She rose to her feet and headed for the library door. "Night."

She'd argue with Bram about the article later.

Olivia followed behind Sabelle, but paused in the doorway. "Marrok will likely be hours with Bram and Tynan. If you want someone to talk to, I'm here. I know what it's like to be among all these guys and have no idea what's going on. I've recently been through the mating thing, so . . ."

She appreciated the other women, really. But she wanted to read up so she could verbally skewer Caden when he returned. She would also wait for Bram's meeting to end so she could talk to him about transcasting. The issue of her article for *Out of This Realm* aside, magickind needed information. And dangerous or not, she was the woman to give it to them.

Sydney awoke suddenly, head tilted awkwardly onto the arm of the sofa, a book still open in her lap, a terrible cramp in her neck—and the magical Mating Call running through her head.

Noises sounded just outside the door. Loud ones. Shouting. Marching. Good God, what time was it? Judging from the weakness of the sunlight outside the northern window, it was early.

With a frown and a pull at her sore neck, Sydney rose and approached the library door. Someone had closed it during the night. The voices streaming down the stairs and in the hall were slightly muffled, but emphatic.

"You're certain?" Bram asked in clipped, authoritative tones.

"Indeed. Saw him myself." Duke. No mistaking that quiet

upper-crust speech. The man scarcely ever raised his voice; as if he expected his words to be obeyed, so didn't bother shouting.

"Splendid. Shock returned five minutes ago. Let me see . . ."

Bram's voice trailed off. Pounding footsteps.

What the devil is going on?

Sydney opened the library door and peeked into the hall. There Duke stood, wearing chocolate trousers and a pristine white shirt, both meticulously pressed. He had wide shoulders and a perfect patrician profile. In a glance, she could see why he was one of England's most eligible bachelors. Funny that few humans knew just how special he was.

A moment later, Bram emerged from his office, Shock in tow.

"Where is Zain?" the tough guy growled.

"Below," said the blond wizard. Despite his disheveled hair, rumpled striped shirt and designer jeans, he maintained that air of authority.

Now if she could just figure out what they were talking about, she'd be loads happier.

"Let me go down," Shock said.

Bram shook his head. "I want to hear where you've bloody been. And he shouldn't see you here. Let Duke get him. We'll need him upstairs anyway."

Shock ground his jaw and crossed his arms, looking quite brassed off. Sydney wondered why. He'd been absent of late. Was he angry that Bram had tracked him down? Or because the Doomsday Brethren's leader demanded a command performance at some ungodly hour of the morning?

After a quick gesture to Duke, who acknowledged with a nod, Bram turned back to Shock. "While we're waiting, want to tell me where you've been these past days? Bloody hard to plan an attack on the enemy when your only spy doesn't see fit to appear."

Sydney smothered a gasp with her hand. They were planning to attack Mathias? Sabelle said they had information that the evil wizard was weak now. It would make sense.

"You summoned me before the sun rose to interrogate me? I'm not at your beck and call."

Bram crossed his arms over his chest. Though Shock was both taller and bigger, Bram carried a knowledge and a lethal aura that even Shock, with those dark sunglasses, couldn't miss.

"So you only answer to Mathias, then?"

"Do you doubt that I have to make my loyalty look real?" Shock tensed, then cursed. "I explained all this. Are you a simpleton?"

Tapping his toe, Bram paused for a long moment. "Simpleton, no. Suspicious, always. Your family reputation isn't the best, Shock. Your parents were rabid Mathias supporters. Your brother still is. When you disappear for days at a time with no communication, I'd be a fool not to wonder if you were really spying on our side for Mathias, rather than the other way around."

A double agent? Sydney's eyes widened. She could completely understand Bram's skepticism. He hardly struck her as Mr. Upstanding.

Suddenly, the object of her thoughts turned his head and looked in her direction. She suspected he was looking right at her, but with those sunglasses, she couldn't be certain. Still, a flush of embarrassment crept up her body, to her face, heating her cheeks. *Bugger!*

"I would hardly call you upstanding, either, considering you're eavesdropping and have been since I joined this conversation."

"Shock, go to my office. Zain shouldn't see you here now. We'll finish this chat in a bit." As Shock groused, Bram turned to her with a scowl and a raised brow. "You've no need to know Doomsday Brethren business. It's not for you to print in your newspaper. These warriors could die if you leak information."

She would never intentionally hurt anyone, but inadvertently she already had. Shame smote Sydney. She understood now how people could die. Bram had no reason to believe that she wanted to help them. But she had to try.

"I'm not listening so that I can steal information for my next story. I'm willing to put that aside and help. When Mr. O'Shea arrived last night, I realized that magickind knows nothing about Mathias's return. I want to help resolve that. I'm an experienced journalist. I've done more than work for a tabloid. I interned at the BBC for a summer, so I can—"

"This is the 'nothing' Caden didn't want me to discuss with you, I presume?"

"Precisely."

"Even if I believed you, it's not that simple. The Council is against notifying the public."

Suddenly, the front door slammed. Tynan O'Shea stood in front of the portal. "And people are dying for that stubborn stupidity. The Pullmans would still be a whole family today if someone had advised them that Mathias had come back with both barrels loaded and in search of Privileged families to destroy. The men killed, the women murdered or taken, the children sliced in two—all of it avoidable. Stop being a bloody coward. You joined that group of codgers on the Council to be its future. Start acting like it now."

"I started the Doomsday Brethren under the Council's nose. If they so much as catch a breath of the fact I've begun an army to counter Mathias, do you think for an instant I'd retain my Council seat? Who would they replace me with? Someone whose mind is more like theirs. That would not benefit us or magickind. We must lay low and think smart until they'll admit what's in front of them."

Magical politics? Fascinating. Sydney couldn't take it in fast enough. How amazing to be one of the few humans to know about this world within a world. Even more amazing to be in a position to help, because despite what Bram said, she thought magickind deserved the truth.

"What about the next family that's attacked?" she asked Bram. "And the one after that? If a few words via transcast might save them, then why not—"

"Who told you about that?"

"Doesn't matter. I'm volunteering. Just show me what to do. No one has to know you're involved. *I* want to do it."

Bram sent her an incredulous stare. "Do you understand the incredible danger you'll be in? Mathias and every Anarki scum will hunt you until you're caught. They are banking on the Council being useless and paralyzed by their fear."

"So if you want to win this war, why give them the very thing they need to flourish?"

"She has a point," Duke said, dragging a bedraggled figure behind him.

The tall figure had long hair and a T-shirt that said *Do Not Disturb. I'm Disturbed Enough Already.* His head popped back when Duke yanked on his hair. Zain!

Well, clearly the T-shirt was appropriate.

"We'll talk about this later," Bram barked.

At least it isn't a no. Close, but Sydney hoped he'd come around.

"Well, if it isn't Privileged's poster boy," Zain sneered at Bram.

"It's better than raping women and killing children."

"Can I kill him?" Tynan asked.

"No. We need him at the moment." Then Bram turned to Zain, stepping closer. "You're going to perform the *helbresele* spell."

That healing spell Sabelle had spoken of earlier?

If Zain hadn't had his hands tied behind his back, he would have assuredly crossed his arms over his chest in defiance. "If I expended the energy necessary to injure someone, why would I bother to bestow a healing spell on them?"

The sod's flippant tone made Sydney furious.

"Because I said so," Bram snarled. "And if you don't . . ." The wizard glanced toward the door, then smiled. "Do you remember Auropha MacKinnett?"

Nodding, Zain added, "I abducted her straight from her bed. The Privileged bitch gave Mathias enough power with her lovely screams to last days. But I can't heal her now. Very dead. So sorry."

"Bastard!" Tynan charged toward Zain.

Bram held up a hand. It wasn't the gesture that stopped him as much as some invisible restraint. O'Shea snarled and scowled, but Bram didn't budge. Zain, however, stared warily at the grieving man, who was more muscular and more enraged. Tynan's gray eyes said he'd rip the man limb from limb, given half the chance.

"If you don't cooperate," Bram began. "I'll be happy to tie you down and let Auropha's mate-to-be avenge her in any way he pleases. Don't think anyone will mourn you, you sodding little shit."

"How does threatening murder make you any better than Mathias?"

Bram cocked his head. "I view your extermination as preventive maintenance. If you choose not to cooperate, then I'll make certain you can't harm anyone else. We all know you attack those who can't fight back, mostly women. If you want to fight a man your size or better, at least it's fair. But a woman? Is that what it takes for you to feel manly?"

"Piss off." Zain flushed an angry red.

Tynan charged toward Zain again, barely held in check by a force Sydney couldn't see.

Over his shoulder, Zain stared at Tynan, who itched for the opportunity to inflict damage.

"Pick," Bram demanded. "Tynan O'Shea or the *helbresele* spell?"

"And that's a healing spell?" she asked. "For Aquarius?"

"Yes," Duke answered softly. "Since he inflicted the damage, only he can repair it."

"And it will cost him a great deal of his energy," Bram explained with a smile. "Nearly everything he has."

Aquarius! The man could heal her friend? Sydney wanted badly to plead with Zain to help. But she felt certain that her pleas would give him pleasure, especially when he denied them. She bit her lip and stayed mute.

"So," Bram said. "What's it going to be? Healing and a new beginning? Or certain death? Choose wisely and choose now."

Chapter Fifteen

Sensing that he was both outnumbered and in danger, Zain agreed to heal Aquarius. Caden still wasn't certain how such a thing worked. Everyday magic he'd been unable to avoid as a child, but this more complicated life-and-death magic was all new to him.

As they made their way upstairs, Bram and Duke prodded Zain. The new bloke, Tynan, growled threats behind him. Caden looked over at Sydney. She was pale but her dark eyes reflected her determination and optimism. He knew exactly how she felt, hoping the magical cure would work. For her sake, he prayed she got the happy ending for her friend that he hadn't gotten for Westin and still needed for Lucan.

As they awaited Aquarius's fate, Caden reached across the space between them and took her hand. They'd had their differences, but at this moment they didn't matter.

Instantly, she whipped her gaze to him. Naked pain and uncertainty showed behind her calm facade, nearly undoing him. He wanted to hold her, bring her close, and assure her all would be well. But he wasn't certain of that at all.

Instead, he murmured, "Squeeze my hand if you need me."

With a shaky nod, she turned and followed the procession up the stairs to the bedroom in which Aquarius rested. Inside the cool, shadowed room, everyone fanned out around the bed where the little woman lay, still bloated and red, lips cracked. Sabelle had removed her clothes and dressed her in a feather-light cotton gown. Aquarius's eyes remained closed, her breathing slightly labored.

Bram drew his wand and held it at Zain. "Go on."

Zain growled at them both, then caught Sydney's gaze. Tears streamed down her face, and she clutched Caden's hand. His heart lifted. She'd come to him for support, trusted him to care for her. Caressing the soft crown of her fiery hair, he squeezed her hand in return.

Behind her, Sabelle patted her shoulder. Standing beside Marrok on the opposite side of the bed, Olivia gave her a reassuring smile.

Tynan shoved Zain closer to Aquarius.

"How does this work?" she whispered to Caden.

"I've never heard of it. But Bram made it sound common enough, so . . ."

Sydney exhaled, clearly trying to calm herself. Caden wanted to reassure her that if Zain did anything more to hurt Aquarius, Bram would let Tynan at him. But he didn't want to say it out loud and give the Denzell bastard any ideas.

Zain finally stepped forward, leaning over the bed, and reached for Aquarius.

With a ruthless grip on his arm, Bram stayed the other wizard.

"I have to hold her against me," Zain explained.

Bram released Zain slowly. "One wrong move, and I swear, I'll have no compunction about making certain your family needs tweezers to pick up your remains."

Sneering, Zain turned back to Aquarius. He sat on the bed beside her and pulled her awkwardly into his lap, bringing her small breasts against his chest. Her hair drifted down to his thighs. Her arms hung limply from her shoulders. Zain took in a deep breath and closed his eyes.

His arms tightened around her, then began to shake. He drew in a sharp breath, his eyes popping wide open as if stunned. Caden could see whites all around the dark irises.

Tighter and tighter, Sydney squeezed his hand. The air thickened with tension and fear. He could smell the worry pouring off Sydney and wished he could do more.

Seconds dragged by, one after the other, and still Aquarius sagged against Zain, unmoving, seemingly not breathing. His whole body began to shake. Sweat rolled in fat drops down his forehead and temples. His face turned ghostly white.

Suddenly, he released Aquarius, collapsing back to the bed. Bram rushed forward. She fell face first in a heap across him. Sabelle elbowed her way between Tynan and Sydney, who let go of Caden's hand and tried to dart to the bed. He held her back.

"Let them," Caden whispered. "Just in case it's a trick."

"She's my friend," she cried. "If anything happens . . ."

Tears took over then, and Caden's heart broke for her. Since meeting her, he'd been dazzled by her beauty and smarts. Her moxie and dedication had impressed the hell out of him as well, even if, at times, they scared him. For days, she'd been tending Aquarius's injuries. Sydney's incredible loyalty and love made him want her all the more. Magic aside, it was no wonder he was falling in love with her.

Caden closed his eyes. This wasn't the time or place—Sydney was hurting. But what a fucking cosmic joke that he should finally meet a woman he adored, only for her to become entangled in the very world he despised.

Gently, Bram rolled Aquarius over, easing her away from Zain. Neither stirred. "Aquarius?" Bram called. "Can you hear me?"

Still nothing.

Sydney looked about her with a desperate glance. "Can anyone else help her? A bit of magic and—"

"Sorry." Bram's face was soft with regret. "Only the one who inflicted the hurt can heal her. Check him," Bram barked at Duke.

Hurstgrove leaned around Sabelle, who was gently brushing Aquarius's hair from her face to reveal healed skin, but an unmoving form. He waved a hand across Zain's face.

"He's out," Duke declared, pulling him to the far edge of the bed.

"Oh God." Sydney's voice trembled.

All of Zain's energy hadn't been enough to bring Aquarius around. Caden squeezed Sydney tighter. He hated to see her pain, but a part of him hoped that she'd finally accept the danger she was courting. And this was just a sliver of the possibilities. The things he'd heard about Anarki attacks in Bram's meetings these past few weeks were bone chilling. He hated using Aquarius as an illustration for Sydney, but if it got her to forget the transcasting idea, then something good would come of this tragedy.

Suddenly, a woman groaned, then coughed. It wasn't Sydney or Sabelle. Caden glanced up and saw Olivia staring wide-eyed at Aquarius. Glancing past Sabelle's bent form, he studied the delicate woman.

Slowly, she opened her green eyes. Groggy, unfocused— but awake.

"What is it?" Sydney demanded, trying to peek around the blond witch. "Tell me!"

Sabelle pulled back from Aquarius, and a last glance at the other woman's face showed her to be perfectly healthy, if still a bit red.

"See for yourself." Caden thrust Sydney toward her friend, as relief poured through him.

Sydney squealed and darted from his grasp, charging headlong toward her friend, arms open wide.

Bram thrust an arm between them, then admonished, "Gently."

With a vigorous nod, Sydney leaned carefully toward her friend, brushing her cheek. "How do you feel?"

"If I said terrible, you'd only cry more. I don't need the bad karma."

Sydney gave a watery laugh. "You scared ten years off me!"

"Can't have that. Who else will put up with me at the office?" Aquarius groaned as she leaned toward Sydney. "Where am I?"

"My home. Where do you hurt?" Sabelle asked.

Aquarius sent Sydney a quizzical glance.

"That's Sabelle. You remember Bram from my flat? This is his sister."

"The cocky one with the angry aura?"

Bram chuckled. "I bet if you look at me now, you'll find my aura much changed."

With a slow turn of her head, Aquarius stared at Bram. "You've traded anger for stress. You should learn to meditate."

"She's better already," Sydney joked, wiping tears from her cheeks.

"Get some rest," Sabelle suggested to Aquarius.

Sydney patted Aquarius's shoulder, then urged her to sit back in the bed, against the pillows.

She touched her cracked lips. "I'm dry everywhere. Water?"

Sabelle waved a hand, and instantly a cool glass of water appeared in a delicate crystal cup. "Drink."

Aquarius didn't look very surprised. "Nice trick. Thank

you." She tossed back the entire glass at once. Once finished, she handed it back to Sabelle. "So what happened to me? To say I feel run over by a train is an understatement."

"What's the last thing you recall?"

Aquarius paused. "Coming by your flat to talk to you about—" She gasped. "Has anyone found Anka yet?"

Sydney looked back. Over her shoulder, she sent Caden a silent apology, then turned back to her friend. "No. We're still looking."

"She was weak the morning she left. Talked about needing energy. I offered her green tea, but she wouldn't have it."

Caden froze. Of course, Anka had been weeks without contact from Lucan. As often as they'd tried to force feed Lucan energy, had Anka been without any contact that would build up her power? So who had she found to recharge her? Or had Mathias seized her again before she could take a lover?

Either possibility would kill his brother—if he ever emerged from this mourning.

After Sydney and Aquarius had hugged, cried, and reassured each other, Sydney listened to her friend's horrific description of Zain's torture. Seeing what Mathias and his henchmen had done to both Anka and Aquarius made Sydney more determined to help protect others. When she'd spoken to Bram earlier about transcasting, he hadn't said no. Now she was going to get assertive, Caden be damned. Why should anyone suffer because they were uninformed about the danger about to descend on their doorsteps?

Fire brewing in her belly, Sydney jogged down the stairs to find Bram. The Council was against spreading word of Mathias's return, but she knew that Bram *wanted* others to know. Was itching to tell them, in fact. She was going to help him do what he wanted to.

As soon as she entered the hallway, she heard raised voices to the left, behind closed doors. Damn and blast! They were all in Bram's office, except Caden, who'd departed with Sabelle to begin cleaning up Lucan's house.

Sydney approached the door and raised her hand to knock. Before she could, a voice boomed through the heavy wood separating her from the men, "Are you out of your bloody mind?"

Ice. The warrior everyone else believed mad. The irony of his question wasn't lost on her.

"For the first time in nearly two hundred years, we agree on something," Bram quipped.

"Are any of you sods listening to me?" Shock growled. "What are your better ideas? I can't lead you to Mathias in his lair with your hands tied and your wands confiscated. Mathias fell for that trap once, and it led to his exile."

"Aye," Marrok agreed. "We may call the man many unpleasant things, but he has never shown himself to be stupid. We cannot underestimate him. We will get but one chance to undertake a surprise attack."

"Indeed," Duke added. "Besides, if you pretend to lead us to Mathias, then we unleash our fight, he'll be suspicious of you in the future, Shock. I'm not certain that serves our long-term interests."

"But a pair of us claiming to be traitors and offering to bring him the book?" Ice again, his tone saying all on its own that he thought the idea absurd. "Why can't we simply lure him out and whip his arse?"

"That plan leaves him a base to run back to and regroup, should he escape the ambush," Bram said. "I want to destroy his home turf, disrupt his operations. And if Shock lured him out, again, Mathias would suspect him in the future."

"Here's another snag: if we want to be certain we can use

the diary as bait, a woman *must* carry the book. After Caden tried to steal it from Sydney, we can't discount its rules."

Sydney thought that line was as good a cue as any. With an assertive push on the double doors leading to Bram's office, she swept into the room, trying to quell her quaking.

"I'll take it to him."

Six pairs of male eyes all swiveled her way, expressions ranging from stunned to considering. Bram was the first to speak.

"You're not a witch."

A hot protest leapt to the tip of her tongue, but she had to play this smart. "I am female, but if you insist on someone magical, I suppose you'll use Sabelle."

Bram reared back. "Absolutely not!"

Ice glared at her from beneath heavy black brows.

Sydney laughed, as if she'd been incredibly daft. "Of course, you're taking Olivia. Married to the ultimate warrior, descendant of Morganna, she's likely a gifted witch."

Marrok stepped forward, hand on the hilt of the everpresent sword at his side. "I know not what game you play, but my tender, untrained wife will be nowhere near this battle."

Sydney feigned confusion. "But if you need a woman to pretend to deliver the book to Mathias in order to breach his defenses and you're against using Sabelle and Olivia, who did you have in mind?"

Bram looked straight ahead, meeting no one's gaze. The others looked at him, then at one another. Clearly, they hadn't gotten this far in their planning.

Sydney cleared her throat. "Might I suggest that I'm the perfect candidate. I loathe Mathias for what he's done to Anka and Aquarius, and I relish the opportunity to be a part of an attack that could destroy him."

With a furious scowl, Bram turned to her. "How do you know what we're about?"

"Your voices are louder than your doors are thick. I'm merely volunteering because I know you need the assistance and I'm not personally valuable to anyone here. Unless you prefer to try the trick that felled Mathias once before . . ." She tried to suppress a smile of triumph, but she had them by the balls and they knew it.

"Caden would not think you expendable," Duke said from the far side of the room. "Quite the opposite."

"Since he hasn't seen fit to kiss me—ever—to ascertain pertinent facts or speak certain words . . ." Their jaws gaped. "Yes, I'm informed about your mating rituals. Given all that, if I have your blessing to assist, this decision is mine alone."

A long beat of silence passed, and she waited it out.

"She makes excellent points," Ice conceded.

"She's got more gumption than half the men I know," Tynan admitted.

"Aye, a warrior spirit in a small body. You know if you attempt this, you risk grave danger?" Marrok asked.

Did he think she was a fool? "Of course. But just as you're willing to risk your very lives to stop terrible evil, so am I. I may not have the brawn or magical ability you possess, but my wit has saved me from a scrape more than once. I may be more helpful than you imagine."

"This isn't fodder for one of your stories," Bram growled.

"At the moment, my only thought is to help. We can negotiate the rest later."

"This isn't your fight," Bram pointed out.

"When that bastard hurts my friends, it is."

Bram tapped his toe against the expensive Persian rug and glanced at Duke. Hurstgrove shrugged.

"We need a woman to carry the book. Unless you know of a female warrior . . ."

The jerky shake of Bram's head told Sydney she'd won. She pasted on a smile and couldn't resist fluttering her lashes. "Well?"

"You are a minx." Bram sighed.

His toe kept tapping, which told Sydney that his mind had already reached the right conclusion, but his pride simply wasn't allowing him to utter the words. Wisely, she stayed silent.

Finally, he conceded. "Very well. But there are rules."

"Indeed?"

"If you want to stay alive, you must behave as if you're delivering the book to him because as you researched your articles, you agreed with his message of equality."

"Easy enough." And most likely the only tactic that would allow her to escape in one piece.

"You don't go alone."

Sydney thrust a hand on her hip. "I'd prefer not to. But who can I take without arousing his suspicion?"

A moment of silent thought passed before all eyes in the room drifted to the warrior in leather with the very bad attitude.

Shock bristled. "I'm not here to babysit."

"Too bad." Bram's tone was unequivocal. "You tell Mathias that you met her through Zain and that you persuaded her to come with you to give him the book. Tell him that you promised her protection in exchange for the diary and some positive press. This buys you credibility and Sydney's freedom. And a way to 'accidentally' leave the protections around his base open."

"You want me to escort her in, keep the trail to his compound cracked for you to enter, then leave?" Shock exploded.

"You want me to deliver the book into a madman's hands and walk away?" she asked.

"Yes and yes." Bram crossed his arms over his chest.

"I'll take Shock's protection. But your plan has two flaws: first, it keeps the book in Mathias's hands."

"Not at all. If you make him take it from you instead of handing it over, it will return to you. If you give the book to him, then it may remain. We don't know for certain. Simply use that wit of yours and make him filch it. As soon as you leave, so will the book."

Clever. Quite clever. Bram was more intelligent than she'd thought. "Fine. But there's still flaw number two: I refuse to help you unless you allow me to capture video so I can later transcast proof of Mathias's return to magickind. Do you have a small camera?"

"Do you know what you're asking of me?"

"Indeed. You also know it's the right thing to do. Man up."

Bram hesitated, then sighed. "Well, fuck. There goes my Council seat."

The following morning as the sun rose, Caden burst into the bedroom Sabelle had assigned Sydney and crossed his arms over his chest. "It's one thing to talk about transcasting, but to meet with Mathias? No. You are *not* going."

The words rang with authority, but his gaze wandered. Good God, what was she wearing? Or rather, what wasn't she wearing? Having barged in before she was dressed, he stared at her body clad only in her bra and very tiny knickers. With effort, he dragged his stare to her face, squaring his shoulders with determination. He'd come to save her from a fatal mistake, not gawk.

But Sydney taunted him, making a great show of adjusting her bra, flashing a bit of creamy breast. One strap fell off her shoulder, and she lifted it in place with a coy smile.

Caden swallowed. He would *not* let her lead him around by his cock. He simply was not going to—bloody hell, her lacy knickers were actually a thong! When she bent over to don a pair of socks, the sight of her bare backside and graceful legs stopped all thought. Sydney followed up with a sly look over her shoulder.

"Actually, it's none of your business." She shoved her shirt over her head and reached for her jeans.

That snapped him out of his trance. "By God, woman, it is. Bram tasked me with returning the book to him and shutting you up. I've managed the first. And I will make good on the second today. No joining this attack and no transcasting."

"Bram and I have changed your plans." She shrugged. "Sorry."

She fastened her jeans, grabbed her trainers, and tried to slide by him. Caden grabbed her and pulled her near. God, it felt good to hold her. She was addicting, especially when she glanced up at him, lips pursed and glossy and right there beneath him.

"Did you want something?"

To take that mouth and make it his in every way known to human and magickind. To make certain that she understood precisely who she belonged to.

"Spit it out or let me go."

If only it were that simple. "It *is* my business."

"Based on?"

He tightened his jaw. Since he hadn't finished speaking the Mating Call, he had no basis; they both knew it. His head knew that he had no claim on her—unless he wanted to be roped into magic and put her in deeper danger. His body, pride, and heart, however, weren't prepared to give up. How had one fiery woman stolen into his life and turned his world completely topsy-turvy in scarcely more than a week?

Finally, he murmured, "I care about you."

"Really?" Something really angry came across her face. "Prove it, then. Kiss me."

Her words were like petrol on a roaring fire. She had no idea how badly he craved to know the taste of her.

Last night, after hours spent searching for Anka and righting his brother's house so he could move Lucan there, Caden had stopped by a pub in which he'd been fortunate to find temporary female companionship in the past. As before, he'd received inviting glances and even two promising offers. The only thing he'd been able to muster enthusiasm for was another ale. Sydney had so invaded his mind and heart, there wasn't room for anyone else.

But that didn't change their situation.

"Sydney. I can't," he said with regret.

"You *won't*. Just like you won't finish speaking those words to me that you began in the library."

He froze. Someone had explained magical mating to her. And she was clearly furious.

Frustration boiled over, blending with pain, uncertainty, fear for her, and the goddamned longing he couldn't seem to shake.

"You're right," he growled. "I won't put you in danger, which is exactly where you'll be if I let you join this attack. Same if I mate with you. I can't drag either of us deeper into this magical muck."

"Why not?"

"What if Mathias takes you? What if something happens and I lose you? I just . . . can't."

He expected her anger, but was surprised when her face softened. "What happened?"

"Happened?"

"To make you distrust magic? You didn't choose a human path without reason. You haven't avoided helping magickind and their cause because you fear battle. You've hardly avoided women and relationships in your past, but you've avoided me because you suspect I'm your magical mate. So what tragedy made you afraid?"

Caden froze, paralyzed. He shouldn't be stunned that Sydney had figured that out, but shock thrummed through his system. Mind racing, he wondered what the devil to say. She deserved answers, but opening up the wound Westin's death had left inside him would solve nothing.

"Leave the past in the past. Please."

Something sad settled into her expression as she dragged a brush through her hair and braided it. "Bury your head in the sand, then. I can't. We'd best go downstairs now. They're waiting."

"Move, whelp," Shock said suddenly from behind him, then motioned toward Sydney. "Ready?"

She moved toward Shock and sent Caden one last resolute expression that chilled him to the core. "Ready."

Fog hung in eerie patches as Caden assembled with Sydney and the Doomsday Brethren outside. Dressed head to toe in battle gear and dripping enough weapons to make a third-world dictator salivate, he approached Sydney, who held the Doomsday Diary and stood close to Shock. She looked to Caden for comfort, but to the leather-clad warrior for protection. The thought stung his pride.

"Everyone knows their assignment, right?" Bram said more than asked.

"Aye." Marrok loaded a wicked Glock with a smile, his sword hanging at his side.

"Got it." Ice looked as if he was looking forward to this. Then again, given the fact Mathias had brutally murdered his sister nearly two hundred years ago, he probably was.

"Can't wait." Tynan was all business, but his eyes glowed with pleasure.

"Ready." Duke managed to look like a cover model even in clothes meant for stealth and a pair of guns slung low on his hips.

"And I'm with the skirt," Shock groused.

"She's not a 'skirt,' " Caden snapped. "She's a very worthy female, and you're crawling on my last nerve."

Shock responded with an obnoxious finger gesture.

"Why are you here?" Bram asked.

"I'm coming along," Caden said, strapping a blade to this thigh and securing the clip in his S & W.

"Why?"

What the hell? "Does it matter?"

"It does. Every one of the warriors here has a vested interest in our success, except you. You're thinking with your cock and only joining us to protect the woman you don't have the balls to claim. Admit it."

Bram simply didn't understand. Then again, if Sydney hadn't convinced Bram and the others to let her go, Caden wouldn't have been as committed to today's attack. Not because he was against it or afraid. Any hint of joining the group, and he could find himself permanently entangled in magic and losing people like Duke, who he'd come to admire. But this once, Sydney had boxed him into a corner.

"I've got your six," Caden insisted.

"Even though you don't give a shit about this mission and won't join us, we're expected to accept that you'll protect us with your life?"

Bram's question was fair. In his position, Caden would ask

the same things. His respect for the group's leader notched up.

"You, Shock, and the rest are protecting Sydney. So yes, I care." He looked right at her, dwarfed by Shock standing beside her. "I'll give my life for hers—and anyone protecting her."

Tears collected in the corners of Sydney's eyes before she looked away. Bloody hell, he hated the distance between them.

Finally, Bram nodded. "We need all the warriors we can get. I'll provide you a wand. Practice would have been advisable, but under the circumstances, your instinct will have to do."

"I don't want a wand," Caden insisted, chafing at the thought of magic. "The Marines taught me everything I need to know."

Bram rubbed his forehead. "Fine. Your knowledge of explosives will be helpful. Let's review the plan. Not a word of objection, understood?" At Caden's reluctant nod, he went on. "Shock says the gift of hypnosis runs in his family. He will put Sydney into a trance . . ."

Sydney came to at the sound of a snap. She blinked once, twice, her fuzzy vision coming into focus. Then she looked up into the dark lenses of Shock's sunglasses. As always, his face told her nothing, and she still wasn't sure she trusted him. She clutched the book tighter.

Around her, she was aware of tall ceilings, hard floors, relatively bare walls. She glanced around. Through a partition door, she could see this warehouse had been transformed into a trendy industrial loft. Inside the makeshift office sat a black leather sofa and glass tables. The partition walls hid the rest of the space, but she could hear shuffles and grunts beyond. This was Mathias's lair?

"Welcome." A smooth, cultured voice snagged her attention.

Glancing to her right, Sydney took in its source. Stared, really. The bloke was gorgeous. Dark hair threaded with streaks of golden brown lay in loose waves around his neck, nearly to his bulging shoulders. He wore a tight black T-shirt that hugged every ripped bulge of his biceps, chest, and abdominals. A sexual animal in his prime with enough magnetism for ten men. Sydney sucked in a breath.

Exotic cheekbones framed a lush mouth, smiling widely. His pale blue eyes, rimmed with heavy black lashes, grabbed attention, at first for their utter beauty. But when she looked again, she saw the eyes revealed the cruelty of Jack the Ripper and Hitler combined. They chilled her.

Sharp expression, glittering eyes, carefully controlled upturning of lips, he compelled and repelled at once. Maybe she'd been listening to Aquarius too long. She couldn't see this man's aura, but she felt it. Calculating, soulless. Evil.

Self-preservation kicked in. She played her rehearsed part. "Thank you."

"I'm Mathias." He held out his hand.

Knowing the crimes he had committed, certain he was capable of far worse, Sydney was loathe to take it, but maintaining the charade was critical. She shook his hand, scorched by the fire that burned across her palm, up her arm. She pulled back quickly, resisting the urge to rub her offended skin.

"Would you care to sit?" He gestured to the sofa behind Shock.

She glanced at Shock out of the corner of her eye. He gave her an imperceptible nod.

"Certainly." Sydney clutched the book tighter as they sat on the black leather grouping. As she settled onto the cushion, she pressed the play button on Bram's tiny video recorder, which was hidden in a pocket on the outside of her handbag with a little hole cut to accommodate the lens, which she pointed right at Mathias.

Gotcha! She thought. *Let's see what we can get this bastard to admit to on film.*

"Shock has told me about you. Anyone who brings the Doomsday Diary to me is to be rewarded."

"I-I stumbled across it in my research. Actually, a stranger gave it to me after my first article printed. But after hearing of your quest for equality among magickind, I thought it might be best in your hands." And she nearly choked on those words.

"In that case, why don't you give it to me now?"

CHAPTER SIXTEEN

GIVE IT TO HIM now? Caden watched Mathias commanding Sydney through a crack in the warehouse's window.

Earlier, Shock had snuck them all past Mathias's security spells, which didn't surprise him. Getting out in one piece was another matter altogether.

Looking around, it was clear that Mathias didn't believe in anything so human as guards, so there had been none to overtake. Though he and the Doomsday Brethren now waited near Mathias's stronghold for the "go" signal from Shock, he was more interested in Mathias and Sydney's conversation.

The evil wizard was testing her, toying with her. It took every ounce of restraint not to burst into the building and slay him on the spot. Clutching the butt of his semi-automatic, he had second thoughts about refusing a wand. Embracing magic wasn't on his agenda, but could he fight an evil wizard with a 9 mm? He knew from their battle in the tunnel that bullets had little effect on Mathias. To add a human element Mathias would never think to combat, Caden had placed C4 at every corner and window of the building. Once inside, his mission was to place more around the support beams so the building would come down at the touch of a button, preferably with Mathias in it.

"That's why I came here," Sydney said. "To give you the Doomsday Diary. But I wonder, you're such a powerful figure in magickind, could I persuade you to answer a few questions first?"

She managed to look both starstruck and sheepish. The fact she had the temerity to ask such a man questions without looking nervous staggered Caden. She was baiting a very dangerous bear. Even the look on Shock's face was, well, shocked.

Mathias crossed his legs and leaned back in his black leather chair. "A woman with backbone . . . I haven't known many human females. Perhaps I should remedy that."

Sydney looked down with just the right amount of coyness. "Is that a yes?"

Mathias laughed. "Amusing *and* lovely. I smell a man on you. A wizard."

Her eyes widened, and Caden's heart stuttered. Could Mathias identify her lover? Would he know that she'd been intimate with someone aligned against him?

She glanced at Shock, who said, "She fancies my brother. They've been nearly inseparable for days."

Mathias regarded her carefully. "That's where he's been. And he convinced you to bring the book to me?"

She shook her head. "It was my book and my choice. Actually, Shock suggested I give it to you. I just have a few questions first."

Leaning forward, Mathias leveled a bland stare at Sydney, but Caden saw the lethal way his gaze dissected her. If she couldn't read men, she was screwed.

Nodding, she adjusted her handbag in her lap, perching it on the edge of her knees. *What the . . .*

Suddenly, Caden understood. The camera was in her handbag, now close to Mathias. *Brave little fool.* She was going to get herself killed. Everything inside him clenched. Somehow, he had to get her out of there without compromising the mission.

Sydney bit her lip in a nervous gesture. "I understand the book has awesome power."

"An object with this much magical ability has not been seen in centuries. It will give me the power to provide the Deprived a chance at equality."

"A commendable goal, but how exactly can the book help you achieve it? What will you *do* with the Doomsday Diary? Could you control, say, an entire class of magickind if you chose?"

"Before acting, I must study the book carefully. An object like this deserves respect. To answer you now would be premature and rash."

"Naturally," Sydney countered. "But give me an idea of the things you anticipate being able to do with this diary."

"Forgive me if I decline to answer your question. Shock looks quite protective, and you're Zain's current amour. To keep my plans secret, I would hate to be . . . impolite." The wizard sent her a tight smile. "The book, please."

Mathias's tone hadn't changed. Nor had his expression. But Caden could tell the wizard was done indulging Sydney. He hoped she realized it. She needed to get the hell out. Heart racing, fear burned his veins as Caden mouthed to Bram, *Now?*

Bram shook his head. Caden clutched his gun so tight, his fingers turned white. When it came to her job, Sydney didn't understand the word "stop." If she pushed Mathias further, what happened to Anka and Aquarius would look like fun.

"In a moment," Sydney assured. "What about your background makes you willing to lead the Deprived out of their poverty? It sounds like an admirable cause, and a favorable story about the inspiration behind your dedication might help your cause."

With a brow raised, Mathias leaned forward and spoke softly. "The time for reporting magickind's news in your human rag has ended. My presence is still something of a surprise, and I prefer to keep it that way. No more questions. The book. Now."

Though the plan entailed making Mathias steal it, screw Bram's plan. *Give it to him before he kills you and get out!*

Instead, she frowned. "You understand why I'm reluctant to turn over what is, by your own admission, an awesome weapon without more information."

"I'm a busy man. By your own admission, my cause is an admirable one, and my attention is better spent on the war and the matter of equality."

Sydney pursed her lips. "Indeed. But I have heard troubling rumors about your treatment of witches. Can you comment?"

Horror washed over Caden, and he bit the inside of his cheek until he tasted blood. Mathias would have no compunction about killing her for merely asking the question.

"Give him the book, damn it," Shock snarled and ripped it out of her hands, then shoved it into Mathias's outstretched arms. "You came to do that, and now you have. Let's go."

Sydney managed to look flustered and irritated. "I wasn't done asking questions. What about—"

"Yes, you were." Shock warned.

Caden hoped to God Sydney heeded him. *What in hell had possessed her to interrogate a man who could squash her like a bug?* If she walked out of this warehouse alive, she had no idea the tirade he planned to unleash on her.

"What about Auropha MacKinnett, Anka MacTavish, Elmira Craddock?" She kept aiming her handbag and the video camera in the dark wizard's direction.

Mathias's expression looked empty, yet Caden saw fury creeping through the wizard's black magical signature. He held his breath, terrified the evil bastard would draw his wand and end Sydney in one flick of his wrist.

"Come on!" Shock grabbed Sydney's elbow and hauled her to her feet.

Normally, Caden would be furious that Shock had touched her and dragged her to the door, even as she held her bag in Mathias's direction. But now, he was grateful to Shock for every centimeter of distance he put between Sydney and Mathias.

As they neared the door, Mathias stood, his weighty gaze on Sydney. "Stop."

Instead of walking—or better yet, running—out of the warehouse, Sydney turned to him.

"The wizard I scent on you doesn't smell like Zain."

Caden's heart nearly beat out of his chest. A flush stained her cheeks, but she shrugged. "If you're not inclined to tell me all about your intentions concerning the book or your past actions, I hardly feel obligated to explain my sex life."

"It's in your best interest to reconsider. Are you fraternizing with my enemies? Maybe one of the Doomsday Brethren?"

Terror struck Caden cold.

She tilted her head and glared at Mathias. "Would I be bringing you the book if I was?"

Because she was a minx, Sydney didn't wait for the answer, but turned and headed for the door, exiting the little room.

Then all hell broke loose.

As she crossed the threshold, the Doomsday Diary vanished from Mathias's hands. The wizard looked down as it dissipated. Letting out a horrific roar, he tried in vain to grab the little red volume, then whirled toward the warehouse's interior door—and Sydney.

Caden didn't bother waiting for any "go" signal. He kicked in the window and leapt through, dropping to the concrete and rolling to a crouch, gun drawn. He'd have one chance to surprise the fucker and he meant to make the most of it.

The evil wizard whirled toward the noise, then grabbed his wand and raised it, his enraged blue eyes ringed in red. The plastic grip of the gun heated Caden's hand. Its weight was nothing compared to the gravity of Mathias's magic. Again, he wondered if he'd have been better off with a wand and magic he could use.

Before Mathias could level Caden with a lethal spell, Bram jumped through the window, wand drawn, and faced their nemesis.

With Mathias's attention momentarily divided, Caden fired. One of the bullets tore through Mathias's stomach, and he grunted, surprise transforming his expression. Quickly, blood spread, darkening an ever-widening circle on Mathias's black T-shirt. He clutched his gut, glaring at Caden with even redder eyes.

"You are going to die," he growled. "Along with Rion."

Mathias jerked his wand in their direction. Bram waved his own and deflected whatever the bastard had hurled their way. But the effort cost Bram as he stumbled back with a gasp. Caden popped off another shot, but the element of surprise was gone, and Mathias dodged the bullet.

Bram flicked a wrist at the wall behind Mathias, and it came crashing down in a tumble of plaster. Sydney stood behind the door with the book in one hand and her handbag in the other. Why the hell hadn't she departed with Shock as planned? Caden wanted to blame the other warrior, but knowing Sydney, she'd stubbornly stayed.

Mathias raised his wand to Sydney. Caden roared forward, gun at the ready. On the far side of the warehouse, Marrok and Tynan broke through another window, distracting Mathias again. Ice charged through the warehouse's front door. Apparently getting the signal, Duke teleported into the room behind Mathias.

Now the wanker was completely surrounded. Time to play. . . . As soon as Sydney left.

"Go!" he shouted at her.

She ignored him. Damn it, would the woman never listen! Fury and fear juiced his bloodstream that had his adrenaline on overdrive. He itched to snap Mathias's wand—and neck—in two.

"Lower your wand," Bram shouted at Mathias. "You're done tormenting and raping magickind, tearing apart families. You'll never get your hands on the Doomsday Diary."

"You overestimate your ragtag band, Rion." With a wave, Mathias pointed his wand at the wall behind Duke. In a hiss, it disappeared—no rubble, no mess, just—dissipated.

Behind the missing wall stood a sea of Anarki, all zombies, dead on the outside, malevolent on the inside. Their sheer numbers shocked Caden. Not a dozen or a hundred . . . at least a thousand with grave-white faces and vacant expressions.

Beside him, Bram sucked in a breath. "So many. How?"

Clutching his bleeding gut, Mathias smiled. "You have your secret weapon; I have mine."

The Anarki army surged forward, revealing the far corners of the room. Over the top of the Anarki's heads, Caden saw a soldier in fatigues—a U.S. Marine—fighting two wizards.

"No! *No!*" the soldier screamed, struggling against them, kicking out. The wizards overpowered him and managed to shove him against a raised, slanted dais, and with a flick of their wands, strapped him down. If Caden had a wand, he might be able to free him.

An instant later, they passed a round object over his skull. The man belted out a spine-chilling yell of pain.

Once the object was pulled away and moved to the next victim, Caden looked at the limp man. In his early twenties, he'd been strong, healthy, vital only moments ago. That man was gone now. In his place was an Anarki zombie, like all the others coming toward Caden, a puppet whose flesh was already whitening. The eyes staring back were devoid of life as he melted in with the attacking crowd.

There were at least fifty soldiers strapped to tables, lined up one after the other against the warehouse's back wall. The two wizards were passing the round object over one head at a time, all to horrific screams. A few moments later, they left behind corpses, alive only by Mathias's magic and will.

Shit! Time to save who they could, lay the C4, and blow this joint—literally. With Mathias's attentions engaged by the others, Caden raced to complete his mission, darting to the first visible support beam and applying the explosive putty.

Marrok stepped toward the crowd of Anarki zombies, sword drawn. Bending low, he swung, cutting several in the front row in half. Black blood spurted in every direction. With a fist pump, Caden dodged his way to the next support beam, in and out of the battle—stopping to slice and dice any Anarki intent on stopping him. Duke joined him, shooting down several zombies in his way.

While Caden bent to secure the next explosive, Mathias snarled, eyes narrowed at Bram as he closed in on one side. Ice approached from the front, Tynan from his opposite side.

"Your Anarki can't stop us. We're not going to rest until you're back in exile," Bram said. "You're surrounded. Give up."

Mathias snorted, the sound abrasive and amused. "You may have Merlin's blood in your veins, but I will still decimate you and your worthless bunch."

He whooshed his wand toward the crowd. Shrieks sounded all around. The frigid zombies crushed in, forming a protective circle around Mathias. Those close to a Doomsday Brethren wizard attacked.

Marrok and Duke cut through them as fast as they could. Bram dodged his would-be killers with a blade here and an elbow there, charging after Mathias. Tynan followed, determined to get his pound of flesh.

Mathias leapt toward the exit. As the wall of Anarki encircled him, now closer to the warehouse door, Sydney set her handbag on a nearby ledge, shoved the book inside, and peeked into the bag. A moment later, she grabbed an aerosol can and a lighter.

"Duck!" she screamed, then she flicked the lighter and sprayed the contents of the can into the open flame.

The resulting fireball hit the Anarki dead on. The roar and heat of the blaze singed the heads off the first row of zombies looming near. The second row paused their catatonic march, either tripping over their dead cohorts or falling victim to the fire.

Then the aerosol from the can sputtered, died. The Anarki surged forward again.

One stepped over his fallen comrades and reached Sydney. She grabbed her handbag and tried to twist away, but the door and the wall of zombies trapped her. She slid along the wall, then gasped suddenly and clutched her arm, face contorting with pain.

"Bugger!" she muttered as blood started spreading across the pristine white sleeve.

At the sight, Caden's protective instincts rocketed to life. He climbed a stair rail, jumping over zombies to reach Sydney, shooting down and knifing any who stood in his path.

A corpse grabbed Sydney, pinning her to the wall and

squeezing her neck. As the magical battle raged around them, Sydney's wheezing and choking rose above the din. Her eyes bulged in panic. Red suffused her face as she flailed and fought.

Caden leapt over two more Anarki. A third, wearing fatigues stood in his way, evil pouring from his eyes. His bullets running low, Caden clutched his knife, then looked back up at the zombie in shock.

Brian, his Marine buddy. The pasty white face and vacant eyes had thrown him, but that sandy hair, the scar on his chin, the patch that read *Halstead* across his chest proclaimed him Caden's missing platoon mate. He swallowed, unable to move, breathe.

"Brian?"

No reaction except a malevolent smile as he reached for Caden's throat.

Kill him!

Shock's voice roared in his head. How was that possible? *Kill him before he tears you to pieces*, Shock demanded.

Last chance. "Brian?"

Nothing but a creepy smile and a shivery death grip reaching ever closer. When Caden heard Sydney scream again, he plunged the knife into Brian's neck and ripped down viciously, nearly tearing his head from his neck.

Brian crumbled to the ground. Guilt, grief, and relief crushing him inside, Caden stepped over the body and scrambled to Sydney's side. He had to compartmentalize Brian's death now and deal with the present.

He grabbed the zombie holding her throat and pushed him face first into the concrete wall. It was still fighting after the first blow, so Caden delivered two more. The undead soldier went limp.

Whirling back to Sydney, he saw that another zombie

had her in its grip, dragging her along the wall. More blood spread across the shirt at her waist. The white cotton was torn and a few inches of ragged flesh peeked through. She cried out and fell to her knees, pain slashing across her expression. The zombie was following her to the floor with murder in his eyes.

And Caden wasn't going to reach her in time.

Panic burned through him, even making his fingertips tingle. A swell of energy bounded inside him. Suddenly, he pictured the broken glass on the floor flying toward the Anarki. Seemingly of their own volition, his arms raised and hurtled forward. He snarled his rage and glass shards flew past him and embedded sharp points into the zombie's back. Black blood flowed, gurgled, and the creature fell to the ground.

He'd done magic. *Dear God.* No time to dwell on it, whether to rail or cheer. Instead, Caden charged toward Sydney. A fresh swarm of Anarki were headed her way. With one hand, she clutched her handbag. With the other, she scooted away from the zombies, wearing an expression of utter terror.

Caden couldn't see Bram and the rest of the Doomsday Brethren, but it didn't matter. He was done risking Sydney.

With superhuman speed, he reached his little firecracker before the Anarki and grabbed her against his body, avoiding her injured shoulder. She wrapped one arm and her legs around him. Her handbag bobbed against his side as he raced out the front door of the warehouse and reached into his pocket to set off the warning charge. An explosion just outside the building rattled the walls and sent up flames.

The Doomsday Brethren had sixty seconds to get out before he blew the whole building to kingdom come.

Outside, the weak morning sun filtered through gray clouds, lending barely enough light to see Sydney's wounds. The shape of the slashes told him she'd gouged her flesh on a nail—or those Anarki bastards had pushed her on it—as she tried to get away. She needed direct pressure and stitches immediately.

Caden stripped off his shirt and rolled her to her back, easing the cloth against the deepest of her wounds. "Lie still. We'll be out of here soon."

She nodded. "I got the film. As soon as I put it together, I'm transcasting it to all of magickind. This will save lives."

And who was going to save hers? But now wasn't the time to debate. It simply wasn't going to happen.

Bram emerged from the warehouse, two of the captured soldiers who hadn't yet been converted into Anarki behind him. Duke emerged next with another three. Ice and Tynan each brought a handful more. Caden wished one of those saved could have been Brian. He didn't even have to close his eyes to relive the horrifying moment he'd plunged the knife into his friend's neck. *God, Brian.*

Still, Mathias had killed him, and Brian hadn't been Caden's friend anymore. War meant kill or be killed. The guilt would hurt like hell, but he had saved Sydney.

And he'd used magic to do it. Even though his palms burned, his head hurt, and he felt so weak his thighs trembled, Caden couldn't deny that without magic, she'd likely be dead.

Shoving the thought aside, Caden looked at his watch. *Five, four, three . . . where was Marrok?*

Just then, the medieval warrior emerged with nearly twenty of Mathias's prisoners. They all looked shell-shocked and confused by what they'd seen. And why not? It wasn't every day a man saw another's soul ripped out via magic.

"Blow it!" Bram shouted.

Caden didn't hesitate. He pressed the button in his pocket. The entire warehouse detonated in a flash of fire, glass, and dust. The Doomsday Brethren stepped back as bodies flew. Sydney shrieked. Flames licked out, heat ripped through the morning air, and the structure collapsed. What was left of its walls were singed black as the pop and hiss of fire ate anything in its path.

Mission accomplished. He only hoped that Mathias was still inside.

Bram tossed one soldier a cell phone. "Dial nine-nine-nine. Tell them you're captured soldiers standing in front of the American Embassy."

"But we aren't there," the confused soldier challenged.

Just then, Shock appeared and waved his wand. They all tumbled to the ground in a deep slumber.

"Damn you!" Sydney barked at Shock, clutching Caden's shirt to her wound. "I wanted to interview them."

"Hell no!" Caden barked.

Shock and Bram exchanged a glance.

"He's right. No time. Too dangerous," Bram decreed. "I know it's not easy, Shock, but see if you can do anything with their memories."

"Damn near impossible," he grumbled. "I'll try."

Shock gathered grabbed three and teleported out, only to appear moments later and repeat the process.

Clutching Sydney against him, Caden smelled her feminine scent tangled up in his own and thanked God she was alive. They had to get her medical attention now. For that, they had to get to safety.

Duke sidled up to him a few moments later.

"Ready?" Even after a battle, the titled wizard looked collected and almost royal.

"Hurry," Caden insisted, watching as Bram took Marrok's arm and they disappeared. Tynan and Ice both teleported out.

"You could learn to do that yourself now, you know?" Duke said.

Yes, he could. Since transition, he'd been "blessed" with common magic like teleporting. But magic was a slippery slope, in his mind. Accept one "gift," and how long before he'd take everything else? Already he'd used it today and prayed that no one had witnessed it.

"Get us back," Caden groused. "She's hurt."

"I'm fine," Sydney insisted.

"You need stitches. No arguing."

She opened her mouth, but Duke grabbed Caden's arm and placed a hand at Sydney's back. Moments later, they tumbled through emptiness, then landed in Bram's office. Sabelle was already waiting, and though Caden wanted to be the one to tend to Sydney, her injuries weren't life threatening. And he was too weak. As much as he hated to admit it, Bram's sister was both talented and capable of handling Sydney.

"Go with her," Caden murmured. "Let her patch you up. I'll be along shortly."

She held up the handbag. "As long as she's quick. I've got good film and the book inside." Leveling a sharp glance at Bram, she challenged, "You're not backing out, right?"

"The matter is too serious for the Council to remain silent. You can transcast."

Fury shot through Caden. Before he could object, Sydney rushed Sabelle out the door, excitement humming off of her. Caden wanted to go along, hold her hand, shout some sense into her, but the fair-haired general stood behind his desk and barked questions.

"Did anyone see Mathias teleport out?"

"Yes," Tynan snarled. "I was just about to blast the bloody sadist when I saw the warning explosion. Unfortunately, so did he. He grabbed that glass globe his followers used to create Anarki and flashed out. After that, I grabbed a couple of the captured soldiers and left."

"Fuck!" Ice spat the word everyone was thinking.

"At least we blew up his facility and damn near a thousand zombies," Duke added.

Including his friend. Pain stabbed Caden in the gut, but even as it did, he knew he had to let go. What was done, was done. War was hell. He just didn't want to suffer any more losses.

"How was he making them in the first place?" Caden demanded. "What is that glass sphere? One of those soldiers was my friend."

Mercy tempered Bram's battle-fierce expression for a moment. "I don't know. A wizard can torture a human's soul from him and replace their will with his bidding. Normally, he can convert but a few at a time at the cost of a great deal of energy. That glass ball his followers were wielding is a mystery to me. I'll start investigating."

Then Bram's mercy hardened, and he glared at Caden. "The bad news is, Mathias got away. We were supposed to have more time to trap him so he'd go up in flames with the building. We agreed to that plan. Why the bloody hell did you detonate off the charge early?"

Caden's temper spiked. He wasn't one of the Doomsday Brethren. Bram wasn't his commanding officer.

But you agreed to help, whispered the pesky voice in his head. He'd had a mission and he'd panicked and jettisoned the mission. Period.

"The Anarki had Sydney cornered and were about to kill her. I got her out."

"Damn you!" Bram charged from behind his desk and

got in Caden's face. "If you'd learn some bloody magic, you might have saved her without aborting the mission."

"I used it!"

Bram raised a brow. "On purpose?" Into Caden's silence, he added, "Because of your stubborn refusal to learn magic, we blew our surprise and perhaps Shock's cover so you could save Sydney. The fact she's your mate and you won't claim her is clouding your judgment."

Caden absorbed Bram's words with anger and guilt. He hated it, but the wizard was right.

"You're no longer fighting with us. If your brother needs help, ring me. Otherwise, until you embrace your magic," Bram shook his head. "Get out."

Caden stomped up the stairs. *Get out?* He'd be more than bloody happy to. Bram ordering him gone hadn't hurt in the least. That was fury brewing in his gut. Definitely. He didn't need this group of wizards. In fact, he didn't belong tangled up in magic. He'd take Lucan back to his own house, as the healer recommended. Bram's assistance hadn't helped locate Anka, so Caden would continue that quest alone. He'd grab his belongings, his brother, and go.

But what about Sydney?

She couldn't return to her human life, and unless he mated with her, he had no business taking her with him. She would be safer with Bram and the others, especially now that Mathias had seen her face. It all made sense except . . . the thought of leaving her made him want to tear something apart with his bare hands. How the hell could he protect Sydney from a distance?

He couldn't.

"Ouch! Damn it, I thought magical healing would be less painful. Did you fry my skin together?"

Sydney. At the top of the stairs, he shook his head wryly. Even when his life was shit, she amused him. He had to figure out some way to watch over her and his brother. He wasn't going to leave her when her life was in danger. After all, the diary had been stolen out from under Bram, so clearly the wizard made mistakes.

Lately, Caden had been riding the thin line between the magical heritage he rejected and the human world he embraced. He'd continue doing it to keep Sydney alive. He refused to step over the line while she sought the very world he wanted to escape. As much as he loved her, they wanted different futures. Given that, linking his survival to her as his mate made little sense. She'd never be happy if she followed him to his human existence in Dallas. He had no doubt that if he mated with Sydney, with her so determined to help magickind, she'd end up dead and he'd become exactly like his brother.

Being back in the UK had been a homecoming, but if he remained with Sydney, she'd want him to join the Doomsday Brethren. Today's battle had made him feel vital and part of a unit again, but he'd screwed up. Lost his edge. Maybe losing his platoon had done that. Whatever it was, he didn't want to endure the pain again or put Bram and the others at risk.

As Bram had ceased Caden's involvement with the Doomsday Brethren, he needed to do the same with Sydney. After settling Lucan in at home, he'd protect her, but no more.

As he entered the bedroom, Sabelle left, answering his unspoken question as she did. "Conrad just left. Sydney's fine."

"Indeed," Sydney insisted as she dug into her handbag and extracted the camera. "Help me edit this film? I know you're against me transcasting, but you saw how evil Mathias was. We can't let him continue to run amok. I want to transcast within the hour."

His advice was going to fall on deaf ears, but Caden felt compelled to say it. "You understand that there's no going back? You'll both incur Mathias's supreme wrath and be trapped in magickind forever."

"Trapped?" She frowned. "I have a chance now to save lives and achieve everything I ever dreamed. Nothing worth doing is without risk."

"Pretty speech. I don't think it will comfort you when Mathias tries to kill you. I'm not helping you transcast."

She cocked her head and peered at him, clearly puzzling something out. "You're walking away and leaving this mess to Bram and the others and wasting your abilities when you could be helping, too."

"Bram tossed me out, and I'm leaving something I never wanted to be involved in."

Sydney paused, drew back. "You're leaving me as well."

Caden saw no reason to beat about the bush. "I'll protect you. I can't be this close, care this much, and lose you. I . . . can't."

Clenching her fists, Sydney tried to hold back sudden tears. And failed. "I don't understand you. First, you ran from your parents and your heritage, spent ten years trying to be American and human, when you're neither. You came back to help your brother, why? Obligation? Because you couldn't avoid it without feeling like a heel? You're not running from the Doomsday Brethren and me. You're running from yourself—like you have been your whole life."

Caden accepted the rebuke in silence. Sydney simply didn't understand. Nor could she relate to the tangle of affection and duty he felt for Lucan after losing Westin. And she had no way of comprehending the disastrous results of a failed magical mating. Would it make a difference if she did? No, it was too late now. Some things simply weren't meant to be.

"You've oversimplified everything," he said.

"Have I? Explain to me exactly how this isn't running from your destiny."

CHAPTER SEVENTEEN

"Sydney, I don't expect you to understand."

Which meant he wasn't even going to try to explain. Grief felt like a blow to the chest.

"*Make* me understand. Why?"

He raked a frustrated hand through mussed brown hair. "Magic isn't always . . . good."

"Mathias proves that."

"I mean that using magic, even the sort you think is good, can change your life in terrible ways."

His words renewed her dread. She'd fantasized about him in the Doomsday Diary to lure him to her side. Had that changed their lives in terrible ways? The possibility sounded ugly. How much, if any, of their affection and passion was due strictly to the book's magic?

"You're always so bloody vague, raising more questions than you answer."

Sighing, pacing, he grasped for words. "Magic is all new and interesting to you now, but it's ripped apart my life more than once."

"Change happens in everyone's lives, whether you're magical or not. Tell me what's so terrible—"

"No point except to dredge up bad memories and burden you with tragedies you can't change. I just need to go."

"You belong here, fighting beside these warriors. I think you belong beside me, as well." She pressed her lips together to hold in tears. "I've fallen in love with you. You used magic today to save me, though you hate it. You must care about me a bit. Perhaps, in time, it could be real—"

"It *is* real." His blue eyes burned with truth.

But a niggle of doubt remained.

Caden's slumped shoulders and the exhausted lines bracketing his eyes and mouth made him look like defeat on two legs. "I wish the answer was as simple as love, firecracker. But taking the next step with you means accepting magic I don't trust. It's too uncontrollable."

Though she knew better, Sydney couldn't stop fighting for them. "So is life!"

"I've died a hundred times with the desire to kiss you, but if I do, we would be mated for life. You would adopt my lifespan, so that means *hundreds* of years, literally." He wrapped warm hands around her shoulders, and Sydney wished he'd welcome her farther into his embrace. "But if you keep to this path, you're going to die—and take me down with you. I can't stand by and watch. It will drive me mad."

His every word was a pick ax to the heart, and she struggled to comprehend his reasons for walking away from greatness and love for the mundane and lonely. "So you'd prefer to end it, just to be safe?"

Caden hesitated. "You've chosen to remain, and I'm going to protect you. But mating in the middle of a war with both of us on the front lines, there would be consequences you can't begin to comprehend."

"Explain them."

He sighed. "Even if I did, it would change nothing. We want different lives. I won't lie and say I don't love you or that I don't wish things could be different. But I'd be doing us both a disservice if I spoke the Call." Caden looked at her then with bleak, hollow eyes. The expression magnified as he touched her cheek and leaned in to hold her close and kiss her forehead. "I'll remain your bodyguard, nothing more."

Sydney pulled away from his embrace. A deep, heavy ache spread across her chest, shattering her heart into a million pieces. "I'll do my damnedest to make you regret your choice."

She grabbed the video camera, hurt pounding inside her. But she hesitated. That tousled hair that curled at the ends, those electric eyes, the ripped body . . . yes, at first he'd been a walking fantasy, and she'd lusted after him. But soon, she'd discovered the man beneath, the one who put his brother first, who believed in her, who made love passionately, who fought to protect her even when he wanted to run away.

But it appeared that magic was a hurdle they couldn't overcome. Sydney wasn't going to walk away from magickind. This had become more than a story to her. Bram and the others were a handful against a powerful evil. If she could help them, she would. She'd proudly do this job until she could return to the human world to tell the best story ever about magickind.

Pity she'd take the spotlight alone.

"No doubt you'll achieve all your ambitions. I'll miss you."

Tears burning her eyes, she watched Caden leave.

" . . . sobering video from a fight that took place earlier today. Mathias D'Arc is definitely back and, as you saw, is abducting soldiers from around the world and converting them to zombies to make his army. He and his followers have attacked at least four Privileged families, killing many and abducting the women. Take precautions. Keep close watch on all family members. Never stray far from your wand. Have some means of communication nearby. If you're being attacked, contact

Bram Rion. Updates will follow as necessary. I'm Sydney Blair. Stay safe. Good afternoon."

With that, Bram waved a hand in front of the ancient, heavy mirror hanging in the library. Beside him, Sabelle stood with a smile, despite the strain on her face.

"Good job," Bram praised, exiting into the hall. "Angry Council members will scream their displeasure in mere moments, I suspect, but at least innocent people have been warned."

"You've done the right thing," Sabelle added, following Bram.

Nodding, he sighed and approached Sydney. "Are you all right?"

Define all right, she thought. Transcasting the news of Mathias's return had been both exhilarating and bittersweet. Without Caden here to cheer her on, hold her hand, love her afterward . . . a part of her was missing.

"Fine." Melancholy and exhaustion made holding her plastic smile a Herculean task.

"I'll pretend I believe you and wait for the deluge of messages in my office. The rest of the warriors and I should talk, plan our next moves." He paused and placed a hand on her shoulder. "You've done us a great service at much risk to yourself. I appreciate you. I know the others do as well."

Looking tired but determined, Bram left.

"I don't know what he's going to do," Sabelle murmured after he'd cleared the room.

"Do?"

"He's nearly out of energy and cannot find his mate," the witch explained. "Thus far, he's only skimmed the barest amount from a surrogate. I hope he finds this mystery woman soon. Or takes more energy. He's too important to the cause to go on like this."

"What will happen if he doesn't?"

"He'll die. It's why I've been tending Caden's brother. Technically, he's no longer mated since Anka broke with him, but he rejected all females until I duped him into believing I was her. His condition is awful. He's keeping his strength now, but his mind . . . I don't know if he'll recover."

Caden had returned to the UK for his brother and had reluctantly admitted that Lucan had a mental imbalance, but nothing more. Now she saw the truth he'd avoided telling her. Sabelle's explanation made all the pieces click into place. Lucan's magical "divorce" from Anka had caused Lucan's condition. *Could Caden be rejecting a future with me, not because I'd written in the diary, but because he feared becoming like his brother?*

Oh. Dear God.

Suddenly, Sabelle speared Sydney with a direct stare. "You're right. Sorry to read your mind. Terrible habit. Caden *is* terrified of becoming like Lucan." She shook her head. "I hope Caden finds Anka before it's too late."

She had to see the man, had to know what had spooked Caden. Trying to fight something she couldn't see and scarcely understood was both stupid and impossible.

"When Caden left, I told him I would be by shortly to see Lucan. I'm certain they're settled in at Lucan's townhouse. I think it's time you see the dangerous side of magic."

She hardly needed more proof to understand magic's potential peril. But perhaps this would unravel the rest of the complicated puzzle of Caden.

"Of course."

"No pictures. I simply want you to understand, not report."

Naturally. *If I reported on Lucan's condition, it might spur Mathias to take the mates of other Doomsday Brethren.*

"Just Bram," Sabelle provided. "Marrok isn't a wizard, and none of the others are fully mated."

"*Fully* mated?"

Sabelle began trudging her way up the stairs. "Remember when I told you about the Call? They ask, you answer, then you're mated?"

She nodded. "It sounded simple enough, so how can someone be partially mated?"

"They ask and they're refused."

"But if they're refused, how can the bond be established?"

"The wizard takes a mate in his heart when he speaks the words. Whether or not he genuinely means them or the feelings are reciprocated, he is bound by that Call. Until the woman dies, he is hers exclusively."

Sydney's jaw dropped as she followed the woman. "And one of these big warriors—"

"Shock. He Called to Anka shortly before Lucan did and was eventually Renounced."

Another jaw dropper. *Lucan and Shock quarreling over the same woman?*

"For over a century. When Lucan slipped into mate mourning, we called Caden here to care for his brother. He's afraid because he knows you're his, but has seen firsthand the tragic possibilities of mating."

Sabelle reached the top of the stairs and headed for a corner room in the family wing. Sydney had never been to this side of the estate, and when the witch pushed her way into a glamorous room, Sydney's jaw threatened to drop once more. Sumptuous cream silk bedding with golden touches was relieved by hints of melted chocolate. The walls were warm, the drapes swagged, the furniture of dark, glossy wood. Crystal candlesticks gleamed, plush furniture lounged. The room fit Sabelle completely.

"It's lovely."

Sabelle smiled. "My haven. I just need to grab a few things. Should only be a moment."

Why not just summon objects? Sydney wondered.

The beautiful witch sent her a chiding stare. "I'm saving my energy for what's to come."

She grabbed a cape, a length of silk, rope, and a pair of handcuffs. Sydney's brows raised.

"I don't know what I'm facing over there," Sabelle explained. "Here, we had Lucan well restrained so he wouldn't be a danger to anyone."

Suddenly, Sydney wasn't sure she wanted to see Lucan after all. But Sabelle grabbed her arm. Blackness and that topsy-turvy feeling invaded her stomach. A weightless feel left her at odds and ends.

Then the floor appeared beneath them, and they zoomed into a room straight out of Tuscany, with walls like an autumn afternoon and drapes the color of wine, accented by a gleaming hardwood floor.

The only thing out of place was the snarling man secured by rope to all four corners of the bed. His dark hair had been pulled back, revealing a face that would normally be considered handsome. It was so like Caden's with high cheekbones, a wide mouth, a sculpted jaw. But instead of the familiar vibrant blue, Lucan's eyes were just angry black pinpricks. No warmth or passion, as feral as a wild wolf's.

Lucan snapped his unfocused gaze in their direction and roared, struggling against his bonds as the bed creaked. Surprise pinged through Sydney. She stepped back. Way back.

"Losing Anka did *this* to him?"

Sabelle nodded solemnly.

He missed his mate so much that he'd lost his mind? Sydney had never met Lucan, but she ached for him and the pain he was obviously enduring.

"Because she's no longer mated to him? Doesn't that release him? Or does he suffer because the break was against his will?"

"It doesn't matter why the mating ends. Magic makes the ties between mates stronger than humans. Unlike divorce, there's a magical connection that doesn't simply disappear because the union is over."

"Even under all his madness, he misses her?"

"Lucan doesn't remember who he is but, he knows Anka at a core level. I can only give him energy by tricking him into believing I'm her. I use her soap and shampoo, wear her clothes, whatever is necessary."

Under all that torment, Lucan waited for his one true love. And she might be gone from him forever. Tears welled.

"But if Anka is free of Mathias and has left Aquarius, why doesn't she return to Lucan?"

"She doesn't remember him. Magic's way of ensuring survival of the species, I suppose. She's currently mateless and in need of a male with whom she can charge her energy. If she remembered Lucan and suffered as he does, she'd never allow another to mount her and potentially impregnate her. Conceiving is possible, but difficult if unmated, and with Lucan in her memory and heart, she'd likely never mate again."

"Nor will Lucan."

"Men who have been well mated usually emerge from their mate mourning with a strong yearning to mate again."

"Usually? I hear uncertainty in your voice."

Sabelle winced. "Lucan may be different. . . ."

Sydney dared to glance at Lucan again. His gleaming chest and shoulders rippled with each strain against the ropes. His growl was a threat that sent shivers down her spine. His love must be powerful, indeed. And Sabelle had tricked him into bedding her?

"It's the only way to keep him alive."

Caden's reluctance to mate made sense now. He liked being in control. Lucan's descent into madness because of magic would be the worst horror to a soldier with such self command.

They were in the midst of a war, and Sydney had put herself straight in the path of danger. Coupled with the fact she'd brought Caden to her side by foul means—even if the book no longer played a role between them—his retreat made a sad sort of sense.

She bit her lip. She needed to talk to him, if only to say that she understood. "Is Caden here?"

"I'm sure he is. He doesn't know we're here. Lucan long ago allowed Bram and me to visit without chiming in." Sabelle handed her a little white rock. "I'm leaving, since Lucan's energy is holding and I'm not needed. When you're ready to return, just toss this stone in the air and say my name. I'll return for you." Sabelle hugged her, then warned, "Given his worries about Lucan and Mathias's backlash, Caden may be a bit on edge."

A shuffle and a quiet knock on the family room door, Caden twisted around in the plush recliner, expecting to see Sabelle. The sight of Sydney punched him with a breathless rush of thrill and need.

He'd been away from her for four hours and missed her with a frightening intensity, like a junkie craving a fix. After settling Lucan back into his home, Caden had done little except pace and sweat and wish to God he could hear or smell or touch Sydney. Or taste her. He had to get his desire under control before he could protect her. Worse, his energy was waning, and he realized that as an unmated male, he could bed anyone. And must do so soon.

But he only wanted her.

Then his brain kicked in. Why was she here? Sabelle, he realized. And the only reason for the witch to visit was Lucan.

Anxiety buzzed his blood, and he fought to rein in the curse on the tip of his tongue. Sydney now knew far more about his objections. That fact softened her normally sharp gaze.

Damn it, she felt sorry for him.

"I know you're not expecting me." She took a hesitant step into the room, eyes flicking to the book on the nearby table. "I don't mean to barge in, but I had to see you. Why didn't you tell me about Lucan and his mate mourning?"

Caden took a hesitant step closer—but not too close. That would be dangerous. "It doesn't change anything."

"But your refusal to share with me does. I only wanted the truth."

She rushed across the room to stand by his side. Her smell blindsided him with hunger and longing. He dug his fingers into his thigh to keep from reaching out and hauling her into his arms.

"I understand now what you fear," she murmured. "Why you've avoided mating with me. Your brother has lost all control, and that's something you strive to retain. I'm sorry for him, but you don't know that Lucan's condition would become yours—"

"Given the way you've thrown yourself into a war, I do. Your bravery is commendable, but it's placed you in grave danger. You don't take precautions, and I know you'll try to refuse my protection, even if I insist you follow my rules—"

"*Your* rules? I'm hardly a child in need of guidance."

He stepped closer, toe to toe, towering over her. That spicy-sweet scent of hers infiltrated and intoxicated his senses, tightening his gut. The inevitable erection sprang to life moments later. He had to get rid of her quickly. His resistance to her kiss was weakening.

"You met Mathias face-to-face and duped him. Angered him. He won't forget that. Or the fact you revealed him to magickind. He *will* hunt you down and torture you. Why didn't you use caution? Bow out?" he growled, ready to tear his hair out. "Now it's too late. In less than two weeks my desire for you has grown far beyond rational. If we mated, there's no question I *would* become like my brother."

"I'm clever, and you'll protect me. Bram and the others will, too."

"No. I'm no longer involved."

"You should be. Don't you see? Strength in numbers. If you stayed with the others, we'd be safer and making a difference. If we mated, we'd have each other. I don't need more." She paused, bit her lip. "I should tell you something—"

"I feel the same and more, but if I mated with you, I could probably count our time together in days on the fist of one hand. This is *war*. Mathias is like . . . magickind's ultimate sociopath. Determined, smart, charismatic, powerful and willing to kill. And he won't die by a simple bullet, as you saw in his warehouse."

"We've weakened his army," she argued. "Taking the fight to him was the right thing to do, and using the book as bait was perfect. Maybe peace will come shortly, and we will have wasted precious time together."

Caden raked a frustrated hand through his hair. They were talking in circles, and still she wouldn't understand. "Peace? Last time Mathias was vanquished, it took decades and an army of experienced wizards. Many died. Too many were sacrificed."

"The same is true in human wars. And like those, we don't have any control over who lives or who dies. We only have control over what we do with our time together." She squeezed his hand. "If Lucan and Anka's separation has shown anything, it should be that, while lovers can suffer, love itself endures. Even without remembering Lucan, Anka *knew* she was missing someone dear."

"And Lucan has been reduced to an animal."

"Who still pines for his mate. You fear becoming like Lucan so much you would rather skip whatever time we might have together? If that's so, you don't love me as I love you." She sniffed. "And maybe I've no one to blame but myself."

"I love you." Caden couldn't stand it anymore, and he grabbed her shoulders. "But I won't be able to endure the pain of losing you!"

"People live, they love . . . and they die. That's unavoidable."

"But I lose over and over again." A well of memories and fears rose inside him, drowning out logic and caution. Opening his past to her would change everything. But continuing to hide the truth was hurting her, and he couldn't bear that anymore.

"I can't find Anka, and Lucan is likely going to die. Just today, I had to kill one of my old Marine buddies in Mathias's warehouse. It was one of the hardest things I've ever done. And still not as terrible as the day I lost my younger brother, Westin."

Sydney paused, then wrapped warm hands around his biceps, offering silent support.

Caden swallowed. "I was twelve. After Lucan, my parents

had tried for over two hundred years to have another child. They were elderly when I was born, but Westin surprised them ten years later.

"He wasn't quite two when we went out one summer morning to play. Westin was my shadow. He looked up to me. And I loved him . . . God."

Tears hacked at the back of his eyes, stinging. He hadn't let himself think about that day or cry since Westin's burial. Remembering his chapped little cheeks and happy giggles now was like opening a chasm in his soul.

"It's okay if you can't say more now."

But he couldn't stop. "I was chasing him, pretending I was going to scoop him up and tickle him until he cried uncle. He ran, as always. But that day, he tripped."

He could see it in his mind, those little feet stumbling, chubby hands flying. Why didn't closing his eyes make the vision go away?

"And he fell?" Sydney promoted softly.

The only heat in his body came from her soft stroke of his arm. Everything else inside him was dead cold. He swallowed.

"Yes. And hit his head on a stone wall."

As he said the words, he could see Westin collide with the wall, then crumble to the ground, blood spewing from a cut on a ragged rock, bruise bursting across his forehead.

Sydney gasped.

He stabbed his eyes with a thumb and forefinger. *Choke out the rest. Get it over with.* He owed her a reason for breaking her heart. "I screamed, and my mother came running. She was rattled but promised that simple magic would make him 'right as rain' again. She squeezed my hand, and I remember feeling utter relief as she hovered her wand over Westin's wound. Instead of healing, he choked, sputtered, suffocated."

Beside him, Sydney frowned. "I don't understand."

"Her magic, meant to heal him, went awry and killed him. She was rattled, perhaps applied the wrong spell. After my mother stopped screaming, I remember the song of the same fucking birds that had been singing ten minutes ago, before my life changed."

"Oh, I'm so sorry, Caden." Sydney wrapped her arms around him tightly.

How easy it would be to lean against her, let the balm of her love fill the festering wound inside him.

Easy but dangerous.

"After that, my mother and I barely spoke. She retired to her bed and never left. I wouldn't blame her for hating me. I ran him into a wall and—"

Tears. Scalding drops made a path down his face and he wiped them away angrily, then drew in a rattling breath. "I can't be with you. I shouldn't even love you. Because I'll lose you like I've lost Westin and my mother, all my friends. And now Lucan. They all hurt like hell. But losing you too." He shook his head. "I'd lose *me*. I'd collapse inside myself and never come out. No reason left to live without you."

"You have every reason to live. Lucan isn't gone, and you're not going to lose me. We're going to fight this bastard and win."

He shook his head. There was too much at risk. "My freedom, life, and heart are gone. I'd like to keep my sanity."

Resignation stiffened her expression, and she stepped out of his embrace. "I've lost those things as well—and I embraced those losses. I think they could lead to something wonderful."

Caden opened his mouth—to say what, he had no idea. But just then a shrill female scream ripped through the house. Adrenaline surged through his bloodstream, and he pushed past Sydney and charged out of the room and down the hall. "Sabelle!"

Sydney was on his heels. "Perhaps she didn't leave. Is Lucan hurting her?"

Likely so, but if he confessed that, then Sydney would insist on helping. The woman truly didn't understand the peril she put herself in. Since he refused to assume the risk of mating with her, he had no right to dictate to her, but be damned, he couldn't hold his tongue.

As he reached Lucan and Anka's bedroom, he grabbed the knob and barked, "Stay here!"

He threw the door open and tried to slam it in her face, but Sydney resisted. As Caden saw the unfolding drama within, he stopped fighting her and stared in mute horror.

Lucan had been released from his bonds and scrambled to the end of the bed where he'd captured a female underneath him, her blond hair twisting in ringlets across the bed and down to the floor. His face contorted with menace as his hands encircled her neck and squeezed.

Instead of struggling beneath him, the woman embraced him, holding as tight as possible, her whole body shaking. Something gentle and magical poured off her, flowing into Lucan. But Lucan and the witch weren't intimately entwined.

They were locked in a death struggle.

This witch didn't have Sabelle's magical signature, but a different one entirely.

She struggled to free her neck and turned her head, revealing a red, distressed face.

"Anka!" Sydney gasped.

Caden didn't have time for surprise, not when Lucan was about to kill his own mate. Why didn't he recognize her? Somehow, someway, Caden had to stop Lucan from choking the life out of his beloved.

Shoving aside his dismay, Caden jumped into action, body slamming Lucan to drive him away from Anka.

"No!" the witch choked out, the sound barely discernible above the din.

But primal instinct gave Lucan ferocity. He lifted one hand away from Anka's slender neck and backhanded Caden away with a roar. Caden hurtled across the room until his head hit one of the bedposts with a thump.

Pain exploded through the back of his skull. Cursing, he reached up to the sore spot. His hand came away sticky and wet with blood. Bloody hell!

Another choked scream made Caden struggle to his feet. Lucan again had his fingers wrapped tightly around Anka's throat. As before, she clutched Lucan to her, rather than shoving him away. Did she want to die?

Caden pulled his mobile phone from his belt, Bram on ready speed dial.

"Help is on the way," Sydney said through a cloud of white smoke. "Sabelle gave me one of those enchanted rock things. I've just used it."

That impulsiveness and acceptance of magic might get her into trouble on occasion, but right now it just might save the day. He tucked the phone away, then crept toward his brother.

It was up to him to stop another tragedy, another loss.

"Lucan," he murmured, panic invading his bones. God, he had to stop this. Lucan would never forgive himself if he killed Anka. "You're hurting Anka. Remember Anka? Your mate."

Lucan's face turned more feral. "Shock Denzell!"

What did Shock have to do with Anka nearly gasping her last breath?

With that growl, Lucan's fingers again tightened on

Anka's neck. Sydney stepped in, and Caden thrust out an arm to hold her back. He was about to have a tragedy on his hands. He didn't need two.

"No. Anka. *Your* Anka," he insisted. "Let her go."

Still, the little witch beneath him gripped Lucan tightly and trembled, even as her face turned red and her eyes began to roll back in her head.

Caden grabbed Lucan's wrists, but couldn't pry them apart. Anka drew in a wheezing gasp of a breath—and brought Lucan closer to her. Caden tried to wedge himself between them, but both were frozen into place by determination, emotion, and that blasted magic.

Suddenly, Lucan stiffened. His eyes flew open wide as Anka melted beneath him, either unconscious or . . .

Dear God, no.

The expression on Lucan's face mirrored that thought. Caden could see the whites of his brother's eyes for the first time in a month. He focused as if he could actually see.

As if scalded, Lucan ripped his hands from Anka's neck and sucked in a panicked gasp.

Caden rushed closer. Check Anka or restrain Lucan first? Ask questions or just start performing CPR and hope Lucan didn't kill him?

His brother saved him from answering that question by rasping out, "What have I done?"

Then he promptly melted into unconsciousness.

CHAPTER EIGHTEEN

CADEN STARED AT HIS brother, who sat on the couch in his family room, cradling his head in his hands. Lucan was alive and lucid . . . and broken.

If Caden had needed more proof of magic's capricious nature, he'd gotten it today.

He didn't ask Lucan if he was all right. Such a stupid question. Caden knew the answer. How did a man face the sort of stunning twist of fate magic had forced Lucan to suffer today, nearly strangling his beloved wife?

Sabelle had arrived in Lucan's bedroom, Bram, Duke, and Ice hot on her heels. Quickly, they'd surmised that Lucan had entered a healthy, restorative sleep. Anka, though pale as death, had depleted her energy.

While Lucan had been trying to kill her, she'd been holding onto him with every ounce of her energy, bravely fighting certain death to perform the *helbresele* spell. To heal his mate mourning. She had drained herself and nearly died in the process.

The good news was, Lucan came around quickly and assessed the damage, thrilled to have his mate back. An elated Lucan had curled his body protectively over Anka's, chanting his apology against her lips over and over. He clung to her, trying to share a bit of his energy with her with simple touches. It worked. The bad news? The first person Anka asked for was Shock.

Caden couldn't forget the way Lucan had staggered back, his guilt morphing, blending with betrayal.

Lucan had sat back on the bed, his face sharp with pain. "That's why you smell like Shock. You've been with him."

Anka's amber eyes welled up with tears, and the terrible truth became clear before she said a word.

"I didn't remember you," she whispered. "I stayed with my human cousin, Aquarius. I hoped Mathias would never think to look for me there, in case he wished to torment me further. I remembered almost nothing about myself or my life."

Caden had gone to his brother's side and braced his hand on Lucan's shoulder in silent support. He wanted to be angry with Anka for hurting his brother, putting him through so much, and now betraying Lucan with his greatest enemy. But her sweet face and bowed mouth crumbled into pain and fear and anguish. She'd been through a great deal, too.

Looking back on the incident three hours later, Caden worried. Despite the fact they seemed meant for each other, could all ever be well between them again? Or had blasted magic ruined something wonderful forever?

He already knew the answer to that question for him and Sydney.

"But you remembered Shock." Lucan had tensed beneath Caden's palm. "Before you recalled me."

Anka then nodded, and fresh tears fell unimpeded down her pale cheeks. "Once Mathias broke our bond, I remembered nothing. I suspected I'd been mated, but I was weak and needed energy. I remembered Shock's Call."

Lucan looked away, clenching his jaw. Caden was certain that his brother was picturing his wife and his enemy embracing. Sharing pleasure. He hurt for Lucan. Imagining Sydney with another man was like an open wound in Caden's gut.

No one else in the room said a word.

Drawing a few deep breaths, Lucan finally turned back to his former mate. "You remember me now. Come home."

"I'm not the same woman," the exhausted witch said sadly.

"You no longer need Shock anymore. You have me."

Anka gathered her strength and grasped Lucan's hand. "I do need him. Everything between you and me is a treasured memory. But I need time . . . I can't simply step back into my old life and be the same woman I was."

Lucan grabbed her shoulders. "Because I failed to protect you?"

She barely managed to shake her head as tears threatened to overtake her. "What Mathias did to me *changed* me. I can't just . . . be happy again. I don't know what I want, what to believe."

"You don't have to." He squeezed her hands tight. "I'll heal you."

"I don't deserve you. You don't know what I did with him." Her eyes squeezed shut as shame washed over her.

"Against your will!"

"It started that way. But then . . ." She squeezed her eyes shut as tears streamed down. "I begged him."

Lucan swallowed. "He compelled you. Don't think for a second that I fault you. I left you unprotected, and Mathias abducted you. I love you—"

She withdrew from his grasp. "Don't. I came to see you as soon as I remembered. I'm sorry for the way our mating ended. I wanted to make certain you weren't suffering."

"Without you? Every day. I have no one to blame but myself for—" Lucan choked on his next words. "For Mathias violating you."

"He hurt you, too," she breathed, her eyes nearly closing as her energy waned. "Until today, I never imagined how deeply. Had to perform the *helbresele* spell."

Her eyes slid shut.

"It nearly killed you. *I* nearly killed you." Lucan eased her onto her back and leaned over her, stroking her pale curls. "Yet, rather than teleporting away, you've stayed."

Silently, Caden had to agree with the unspoken part of Lucan's sentence; Anka's actions revealed strong feelings for her former mate. But her eyes fluttered open and she crossed her arms over her chest and eased from beneath him.

Confusion overtook Lucan's expression, and Caden's heart broke for him. Though this tense moment wasn't his, he found himself holding his breath, wishing for a happy outcome for his brother. After what he and Anka had endured, surely they deserved as much. But magickind wasn't a Hallmark world.

"I had to make things as right for you as I could," she slurred. "Now I must go."

"No!" Lucan clenched his fists at his sides looking somewhere between blindsided and helpless. "Don't. I'll care for you."

"And you'll expect everything to be as it was." Her mouth trembled as she began to cry. "I've experienced too much. I've been with Shock. We can't sweep that under the rug. He will always be between us. Maybe he always was."

Lucan looked like he wanted to refute Anka—and couldn't.

"In time, we could recover."

"I'll always treasure our time together. But Mathias . . ." She choked on tears. "You're a wonderful man, but you must see that I'm ruined. I won't make you endure that," Anka murmured, then turned to Bram. "Will you take me to Shock?"

Though Lucan fought and argued, Anka sent him a contrite stare, then allowed Bram to teleport her out.

Sydney lingered, looking as if she wanted to talk, but there was no need. The regret on her face told him that she understood his reluctance to mate now. He couldn't have illustrated it more clearly if he'd drawn her a picture.

Finally, she left with Ice, Sabelle, and Duke.

Then Caden was alone with Lucan, who quickly decided his best friend was a bottle. Lucan hadn't had a sober moment since.

Shadow crept into the room as Caden looked over at his big brother, cradling his head in his hands, a mostly empty whiskey bottle on the table in front of him. Caden had no idea what to say. Platitudes that all would be well and time healed wounds seemed inane and insulting. He wasn't sure time would heal this wound, ever.

"Don't stare at me. Say something," Lucan growled.

"I don't know what to say."

"I haven't seen you in years. Your presence is a surprise." Lucan laughed bitterly. "One of many. When did you arrive?"

"When your mate mourning began."

A reluctant smile tugged at Lucan's mouth before he took another swig. "Bram come after you?"

"Sabelle, on Bram's orders."

"Bet you hated returning."

Words couldn't express how much, but saying that to Lucan would only increase his guilt. "I'm fine."

"I'm glad you're back. You can't be truly happy in the States. You loved home so much when you were little."

Loved home? Caden remembered the wonderful summer days before Westin's death. A lifetime ago, really. He hadn't thought of those times in decades, romping with his father and younger brother in the fields, playing magical hero, his mother vowing that would be his future.

How much everything had changed.

"The States are home now."

"You'll be going back, then?" Lucan scowled.

Not until he was certain Lucan was okay and settled. Not until he found some way to protect Sydney from danger. "Eventually."

Lucan sighed. "I see you transitioned. Recently?"

Caden nodded. "Last week. Terrible stuff."

Lucan took another long swallow. "You have a strong signature. Powerful magic. Have you used it yet?"

"Not much." Caden couldn't meet Lucan's eyes. His brother had chosen a magic life for himself, and Caden wondered if Lucan would understand his decision otherwise. "I'd rather not. Magic brings nothing but destruction and heartache—"

"And days filled with endless possibilities. Westin's death wasn't your fault. Or Mum's."

Caden looked at him with burning eyes. "Westin should never have died. I should have taken him elsewhere to play. Mum's spell—"

"In both the human and magical world, accidents happen."

"Magic killed him—and took Anka from you, through no fault of your own."

"No." Looking down into the bottle, Lucan hesitated. "I hold the blame."

"What? Don't assume Mathias's guilt. You couldn't be with Anka all day, every day. You did your best to protect—"

"Not enough. Mathias took her and . . . I didn't save her."

"Damn magic threw you into mate mourning. If not for that—"

"Even if I hadn't been in mate mourning, I still would have been out of my mind with worry. The truth is, I failed to consider that Mathias might make her a target when I joined the Doomsday Brethren. Now, I'm reaping what I've sown."

Caden wanted to reassure Lucan that he couldn't have known, but the first rule of combat was to expect the unexpected.

"I haven't a clue what will happen," Lucan went on. "I don't want to give up on Anka, and the fact she hasn't accepted Shock's outstanding Mating Call gives me hope, but I nearly killed her. I didn't protect her when I should have. How can she forgive me?"

No doubt, Lucan still loved her. Profound sadness crept through Caden, and the tragedy wasn't even his. "I'm sorry."

Lucan shrugged. "Who gave me energy while I was out of my mind?"

"We hired surrogates. Do you remember?"

"I remember women who smelled terrible. I remember being angry. I could see nothing, hear very little, but smell guided me. Then I remember a woman who smelled much like Anka . . . at first. The last time she came to me, I scented Sabelle." Lucan winced. "Tell me I didn't use my best friend's sister."

"I'm sorry." Caden could only apologize. Lying would do no good.

Lucan cursed. "I owe her an apology for my rough behavior, I'm certain. And a great deal of gratitude. She's an amazing woman."

Caden couldn't argue that. "Indeed."

A long silence followed, and Caden reached for his own bottle, swallowing the sting of the alcohol, letting it burn a path from his throat to his stomach.

"Let's talk of something more pleasant," Lucan suggested. "Tell me about the saucy redhead who left with Bram and the others."

Caden tensed. "Sydney Blair. She's a reporter for a human tabloid."

"She has feelings for you."

Damn, Lucan had always been perceptive. Caden nodded.

"You have feelings for her, as well. You've adopted a bit of her color in your signature. Despite the fact you haven't spoken the Call, she's your mate."

Too perceptive. "It doesn't matter."

"Would she refuse you?"

"Can we change the subject?"

"Talking about your problems gets my mind off my own." Lucan grabbed the whiskey off the nearby table and took another swig with a lopsided grin. He'd had just enough alcohol to numb his pain and enough mischief to exploit Caden's pity. Sod. "Would she say no?"

"She'd accept."

"You haven't mated with her because . . . you want a witch?"

Caden snorted. Lucan must know better than that. "Of course not."

"You don't love her?"

"I do."

Lucan stroked his chin as if perplexed. "She's against magic?"

"Quite the opposite. She persuaded Bram to allow her to transcast news of Mathias's return."

"The Council agreed?" Lucan looked genuinely shocked.

"No. Bram finally agreed that distributing the information without their blessing was best."

"There will be hell to pay. Good for him, doing the right

thing. Sydney wants to help, then? That's why she's transcasting, despite the danger?"

"Yes." Caden sighed, knowing where Lucan's line of questioning was headed. Might as well beat him to the destination. "And that is precisely why I haven't spoken the Call. The more she involves herself in magickind, the higher up Mathias moves her name on his hit list."

"You don't want to lose her the way you lost Westin. Or the way I lost Anka."

Either would devastate Caden. "Something like that."

Lucan slammed his bottle down on the table and lunged in Caden's face, bracing his fists against the back of the sofa, effectively pinning Caden there. "You stupid fuck! You have a woman who loves you and would accept your mating call. Yet you're willing to flush it down the toilet to avoid possible pain." He scoffed and backed away. "You have no idea—"

"I do!" Caden shoved Lucan aside and jumped to his feet, anger roiling through his body. "You weren't there when Westin died. *I* was!"

Lucan sighed. "An accident."

"That doesn't make him any less dead. And then you—I saw you chained to a bed for weeks. I watched you with Sabelle." Lucan winced, but Caden pressed on. "You nearly killed her for trying to save you. For as long as Anka stays in Shock's bed, there will be an infinitely deep hole in your heart. Why the hell would I sign up for that?"

"Because I wouldn't trade a moment of what Anka and I had together. For any reason. It's my own bloody fault for not protecting her, but I adore her. Love her. I'd never known true happiness until I mated with her. Would I give up all that bliss because I'm hurting now? Never. You have the advantage, idiot. I didn't find Anka until I was nearly three hundred. You're only thirty. You and Sydney could have hundreds of years to enjoy each other."

"Or she could goddamn die tomorrow." Caden shouted. "She constantly puts herself in danger. I do everything in my power to keep her safe, but she doesn't want my protection. She'd rather make a difference for magickind. How can I protect her against a monster like Mathias? Magically, I'm no match for him. Knowing my mate was in his clutches would kill me."

"I'm living proof that it won't. You don't want the pain or the mourning that goes with losing a mate, so you're going to toss her away now? Bloody stupid." Suddenly, Lucan growled and lifted him by his shirt. "Love rarely comes more than once in a lifetime. If you piss her away, be prepared for centuries of emptiness. And without your longer lifespan, you'll see her grow old and turn to dust so quickly your head will spin. Then you'll stand alone, a young wizard on the outside, an old, withering man on the inside, wishing for just ten minutes with your one true love. And she will be gone. I'll be standing there to say I told you so. Because ten minutes with your beloved is better than a lifetime without her."

Like needles piercing her skin, her soul, Sydney felt the pain of Caden's departure. Inside, she ached—even while she wanted to throw half of Bram's priceless knickknacks against his pristine wall. And yet . . . after the up-close view of what Lucan had become and hearing of Westin's heartbreaking death, Sydney couldn't really blame Caden.

She wanted to be furious. Mostly, she was sad.

Maybe if she found some way to end this war sooner, take Mathias down now. . . . If the evil wizard's threat against her ended, she and Caden could deal with the rest of their issues one by one. Likely, it would take time, but as long as they ended up together, she could learn patience.

Evening lengthened into night, then into early morning, and still Sydney paced her room, turning over ideas, rejecting them, starting over. After hours of filtering through ideas, two remained. First, she had to find that magical book and discern once and for all if the feelings they shared had originated from the book. If so, she had to undo the magic. And let the chips fall.

Second, she had to help magickind in a larger way. Transcasting Mathias's return was a start. Bram hadn't let her give details about the attacks—yet. But if magickind knew what Mathias had done, what he planned to do, and got angry at the horrific violence Mathias was inflicting, magickind might band together. If so, Mathias didn't stand a chance. But they needed an advantage.

One sat languishing behind bars downstairs.

Sydney glanced at the clock. Nearly three in the morning. *No time like the present.*

Down the dark stairs she traveled, creeping into Bram's office. In a secret compartment behind the sofa, she located the book. After they'd returned from attacking Mathias's warehouse, Bram had disclosed his hiding place to all the females in the house . . . just in case.

Extracting the little book, she lit a small desktop lamp and spread the pages open with a pen. Quickly, she leafed through the book, looking for her previous two entries. She couldn't find the first. Or the second. *What the hell?* Blasted book made no sense. Then again, it was magic.

With a sigh, Sydney stared at the blank pages. *What to write?*

Within a few minutes she crafted another message to her "Magical Diary," wishing that she hated Caden and he

loathed her as well. They would give each other coal for
Christmas, dead roses for Valentine's Day, and snarl like pit
bulls every day in between. Then she stared at the page,
waiting for the diary's inevitable message.

> *To wish for enmity, you are too late.*
> *This fantasy cannot be your fate.*
> *Because true love has claimed your*
> *hearts, you two are sworn never to part.*

True love? A smile burst across her face. Hearing that her
fantasies hadn't incited false feelings was a huge relief—and
made her all the more impatient to get on with task number
two. The sooner she found a way to rally magickind around
Bram, the sooner she and Caden could work through their differences. That meant trying to talk information out of Zain.

Though he was likely to be a hostile interview subject
and it was the middle of the night, she wasn't waiting. Who
knew whether Mathias could do extra damage to magickind
while she waited for a more polite hour? Zain was behind
bars, had no wand, and Bram had explained that only his
houseguests could teleport in and out. The dungeon dampened magical ability, too. She'd be safe long enough to ask a
few questions.

But how? Snark wouldn't serve her. Zain's T-shirts suggested he would snark back, which would be counterpro-
ductive. She'd be better served using their previous work
connection and playing the stupid human card.

Sydney grabbed Bram's little video camera and made her
way through the dark house, down to where Bram kept Zain
locked away.

She eased the door open. It was pitch black inside. No

windows, no lights. The room smelled like damp stones and despair. She shivered.

"Why are you here, Sydney?" Zain rasped out. He sounded weak.

"How did you—"

"Your scent."

She didn't think taking a shower would fix that. "Where's a light?"

"There isn't one." He barely got the words out.

Sydney recoiled. "I'll return."

Trudging upstairs, she wondered why there was no light in the dungeon. Even during the day, with the room underground and no windows, the room would remain black as midnight. A magical form of torture? Either way, she couldn't find the buttons to start the video camera without a bit of light.

In the library, she found a candle. She had to search harder for a match. Probably not a necessary item in a magical household, but her handbag still had a book of matches from the pub near her house.

Lighting and clutching the candle, she descended the stairs again and pushed open the door. Setting the candle on a nearby table, she turned on the video camera. Its light burst into every corner as she stepped into the middle of the room.

"What the devil?" Zain shielded his face with his hand, his longish hair wild.

"Sorry. I'd hoped to interview you."

"I don't want to talk." He sighed. "I'm exhausted. I need more time with the surrogate. I'm still weak after healing your friend. Bram allowed me very little energy."

Perhaps he was faking it, but he looked like death warmed over. Pale and gaunt, several days' growth shadowed his jawline, nearly overwhelming his face. His clothing was dirty. Of course, he deserved every bit of it for what he'd done to Aquarius.

"If you talk to me, I'll talk to him."

Zain frowned. "Why should I trust you?"

"What have I done to earn your distrust? I'm just trying to understand what's happening. Caden wants nothing to do with magic and won't talk about it. Bram is too busy. The others . . . well, you know far more than I."

Zain leaned against the bars. "Of course I do."

The stroke to his ego. She bit her lip, putting on her best earnest face. "Help me. I *am* a reporter at heart. Even if this story will never see daylight, I want to understand . . . when you first came to work for *Out of This Realm*, you said you had a mysterious someone who left you information. That wasn't true, was it? Did Mathias tell you? Or did you just know?"

"I knew. I know most everything Mathias does or plans."

"I thought as much. I've heard Bram's side of this war, but I want to understand Mathias's. I'm intrigued by his struggle for equality. It sounds so . . . utopian. But I allowed myself to be swayed by Anka's story of rape and Bram's tales of Privileged attacks without checking the other side of the story. It wasn't professional of me. What is Mathias's side to those stories?"

Zain drew in a ragged breath. "Everyone has enemies, some willing to exaggerate the truth."

"That's true, but I saw Anka after Mathias released her. Did he break her bond with Lucan, then force her to his bed?"

"That was her view of events. Mathias's version of the story is much less melodramatic."

Doubtful, but she had to keep him talking, find proof for

magickind that Mathias was up to something terrible so they would rally behind Bram and the Doomsday Brethren.

"Right, then. What are Mathias's plans to help the Deprived overcome their oppression?"

Zain moaned. "Come closer. I can't hear you."

Sydney bit her lip. Was he lying? Perhaps, but so far he was doing nothing more menacing than begging. He had no wand, no energy, could barely keep his eyes open. How could he be a threat?

"What are Mathias's plans?" she repeated.

"Closer," he pleaded. "Please. Give me your hand. I need a bit of your energy."

She stilled. "You can get it from a simple touch?"

"Some."

His request disturbed her. She didn't trust him to touch her. "Answer me first. What does Mathias plan?"

"To eradicate inequality, of course."

"How? How will obtaining the Doomsday Diary help him do that? Will he simply write that as a wish?"

"What else would he do?"

"I don't know. You're familiar with him. All I've heard are the . . . rumors."

"They're crap!"

Sydney was tired of Zain's coy answers. She had to break him out of this mode. "Are they? I understand the opposition telling lies and whatnot, but if you're anything to go by . . . What you did to my friend Aquarius was unforgivable. You threatened to kill me!"

The more she thought about it, the more angry she became.

"Worthless pawns, both of you," he spat. "Just like your wizard lover."

Zain's remark was meant to get under her skin, and it did.

But she refused to show it. "Why should anyone get behind your 'cause' if half the goal is simply to kill people?"

"Stupid prats blame someone brave enough to challenge the establishment. Mathias should be hailed as a hero." Zain lunged at the bars and shook them.

They rattled, clinked. Dust and grit fell from the ceiling. Was the plaster disintegrating?

Sydney glanced up to where the bars joined the ceiling. They were working free.

She gasped and peered at Zain. Had he seen it, too?

Too late. He had. He might not be able to do magic, but he could use his strength to get out. Fear laced her veins as she turned to run. She had to get help.

Two steps later, she heard the bars rattle—then thud to the ground. She kept moving, but Zain grabbed a fistful of her hair and whirled her around.

"The delicious energy from your anger and fear was just what I needed."

He wore a sick, almost sexual smile that turned her stomach. She looked away, mind racing. How could she get away to alert Bram and the others? What had she done?

"Look at me," he barked, using his grip in her hair to force her to comply. "Now, be a good girl and retrieve the Doomsday Diary."

"Why?" she asked wanly.

"For Mathias, of course."

"But he'll take it and kill me."

Zain pulled her close and stroked her cheek. "Think of yourself as an important sacrifice for a very worthy cause. You'll make the news."

Fear lanced Sydney. *Oh God!* She had to fight.

"Don't try anything, or I'll roast you and make what I did to Aquarius seem like a sunburn."

She drew in a deep breath, battling her fear. She refused to be bullied. "Do it. I won't give up the book."

"Then I'll kill everyone you work with at that silly human tabloid. Do you want that many deaths on your conscience?"

Bastard! Zain had her and he knew it. As he pushed her up the stairs to Bram's office, Sydney tried to think of a way out of this mess. But he'd boxed her in completely. Holly and the others were all human and no match for what Zain could unleash on them.

Quickly, she deposited the video camera on Bram's desk, then dragged out the hidden book once more. Trembling and dismayed, she handed it to him.

Chapter Nineteen

With a gasp, Caden sat straight up in bed. He looked around the darkened room at Lucan's house, panting, sweating.

Something was wrong.

Bounding out of bed, he grabbed his jeans and shirt, thrusting them on as he ran down the hall to Lucan's room and shoved the door. Empty. *Shit!*

Backtracking, he raced toward the front of the house, wondering if his brother had slipped out, gone to challenge Shock for Anka, decided to end it all. . . . Instead, he found Lucan sleeping fitfully on the sofa.

As Caden's gaze latched onto his brother's face, Lucan opened his eyes. "What is it?"

Hesitating, Caden wasn't certain what to say. Lucan was well enough—in one piece, anyway. But Caden *knew* something was terribly wrong.

"I have this sense of foreboding . . . this dread." It throbbed inside him, an echo of someone else's real fear.

Lucan rubbed his hand over his shadowed jaw. "Have you opened your magical senses?"

"My what? No."

Lucan sighed. "Close your eyes. Look inside yourself for your magic. That thing that sparks and burns at your core."

His eyes slid shut, and he shook his head. "It's not in one place; it's everywhere."

"Find the heart of it. Look inside," Lucan snapped impatiently.

As Lucan said the words, Caden focused deeper inward. There it was. As soon as he found the heart of his magic, it expanded, growing exponentially, as if it had been waiting for him to acknowledge its existence. Now, it woke a sleeping giant. Desperately, Caden tried to shrink it, shove it aside—something.

"No!" Lucan commanded. "Grab onto it. Let it take you."

"Hell no! It's going to drown me. It's massive."

"Excellent." Lucan jumped to his feet. "Size . . . um, matters. Magically speaking."

"I don't want it! Damn it, I just want to be normal."

"You're not," Lucan snapped. "And the sense that something is wrong often involves a wizard's mate. If you want to know if something happened to Sydney, I suggest you give your senses free rein. Now."

Caden caught his breath. *Sydney in trouble?* Yes, he sensed it. *Her* fear and panic. Her regret. Her cry for help. And for her, he'd move mountains, scale skyscrapers.

Embrace magic.

Most of the night he'd spent pondering Lucan's admonishments about embracing love and accepting his mate. His heart wanted it so damn bad. All evening, logic had urged him to resist.

But everything changed the moment he knew Sydney was in danger.

Without hesitation, he looked inward again, mentally touching his magic. It burst inside him, burning down his arms, reaching its tentacles through his brain—and grabbing on. As it did, he looked outward for Sydney, trying to feel her, find her.

He did, and horror washed over him.

"Oh, God," Caden gasped, heart drumming furiously.

"For a moment, I saw everything through her eyes. And he's got her. Mathias!"

Lucan cursed. "Don't panic. Close your eyes. See if your magic can locate her."

He concentrated, frowned. Vague images pinged back at him. Her arms curled around the book, Mathias barking questions. But no location.

"I-I can't. I don't know how. You couldn't do it when Anka was taken from you."

Would Sydney be ravaged by that monster, as Anka had been? If an experienced wizard with a long-term mate bond had been unable to find her, what hope did Caden have?

"He took Anka suddenly," Lucan explained. "I felt only a vague sense of uneasiness before the bond was broken."

"We aren't mated. How can I find what isn't technically mine?"

"Mother said for years that your magic would cross rare lines. Try."

A deluge of thoughts and emotions pounded him. Fear. Anger at himself for not mating with Sydney. Dread. The sensations that kept pouring across the tenuous thread of consciousness he shared with her. Determination.

There! "A house. Remote." Frustration crashed over him. "That's all I can see. It could be anywhere."

"Have you teleported on your own yet?"

"No."

Lucan sighed roughly. "Remind me when this is over to beat you within an inch of your stubborn life. Close your eyes. Envision yourself getting as close to Sydney as possible. Focus on your sense of her, not the appearance of the location. Your instincts should guide you to her."

His first time to teleport, and he wasn't even sure where he was headed? No time to worry about that. "If I fail?"

Wincing, Lucan slapped his shoulder. "Best not to dwell on that."

Perfect. But as a fresh surge of terror clawed at his magical senses, and he actually felt Sydney's fear like the taste of blood in his mouth, he had to try now.

"Here I go."

Lucan grabbed his arm. "I'll pop in on Bram. He'll help."

Caden shook his head. "He coerced me to temporarily join the Doomsday Brethren in exchange for helping me find Anka. After flubbing a mission a few days ago, he ousted me."

With a raised brow, Lucan predicted, "I think you'll be surprised. But if I'm wrong, then I'll go to Shock. He'll know best where Mathias is keeping Sydney."

The gesture stunned Caden. "You'd do that? Even though the bastard has your mate?"

"To keep you with yours so that you could have your happy ending? Yes. Shock may well work for Mathias, and if so—"

"He claims to be a double agent."

"Not relevant now, except that if he's truly on our side, then getting him to help me find Sydney should be much simpler. Go. I'll sort the rest out."

Suddenly a scream rent his mind. Pain and fear scraped every nerve ending raw. The time for deliberation was gone. He had to act now.

He closed his eyes, focused on Sydney and how to be as near her as possible. Then he was tumbling through the dark.

"How lovely of you to bring the Doomsday Diary to me." Mathias sent her a tight smile. "I'll reward Zain later. But now, my dear, you must tell me how the book works."

Sydney staggered as Zain completed teleporting and the room tilted. She blinked, trying to get her bearings. But all she saw was an unfamiliar house. And Mathias waiting for her.

Fear zipped down her spine. It was one thing to sit across from Mathias with Shock present and the Doomsday Brethren just outside. This face-to-face now? Disturbing, to say the least.

She clutched the book to her chest. "What will you do with it?"

He sifted his fingers through her hair, and Sydney tried not to show just how distasteful she found his touch. "Put an end to all this silly fighting. Magickind needs to unite."

Under the banner of false equality and his cruel thumb? No.

"How does the book work?"

Sydney figured in this instance, her best defense was to play dumb. "I don't know. I'm not a witch."

"Precisely my point." Mathias leaned closer, and she shivered. "How can a human control that book?"

His eyes, so icy blue, were nearly silver—and alive with intelligence and evil. Sexuality oozed from every pore. To the woman who didn't know what he was, a man this good looking would be a powerful lure. Yet Sydney was not only repelled, but disgusted. His closeness spiked nausea through her.

She had no idea why he wasn't reading her mind as Sabelle did. Different powers? Whatever. She wasn't looking a gift horse in the mouth.

"I d-don't."

Without using his hands or feet, he scooted both himself and the sofa he sat upon closer. It just moved. Then he leaned in, grabbing her arms. "It's attached to you. The minute you left my office in the warehouse, it dissolved out of my hands, back into yours. Tell me why."

If Mathias didn't know the secrets of the Doomsday Diary, she wasn't going to explain them. She was pretty certain he regarded humans as little better then pond scum, so convincing him of her stupidity shouldn't be difficult.

She shrugged. "Something Bram did?"

Mathias stared, deep, hard. Sydney tried not to give the prick the benefit of her fear, but he seemed to reach inside her and bring it all out. "Do you know what I did to one of the Doomsday Brethren's mates?"

Despite her vow to stay strong, she shrank back in her chair. "You raped her."

He smiled as if reliving a fond memory. "Indeed, I rent her bond with her mate and stole most of her life essence. She was a strong witch, and that took time. You I can decimate in three minutes. Then I'll hunt down the cowardly wizard who hasn't completed his Mating Call and make him watch while I waste you completely under the pounding of my cock."

"You vile son of a bitch. You stay the hell away from us!"

Mathias laughed. "Or what?"

Sydney clutched her hands in her lap, her brain furiously whirling for a way out. Why had she ever imagined that Zain locked up without a wand was harmless? That she understood magic enough to know what was safe? Caden had been telling her for days now that it was unpredictable and dangerous. She hadn't listened.

"Let's try again," Mathias suggested. "You tell me what I want to know, and I'll spare you."

"You're going to kill me anyway. Let's be honest."

"Hmm." Mathias frowned. "It occurs to me that the Doomsday Brethren will converge on me en masse to save you, the book, or both. You're excellent bait. As soon as all the Doomsday Brethren are dead, *then* I can kill you. Unless you'd like me to show some mercy. Tell me what you know about the diary, and I might."

Sydney highly doubted that, but if they were still talking, she was still alive and still able to try to find a way out of this. "I don't know anything that will help you."

"I grow tired of this game."

Mathias flicked a hand in her direction. A fireball burst inside her. She screamed as if her insides had suddenly been boiled in acid. She clutched her middle, fearing imminent death.

Caden! her mind screamed. She loved him and wished everything could have ended differently between them. She would have liked to kiss him and know one perfect night as his mate. But even dying like this, she wasn't sorry she'd become involved with him. She was only sorry that she didn't know how to fight this evil and couldn't keep the others safe.

"Didn't like that, did you?" he asked smugly. "Maybe you'll be more cooperative now. Right, Shock?"

Sydney's eyes flew open, and Shock stood beside Mathias, wearing those sunglasses that hid his every thought. He smirked at her, his look suggesting that she was getting what she deserved. But he'd helped Bram and the others attack Mathias's warehouse. The attack had been a success . . . or had it? Mathias had escaped, and with that terrible glass sphere he used to make Anarki soldiers at will. *Whose side was he really on?*

"Hello, Sydney." Shock's voice held all the warmth of a glacier.

"You treacherous, two-faced bastard!"

"You do have the Doomsday Brethren convinced that you have their best interests at heart." Mathias laughed.

Shock sent Mathias a brash smile. "Of course. How can I help you?"

Sydney reared back. Every time Shock opened his mouth to Bram he was challenging, disrespectful. When he spoke to Mathias, she'd been surprised not to hear a "master" at the end of his greeting.

"Read this stupid chit's mind, please. What does she know about the Doomsday Diary? Where did she get it?"

Shock turned toward her. She used the techniques Sabelle had given her to ward him out of her mind, but even her dull thoughts of computer maintenance and a dreary lullaby didn't stop him.

"It was a gift to her, from a friend. She isn't certain where the friend got it."

"What else does she know?" Mathias scowled.

"She was told it granted sexual fantasies. It came with no further instructions."

"Did she use it in that capacity?" he asked Shock.

"No," Sydney said.

"Of course," Shock corrected immediately. "Twice. It worked both times."

"Is she a witch?"

She could actually feel Shock tromping through her mind, his steps as subtle as an elephant's. Gripping her head to stop the pain, she willed him to get out. A moment later, his heavy presence left her.

"If she is, she is unaware of it."

"How old are you?" Mathias snapped.

She sighed. If she didn't answer, Mathias would just send Shock back in to pillage her mind.

"Twenty-seven."

"Not a witch," they said in unison.

"Females transition into their powers around twenty-five," Shock supplied.

Mathias focused on her utterly, the same way a snake

probably watched its prey before swallowing it whole. "The book has conferred some sense of ownership to you. Because you used it?"

Suddenly, Shock was in her head again, crashing through her skull as if he was looking for answers with a machete. She screamed at the skull-cracking pain.

"She does not know."

Mathias waved him away. "That's all. Go round up the Anarki. I'm expecting company soon. You'll greet them, I hope."

Shock shot her an evil grin. "With great pleasure."

Sydney watched him with horror as he strode out, long leather duster trailing behind him.

As soon as he was gone, Mathias snatched the Doomsday Diary off of her lap and rose, his long stride eating up the space to the door out of the makeshift office. The moment Mathias stepped over the threshold, he cursed.

The book reappeared on her lap.

When he turned back to her, he fixed his stare on the diary, then lifted his terrible gaze to her. The force of his anger was like a missile. Even across the room, she knew the fury rimming his eyes with red could be fatal.

He took a deep breath. Another. Then strode across the room again in measured steps and sat on the sofa once more. "It's because you're female. Damn Morganna. Did a woman give this book to you?"

She wanted to tell him to go to hell, but he'd kill her for it. At the very least she had to stay alive long enough to help any of the Doomsday Brethren who came.

"Yes."

"Human?"

"I believe so."

"Even more puzzling . . ." Mathias sat back against the

red velvet sofa, looking perplexed. Suddenly, he snapped.

Moments later, a bony woman with glossy black hair and black-rimmed brown eyes glided to his side. She wore a blue bra that supported pert breasts, but was cut low, nearly exposing her hard nipples. Her matching knickers were nearly transparent.

"Sir?" she breathed.

He stood and dropped an open-mouthed kiss on her neck, his thumb idly strumming her taut nipple. She keened and writhed under his touch. Surely he was forcing her response by magical means, because the wizard made Sydney's skin crawl. When he caressed her hip and buttocks, pulling her close, the woman lifted her leg over his hip and writhed sinuously.

They needed privacy. If she had to watch another moment, she would be ill.

"Rhea, be a good girl and grab that book from the human's lap."

With an absent nod, the thin woman slinked across the distance between. Sydney clutched the book. The woman tugged, but Sydney refused to let go. Once she did, she was pretty sure she'd lose control of the Doomsday Diary. Mathias had it right; the little journal didn't seem fussy about *which* woman handled it.

"Let go," Mathias instructed.

"Sod off."

"You'll pay for that backtalk."

Mathias flicked his hand in her direction and the scorching bomb burst under her skin again. Reflexively, she released the book and doubled over, clutching her stomach. Oh God, she was going to die at the hands of this madman.

"Take the book to my bedroom, sweet. I'll join you there."

The tall woman smiled, and Sydney wondered if she'd lost her bleeding mind. Likely so. Rhea strutted toward the door on four-inch stilettos, as if she'd been born on them. When she reached the door, she strode through with her head held high, then kept walking—taking the book with her. This time, it didn't reappear on Sydney's lap.

Sydney's stomach sank. She'd lost magickind's greatest weapon and put it in the hands of a madman who'd likely use it to kill her and all the Doomsday Brethren, including Caden. Her reckless need to tell the story, her voracious curiosity to explore the amazing world of magic had been her downfall. Why hadn't she listened?

It was her last thought before darkness overtook her.

After free-falling through black weightless space, Caden slammed to the ground in a cold field. Fresh snow had fallen and seeped under his clothes. Every exhalation misted the chilly air. The crisp smells reminded him of the north country. He had no idea how far he'd traveled, but he closed his eyes, feeling for Sydney, and knew he was closer.

Her earlier panic had been replaced with a muffled unease, as if she had a disturbed sleep. Now he prayed it was slumber, not something tragic.

He followed the feel of Sydney, closer, closer with each step through the dark. He almost thanked the snow for lighting his way with the reflective moonlight.

Through spindly trees, he saw a huge estate rise in the distance. More Italian Renaissance than Middle Ages, the beautiful limestone glowed in the golden light as pristine snow surrounded it. She was in there, his Sydney. He knew it, just like he knew if he took too many more steps around the perimeter, he could set off magical traps.

He took a deep breath, closed his eyes. He was a trained

soldier, often able to find and disable security. Mathias's would be magical, but should be disarmable. Thinking with his magical senses would be critical.

Magic buzzed through his system, raced through his veins. His legs were a bit wobbly after the teleport, and this level of energy wasn't going to last. But he had to endure until he saved Sydney.

Caden skirted the perimeter of the building, looking for traps and holes in the security. A few feet ahead, he encountered a wall, presumably for humans since it did nothing more than put off a "keep out" vibe. It included a very mild electrical surge—more than enough to deter a normal human.

Too bad for Mathias he wasn't "normal" anymore.

Closing his eyes, Caden let his senses crawl around the wall. About ten feet high. Simple.

While he didn't know the limits of his magic, there was nothing he couldn't do if it helped him reach Sydney. For all he knew, he was bloody Superman. When he was a tot, his mother had certainly made it sound as if he would be. Besides, he'd already performed some magic. Lifting Sydney's password off her computer at *Out of This Realm*, sending a wall of glass flying into Anarki when the Doomsday Brethren had attacked Mathias. How hard could leaping a wall be?

Squeezing his eyes shut tight, he jumped—and quickly discovered that when he tapped into his magic, jumping ten-foot walls was no problem. One step closer to Sydney.

Moments later, Caden noticed a shifting of the air. Then he saw something unexpected. Someone.

Shock strode toward him as if rising up out of the mist. Even at night, he wore those blasted sunglasses, so Caden had no idea what he was thinking. He'd never really trusted the sod, and now that the man had all but stolen his brother's mate away, he didn't trust Shock at all.

"You're here for Sydney. I'll sneak you past the alarms and take you to her."

"Why should I trust you? You had Anka under your roof and in your bed for days and told no one. Nor did you return her to my brother."

"She was *mine* before your brother stole her from me," he growled. "I owe Lucan nothing. She was abducted and hurt on his watch. It won't happen on mine."

Caden hesitated, mulling over Shock's words. In all likelihood, that's exactly how Shock saw the matter. But that didn't piss Caden off any less or make him trust Shock any more.

"I don't really care about your tender sensibilities," Shock mocked. "If you're here for Sydney, I'll take you now."

Caden glared at the leather-clad wizard. "Just like that?"

Shock looked past Caden. "You come alone?"

The truth gave Shock the green light to overpower him. But Shock would only read his mind if he lied.

Caden nodded. "This is my fight."

He raised a skeptical brow above those dark sunglasses. "So Bram and Lucan and the others are leaving you to rescue Sydney and the book by yourself?"

"Sydney is my responsibility. The book isn't my first priority."

"But you're going to try to rescue it." It wasn't a question.

And Shock was right. Since opening his magical senses, he'd come to understand that if he didn't, he could save Sydney, but Mathias could use the book to consign them all to hell on earth ten minutes later. If he genuinely wanted her safety and the chance to live happily ever after with her, then he had to snatch the book.

Shock sighed. "Well, of course, you'll want to save the book. It shouldn't have been a hard decision."

"Get the hell out of my thoughts."

"Look, you did a good job getting this close, but once Mathias took your woman, he knew you'd come. I suspected you'd come after the book, as well. Despite what you think, the others *will* come. Now I'm going to restrain you and drag you to Sydney's cell, to make it all look believable."

He shook his head. "Mathias seems like a natural ally for you, since your brother is all cozied up with him. How do I know that I can trust you, mate thief?"

An acrimonious smile split his mouth. "You don't."

Caden roused with a groan and opened his eyes to find a dank limestone floor—and realized he was hanging upside down, a shoulder in his midsection. A throb ripped through the peace in his head, and he groaned.

"Awake, are you?" A male voice groused. Shock. "That was a quick recovery. Your magic is strong. I'll have to keep my eye on you. On your feet."

With a grunt, Shock set him down. Shadowed, underground. Prison-like. Shit.

"You're not locking me up!"

Shock shoved him around a corner. "Don't be difficult, whelp. You wanted to see your woman, and I'm taking you to her. I have to wait for the rest of the company."

With a downward slash of his wrist, Shock opened the cell. Its rusty door squeaked open. Sydney appeared out of a dark corner, looking no worse for the wear. She ran to the open door, but Shock held up a palm, creating an invisible wall to stop her. Caden tried to focus on tearing down that wall, to no avail. Shock's magic didn't bend.

Damn, there was always Marine-style brute force.

Caden whirled and punched Shock in the stomach, and he grunted, doubling over. Running toward Sydney, Caden was determined to get her though Shock's force field. He grabbed her hand, and when his fingers closed around hers, a sense of home and thankfulness curled around him. Warmth, relief, need.

Until he felt a boot right in his arse.

Caden tumbled into the cell, falling into Sydney. They toppled over, to the cold floor, in a heap of arms and legs.

With a rusty screech, the cell door closed, and Shock used his magic to seal it.

He sent them a sly smile. "Wait here. If your friends don't appear, Mathias will send you back to Bram and the others with a message. Your woman . . ." Shock shook his head. "You should know, it doesn't look good."

Scrambling to his feet, Caden raced to the bars and screamed at Shock's retreating back, "You traitor! How the hell could you do something so miserable and underhanded when people are dying? Do you care more about your own power than the fact Mathias is going to wipe out entire families?"

Shock paused, then slowly turned to glare at Caden over his leather-clad shoulder. "You don't know a damn thing about me."

Then Shock was gone, and Caden sighed as failure settled over him, heavy and oppressive. How bloody stupid had he been, believing that he could rescue Sydney from the most powerful wizard in a millennium by himself?

"Caden, how did you get here?" she asked.

He turned to her, drinking in the sight of her, loose sweat pants, baggy T-shirt, hair blazing like a wildfire around her shoulders. The impact of her slammed into him.

She was his, the past he should have grabbed with both hands, the future he could have if they found a way out of this bloody mess. He wasn't going to give it or her up for another second.

"Sydney, I'm sorry. I love you." Refusing to waste a second, Caden cradled her face in his hands and did something he should have done the moment he met her: He kissed her.

His mouth crashed over hers, open, seeking, dying for a taste of her. Their lips joined. Their tongues met. Her taste boomed across his senses, spicy, sweet, slightly tart—all woman. His senses revved up, both magical and male. In concert, they demanded more, everything, from her. A chorus of *now, now, now!* chanted in his head. His body tensed, his cock hardened, and he grasped her tighter.

Under him, Sydney surged, throwing her fervor into the kiss. She grabbed his hair, clutched his sweater, moaning, writhing, accepting in every way.

Lucan had been right. Ten minutes with Sydney was better than an eternity without her.

Familiar words burst across his brain, and he embraced them, then tore his mouth from hers and panted, "Become a part of me as I become a part of you. And ever after, I promise myself to thee. Each day we share, I shall be honest, good, and true. If this you seek, heed my call. From this moment on, there is no other for me but you."

She gasped, her eyes welling. "You're certain?"

Caden took her mouth again, her flavor bursting across his senses, and he knew without a doubt she was his one true mate. Always had been. Always would be. "Completely."

"Mathias is going to kill me. Soon. You'll be like Lucan—"

"I'll do everything I can to prevent that, but if not, I would rather have had you for a few moments than not at all, firecracker."

"Promise me, if you make it out alive, that you'll continue fighting. Not for revenge, but for what's right. For magickind."

"I won't let you go easily. You won't be unavenged. I won't let this scum take over *my* people."

Warm tears rolled down her cheeks. Then she smiled, lighting up the cell, his world. "I'm so proud of you, and I love you so much." She sniffed. "But there's something you should know. I wrote about you in the Doomsday Diary. I wanted you so badly . . ."

Caden searched his memories. "The night I crashed through the door of your flat and we made love against the wall?"

"Yes. And again before you took me on my kitchen table."

"You minx." He caressed her cheek lovingly. "You had *no* idea what you were in for."

"I wouldn't change it for the world. I tried to . . . I wrote a reverse 'fantasy' in the Doomsday Diary to see if your feelings for me were all magically manufactured."

"They're not. I swear."

She sent him an impish smile. "I know. The diary told me."

With a growl, he pulled her against him. "Don't you have an answer for me? Do you know the words?"

She nodded. "Bram and Sabelle have a great library." Happiness broke over her face, like the sun from behind storm clouds, illuminating everything in joy. "As I become a part of you, you become a part of me. I will be honest, good, and true. I heed your call. 'Tis you I seek. From this moment on, there is no other for me but you."

A powerful jolt slammed into Caden's body, and his sense of Sydney as his mate jumped into the foreground of his consciousness, fusing into his heart. She had been important; now she was his everything. She gasped, clearly feeling it as well.

But with the sealing of their bond came another crashing need—to test her, taste her, claim her—all of her.

Without a thought, he dragged the baggy shirt off one shoulder to reveal a bare breast, then he cupped it.

"Caden! They're going to come back. We should focus on—"

He cut her speech off with a kiss, deep, blistering, the kind that sent sizzle all the way through his body. Slowly, she melted against him.

Caden eased back until he sat on the room's lone bed, bringing her down to straddle his lap. Narrow and squat, the little bed wasn't the haven he wanted the first time he loved his mate, but he wasn't going to quibble. She was in his arms. The future was coming, he knew. But he'd face it stronger if he joined with her first.

"This might be our last chance," he whispered against her mouth. "Our only chance. Let me love you."

Sydney didn't hesitate. She grabbed Caden's sweater, tugging and pulling until she managed to yank it over his head. Rapaciously, she ran her hands over his hands and shoulders, and he thanked his years of daily running and training in the Marines and beyond that kept him in shape.

But he wasn't content to just have her hands on him; he wanted her open to him. Lifting her off his lap, he dragged the large sweatpants down one thigh. Another adjustment, and his own pants rested south of his hips.

As he brought her back to his lap, he captured her mouth again, brushed his knuckles over her collarbone, across her nipple, skipped the shirt covering her abdomen, then delved into the red curls between her pale thighs. Slick, steamy—ready. He'd missed her so, so much, trying to separate her from him, and thus from danger. Keep himself safe from the whims of magic. But he'd been foolish, wasting time. If they managed to escape this place in one piece, he'd never waste another second together. If they didn't . . . he didn't regret their mating in the least.

Raking his fingertips over her clit, he basked in her sighs and moans. She melted, all delicious and sweet, around his hand as he plunged his fingers inside her and rubbed her sweet spot.

Her fingernails found their way into his shoulders, and he smiled when she dusted his neck with urgent kisses. The smile turned to desperate hunger when she caught his mouth in a searing kiss, grabbed his aching erection, and pushed her hips down to it.

Slowly, she sank over him, and the tight clasp of her body was both a homecoming and a pleasure unlike any he'd ever known. His mate. *His.* No matter what.

Their time was short, but their love unlimited. Grabbing her hips, he tutored her in a long, slow stroke as he brushed his lips over hers again, then settled deep, mating with her body, her mouth—her heart.

Gripping his biceps, she stroked her way up and down his cock, and the inferno-hot pleasure singed him. She tightened around him. Her cheeks grew pink, then flushed a darker rose. Her nipples swelled, her head tipped back, and she looked like the ultimate goddess of pleasure. Smart, brave, loving. His.

Caden's heart swelled with need, with love. His body did the same. Grimacing, he tried to stave off the orgasm about to overwhelm. But Sydney's pace quickened. She dug her fingers deeper into him as she bounced on him, chanting his name. Caden curled his arms around her and fused his mouth to hers as her sex clamped down on him. He swallowed her scream of pleasure and joined her over the abyss, in an ecstasy that not only suffused him with a warm satiation—but a jolt of power so intense, it nearly overpowered his system. And love. God, so much of it. That love gave him a new dimension of strength. He was determined that, while that may have been their first time making love as mates, it damn well wouldn't be their last.

Quietly, they dressed, pausing to kiss. He touched her, wrapped her in his embrace to reassure her, then sat on the bed to cuddle her in his lap.

"Caden?" she turned worried brown eyes on him.

He knew everything on her mind. It was on his too. But damn it, he hadn't come this far, been born with the sort of magic that his mother, as a good seer, had praised, and found this amazing woman, only to have her ripped from him.

Time to fight.

"Shh. It's not over."

"Your time alone is." A man's voice intruded on their intimate cocoon. Shock. Then he opened the cell and motioned to Sydney. "Come with me."

CHAPTER TWENTY

SYDNEY TREMBLED AS SHOCK held her by the elbow and dragged her toward the middle of the house. "Where are you taking me?"

"Where Mathias asked me to."

His complete lack of inflection, of guilt, incensed her. Rage bottled up inside her, then she wondered why she was keeping a cork on it. She was going to die, regardless. Why not tell Shock what toilet scum she thought he was?

"So you enjoy watching innocent people be tortured to death? Or you just don't care?"

He glared down his shoulder at her, his expression unreadable. "You're playing games you don't understand."

"You're betraying people who count on you."

"More than you know," he muttered, then tugged on her elbow and dragged her behind him.

As she feared, Shock lugged her back to the cold sitting room of black, glass, and chrome in which she'd been earlier. There, Mathias sat, waiting, his expression cool but impatient. She had the distinct impression he was concealing the depth of his rage. And it scared the hell out of her. The Doomsday Diary sat on the table in front of him. The half-dressed witch who'd taken the book from Sydney slept in a corner. At least she hoped the woman was asleep.

Shock shoved her into a chair across from Mathias.

"These meetings are too frequent, my dear," he said.

"Rhea is unable to use the book. Everything she writes disappears. I cannot see the words at all. Care to explain?"

Sydney glanced at Shock. As long as the traitor was here, she stood no chance of keeping her thoughts to herself. "I just wrote what I wanted in the book and . . . poof."

"It came true immediately?"

"No. It took a few days."

Mathias glanced at Shock.

"She's telling the truth as she knows it." Shock supplied.

Mathias relaxed against the back of the sofa. "It's possible that larger magic takes time to collect and organize."

Shock nodded. "She was looking only for a shag. Hardly difficult magic, but she's not a witch . . ."

A feral grin stretched across the evil wizard's mouth as he turned to her. "If you need a man in your bed, I'm more than happy to oblige."

Ewww. "I don't."

"I can change your mind . . . whether you want it changed or not. Regardless of whether your new mate is languishing in the cell downstairs or not."

How did he know?

"Your magical signature," Shock said. "You now have one that brands you as Caden's. Most anyone magical can see it."

Sydney liked that idea, and hoped that she'd have years and years with this signature—and a happy life to go with it. But she had to get out of here first.

Shock merely raised a brow at her, but thankfully kept commentary to himself.

"You used the book twice with success. Rhea could not use it at all," Mathias mused as if solving a puzzle aloud. "Of course, you're a smart girl, and she's a stupid slut. But she's magical and you're not. I know it works for witches, or Morganna le Fay would have never created it. There is something I'm missing. What?"

Sydney wasn't even certain herself, but Sabelle and Olivia's theory that the woman using the book had to be wishing for her heart's desire made sense. She had when she'd wished for Caden. Who knows what Mathias's witch whore had wished for?

"She doesn't know." Shock's tone was both annoyed and dismissive. "She's human. She stumbled into magic and got lucky. That's all."

Sydney frowned. If Shock could read her mind, why hadn't he regurgitated her every thought to Mathias?

"Any chance she's able to mask her thoughts from you?"

Shock snorted in answer.

"Take her to my bed. I think I'll enjoy finding out how much energy this feisty human can give me before she dies."

Zipping her gaze up to Shock's face, Sydney's heart beat triple time. *Oh, dear God.* The last thing in the world she wanted was to endure a moment of Mathias's touch. But to die in his bed . . . she shivered.

Now Shock was the only thing standing between her and death. His bland expression didn't give her much hope.

"In order to bed her, you'll have to break her mate bond. That will likely kill her. Let me spend a little time with her. I have ways of getting deeper into a woman's mind."

"Unpleasant ones, I hope?" Mathias perked up.

"Absolutely."

Mathias paused, then smiled. "Take her, then. Don't bring her back unless you've extracted everything from her mind—or she's dead."

As soon as Shock magically shoved him back in the cell and locked him in again, taking Sydney away with him, Caden broke out in a cold sweat. *Damn it, now what?* He doubted he could break Shock's magical seal on this cell. But he couldn't sit here while the traitor and mate thief took Sydney to his boss like a lamb to slaughter. Even the thought made him want to roar the entire house down.

He knew more than a little martial arts, but every attempt to kick at the walls or bars proved fruitless. He'd looked around the cell for a trapdoor, back exit, ceiling vent . . . nothing.

He was going to have to get creative with magic. Damn it, he scarcely knew enough to be dangerous. He had the instincts to complete simple tasks, and had been so foolishly adamant about not learning more.

Swallowing hard, Caden forced his recriminations away and willed himself to think. He had to know *something* that would help her. Sitting trapped while his mate died at Mathias's hands was not an option. But he'd never done big magic.

Except at transition. His one special power.

Hope soared, but he tempered it. He had to be logical. The fact was, he'd been almost high on magic when he'd cloned himself, he really had no idea how he'd done it. Common wisdom said that a witch or wizard should not reveal their special power unless it meant the difference between life and death.

Saving Sydney *was* his life or death.

Vaguely, Caden recalled fusing his clone back to his body by visualizing the event. He hoped, prayed, the reverse worked.

Sitting on the cot on which he'd so recently loved Sydney, he squeezed his eyes shut. In his mind, he pictured his clone morphing separately from him—on the other side of these bars. His entire body tensed as he clutched the bed frame.

His arms shook, and he could feel the veins swelling as he concentrated. Seconds became a minute. A minute became three. But nothing happened. He cursed under his breath.

Then he felt his insides ripping in half.

Caden clenched his teeth against the horrific sensation of someone opening his chest and sucking out his insides. His whole body trembled. His head exploded with pain.

Suddenly, it ended, and he slumped back against the wall, utterly drained, wishing he had something to show for his effort.

"I'll come back with help." The voice sounded eerily like his own.

His eyes flew open wide, and he saw himself—his other self—standing outside the cell.

Thank God. He'd done it.

"Save her," he rasped in exhaustion.

His clone nodded and disappeared. And he bloody hated it, but now all he could do was wait.

At Shock's urging, Sydney rose on wobbly legs. She'd never imagined he was a good guy, but now she'd find out exactly how bad he was. Even if Shock didn't lay a hand on her, she had no doubt he could think of a hundred magical ways to torture her.

"Faster," he snapped. "You're keeping me from my fun, and Mathias from valuable information."

The cold calculation of his command pissed her off. If she was going to die, she might as well let the bastard know how much she loathed him.

"How inconsiderate of me not to run to my death. Must be a real bitch for you."

Mathias laughed, the sound scratching an icy path up her spine before his expression fell into pure menace. "You'll give her extra pain for that, I hope?"

"With pleasure."

"Wait!" Mathias barked. "A disturbance in the security. I think the Doomsday Brethren have arrived. With them out of the way, we won't need this chit anymore. If we kill all the warriors, Olivia Gray and Sabelle Rion will be alone, unprotected. Certainly one of them can be persuaded to help our cause."

"Don't touch my friends!" she screamed.

"You're in no position to issue orders." Mathias smiled tightly, then looked at Shock. "Why don't you go greet our company? Take the Anarki with you. I'll stay with our lovely guest."

Sydney could just imagine Shock's greeting. The Doomsday Brethren trusted him—at least a bit. Because of it, they could be easily duped—and quickly dead. Any chances of escape or a future for magickind would walk out the door with the big, bad wizard.

She grabbed his arm. "Please, no. Don't do this!"

Shock sent her a glare, shook off her hold, and walked out the door.

Caden shivered in the cold cell. But he shoved the discomfort aside and focused on the "movie" in his mind that was spooling from his clone. Soon, his replica made his way out of the basement to the first floor—and Mathias's sitting room.

As he crept in shadow up the stairs and around a corner, a small lamp on the table illuminated Sydney, a small form in an oversized black leather chair, pale and hugging her knees to her chest. She stared at Mathias with undisguised hate.

Though she couldn't see him, he was damn glad to see her alive.

Sunlight was beginning to creep through the east-facing windows above him. Soon, his hiding place would be compromised. He was going to have to think and act fast to get Sydney out of here and snatch the Doomsday Diary. No way was he leaving such a weapon in the hands of someone like Mathias.

He was only going to have one chance to surprise the evil wizard, and Caden didn't know if his clone could perform magic. Even if he could channel energy to the duplicate, did he have enough energy left in him to kill Mathias?

As the sun crept farther into the room, and he heard the sounds of battle erupting outside, Caden figured it was now or never. Either the Doomsday Brethren would fight their way inside and chaos would erupt, or the Anarki would come in and kill them all. If he was going to get Sydney out before things got dangerous, it had to be now.

Caden positioned himself into a crouch, ready to run. Sydney spotted him out of the corner of her eyes. She stifled her surprise quickly, but Mathias saw or sensed something. Whirling, he pulled out his wand. Using his instincts, Caden flipped a hand toward Mathias, picturing a fireball hurtling toward the wizard. Invisible energy ripped out of his body, burning down his fingers toward Mathias.

The other wizard couldn't scramble a defense fast enough. He jumped aside, but the ball struck him in the gut. Mathias doubled over, clutching his abdomen. Sweat dotted his temples and his face strained with pain as he looked up at Caden with hate.

"You'll pay for that."

"Not today," he quipped, then pulled Sydney to her feet. "Grab the book and run. It's still dark; you can get out. Stay in shadow. Bram and the others sound like they're fighting on the northeast side of the house. Run out the back and stay close to the walls. I'll be there as soon as possible."

Sydney shook her head. "I'm not leaving without you."

He loved her more than ever, marveled that he had a mate who was his, but locked away in a cell below, the real him couldn't defend her and both he and the clone were running out of energy. Why the hell wouldn't she listen? "You and the book are all that matter. Go!"

"We go together! Zap him again."

Her gaze flicked over to Mathias, beginning to straighten up, still clutching his wand with a groan. Below, Caden focused, trying to summon his energy to send to the clone to protect Sydney. His gut cramped, and he trembled, sweating and straining for something.

He had no magical energy left.

"Stupid neophyte," Mathias scoffed. "I'm looking forward to watching you die."

Caden had no idea why Mathias hadn't yet blasted him. Either he hadn't fully healed from the injury Olivia had delivered to him last month, or the blast he'd just given the wizard had done more damage than imagined. Whatever. Time for some old-school ass kicking.

Dropping into a fighting stance, his replica delivered a blistering roundhouse kick to Mathias's jaw. He reeled back, staggering.

Below them, doors banged against the limestone walls, grunts, shouts, and the sounds of fistfighting erupted below.

Mathias smiled. "Your friends are coming. Too bad they'll be too late."

Fast as lightning, Mathias whipped his wand toward Caden's clone. A split second later, something hit him that weighed twenty tons, was as hot as lava, as destructive as acid. The spell spread throughout the clone's body. In his cell below, Caden absorbed the immense pain, felt the duplicate's organs shut down as he crumpled to the ground.

Sydney fell to her knees over him, grabbing his hand. "No. No! You can't . . . Caden, listen. Please!"

"Take the book," the clone panted. "Get out."

Every muscle in Caden's body jolted in pain, and when the clone shut his eyes, Caden could no longer see Sydney. He panicked as pain ripped through him, shredding his insides.

The fighting reached the top of the stairs. The clone's hearing discerned shouts.

"I've already killed your friend. So glad you'll be next, Rion," Mathias taunted.

The fighting around him resumed in a fierce clash. He sensed his replica's consciousness fading when a strong hand landed on his chest. Lucan. Funny how he sensed his brother from just a touch. Oddly, tragedy had made them closer, and he regretted that he wouldn't know what tomorrow might have brought for them.

"Thank God you mated. The others are keeping Mathias busy. Quick! Kiss him, Sydney."

Moments later, Caden felt Sydney brush her lips gently over his. Nice. He floated, his consciousness like a cloud drifting in a clear, blue sky. The pain was receding, and he welcomed peace.

"Fight, damn it!" Lucan growled. "Take energy from your mate."

Sydney redoubled her efforts, her mouth growing insistent and frantic as the battle around them raged, others holding off Mathias and the Anarki. "Don't. Leave. Me." She peppered him with kisses between each word. "Stay with me!"

"Can't. I'm in a cell," he managed to get out.

"What the hell is he talking about?" his brother asked.

Caden didn't have the energy to answer.

"I—I . . ." Sydney seemed to flounder for an answer, then she gasped. "You cloned yourself?"

"Hmm . . ." He didn't have the energy to say more. He felt his life force draining, dwindling more with each minute.

"Take me to him," Sydney commanded Lucan. "This is a clone. The real him is downstairs. Bring that body."

"No," he protested, but it was a weak whisper. The remnant of his energy. "Go."

Lucan ignored his pleas and lifted him, jolting every muscle in Caden's body. The agony twisted through him, and he had no idea if he could withstand more of the excruciating pain. Sweat rolled down his body, despite the chilly temperatures in the cell. He gripped the bed, wondering if it would break in his hands. He focused all his energy on staying conscious, not throwing up, waiting for Sydney.

As Lucan carried him down the stairs, the sounds of the raging battle faded in the distance. Caden nearly passed out, but he felt every step his brother carried his cloned body with a teeth-jarring agony.

A crash told him that Lucan had exploded the door wide open. Suddenly, Sydney was beside him, pressing her lips to his. Energy trickled into his system, a bit more as the seconds ticked by. Between them, Caden could feel the book. But it was her urgent touch that brought him around.

He opened his mouth beneath her and dipped inside, mingling with her, inhaling her essence. Energy now flooded his senses. He deepened the kiss, and she responded with all the fire and love inside her. His vitality spiked. The energy derived from the kiss was temporary until he could claim her body fully again, but it would hold for now.

Reluctantly, he ripped his mouth away. "Better, firecracker. Thank you."

Squeezing his eyes shut, he pictured the barely alive replica merging with him, becoming one being. A sucking sound and a jolting collision later, the duplicate settled under his skin again.

"You can clone yourself?" Lucan smiled. "Impressive, little brother. Mum was right."

She'd predicted he'd be a once-in-a-lifetime hero. He wasn't—yet.

"The others?"

"Upstairs fighting off Mathias and the Anarki."

"Take Sydney and the book back to Bram's for me. I have unfinished business."

Lucan frowned. "You have little experience in these battles, and I—"

"I have energy." He gripped Sydney's hand. "And the means to get more, if need be. Until you find someone to merge with, you're going to be weak. Take her. For me."

"Come with us," Sydney pleaded. "Don't risk yourself."

He swallowed. "Bram came back to help me and fight for you, even after he dismissed me from the Doomsday Brethren. He's remained fighting, even though we brought the book to safety. I can't leave him and the others without helping."

Lucan's smile tilted with pride. "Go. We'll be waiting."

They exited the cell and began to make their way up the stairs, Caden to join the battle, Lucan and Sydney to get out of the house and teleport. Shock stood at the top blocking their entrance.

"Do you have the book?" he barked.

Sydney clutched it to her chest. "You're not taking it from us."

With a growl, Lucan reached for his wand, then stopped. "I want to do this by my own hand."

Without warning, he charged Shock and punched him in the jaw. Shock reeled back, stumbling until his backside hit the stairs. Then Lucan drew out his wand. The leather-clad wizard froze instantly, as if his arms and legs had been bound tightly. Caden worried that Lucan had drained too much of his energy doing it, but understood that his brother needed to hurt the man who had stolen his mate.

"I hope you enjoyed your cheap shot," Shock growled. "It's the only one you'll get."

"If I had more energy, I'd kill you. This isn't over."

"Anka is with me." Shock managed to look menacing even immobilized.

"For now," Lucan conceded. "Not forever."

Then he took Sydney by the hand, led her past Shock, up the stairs, and into the morning.

Caden turned the other way and headed toward the sounds of battle to his right.

He rounded the corner to find disaster. Marrok and Tynan had engaged a dozen Anarki zombies and were quickly hacking their way through the men. Caden thought of his friend Brian with a pang and vowed that he'd take that damn glass sphere from Mathias somehow, someway.

Duke and Ice had engaged a trio of wizards in robes who had appeared since the last time Caden had been in the melee. And near the fireplace, Bram and Mathias faced each other.

"You're outnumbered," Mathias pointed out.

Bram shrugged. "We're better trained."

And sneaking up behind him, Caden had the element of surprise. Bram never looked his way, but sent him an imperceptible nod. Time to play . . .

"Even as Merlin's famed grandson, you're no match for me," Mathias snarled.

He whipped his wand out suddenly, then swung his arm toward Bram. A cloud of black smoke blazed between them, headed for Bram.

Before Mathias could do anything more, Caden snuck up behind Mathias and kicked him viciously in the knees. With a grunt, the evil wizard fell forward, catching himself on his hands, while his wand clattered to the tile. Brimming with fury and determination, Caden grabbed him by the hair and pounded his head directly onto the tiled floor. He heard an audible crack, and Mathias screamed. Caden raised a hand in the wizard's direction and pictured wrapping invisible ropes around Mathias to secure him. Once the wizard was still, Caden kicked him onto his back. His bloody forehead was already starting to bruise, looking darker than his blue eyes, now spitting hatred. He struggled, but seemed to be held by invisible bonds.

Marine training and magic working together. Perfect.

"You should be dead," Mathias choked.

"You missed."

Now he just had to find the bloody Anarki-creating glass sphere. Dropping to his knees beside Mathias, he patted the wizard down. It might not be hidden in his clothes, but Mathias struck him as a control freak who would want it near him as often as possible.

One of his pockets bulged, and Caden reached in. Sure enough, he pulled out the familiar glass sphere. "This won't be ripping out another soul."

"I traveled to Africa to find that," Mathias spat. "It's rare. If you destroy it, there won't be a hell deep enough for you to hide in."

"If you keep turning my friends into Anarki, I'll rip your stones out through your nostrils, then spit in the hole."

With that, Caden slammed the sphere against the tile. It shattered into a thousand tiny pieces.

"Bloody stupid neophyte! I'm going to kill your pretty little mate slowly and make you watch."

"Right now, you're going to die," Caden snarled. It might take every last bit of his energy, even kill him. But he was looking forward to seeing Mathias as a corpse.

Suddenly, Bram screamed behind him, and Caden whirled. The black smoke from Mathias's spell was smothering him, and Mathias's bed-warming witch screeched as she charged toward them, fury in her gaze, her wand raised in threat.

Tynan took her to the ground, but several of the Anarki rushed toward Caden and Bram. He crouched into fighting stance to face the new threat, glancing over his shoulder to glare at Mathias.

The evil wizard was gone.

"Fuck!" Ice yelled.

"Where did he go?" Caden shouted.

"Coward teleported out."

Fury and disappointment pounded. Caden wanted to be the one to waste Mathias. For Bram, for Brian. To ensure Sydney's safety. He hated that the bastard would live another day.

Caden fought off the attack of the Anarki zombies, kicking one in the gut. It broke in half, bleeding black. The other he elbowed in the jaw. His head rolled off his rotting body. Another crept up behind him and jumped on his back. Caden cursed then backed up at a jog until he hit a wall. The Anarki squashed like a bug.

Looking around, Caden saw that the other Doomsday Brethren were currently mopping up the last of the opposition. Thank God.

Another Anarki scrambled away from Tynan to Bram's side, holding a knife high above Rion's heart. Racing across the room, Caden leapt onto the ghoul, grabbed his blade, and shoved it deep into his chest. The zombie gasped as black ooze gurgled from his chest, then he slumped into death.

Breathing hard, Caden dropped to his knees next to Bram, who writhed and shouted, fighting an invisible battle with the black cloud. Caden lifted him into his arms just as Duke reached his side, looking sweaty and disheveled. An eerie calm fell over the room, now littered with black blood and dead Anarki wizards.

"We have to get him help," Duke said.

Caden nodded. "What is this black cloud?"

"I don't know. Something very bad, I'm sure. Sydney, Lucan, and the book safe?"

He nodded. "And that damn glass sphere destroyed. Mission accomplished."

With a glance back at Bram, Caden wondered at what price?

Back at Bram's house, with afternoon sunlight streaming through the windows, Caden watched Duke and Sabelle prepare the transcast mirror so Sydney could keep magickind informed. Lucan burst in—with most everyone else behind him.

"What is this, a bloody circus?" Caden demanded.

Lucan thrust his hands on his hips confrontationally. "You're not going back to Texas."

If his brother was expecting an argument, Caden hoped Lucan wouldn't be too disappointed.

"I'm not," he agreed. "I'm staying to fight. A weapon like the Doomsday Diary needs all the protection it can get. I can help."

A smile burst across Lucan's face. "In that case, you'll need this." He pulled an ornate golden box with some sort of family seal across the top. "Will you take your wand?"

"With pride." His chest swelled just thinking about holding the magical instrument made especially for him.

"Kneel."

Caden did, head bowed.

"In the name of MacTavish, brandish this well and do good. Protect yourself, those you love, and guard this with your life. If you swear to do thus, I give this wand to you."

"I swear it," he vowed as Lucan put the instrument in his hands.

Goosebumps broke out across his skin, and power vibrated through him. He was truly a wizard now. Caden looked up at his mate, who smiled proudly.

Lucan slapped him on the back. "Congratulations on transitioning, mating—everything. I think Mum was right; you'll be a gifted wizard."

"I hope you'll consider me one of the Doomsday Brethren, too." Caden addressed the others assembled: Lucan, Ice, Duke, Marrok, and Tynan. "I'm here to fight with you."

Lucan and Duke both stepped closer, and his brother spoke. "Absolutely. If Bram was well, he'd approve."

Sabelle sniffed, holding back tears, and Lucan rushed to put an arm around her. "I'm sure your aunt and the healer will find a cure for Mathias's spell. Remember, I'm here for you." He caressed her cheek. "You cared for me when I needed help. Let me help you."

She hesitated, then nodded. "Thank you."

"We'll get through this," Lucan assured softly.

"Where's Shock?" Ice challenged, glaring as Lucan touched Sabelle.

Lucan glared back. Reminders that the elder Denzell still kept Anka was a sore spot, and Caden cursed under his breath.

"I hope the mate thief and traitor rots."

Caden agreed.

"Actually," Sydney spoke up. "Shock did seem to be on

Mathias's side . . . except that he could have told Mathias that the Doomsday Diary only granted the heart's true desire. The thought was right in my mind to pluck, as he had all the others. But he lied to Mathias about that."

A puzzled silence fell over the group.

Finally, Duke offered. "I don't know if we'll ever know exactly whose side Shock is on. I suspect it's his own. He'll help us . . . if it suits his purpose."

That way Shock wouldn't suffer, regardless of which side ultimately proved victorious in the war. Caden didn't respect that position, but Shock wouldn't be the first to take it.

"What do you think he'll do next? Or Mathias, for that matter?" Caden asked the others.

Duke shrugged. "I have no idea. All we can do is stay prepared for any eventuality and stand strong.

Amen.

"The mirror is ready," Sabelle said, stepping away from Lucan.

In moments, Sydney snapped into action, got into place, and began her transcast. Yes, the Council had sent missives, likely objecting, but with Bram so ill, no one was reading his correspondence.

"During a battle earlier today, a group of wizards destroyed a weapon Mathias claims he retrieved from Africa that ripped the souls from unsuspecting humans and made them Anarki instantly. Mathias escaped, but his forces have been badly damaged. As always, updates will follow as necessary," she concluded. "I'm Sydney Blair." She cut a glance over at Caden and winced at his scowl. "Sydney Blair Mac-Tavish. Stay safe. Good afternoon."

The transcast ended. Caden was still afraid for his mate's safety, but pride beamed all through him. She was vital to him and magickind. He had no idea what he'd do without her—and thankfully he hadn't learned the hard way this morning.

He held her close and pressed his lips to hers. "Perfect."

"The transcast?" she asked hopefully.

"Yes, but I meant you. I'm very proud of you."

"Ugh. New mates." Duke rolled his eyes. "I'm leaving."

The others followed suit and closed the door to the library behind them, sequestering Caden and Sydney alone.

"I hope you mean that," she whispered. "Because I called Holly today and quit my job."

Fear for her speared through him, but he took a deep breath. This was war; they were mates and in this together. "She hadn't already sacked you?"

"Aquarius told her I was working deep undercover on a new magickind story. It satisfied her until I called. She wasn't happy."

"Are you?" he asked gently. "Do you truly want to give up your human existence and work exclusively for magickind? What about proving to your parents that you're a journalistic star?"

"I don't need their validation anymore. I know I'm doing something good. That's all that matters." She bit her lip in uncertainty. "What about you? Once, you wanted to return to Texas and resume—"

"I thought I did. You said it best when you accused me of running from my destiny. It took nearly losing everything and everyone I love dearly to make me realize I had to stand and fight for what I want. I'm a wizard now, and magickind needs those trained to fight during what's bound to be dark times ahead. And I wouldn't leave your side for anything in the world."

"What about your job in Dallas?"

"I called and resigned an hour ago. You're stuck with me."

"Promise?" she laughed. "Where is that little red book? I have a few untapped fantasies I want to jot down."

"Oh, no, you don't. If you want something, from now on, you only need to tell me."

"Looking forward to it," she murmured, then pressed her lips to his.

Turn the page

for a special sneak peek

at the next exciting Doomsday Brethren novel

from nationally bestselling author

Shayla Black

POSSESS ME AT MIDNIGHT

Coming soon from Pocket Books

WHEN THE CEILING THUNDERED, and Ice heard a woman scream, his blood ran cold. *Sabelle!*

He and Tynan hadn't quite finished stashing the weapons when he heard the first rumblings. They were under attack. In a choice between preserving the hardware and saving Sabelle . . . no choice.

After collecting a few weapons for the warriors to carry, Ice quickly conjured thigh-deep water and doused the rest. That done, he whirled around and pumped his way up the stairs, to the first floor of the enormous house. Amid the smoky chaos and ceiling's crumbling plaster raining down, Ice scanned the corridor.

"Sabelle!" he shouted over and over as he stalked to Bram's office, the library, the dining room, broken glass crunching under his boots. All empty.

Duke stumbled toward him from the front door, bleeding from a gash in the forehead. "The Anarki will be inside the house in less than five minutes. Find Sabelle. Get her and the book out of here. And take Lucan."

With a curse under his breath, Ice nodded. The annoyance at taking Lucan was minimal compared to his fear. Sabelle, though he'd never hold her, was . . . everything. He'd never understood a wizard's urge to mate. After one look at her, he comprehended perfectly.

Though she might become Lucan's, no way would he lose her to Mathias.

"I've been screaming my throat raw to find her. Know where she is?"

"Sorry . . . ," Duke said and ran toward the back of the house.

Ice cupped his hands around his mouth. "Sabelle!"

"Up here."

Ice barely heard her reply above another explosive boom, but the siren call of her voice was enough. He charged up the stairs and flung into one bedroom after another. In the middle of one that was golden and silken and sumptuous, he found her.

He resisted the urge to gather her in his arms. She would neither welcome nor allow it.

Sabelle had thrown on a pair of jeans, a creamy white sweater that was snug across her breasts. She shoved a few items into a black backpack. "I'm ready."

"The Doomsday Diary?"

She pointed to the backpack and darted past him, out of the room.

The closer he stayed to her, the safer she would be. He grabbed her arm to guide her down the stairs. Instead, she ripped from his grasp and sprinted down the hall.

Ice chased after her. "Where the hell . . . we must leave now!"

"Not without my brother," she called over her shoulder.

It was on the tip of Ice's tongue to suggest leaving the imperious bastard to rot, but Sabelle would waste valuable time arguing and trying to cart Bram down the stairs. The longer she stayed here, the greater the danger.

"Bloody hell," he muttered, on her heels.

Bram's room of heavy curtains, dark wood, and luxurious damasks was a study in wealth. Ice didn't spare the time to shake his head in annoyance. Right now, Sabelle was trying to use her magic to levitate her brother and evacuate him. A whole lot easier to sling the prat over his shoulder.

With a curse, he edged past Sabelle and grabbed Bram, slinging his dead weight into a fireman's carry.

"Be careful! He's very ill."

As if he didn't know that. With his free hand, Ice grabbed Sabelle's hand and ran. "Let's go!"

Another boom resounded, shaking the whole house. Halfway down the stairs, the front door began to groan and heave intermittently under the magical equivalent of a battering ram. Collectively, the Anarki threw energy at the house as one, trying to shatter its magical protections. And Ice knew, soon, they would succeed.

Outside, a sea of voices chanted. Mathias's entire fucking army was here, and the Doomsday Brethren would be lucky if they managed to get out alive. Ice hardly cared if he did, but Sabelle . . . she mattered. Magickind needed her and the Doomsday Diary safe.

At the bottom of the stairs, he shoved her toward the back door. "Peek out the back windows. Have the Anarki surrounded the house?"

She stared at him, her gorgeous blue eyes rimmed in fear. But she bravely nodded and scampered off, dodging projectiles as another rattling boom shook the house. She was everything worthy in a female, and if he had more time, he'd tell her so.

But for now, he unloaded Bram's unconscious form on the floor, then took up a defensive position by the front door to face the pounding threat. Marrok, Olivia, and Tynan raced down the stairs. With a glance, Marrok saw Sabelle at the back of the house and sent Olivia in her direction. The once immortal warrior and Tynan lined up beside him to face the threat about to crash through their door.

Duke stumbled from Bram's office and joined them. "I've alerted the Council that we're under attack."

Old curmudgeons wouldn't do a damn thing, but Duke's

belief in the nobility of the ruling class was understandable, given his title and background.

"Where are Lucan and Caden?" Duke barked.

He shrugged. Not his problem. His sole focus was to secure this door long enough for Sabelle to make it out alive with the book.

"I don't see Anarki in back," Sabelle shouted.

Hardly meant they weren't there. They could be concealed, but if he and the rest of the Doomsday Brethren waited much longer to take the women and leave, Anarki would be crawling everywhere. Escape would be impossible.

To his right, Caden and Sydney flew down the stairs, Lucan staggering behind, clutching a bleeding shoulder.

"What happened?" Duke asked.

"Flying glass. Someone can heal him once we're safe," Caden suggested.

At her mate's urging, Sydney darted for the other women. At the back door, Sabelle drew her wand, ready to fight, and Ice turned his body so he could see both doors with a subtle turn of his head. Sabelle wouldn't be the one battling for their survival.

Duke lifted the creamy silken drapes covering the windows on either side of the front door. Outside, the swell of black robes grew and grew. They began to fan around the house, scurrying like ants from one place to the next. More joined seconds later. Then more, until there weren't hundreds, but thousands.

Lucan and Caden exchanged a glance as they fell into the battle-ready group. The front door groaned and splintered. It was going to break any minute, and Ice wanted Sabelle nowhere near the hell about to break loose.

"Take the Rions and the book. Lucan can help me defend the door. As soon as you're prepared, I'll send him with you," Duke insisted.

Instead, Lucan ran toward Sabelle.

Quarreling was a waste of time they didn't have, but Ice still had to bite his tongue to keep the argument inside. "Fine."

"Initially, we'll split up to confuse them, cut down their forces and make them chase us in all directions." Duke's face was grave with concern. "The book is most important. Keep it from Mathias no matter what."

"I'll contact you when it's safe. Where will you go?"

Duke winced when the door splintered again, and gray smoke crept in. The same sort of smoke that was slowly killing Bram.

The warriors shouted, cursed, began to back away as the insidious smoke clawed and crawled its way across the floor and walls. Mathias himself was likely here.

"Go now!" Duke shouted.

Ice didn't wait to be told twice. With Bram on his shoulder, he dashed to the back door, then pressed an urgent hand to the small of Sabelle's back. "Grab your backpack. Ease out the door. Stay in shadow. We've got two minutes, at most."

She sent him a shaky nod, but didn't panic. "Lucan?"

Who gives a shit? After losing his mate, the bastard thought to use Sabelle because she was beautiful, kind, and convenient? "Right behind us."

With a nod, she grabbed her belongings. "We're safe for the moment. Bram had more protection here, just in case we ever needed to escape."

Good to know. Still, as Ice opened the door, he checked to make certain no Anarki had made their way around the massive estate. He couldn't see any, but he could hear them, attacking Bram's weakened magical defenses, zapping and gnashing their way ever closer to the Doomsday Brethren's fallback position at the back door.

Ice urged Sabelle onto the terrace, in the shadow provided

by the overhang, then slid out behind her, covering her body with his own. The December chill wrapped around him in welcome, and he thrived on the bite against his skin. Snow was beginning to fall. He hoped the Anarki bastards were having a miserable time. He'd be happy to speed the process along if they threatened his Sabelle.

Damn it, she isn't yours. Ice shushed the unwelcome voice in his head, then wrapped an arm around Sabelle to guide her into the terrace's corner while laying Bram at her feet in case he needed both hands to fight. With concrete at her back and sides, he could protect her. Holding his back to her, he pinned her against the wall and scanned for potential threats, watching as Marrok, Olivia, and Tynan poured out of the house. They took a few steps forward before the wizard grabbed the other two and teleported them away. Sydney and Caden followed.

Where the hell was Lucan? The prick had ten seconds before Ice left him to his own defenses.

Duke stumbled through the door, dragging an injured Lucan behind him, who was now bloody from head to toe.

Behind him, Sabelle gasped and tried to wriggle free. Ice whirled on her and mercilessly flattened her to the wall with his body, pressing her deep into the corner. "Can't you hear the Anarki? They're nearly upon us. You are not rushing through the danger to tend MacTavish."

"But he may need—"

"He is a full-fledged wizard with others around who can care for him. He'll escape."

"But I've been caring for him since Anka . . ."

Something on his face must have shown his fury and the soul-deep willpower he used to squeeze it down. He'd known that Sabelle had become MacTavish's willing carnal sacrifice as he healed, and it lit a fire of jealousy and hatred in his gut. Lucan loved Anka still, but he'd use Sabelle's body, her sweetness and softness, for his own ends. And Sabelle encouraged him. Because she loved him? Ice knew Sabelle would never be his, but he'd be damned if he stood by and watched Lucan use her.

"Would you rather have Lucan die or the Doomsday Diary fall into Mathias's hands?"

She drew in a shuddering breath, and the feel of her breasts against his chest was damn near his undoing. But this wasn't the time or place.

"You're right. I—I wasn't thinking." Her breath misted the cold air, and he wanted to kiss her so desperately. He didn't dare.

"Ice!" Duke called through the dark chill.

Damn it! He pinned Lord High-and-Mighty with a stare and a raised brow.

"The Anarki is through the door and into the house. That gray smoke is everywhere. Take Sabelle and go. Lucan is too injured to be anything but a liability to you now. I'll bring him with Caden and Sydney."

Best notion he'd heard all day. "Let's go, princess."

He grabbed her around the waist. She clutched his wrists and, panting, tried to pull him away. "Where?"

Ice knew of many remote places between here and his boyhood home. He could find a million places to hide—and stay hidden as long as necessary to ensure Sabelle stayed safe.

"Anyplace they're not."

Curling his arm more tightly around her waist, Ice tried not to think about how perfectly she fit against him, how soft her breasts felt cushioning his chest, how easy it would be to curl one hand under her backside and urge her legs around his waist as he rode her . . .

Not happening, he chided himself.

Focusing on Wye Valley in the Welsh Mountains, he willed

himself, Sabelle, and Bram there. His knees left him as darkness and a keen sense of weightless disorientation swallowed him. But he was conscious of his arm around Sabelle, of her clinging to him as he hoisted Bram's limp form.

Moments later, the ground rushed up under them, and they landed in a heap within a cluster of trees, the river trickling nearby. Lights from the adjoining village glowed in the distance.

Ice helped Sabelle to her feet and began leading her in the opposite direction. "Are you all right?"

In the silvery moonlight, she nodded, all those pale curls of hers shimmering around her face, cupping her breasts. "Where are we?"

Not a good idea to think about her breasts now—or ever. "Herefordshire. I know it well. Let's go."

Ice secured Bram over his shoulder, took her hand, and hauled her deeper into the copse of trees. If memory served him, there was an abandoned house built into the nearby hillside. It would be easy to defend and should shelter them for the night. After he re-established communication with Duke and the others, they could decide on a rendezvous point.

They'd taken only a handful of steps under the shelter of the trees when he heard a *whoosh!* behind him.

"Where are they?" a deep voice boomed. "Find them. The spell Rhea cast on the book told us that it's been transported here. Spread out!"

Mathias. Motherfucking hell. The evil bastard himself had given chase. Not good.

Ice had no idea who Rhea was, but evidently, the witch had put a spell on the diary. The Anarki would know the Doomsday Diary's exact location as soon as someone teleported with the book.

Question was, could the spell track them as easily on foot?

Sabelle gave the tiniest of gasps, and Ice gripped her hand more tightly and ran faster, hoping she could keep up. If she couldn't, he'd carry her—whatever was needed for her and the Doomsday Diary to stay safe. Despite the fact that his legs were longer, Sabelle stayed with him, every step. His admiration for her went up another notch.

Quietly, they zigzagged around trees, gradually turning toward the abandoned house. They couldn't stay there now, of course. Likely the first place the Anarki would look. He and Sabelle would have to keep going.

Thanking God for the darkness that covered their tracks in the mud and for the fact that it hadn't snowed in Herefordshire today, he and Sabelle trekked toward the hill on the west side of the valley. Behind him, Ice heard the pursuit of several wizards, the curses when one tripped over a branch.

"Are you certain they ran in this direction?" one asked.

"Dunno. If she teleports anywhere, we'll find her," Mathias assured. "Whoever the bitch is, she cannot outrun us. When we find her, I will happily strip her bare and make certain she knows who her master is."

Over my dead body, Ice mentally growled.

But the conversation told him one thing: as long as he and Sabelle were on foot, unless the Anarki spotted them, they couldn't track the book. He thought briefly of hiding the book in a tree and teleporting away, but the risk was too great. If the Anarki found it. . . . No, they must press on.

Sabelle stumbled in the dark, tumbling into him. Ice secured her with an arm around her waist. She must be getting tired, yet he didn't dare slow their pace.

"Can you go a bit farther?" he whispered.

"I will," she panted.

Ice wasn't certain she could manage, but he prayed she'd find the strength.

Without a word, he stripped the pack from her back and carted it over his shoulder. Bram's dead weight flopped over the other, but like the book, he didn't dare leave Bram behind for the enemy to find—and use against them.

Sweat poured off Ice and his heart pounded a constant, violent tattoo. His lungs were about to burst, and his thighs burned. But he couldn't stop.

Finally, they approached the hill leading out of the valley. Ice was more than ready to be gone from here, find a car in the nearby town and drive to safety.

Just then the moon peeked out from the clouds, shining into the valley below. The trees leading up the sides of the hills were few and far between. Now that Sabelle was no longer carrying the pack, he realized how her white sweater all but glowed in the dark. *Damn it!*

They were going to have to improvise—and quickly. If she was anyone else, he'd simply slop mud over her clothes. Her shiny blond hair, too. But Sabelle Rion? Did she even know what mud was? Regardless, they didn't have time for it. Behind him, Ice heard more Anarki, sounding closer than before.

Though he might be able to coax Sabelle into running north, parallel to the river, he feared running into searching Anarki. Same with running south. The cliff was east, the river west.

They were virtually trapped.

Think, he demanded of himself. *Think!* If they couldn't run safely in any direction, and they couldn't teleport away, how the bloody hell was he supposed to keep the book safe and Sabelle in one piece?

"Ice," she panted in his ear. "I know we shouldn't rest, but . . . perhaps we can take refuge in a tree? Maybe we would be able to spot an escape route if we were up high?"

He turned to her, his jaw dropping in surprise, his heart bursting with gratitude. "Perfect."

With a frantic gaze he looked around until he found a stout old tree with several low-hanging branches. He helped her up, then handed the pack to her. Ice heard Anarki trampling closer. Too close. Perhaps he could teleport into the tree and balance on a branch before Mathias's minions found him? Maybe . . . but he wasn't willing to take a chance. They needed a distraction, something to send the Anarki scrambling in another direction.

"Ice!" she hissed.

Their pursuers were coming closer still. He had to decide—now.

With a silent grunt, he heaved Bram off his shoulder and hoisted him into the next tree over. He wasn't well hidden, but between the dark and Bram's black clothing, this spot might suffice long enough to fool Mathias and his goons.

Still, he needed a distraction . . .

"Careful," Sabelle whispered urgently. "He's so ill."

But not dead yet. He would be if Mathias found him.

A glance at her made Ice pause. Sabelle's white sweater flared in the moonlight like a damn beacon, and as the Anarki crept ever closer, a tree stripped by winter of its foliage provided little camouflage.

"Give me your sweater." He whispered his demand standing at the base of the tree.

Sabelle recoiled. "What?"

So very near now, a muttered curse and footsteps shuffling through dried leaves. The Anarki were maybe a few hundred meters away. He and Sabelle had only seconds left before discovery.

"Your sweater. Now!"

Sabelle glanced down. Understanding dawned a moment later. Without pause, she crossed her arms around her waist and peeled the sweater off, then tossed it to him.

Ice tried not to think about what she might—or might

not—be wearing now that she'd pulled off the thin cashmere. He glimpsed lots of bare, golden skin. Damn it all. Not only was she a temptation, but she wouldn't stay warm for long like that. Then again, time wasn't on their side.

"I'll be back. If the Anarki finds you, transport yourself and the book somewhere you'll have help."

"And leave you and Bram? No." She crossed her arms over her chest.

For a princess, she was terribly stubborn. "Promise me."

She shook her head.

"Now," he demanded in a low voice the wind swept away.

"Bloody cold!" an invading wizard shouted fifty meters to their left. "Hate winter."

Ice dodged around the trunk of the tree and sent Sabelle another demanding glare, mouthing, "Please."

Finally, she rolled her eyes. And nodded.